Eden Phillpotts

Lying Prophets

A Novel. Third Edition

Eden Phillpotts

Lying Prophets
A Novel. Third Edition

ISBN/EAN: 9783337001643

Printed in Europe, USA, Canada, Australia, Japan

Cover: Foto ©Andreas Hilbeck / pixelio.de

More available books at **www.hansebooks.com**

LYING PROPHETS.

MÊN SCRYFA.

Lying Prophets.

A NOVEL.

BY

ELDEN PHILLPOTTS,

AUTHOR OF "DOWN DARTMOOR WAY," "SOME EVERYDAY FOLKS,"
"MY LAUGHING PHILOSOPHER," ETC.

THIRD EDITION.

LONDON:
A. D. INNES & CO.,
BEDFORD STREET.
1897.

TO MY WIFE.

CONTENTS.

BOOK I.

ART.

BOOK II.

NATURE.

BOOK III.

CHANCE.

BOOK I.

ART.

LYING PROPHETS.

CHAPTER I.

NEWLYN.

Away beyond the village stands a white cottage, with the sea lapping at low cliffs beneath it. Plum and apple orchards slope upwards behind this building, and already upon the former trees there trembles a snowy gauze where blossom buds are breaking. Higher yet, dark ploughed fields, with hedges whereon grow straight elms, cover the undulations of a great hill even to its windy crest; and below, at the water-line, lies Newlyn—a village of grey stone and blue, with slate roofs now shining silver-bright under morning sunlight and easterly wind. Smoke softens every outline; red-brick walls and tanned sails bring warmth and colour through the blue vapour of many chimneys; a sun-flash glitters at this point and that, denoting here a conservatory, there a studio. Enter this hive, and you shall find a network of narrow stone streets; a flutter of flannel underwear, of blue stockings and tawny garments drying upon lines; little windows, some with rows of oranges and ginger-beer bottles in them; little shops; little doors, at which cluster little children and many cats, the latter mostly tortoiseshell and white. Infants watch their elders playing marbles in the roadway, and the cats stretch lazy bodies on the mats, made of old fishing-net, which lie at numerous cottage doors.

Newlyn stands on slight elevations above the sea-level, and at one point the road bends downward, breaks and fringes the tide, leading over sand, amongst broken iron, rusty anchors, and dismantled fishing-boats, past an ancient buoy whose sides now serve the purposes of advertisement, and tell of prayer-meetings, cheap tea, and so forth. Hard by the mighty blocks of the old breakwater stand, their fabric dating from the reign of James I., and taking the place of one still older. But the old breakwater is no more than a rialto for ancient gossips now; and far beyond it new piers stretch encircling arms of granite round a new harbour, southwards of which the lighthouse stands and winks his sleepless golden eye from dusk to dawn. Within this harbour when the fishing-fleet is at home lie jungles of stout masts, row upon row, with here and there a sail, carrying on the colour of the ploughed fields above the village, and elsewhere scraps of flaming bunting flashing like flowers in a reed bed. Behind the masts, along the barbican, the cottages stand close and thick, then clamber and struggle up the acclivities behind, decreasing in their numbers as they ascend. Smoke trails inland on the wind— black, as a thin crepe veil, from the funnel of a coal-"tramp" about to leave the harbour; blue from the dry wood burning on a hundred cottage hearths. A smell of fish, where great split pollocks hang drying in the sun; of tar and tan and twine, where nets and cordage lie spread upon low walls and open spaces, gives to Newlyn an odour all its own.

But aloft, above the village air, Spring is dancing, sweet-scented, light-footed, in the hedgerows, through the woods, and on the wild moors which stretch inland away. There the gold of the gorse flames in many a sudden sheet and splash over the wastes whereon last year's ling bloom, all sere and grey, makes a sad-coloured world. The season's change is coming fast, how-ever. Celandines twinkle everywhere, and primroses, more tardy and more coy, already open wondering eyes. The sea lies smooth with a surface just wind-kissed and strewed with a glory of sun-stars. Away to the east, at a point from which brown hills, dotted with white dwellings, tend in long undulations to the cliffs of the Lizard, under fair clouds all banked and sunny white against the blue, rises St. Michael's Mount, with a man's little castle capping Nature's gaunt escarpments and rugged walls. Between Marazion and Newlyn stretches Mount's Bay; while a mile or two of flat sea front, over which, like a string of pearls, roll steam clouds from a train, bring us to Penzance. Then, noting centres of industry where freezing works rise and smelting of ore occupies many men (for Newlyn labours at the two extremes of fire and ice), we are back in the fishing-village again and upon the winding road which leads there-from, first to Penlee Point and the blue-stone quarry, anon to the little hamlet of Mousehole beyond.

Beside this road lay our white cottage, with the sunshine lighting up a piece of new golden thatch let into the old grey, and the plum-trees behind it bursting into new-born foam of flowers. Just outside it, above the low cliff, stood two men looking down into the water, seen dark green below through a tangle of briar and blackthorn and emerald foliage of budding elder. The sea served base uses here, for the dust and dirt of many a cottage was daily cast into the lap of the great scavenger who carried all away. The low cliffs were indeed spattered with filth, and the coltsfoot, already opening yellow blossoms below, found itself rudely saluted with cinders, potato-peelings, fishes' entrails, and such-like unlovely matter.

The men were watching a white fleet of birds paddling on the sea, hurrying this way and that, struggling, with many a plunge and flutter and plaintive cry, for the food a retreating tide was bearing from the shore.

"White spirits and grey, I call them," said the younger of the two spectators. "The gulls fascinate me always. They are beautiful to see and hear and paint. Swimming there, and wheeling between the waves in rough weather, or hanging almost motionless in mid-air, with their heads turning first this way, then that, and their breasts pressed against the wind—why, they are perfect always the little winged gods of the sea!"

"Gods kissing carrion," sneered the other. "Beautiful enough, no doubt; but their music holds no charm for me.

Nothing is quite beautiful which has for its cause something ugly. Those echoing cries down there are the expression of a greedy struggle—no more. I hate your Newlyn gulls. They are ruined, like a thousand other wild things, by civilization. I see them scouring the fields, and hopping after the ploughmen like common crows. A Cornish sea-bird should fight its battle with the sea, and find its home in the heart of the dizzy cliffs, sharing them with the samphire; but your 'white spirits and grey' behave like gutter-fed ducks."

The first speaker laughed, and both strolled upon their way. They were artists; but while Edmund Murdoch dwelt at Newlyn, and lived by his profession, the older man, John Barron, was merely on a visit to the place. He had come down for change, and with no particular intention to work. Barron was wealthy, and wasted rare talents. He did not paint much, and the few who knew his pictures deplored the fact that no temporal inducement called upon him to handle his brush oftener. A few excused him on the plea of his health, which was at all times indifferent, but he never excused himself. It needed something far from the beaten track to inspire him, and inspiration was rare. But let a subject once grip him, and the artist's life centred and fastened upon it until his work was done. He sacrificed everything at such a time; he slaved; labour was to him as a debauch to the drunkard, and he wearied body and mind, and counted his health nothing while the frenzy held him. Then, his picture finished at the cost of the man's whole store of nervous energy and skill, he would probably paint no more for many months. His subject was always some transcript from nature, wrought out with almost brutal vigour and disregard of everything but truth. His looks belied his work curiously. A small, slight man he was, with sloping shoulders and the consumptive build; but the breadth of his head above the ears showed brain, and his grey eyes spoke a strength of purpose, upon which a hard, finely modelled mouth set the seal. Once, in the West Indies, he had painted a picture of two negresses bathing at Tobago. Behind them hung low tangles of cactus, melo-cactus, and white-blossomed orchid; while on the tawny rocks glimmered snowy cotton, splashed with a crimson and orange turban. But the marvel of the work lay in the figures and the refraction of their brown limbs seen through crystal-clear water. The picture brought reputation to a man who cared nothing for it, and Barron's "Bathing Negresses" are only quoted because they illustrate his method of work. He had painted from the sea in a boat moored fore and aft; he had kept the two women shivering and whining in the water for two hours at a time. They could not indeed refuse the gold he offered for their services; but one of them never lived to enjoy the money, for her prolonged ablutions in the cause of art killed her a week after her work was done.

John Barron was a selfish sybarite, and affected absolutely primitive instincts with regard to his fellow-creatures. The Land's End had disappointed him; he had found Nature neither grand nor terrific there, but sleepy and tame as a cat after a full meal. Neither did he derive any pleasure from the society of his craft at Newlyn. He hated the clatter of art jargon; he flouted all schools, and pointed out, what nobody doubts now, that the artists of the Cornish village in reality represented nothing but a community of fellow-workers, all actuated indeed by love of art, but each developing his own bent without thought for his neighbour's theory. Barron indeed made some enemies before he had been in the place a week, and the greater lights liked him none the better for vehemently disclaiming the honour when they told him he was one of themselves. "The shape of a brush does not make men paint alike," he said, "else we were all equal, and should only differ in colour. Some of you can no more paint with a square brush than you can with a knife; some of you could not paint though your palettes were set with Nature's own sunset colours; and others of you, if you had a rabbit's scut at the end of a hop-pole, and the grey mud from a rain puddle, would produce work worth considering. You are a community of painters—some clever, some hopeless—but you are not a school, and you may thank God for it."

John Barron was rough tonic, but the man generally found an audience at the end of the day in this studio or that. The truth of much that he said appealed to the lofty-minded and serious; his dry cynicism, savage dislike of civilization, and frank affection for nature attracted others. He hit hard, but he never resented rough knocks in return, and no man had seen him out of temper with anything but mysticism, and the art bred therefrom. Upon the whole, however, his materialism annoyed more than his wit amused.

Upon the evening which followed his insult offered to the Newlyn gulls, Barron, with Edmund Murdoch and some other men, was talking in the studio of one Brady, known to fame as the "Wrecker," from his love for the artistic representation of maritime disaster. Barron liked this man, for he was outspoken and held vigorous views, but the two quarrelled freely.

"Fate was a fool when she chucked her presents into the lap of a lazy beggar like you," said Brady, addressing the visitor; "and thrice a fool," he added, "to assort her gifts so ill."

"Fate is a knave, a mad thing playing at cat's cradle with the threads of our wretched little lives," answered John Barron. "She is a coward—a bully. She hits the hungry below the belt; she heaps gold into the lap of the old man, but not till he has already dug his own grave to come at it; she gives health to those who must needs waste all their splendid strength on work, and wealth to worthless beings like myself, who are always ailing, and who never spend a pound with wisdom. Make no dark cryptic mystery of Fate when you paint her. She looks to me like a mischievous monkey poking sticks into an ant-hill."

"She's a woman," said Murdoch.

"She's three," corrected Brady; "what can you expect from three women rolled into one?"

"Away with her! Waste no incense at her shrine. She'll

cut the thread no sooner because you turn your back on her. Fling overboard your mythologies, dead and alive, and kneel to Nature. A budding spike of wild hyacinth is worth all the gods put together. Go hand in hand with Nature, I say. Ask nothing from her; walk humbly, be well content if she lets you but turn the corner of one page none else have read. That's how I live. My life is not a prayer exactly—— "

" I should say not," interrupted Brady.

" But a hymn of praise—a purely impersonal existence lived all alone, like a man at a prison window. This carcase, with its shaky machinery and defective breathing apparatus, is the prison. I look out of the window till the walls crumble away."

" And then?" asked one Paul Tarrant, a painter who prided himself on being a Christian as well.

" Then the spark which I call myself goes back to Nature, as the cloud gives the raindrop back to the sea from whence the sun drew it."

" A lie, man!" answered the other, hotly.

" Perhaps. It really matters nothing. God—if there be a God—will not blame me for making a mistake. Meantime I live like the rook and the thrush. They never pray, they praise; they sing ' grace before meat' and after it, as Nature taught them."

" A simple child of Nature—beautiful spectacle," said Brady. " But I'm sorry all the same," he continued, "that you've found nothing in Cornwall to keep you here and make you do some work. You talk an awful deal of rot, but we want to see you paint. Isn't there anything or anybody worthy of you?"

" As a matter of fact, I've found a girl," said Barron.

There was a clamour of excitement at this news, above which Brady's bull voice roared approval.

"Proud girl, proud parents, proud Newlyn!" he bellowed.

" The mood ripens too," continued Barron, quietly. " ' Sacrifice all the world to mood,' is my motto. So I shall stop and paint."

A moment later derisive laughter greeted the artist's decision, for Murdoch, in answer to a hail of questions, announced the subject of his friend's inspiration.

"We strolled round this morning and saw Joan Tregenza in an iron hoop with a pail of water slung at either hand."

"So your picture begins and ends where it is, Barron, my friend—in your imagination. Did it strike you, when you first saw that vision of loveliness in dirty drab, that she was hardly the girl to have gone unpainted till now?" asked Brady.

"The possibility of previous pictures is hardly likely to weigh with me. Why, I would paint a drowned sailor if the subject attracted me, and that though you have done it," answered the other, nodding towards a big canvas in the corner, where Brady's picture for the year approached completion.

"My dear chap, we all worship Joan at a distance. She is not to be painted. Tears and prayers are useless. She has a flinty father, a fisherman, who looks upon painting as a snare of the fiend, and sees every artist already wriggling on the trident in his mind's eye. Joan has also a lover, who would rather behold her dead than on canvas," declared Murdoch.

"In fact, these Methodist folk take us to be what you really are," said Brady, bluntly. "Old Tregenza tars us every one with the same brush. We are lost sinners all."

"Well, why trouble him? A fisherman would have his business on the sea. Candidly, I must paint her. The wish grows upon me."

"Even money you don't get as much as a sketch," said Murdoch.

"Have any of you tried approaching her directly, instead of her relations?"

"She's as shy as a hawk, man."

"That makes me the more hopeful. You fellows with your Tam-o'-Shanters and aggressive neckties, and knickerbockers and calves, would frighten the devil. I'm shy myself. If she's natural, then we shall possibly understand each other."

"I'll bet you ten to one in pounds you won't have your wish," said Brady.

"No, shan't bet. You're all so certain. Probably I shall find myself beaten, like the rest of you; but it's worth trying. She's a pretty thing."

"How will you paint her if you get the chance?"

"Don't know yet. I should like to paint her in a wolf-skin, with a thread of wolf's teeth round her neck and a celt-headed spear in her hand."

"Art will be a loser by the pending repulse," declared Brady. "And now, as my whisky-bottle's empty, and my lamp going out, you chaps can follow its example whenever you please."

So the men scattered into a starry night, and went each his way through the streets of the sleeping village.

CHAPTER II.

IN A HALO OF GOLD.

EDMUND MURDOCH's studio stood high on Newlyn Hill, and
Barron had taken comfortable rooms in a little lodging-house
close beside it. The men often enjoyed breakfast in each
other's company; but on the following morning, when Murdoch
strolled over to see his friend, he found that his rooms were
empty.

Barron, in fact, was already nearly a mile from Newlyn,
and at the moment when the younger artist sought him he
stood upon a footpath which ran through ploughed fields to
the village of Paul. In the bottom of his mind ran a current
of thought occupied with the problem of Joan Tregenza, but
superficially he was concerned with the spring world in which
he walked. He stood where Nature, like Artemis, was a
mother of many breasts. Brown and solemn in their undulations, they rose about and around him to the sky-line, where
the land cut sharply against a pale blue heaven, from which
tinkled the music of larks. He wandered slowly and thoughtfully forward; noted the young wheat brushing the earth
with a veil of green; dawdled where the elms stood, their
high tops thick with blossom; and delayed for full twenty
minutes to see the felling of one giant tree. A wedge-shaped
cut had been made upon the side where the great elm
was to fall, and upon the other side two men were sawing
through the trunk. There was no sound but the steady hiss
of steel teeth gnawing inch by inch to the wine-red heart of
the tree. Sunshine glimmered on its leafy crown, and as yet

distant branch and bough knew nothing of the midgets and death below.

Barron took pleasure in seeing the great god Change at work, but he mourned in that a masterpiece on which Nature had bestowed half a century and more of love must now vanish.

"A pity," he said, while the executioners rested a few moments from their labours—"a pity to cut down such a noble tree."

One woodman laughed, and the other—an old rustic, lean and bent—made answer—

"I sez 'dang the tree! Us doan't take no joy in thrawin' en, mister. I be bedoled wi' pain, an' this 'ere sawin's just food for rheumatiz. My back's that bad. But squire must have money, an' theer's five hundred pounds' value o' ellum comin' down 'fore us done wi' et."

The saw won its way, and between each spell of labour the ancient man held his back and grumbled.

"Er's Billy Jago," confided the second labourer to Barron when his companion had turned aside to get some steel wedges and a sledge-hammer. "Er's well knawn in these paarts—a reg'lar cure. Er used to work up Drift wi' Mister Chirgwin."

Billy added two wedges to those already hammered into the saw-cut, then, with the sledge, he drove them home and finished his task. The sorrowful strokes rang hollow and mournful over the land, sadder to Barron's ear than fall of earth-clod on coffin-lid. And, upon the sound, a responsive shiver and uneasy tremor ran through trunk and bough to topmost twig of the elm—a sudden sense, as it seemed, of awful evil and ruin undreamed of, but now imminent. Then the monster staggered, and the midget struck his last blow and removed himself and his rheumatism. Whereupon began that magnificent descent. Slowly, with infinitely solemn sweep, the elm's vast height swung away from its place, described a wide aërial arc, and so, with the jolting crash and rattle of close thunder, roared head-long to the earth, casting up a cloud of dust, ploughing the grass with splintered limbs, then lying very still. From glorious tree to battered log it sank. No man ever saw more instant wreck and ruin fall lightning-like on a fair thing. The mass was crushed flat and shapeless by its own vast weight, and the larger boughs, which did not touch the earth, were snapped short off by the concussion of their fall.

Billy Jago held his back and whined while Barron spoke, as much to himself as the woodman.

"Dear God," he said, "to think that this glory of the hedge-row, this kingdom of song-birds, should come to the making of pauper coffins and lodging-house furniture!"

"Squire must have money; an' folks must have coffins," said Billy. "You can sleep your last sleep so sound in ellum as you can in oak, for that matter."

Feeling the truth of the assertion, Barron admitted it, then turned his back on the fallen king and pursued his way with thoughts reverting to the proposed picture. There was nothing to alarm Joan Tregenza about him; which seemed well, as he meant to approach the girl herself at the first opportunity, and not her parents. Barron did not carry "artist" stamped upon him. He was plainly attired in a thick tweed suit, and wore a cap of the same material. The man appeared insignificantly small. He was clean-shaved, and looked younger than his five and thirty years seen a short distance off, but older when you stood beside him. He strolled now onward towards the sea, and his cheeks took some colour from the fine air. He walked with a stick, and carried a pair of field-glasses in a case slung over his shoulder. The field-glasses had become a habit with him, but he rarely used them, for his small, slate-coloured eyes were keen.

Once and again John Barron turned to look at St. Michael's Mount, seen far across the bay. The magic of morning made it beautiful, and the great pile towered grandly through a sunny haze. No detail disturbed the eye under this effect of light, and the mount stood vast, dim, golden, magnified and glorified into a fairy palace of romance built by immortal things in a night. Seen thus, it even challenged the beholder's admiration, of which he was at all times sparing. Until that hour he had found nothing but laughter for this same elevation, likening the spectacle of it, with its castle and cottages, now to a senile monarch with moth-eaten ermine about his toes and a lop-sided crown on his head, now to a monstrous sea-snail creeping shorewards.

Barron, having walked down the hill to Mousehole, breasted slowly the steep acclivity which leads therefrom towards the west. Presently he turned, where a plateau of grass sloped above the cliffs, into a little theatre of banks ablaze with gorse. And here his thoughts and the image they were concerned with perished before reality. Framed in a halo of golden furze, her hands making a pent-house above her brow, and in her blue eyes the mingled hue of sea and sky, stood a girl looking out at the horizon. The bud of a wondrous fair woman she was, and Barron saw her slim, yet vigorous figure accentuated under its drab-brown draperies by a kindly breeze. He noted the sweet, childish freshness of her face, her plump arms filling the sleeves of rusty black, and her feet in shoes too big for them. Her hair was hidden under a linen sun-bonnet, but one lock had escaped, and he noted that it was the colour of wheat ripe for the reaping. He regretted it had not been darker, but observed that it chimed well enough with the flaming flowers behind it. And then he frankly praised Nature in his heart for sending her servant such a splendid harmony in gold and brown. There stood his picture in front of him. He gazed a brief second only, and then his quick mind worked to find what human interest had brought Joan Tregenza to this place, and turned her eyes to the sea. It might be that herein existed the possibility of the introduction he desired. He felt that victory probably depended on the events of the next two or three minutes. He owed a supreme effort of skill and tact to Fate which had thus befriended him, and he rose to the occasion.

The girl looked up as he came suddenly upon her, but his eyes were already away and fixed upon the horizon before she turned. Observing that he was not regarding her, she put up her hands again, and continued to scan the remote sea-line where a thin trail of dark smoke told of a steamer, itself apparently invisible. Barron took his glasses from their case and, seeing that the girl made no movement of departure, acted deliberately, and presently began to watch a fleet of brown sails and black hulls putting forth from the little harbour below. Then, without looking at her or taking his eyes from the glasses, he spoke.

"Would you kindly tell me what those small vessels are below there just setting out to sea?" he asked.

The girl started, looked round, and realizing that he had addressed her, made answer—

"They'm Mouzle * luggers, sir."

"Luggers, are they? Thank you. And where are they sailing to? Do you know?"

"Away down-long south'ard o' the Scillies mostly, arter mackerl. Theer's a power o' mackerl bein' catched just now—thousands an' thousands; but some o' they boats be laskin' —that's just fishin' off shore."

"Ah, a busy time for the fishermen."

"'Iss, 'tis."

"Thank you. Good morning."

"Good marnin', sir."

He started as though to continue his walk along the cliffs beyond the plateau and the gorse; then he stopped suddenly, actuated, as it seemed, by a chance thought, and turned back to the girl. She was looking out to sea again.

"By the way," he said unconcernedly, and with no suggestion that anything in particular was responsible for his politeness, "I see you are on the look-out there for something. You may have my glasses a moment if you like, before I go on. They bring the ships very close."

The girl flushed with shy pleasure, and seemed a little uncertain what to answer. Barron, meanwhile, showed no trace of a smile, but looked bored if anything, and, with a

* *Mouzle,* Mousehole.

serious face, handed her the glasses, then walked a little way off.
He was grave and courteous, but made no attempt at friendship.
He had noticed when Joan smiled that her teeth were fine, and
that her full face, though sweet enough, was a shade too plump.

"Thank'ee kindly, sir," she said, taking the glass. "You
see, theer's a gert ship passin' down Channel, an'—an' my Joe's
aboard her, an' they'm bound for furrin' paarts, an' I promised
as I'd come to this here horny-winky * plaace to get a last
sight o' the vessel if I could."

He made no answer, and after a pause she spoke again.

"I caan't see nought; but that's my fault p'raps, not bein'
used to sich things."

"Let me try and find the ship," he said, taking the glasses,
which he had put out of focus purposely. Then, while scan-
ning the horizon where he had noted the smoke-trail, he spoke,
his head turned from her. "Who's Joe, if I may ask? Your
brother, I dare say?"

"No, sir; Joe's my sweetheart."

"There's a big three-masted ship being taken down the
Channel by a small steamer."

"Ah! then I reckon that's the *Anna*, 'cause Joe said 'twas
tolerable certain they'd be in tow of a tug."

"You can see the smoke on the edge of the sea. Look
below it."

He handed the glasses to her again, and heard a little laugh
of delight break from her lips. The surprise of the suddenly
magnified spectacle, visible only as a shadow to the naked eye,
brought laughter; and Barron, now that the girl's attention
was occupied, had leisure to look at her. She was more than
a pretty cottage maid, for she possessed distinction and charm.
There was a delicacy about her, too—a sweet turn of lip, a
purity of skin, a set of limb—which gave the lie to her rough
speech. She was all Saxon to look at, with nothing of the Celt
about her, excepting her name and the old Cornish words upon
her lips. Those the spectator rejoiced in, for they showed that

* *Horny-winky*, lonely; the abode of horny-winks.

she still remained a free thing, primitive, innocent of school boards or like frost-biting influences.

Barron took mental notes. Joan Tregenza was a careless young woman it seemed. Her dress had a button or two missing in front, and a safety-pin had taken their place. Her drab skirt was frayed a little, and patched in one corner with a square of another material; but the colours were well enough, from the artist's point of view. He noted also that the girl's stockings were darned, and badly needed further attention, for above her right shoe-heel a white scrap of Joan was visible. Her hands were a little large, but well shaped; her pose was free and fine, though the field-glasses spoilt the picture, and the sun-bonnet hid the contour of her head.

"So you walked out from Mouzle to see the last of Joe's ship?" he asked, quite seriously, and with no light note in his voice.

"From Newlyn. I ban't a Mouzle maid," she answered.

"Is the *Anna* coming home again soon?"

"No, sir. Her's bound for the Gulf of Californy, round t'other side the world, Joe sez. He reckons to be back agin' come winter."

"That's a long time."

"'Iss, 'tis."

But there was no sentiment about the answer. Joan gazed without a shadow of emotion at the vanishing ship, and alluded to the duration of her sweetheart's absence in a voice that never trembled. Then she gave the glasses back to Barron with many thanks, and evidently wanted to be gone; but stopped awkwardly, not quite knowing how to depart.

Meanwhile, showing no further cognizance of her, Barron took the glasses himself and looked at the distant ship.

"A splendid vessel!" he said. "I expect you have a picture of her—haven't you?"

"No," she answered; "but I've got a li'l ship Joe cut out o' wood an' painted butivul—awnly that's another vessel what Joe sailed in afore."

"I'll tell you what I'll do," he said, "because you were good enough to explain all about the fishing-boats. I'll make a tiny picture of the *Anna,* and paint it and give it to you."

But the girl took fright instantly. "You'm a artist, then?" she said, with alarm in her face and voice.

He shook his head. "No, no. Do I look like an artist? I'm only a stranger down here for a day or two. I paint things sometimes for my own amusement, that's all."

"Pickshers?"

"They are not worth calling pictures. Just scraps of the sea, and trees, and cliffs, and skies, to while away the time and remind me of beautiful things after I have left them."

"You ban't a artist ezacally, then?"

"Certainly not. Don't you like artists?"

"Faither don't. He be a fisherman, an' caan't abear many things as happens in the world. An' not artists. Gen'lemen have axed him to let 'em take my picksher, 'cause they've painted a good few maidens to Newlyn; an' some of 'em wanted to paint faither as well, but he up an' sez 'No!' short. Paintin's vanity 'cordin' to faither, same as they flags an' cannels an' moosic to Newlyn Church is vanity. Most purty things is vanity faither reckons."

"I'm sure he's a wise man. And I think he's right, especially about the candles and flags in church. And now I must go on my walk. Let me see, shall I bring you the little picture of Joe's ship here? I often walk out this way."

He assumed she would take the picture, and now she feared to object. Moreover, such a sketch would be precious in her eyes.

"Maybe 'tis troublin' of 'e, sir?"

"I've promised you. I always keep my word. I shall be here to-morrow about mid-afternoon, because it is lonely and quiet and beautiful. I'm going to try and paint the gorse, all blazing so brightly against the sky."

"Them prickly fuzz-bushes?"

"Yes; because they are very beautiful."

"But they'm everywheers. You might so well paint the bannel * or the yether on the moors, mightn't 'e ? "

"They are beautiful too. Remember, I shall have Joe's ship for you to-morrow."

He nodded without smiling, and turned away until a point of the gorse had hidden her from sight. Then he sat down, loaded his pipe, and reflected.

"' Joe's ship!' " he said to himself. " A happy title enough."

And meantime the girl had looked after him with wonder and some amusement in her eyes, had rubbed her chin reflectively—a habit caught from her father—and had then scampered off smiling to herself.

"What a funny gen'leman ! " she thought. " Never laughs, nor nothin'. An' I judged he was a artist ! But wonnerful kind, an' wonnerful queer wi' it, sure 'nough."

* *Bannel*, broom.

CHAPTER III.

JOAN TREGENZA lived in a white cottage already mentioned—
that standing just beyond Newlyn upon a road above the sea.
The cot was larger than it appeared from the road, and extended
backward into an orchard of plum and apple trees. The kitchen,
which opened into this garden, was stone-paved, cool, comfortable, sweet at all times with the scent of wood smoke, and
frequently not innocent of varied fishy odours. But Newlyn
folk suck in a smell of fish with their mothers' milk—'tis
part of the atmosphere of home.

When Joan returned from her visit to Gorse Point, she
found a hard-faced woman, thin of figure, with untidy brown
hair, wrinkled brow and sharp features, engaged about a pile
of washing in the garden at the kitchen door. Mrs. Tregenza
heard the girl arrive, and spoke without lifting her little grey
eyes from the clothes. Her voice was hard and high and
discontented, like that of one who has long bawled into a deaf
man's ear and is weary of it.

"Drabbit you! Wheer you bin? Allus trapsing out when
you'm wanted; allus caddlin' round doin' nothin' when you
ban't. I s'pose you think breakfus' can be kep' on the table
till dinner, washing-day or no?"

"I don't want no breakfus', then. I took some bread an'
drippin' long with me. Wheer's Tom to?"

"Gone to school this half-hour. 'Tis nine o'clock an' past.
Wheer you bin, I sez? 'Tain't much in your way to rise afore
me of a marnin'."

"Out through Mouzle to Gorse P'int, to see Joe's ship pass by; an' I see en butivul."

"Thank the Lard he's gone! Now I s'pose theer'll be a bit peace in the house, an' you'll bide home an' work. My fingers is to the bone day an' night."

"He'll be gone a year purty nigh."

"Well, the harder you works, the quicker the time'll pass by Theer's nuthin' to grizzle at. Sea-farin' fellers must be away most times. But he'm a good, straight man, and you'm tokened to en, and that's enough. Bide cheerful an' get the water for washin'. If they things of faither's ban't dry come to-morrer, he'll knaw the reason why."

Joan accepted Mrs. Tregenza's comfort philosophically, though her sweetheart's departure had not really caused her any emotion. She visited the larder, drank a cup of milk, and then, fetching an iron hoop and buckets, went to a sunken barrel outside the cottage door into which, from a pipe through the road bank, tumbled a silver thread of spring water.

Of the Tregenza household a word must need be spoken. Joan's own mother had died twelve years ago, and the anxious-natured woman who took her place proved herself a good step-parent enough. Despite a disposition prone to worry and to dwell upon the small tribulations of life, Thomasin Tregenza was not unhappy, for her husband enjoyed prosperity and a reputation for godliness unequalled in Newlyn. A great, weather-worn, grey, hairy man was he, with a big head and a furrowed cliff of a forehead that looked as though it had been carved by its Creator from Cornish granite. Tregenza indeed might have stood for a typical Cornish fisher or a Breton. Like enough, indeed, he had old Armorican blood in his veins, for many hundreds of Britons betook themselves to ancient Brittany when the Saxon invasion swept the West, and many afterwards returned, with foreign wives, to the homes of their fathers.

Michael Tregenza had found religion, of a sort fiery and unlovely enough, but his convictions were definite, with iron-hard limitations, and he looked coldly and without pity on a damned world, himself saved. Grey Michael had no sympathy with sin, and less with sinners. He found the devil in most unexpected quarters, and was always dragging him out of surprising hiding-places and exhibiting him triumphantly, as a boy might show a bird's-egg or butterfly. His devil dwelt at penny readings, at fairs and festivals, in the brushes of the artists, in a walk on a Sunday afternoon undertaken without a definite object, sometimes in a primrose given by a boy to a girl. Of all these bitter, self-righteous, censorious little sects which raise each its own ladder to the Throne of Grace at Newlyn, the Luke Gospellers is the most bitter, most self-righteous, most censorious. And of all those burning lights which reflected the primitive savagery of the Pentateuch from that fold, Grey Michael's beacon flamed aforetime the fiercest and most bloody red. There was not a Gospeller, including the pastor of the flock, but feared the austere fisherman while admiring him.

Concerning his creed, at the risk of wearying you, it must be permitted to speak here, for only by grasping its leading features and its vast unlikeness to the parent tree can just estimate of Michael Tregenza be arrived at. Luke Gospeldom had mighty little to do with the Gospel of Luke. The sect numbered one hundred and thirty-four just persons at war with principalities and powers. They were saturated with the spirit of Israel in the Wilderness, of Esau when every man's hand was against him. At their chapel one heard much of Jehovah, the jealous God, of the burning lake and the damnation reserved for mankind as a whole. Every Luke Gospeller was a Jehovah in his own right. They walked hand in hand with God; they realized the dismay and indignation Newlyn must occasion in His breast; they sympathized heartily with the Everlasting, and would have called down fire from Heaven themselves if they could. Many openly wondered that He delayed so long, for, from a Luke Gospeller's point of view, the place with its dozen other chapels—each held in error by the rest, and all at deadly war among themselves—its ritualistic church of St. Peter, its public-houses, scandals, and strifes, was riper for destruction than Sodom. However, the hundred and thirty-four served to stave off Celestial brimstone, as it seemed.

It is pitiable, in the face of the majestic work of John Wesley in Cornwall, to see the shattered ruins of it which remain. When the Wesleys achieved their notable revival, and swept off the dust of a dead Anglicanism which covered religious Cornwall like a pall in the days of the Georges, the old Celtic spirit, though these heroes found it hard enough to rekindle, burst from its banked-up furnaces at last and blazed abroad once more. That spirit had been bred by the saint bishops of Brito-Celtic days, and Wesley's ultimate success was a grand repetition of history, as extant records of the ancient use of the Church in Cornwall prove. Its principle was, that he who filled a bishop's office should, before all things, conduct and develop missionary enterprise, and the moral and physical courage of the Brito-Celtic bishops, having long slumbered, awoke again in John Wesley. He built on the old foundations. He gave to the laymen a power at that time blindly denied them by the Church—the power which Irish and Welsh and Breton missionary saints of old has vested in them. Wesley— himself a giant—made wise use of the strong where he found them; and if a man—tinker or tinner, fisher or jowster—could preach and grip an audience, that man might do so. Thus had the founders of the new creed developed it; thus does the Church in some measure to-day. But when John Wesley filled his empty belly with blackberries at St. Hilary, in 1743; when he thundered what he deemed eternal truth through Cornwall year after year for half a century; when he faced a thousand perils by sea and land, and spent his arduous days "in watch- ings often, in hunger and thirst, in fasting often, in cold and nakedness;" when, in fine, this stupendous man achieved the foundations of Methodism,—the harvest was over-ripe, at any rate in Cornwall. No Nonconformist was he, though few enough of his followers to-day remember that, if they ever knew it. He worked for his Church; he was a link between it and his party; his last prayer was for Church and king—a fact which might have greatly shocked the Luke Gospellers, had such come to their ears; for John Wesley was their only saint, and they honestly believed that they alone of all Methodist communities were following in his footsteps. Poor souls! they lived as far from what Wesley taught as it is easily possible to conceive. As for Grey Michael, he was under the impression that he and his sect worthily held aloft the true light which Wesley brought in person to Newlyn, and he talked with authority upon the subject of his master and his master's doings; but he knew little about the founder of Methodism in reality, and still less about the history of the Methodist movement. Had he learned that John Wesley himself was once accused of Popish practices; had he known that not until some years after the great preacher's death did his party, in conference assembled, separate itself from the Church of England, he had doubtless been much amazed. Though saturated with religious feeling, the man was wholly ignorant of religious history in so far as it affected his own country. To him all saints not mentioned in Scripture were an abomination and invention of Rome. Had he been informed that the venerable missionary saints of his mother-land were in no case Romish, another vast surprise must have awaited him.

Let it not for an instant be supposed that the Luke Gospellers represented right Methodism; but they fairly exemplified a sorry side of it: those little offshoots of which dozens have separated from the parent tree; and they exhibited most abundantly in themselves that canker-worm of Pharisaism which gnaws at the root of all Nonconformity. This offence, combined with such intolerance and profound ignorance as was to be found amidst the Luke Gospellers, produced a community merely sad or comic to consider according to the point of view.

An instance of Michael Tregenza's attitude to the Church will illustrate better than analysis the lines of thought on which he served his Creator.

Once, when she was thirteen, Joan had gone to an evening service at St. Peter's, because a friend had dared her to do so. Her father was at sea, and she believed the delinquency could by no possibility reach his ears. But a Luke Gospeller heard the dread tidings, and Michael Tregenza was quickly informed of his daughter's lapse. He accused Joan quietly enough, and she confessed.

"Then you'm a damned maiden," he said, "'cause you sinned open-eyed."

He thought the matter over for a week, and finally an idea occurred to him.

"'Tis wi'n the power o' God to reach even you back," he declared to Joan, "an' He's put in my mind that chastenin' might do it. A sore body's saved many sawls 'fore now."

Whereupon he took his daughter into the little parlour, shut the door, and then flogged her as he would have flogged a boy, only using his hard hand instead of a stick.

"Get thee behind her, Satan! Get thee behind her, Satan! Get thee behind her, Satan!" he groaned with every blow; while Joan grit her teeth and bore it as long as she could, then screamed and fainted.

That was how the truth about heaven and hell came to her. She had never felt physical pain before, and eternal torment was merely an idea. From that day, however, she was frightened, and listened to her father gladly and wept tears of thankfulness when, a month after her flogging, he explained that he had wrestled with the Lord for her soul, and how it had been borne in upon him that she was saved alive. She had reached the age of seventeen now, and felt quite confident upon the subject of eternity, as became a right Luke Gospeller. Unlike other women of the sect, however, and despite extreme ignorance on all subjects, the girl had a seed of humour in her nature only waiting circumstances to ripen. She felt pity, too, for the great damned world, and though religion turned life sad-coloured, her own simple, healthy, animal nature and high spirits brought ample share of sunshine and delight. She was, in fact, her mother's child rather than her father's. His ancestors before him had fought the devil, and lived grey lives under a cloud of fear; Michael's own brother had gone religious mad, when still a young man, and died in a lunatic asylum; indeed, the awful difficulty of saving his soul had been in the blood of every true Tregenza for generations.

But Joan's mother came of different stock. The Chirgwins were upland people. They dwelt at Drift and elsewhere, went to the nearest church, held simple views, and were content with orthodox religion. Mr. Tregenza said of them that they always wanted and expected God to do more than His share. But he married Joan Chirgwin, nevertheless, and now he saw her again, fair, trustful, light-hearted, in his daughter. The girl indeed had more of her mother in her than Grey Michael liked. She was superstitious, not after the manner of the Tregenzas, but in a direction that must have brought her father's loudest thunders upon her head if the matter had come to his ears. She loved the old stories of the saints and spirits; she gloried secretly in the splendid wealth of folk-lore and tradition her mother's people and those like them possessed at command. Her dead parent had whispered and sung these matters in Joan's baby ears until her father stopped it. She remembered how black he looked when she lisped about the piskeys; and though to-day she half believed in demon and fairy, goblin and giant, and quite believed in the saints and their miracles, she kept this side of her intelligence close locked when at home, and only nodded very gravely when her father roared against the blighting credulity of men's minds, and the follies for which fishers and miners, and indeed the bulk of the human family in Cornwall, must some day burn.

People outside the fold said that the Luke Gospellers killed Tregenza's first wife. She, of course, accepted her husband's convictions, but it had never been in her tender heart to catch the true Luke Gospel spirit. She was too full of the milk of human kindness, too prone to forgive and forget, too tolerant

 LYING PROPHETS.

and ready to see good in all men. The fiery sustenance of the new tenets withered her away like a scorched flower, and she died five years after her child was born. For a space of two years the widower remained one; then he married again, being at that time a hale man of forty; the owner of his own fishing-boat, and at once the strongest personality and handsomest person in Newlyn. Thomasin Strick, his second wife, was already a Luke Gospeller, and needed no conversion. People laughed in secret at their wooing, and likened it to the rubbing of granite rocks, or a miner's pick striking fire from flints. A boy presently came to them; and now he was ten and his mother forty. She passed rightly for a careful, money-loving soul, and a good wife, with the wit to be also a good Luke Gospeller. But her tongue was harder than her heart. Father and mother alike thought the wide world of their boy, though the child was brought up under an iron rod. Joan too loved her half-brother, Tom, very dearly, and took a pride only second to her stepmother's in the lad's progress and achievements. More than once, though only Joan and he knew it, she had saved his skin from punishment, and she worshipped him with a frank admiration which was bound to win Mrs. Tregenza's regard. Joan quite understood the careful and troubled matron, never attached undue importance to her sharp words, and was usually at her elbow with an ear for all grievances and even a sympathetic word if the same seemed called for. Mrs. Tregenza had to grumble to live, and Joan was the safety-valve, for when her husband came off the sea he would have none of it.

Life moved uniformly for these people, being varied only by the seasons of the year and the different harvests from the sea which each brought with it. Mackerel, pilchards, herrings—all had their appointed time, and the years rolled on, marked by events connected with the secular business of life on one hand, and that greater matter of eternity upon the other. Thus mighty catches of fish held the memory with mighty catches of men. One year the take of mackerel had been beyond all previous recollection; on another occasion three entire families

had joined the Luke Gospellers, and so promised to increase the
scanty numbers of the chosen. There were black memories too,
and black years, casting gloomy shadows. Widows and orphans
knew what it was to watch for brown sails that came into the
harbour's sheltering arms no more; and spiritual death had
overtaken more than one Luke Gospeller. Such turned their
backs upon the light and exchanged Truth for the benighted
parody of religion displayed by Bible Christians, by Plymouth
Brethren, or by the Church of England.

Six months before the day on which she saw his ship through
Barron's glasses, Joan had been formally affianced to Joe Noy,
with her father's permission and approval. The circumstances
of the event demand a word, for Joe had already been engaged
once before: to Mary Chirgwin, a young woman who was first
cousin to Joan, and a good deal older. She was an orphan, and
dwelt at Drift with Sampson Chirgwin, her uncle. The sailor
had thereby brightened an unutterably lonely life, and brought
earthly joy to one who had never known it. Then Grey Michael
got hold of the lad, who was naturally of a solid and religious
temperament, and up to that time of the order of the Rechabites.
As a result, Joe Noy joined the Luke Gospellers, and called
upon his sweetheart to do likewise. But Mary recollected her
aunt, Joan's mother, and being made of stern stuff, stuck to the
Church of England as she knew it, counting salvation a greater
thing than even a home of her own. The struggle was sharp
between them; neither would give way; their engagement was
therefore broken, and the girl's solitary golden glimpse of
happiness in this world shattered. She found it hard to forgive
the Tregenzas, and when, six months afterwards, the sleepy
farm life at Drift was startled by news of Joan's love affair,
Mary, in the first flush of her reawakened agony, spoke bitterly
enough; and even that most mild-mannered of men, her uncle,
said that Michael Tregenza had done an ugly act.

But the fisherman was at no time concerned with Mary or
with Joan. The opportunity to get a soul into the fold had
offered and been accepted. Any matter of earthly love-making

counted little beside this. When Joe broke with Mary, his mentor declared the action inevitable, as the girl would not alter her opinions; and when, presently, young Noy fell in love with Joan, her father saw no objection, for the sailor was honest, already a staunch Luke Gospeller, and a clean liver.

Perhaps at that moment there was hardly another eligible youth in Newlyn, from Tregenza's point of view. He held Joan a girl to be put under stern marital rule as soon as possible, and Joe promised to make a godly husband with a strong will, while his convictions and view of life were altogether satisfactory, being modelled on Michael's own. The arrangement suited Joan. She believed she loved Joe very dearly, and she looked forward with satisfaction to marrying him in about a year's time, when he should have won a shipmaster's certificate. But she viewed his departure without suffering, and would not have willingly foregone her remaining year of freedom. She respected Joe very much, and knew he would make a good partner, and give her a position above the everyday wives of Newlyn; moreover, he was a fine figure of a man. But he lacked mental breadth, and that fact sometimes tickled her dormant sense of humour. He copied her father so exactly, and she, who lived with the real thunder, never could show sufficient gravity or conviction in the presence of the youthful and narrow-minded Noy's second-hand echoes. Mary Chirgwin was naturally a thousand times more religious-minded than Joan, and sometimes Joe wished the sober mind of his first love could be transported to the beautiful body of his second; but he kept this notion to himself, studied to please his future father-in-law, which he succeeded in doing handsomely, and contented himself, in so far as his lady was concerned, by reflecting that the necessary control over her somewhat light mind would be his in due season.

To return from this tedious but necessary glimpse at the position and belief of these people, to Joan and the washing, it is to be noted that she quickly made up for lost time, and, without further mentioning the incidents of her morning's excursion, began to work. She pulled up her sleeves, dragged her dress about her waist, then started to cleanse the thick flannels her father wore at sea, his long-tailed shirts and woollen stockings. The Tregenzas were well-to-do folk, and did not need to use the open spaces of the village for drying of clothes. Joan presently set up a line among the plum trees, and dawdled over the hanging-out of wet garments, for it was now noon, sunny, mild and fresh, with a cool salt breeze off the sea. The winter repose of the bee-butts had been broken at last, and the insects were busy with the plum-blossom and among the little green flowerets on the gooseberry bushes. Beyond, sun-streaked and bright, extended apple trees, with whitewashed stems and a twinkle of crimson on their boughs, where buds grew ripe for the blowing.

Joan yawned, and blinked up at the sun to see if it was dinner-time. Then she watched a kitten hunting the bees in the gooseberry bushes. Presently the little creature knocked one to the ground, and began to pat it and pounce upon it. Then the bee, using nature's weapon to preserve precious life, stung the kitten, and the kitten hopped into the air much amazed. It shook its paw, licked it, shook it again. Joan laughed, and two pigs at the bottom of the garden heard her, and grunted and squealed as they thrust expectant noses through the palings of their sty. They connected the laugh with their dinner, but Joan's thoughts were all upon her own.

A few minutes later Thomasin Tregenza called her, and, as they sat down, Tom arrived from school. He was a brown-faced, dark-eyed, black-haired youngster, good-looking enough, but not at that moment.

"Aw! Jimmery! fightin' agin," said his mother, viewing two swollen lips, a bulged ear, and an eye half-closed.

"I've downed Matthew Bent, Joan! Ten fair rounds, then he gived up!"

"Fight, fight, fight!—'tis all you think of," said his parent; while Joan poured congratulations on the conqueror.

"'Tweer bound to come arter the football when he played foul, an' I tawld en so. Now we'm friends."

"Be he bruised same as you?"

"A sight worse; he's a braave picksher, I tell 'e! I doubt he won't come to school this arternoon. That'll shaw. I be gwaine if I got to crawl theer."

"An' him a year older than what you be!" said Joan.

"'Iss, Mat's 'lebben year old. I'll have some vinegar an' brown paper to this here eye, mother."

"Ait your mayte—ait your mayte fust," she answered. "Plague 'pon your fightin'!"

"But that Bent bwoy's bin at en for months; an' a year older too!" said Joan.

"'Iss, the bwoy's got no more'n what 'e desurved, for that matter. They Bents be all puffed up, though they'm so poor as rats, an' wi'out 'nough religion to save the sawl of a new-born babe 'mongst the lot of 'em."

Tom, with his mouth full of fish and potato-pie, told the story of his victory, and the women made a big, hearty meal and listened.

"He cockled up to me, an' us beginned fightin' right away, an' in the third round I scat en on the mouth an' knocked wan 'is teeth out. An' in the fifth round he dropped me a whister-cuff 'pon the eye as made me blink proper."

"Us doan't want to knaw no more 'bout it," declared his mother after dinner was over. "You've laced en, an' that's enough. You knaw what faither'll say: 'You did ought to fight no battle but the Lard's.' Now clap this here over your eye for a bit, then be off with 'e."

Tom marched away to school earlier than usual that afternoon, while the women went to the door and watched him trudge off, both mightily proud of his performance and his battered brown face.

"He be a reg'lar li'l apty-cock,* sure 'nough!" said Joan.

* *Apty-cock*, brave, plucky youngster.

Mrs. Tregenza answered with a nod, and looked along the road after her son. There was a softer expression in her eyes as she watched him. Besides, she had eaten well and was comfortable. Now she picked her teeth with a pin, and snuffed the sea air, and gave a passing neighbour "good afternoon" with greater warmth of manner than usual. Presently her mood changed; she noisily rated herself and her step-daughter for standing idling; then both went back to their work.

CHAPTER IV.

BARRON BEGINS TO LEARN THE GORSE.

ABOUT five o'clock on the morning of the following day the master of the white cottage came home. His wife expected him, and was getting breakfast when Michael tramped in —a very tall, square-built man, clad to the eye in tanned oilskin over-alls, sou'wester, and jack-boots. The fisherman returned to his family in high good temper, for the sea had yielded silvery thousands to his drift-nets, and the catch had already been sold in the harbour for a handsome figure. The brown sails of Tregenza's lugger flapped in the bay amongst a crowd of others, and every man was in a hurry to be off again at the earliest opportunity. Already the first boats home were putting to sea once more, making a wide tack across the mouth of the bay until nearly abreast of St. Michael's Mount, then tearing away like racehorses, with foam flying as they sailed before the eastern wind, for the Scilly Islands and the mackerel.

Michael kissed his wife and Joan also, as she came to the kitchen, sleepy-eyed in the soft light, to welcome him. Then, while Mrs. Tregenza was busied with breakfast, and the girl cleaned some fish, he went to his own small room off the kitchen and changed his clothes—all silvery, scale-spotted, and blood-smeared—for the clean garments which were spread and waiting. First the man indulged in luxuries. He poured out a large tub of fresh water and washed himself; he even cleaned his nails and his teeth—hyperbolic refinements that made the baser sort laugh at him behind his back.

At the meal which followed his toilet, Tregenza talked to

his wife and daughter upon various subjects. He spoke slowly and from the lungs, with the deep, echoing voice of one used to vocal exercise in the open air.

"I seed the *Anna* yesterday, Joan," he said—"a proud ship, full-rigged, wi' butivul lines. Her passed wi'in three mile of us or less off the islands."

Joan did not hint at her visit to Gorse Point of the previous day; but her stepmother mentioned it, and her father felt called upon to reprimand his daughter, though not very seriously.

"'Twas an empty, vain thing to do," he said.

"I promised Joe, faither."

"Why, then you was right to go, though a fulish thing to promise en. Wheer's Tom to?"

Tom came down a minute later. The swelling of his lips was lessened, but his ear had not returned to a normal size, and his eye was black.

"Fighting again?" Michael began, looking up from his saucer and fixing his eyes on his son.

"Please, faither, I—— "

"Doan't say naught. You'm so fond of it, that I judges you'd best begin fightin' the battle o' life right on end. 'Tain't no use keepin' you to school no more. 'Tis time you comed aboard."

Tom crowed with satisfaction, and Mrs. Tregenza sighed and stopped eating. This event had been hanging over her head for many a long day now; but she had put the thing away, and secretly hoped that after all Tregenza would change his mind and apprentice the boy to a shore trade. However, Tom had made his choice, and his father meant him to abide by it. No other life appealed to the boy; heredity marked him for the sea, and he longed for the hard business to begin.

"I'll larn you something besides fisticuffs, my beauty. 'Tis all well a' fine, this batterin' an' bruisin'; but it awnly breeds the savage in 'e, same as raw meat do in a dog. No more fightin' 'cept wi' dirty weather, an' high seas, an' contrary winds, an' the world, the flesh, an' the devil. I went to sea as a lugger-bwoy when I was eight year old, an' ain't bin off the water more'n a month to wance ever since. This day two week you come along wi' me. That'll give mother full time to see 'bout your kit."

Joan wept, Thomasin Tregenza whined, and Tom danced a break-down, and rolled away to see some fisherboy friends in the harbour before school began. Then Michael, calling his daughter to him, walked with her among his plum trees, talked of God with some quotations, and looked at his pigs. Presently he busied himself, and made ready for sea in a little outhouse where paint and ship's chandlery was stored; and finally, the hour then being half-past seven, he returned to his labours.

Joan walked with him to the harbour, and listened while he talked of the goodness of God to the Luke Gospellers at sea, how the mackerel had been delivered to them in thousands, and how the Bible Christians and Primitive Methodists had fared by no means so happily. The tide was high, and Grey Michael's skiff waited for him at the pier-head beside the light-house. He soon climbed down into it, whereupon the little boat, rowed by two strong pairs of hands, danced away to the fleet. Already the luggers were stretching off in a long line across the bay; and among them appeared a number of visitors— Lowestoft yawls come down to the West after the early mackerel. They were big, stout vessels, and many had steam-power aboard. Joan watched her father's lugger start, and saw it overhaul not a few smaller ships before she turned from the busy harbour homewards. That morning she designed to work with a will, for a part of the afternoon was to be spent on Gorse Point, if all went well, and she already looked forward somewhat curiously to her second meeting with the singular man who had lent her his field-glasses.

Mrs. Tregenza was in sorry, snappy case all day. The blow had fallen, and within a fortnight Tom would go to sea. This dismal fact depressed her not a little, and she snuffled over her ironing, and her voice grated worse than usual upon the ear.

"He's such a hot-headed twoad of a bwoy. I knaw he'll never get on 'pon the water. I doubt us'll hear he's bin knocked overboard or some sich thing some day; an' them two brothers, they Pritchards, as allus sails 'long wi' Tregenza, they'm that comical-tempered every one knaws. Oh, my God, why couldn' he let on larn a land trade—carpenterin' or sich like?"

"But, you see, faither's a rich man, an' some time Tom 'll fill his shoes. Faither do awn his bwoat an' the nets tu, which is more'n most Newlyn men does."

"'Iss, I should think 'twas," said Mrs. Tregenza, forgetting her present sorrow in the memory of such splendid circumstances. "Theer ban't wan feller as awns all like what faither do. The Lard helps His chosen; not but what Tregenza allus helped hisself, an' set the example to Newlyn from his boyhood."

Mrs. Tregenza always licked her lips when she talked about money or religion, and she did so now.

Among Cornish drifters Grey Michael's position was undoubtedly unique; for, under the rules of the Cornish fishery, he enjoyed exceptional advantages, owing to his personal possession both of boat and nets. The owner of a drift-boat takes one-eighth part of the gross proceeds of a catch, and the remaining seven-eighths are divided into two equal parts, of which one part is subdivided among the crew of the boat, while the other goes to the owner or owners of the nets used on board. The number of nets to a boat is about fifty as a rule, and a man to possess his own boat and outfit must be unusually well-to-do.

But it was partly for this reason that Mrs. Tregenza refused to be comforted. She grudged every farthing spent on anything, and much disliked the notion of tramping to Penzance to spend the greater part of a five-pound note on Tom's sea outfit. In a better cause, she would not have thought it ill to expend money upon him. His position pointed to something higher than a fisherman's life. He might have aspired to a shop in the future, together with a measure of worldly prosperity and importance not to be expected from any mere seafarer. But Tom had settled the matter by deciding for himself, and his father had approved the ambition; so there the matter ended, save for grumbling and sighing. Joan too felt sore enough at heart when she heard that the long-dreaded event lay but a fortnight in the future. But she knew her father, and felt sure that the certainty of Tom's going to sea at the appointed time would now only be defeated by death or the Judgment Day. So she did not worry or fret. Nothing served to soothe her stepmother, however, and the girl was glad to slip off after dinner, leaving Thomasin with her troubles.

Joan made brisk way through Mousehole, and in less than an hour stood out among the furzes in the little lonely theatre above the cliffs. For a moment she saw nothing of John Barron; then she found him sitting on a camp-stool before a light easel which looked all legs, with a mere little square patch of a picture perched upon them. Joan walked to within a few yards of the artist, and waited for him to speak. But eye, hand, brain were all working together on the sketch before him, and if he saw his visitor at all, which was doubtful, he took no notice of her. Joan came a little closer, and still John Barron ignored her presence. Then she grew uncomfortable, and feeling she must break the silence, spoke.

"I be come, sir, 'cordin' to what you said."

He added a touch, and looked up with no recognition in his eyes. His forehead frowned with doubt apparently, then he seemed to remember.

"Ah, the young woman who told me about the luggers!" Suddenly he smiled at her—the first time she had seen him do so. "You never mentioned your name, I think?"

"Joan Tregenza, sir."

"I promised you a little picture of that big ship, didn't I?"

"You was that kind, sir."

"Well, I haven't forgotten it. I finished the picture this

morning, and I think you may like it; but I had to leave it until to-morrow, because the paints take so long to dry."

"I'm sure I thank you kindly, sir."

"No need. To-morrow it will be quite ready for you, with a frame and all complete. You see, I've begun to try and paint the gorse."

He invited her by a gesture to view his work. She came closer, and as she bent he glanced up at her with his face for a moment close to hers; then she drew back quickly, blushing.

"'Tis butivul—just like them fuzzes!"

He had been working for two hours before she came, painting a small patch of the gorse. Old gnarled stems wound upwards crookedly, and beneath them lay a dead carpet of gorse needles, with a blade or two of grass breaking through. From the roots and bases of the main stems sprouted many a shoot of young gorse, their prickles tender as the claws of a new-born kitten, their shape, colour, and foliage of thorns quite different to the mature plant above. There, in the main masses of the shrub, mossy brown buds in clumps foretold future splendour. But already much gold had burst the sheath and was ablaze, scenting the pure air, murmured over by many bees.

"You could a'most pick they theer flowers," declared Joan of the picture.

"Perhaps presently, when they are painted as I hope to paint them. This is only a rough bit of work to occupy my hand and eye while I am learning the gorse. Men who paint seriously have to learn trees and blossoms just as they have to learn faces. And we are never satisfied. When I have painted this gorse, with its thorns and buds, I shall sigh for more truth. I cannot paint the soul of each yellow flower that opens to the sun; I cannot paint the sunny smell that is sweet in our nostrils now. God's gorse scents the air; mine will only smell of fat oil. What shall I do?"

"I dunnaw."

"More does anybody. It can't be helped. But I must try my best and make it real—each spike, as I see it—the dead grey ones on the ground, and the live green ones on the tree, and the baby ones, and the old grey-pointed ones which have seen their best days and will presently die and fall—I must paint them all, Joan."

She laughed.

"Don't laugh," he said very seriously. "Only an artist would laugh at me—not you who love nature. There lived a great painter, Joan, who painted pictures that nobody else in the world could paint. He is dead now, but he took trouble to the last day he had power to hold a brush. Once, when he was a young man, he drew a lemon tree far away in Italy. It was only a little lemon tree, but the artist rose morning after morning, and drew it leaf by leaf, twig by twig, until every leaf and bud and lemon and bough had appeared. It was not laboured and false; it was grand because it was true; a joy for ever; work Old Masters had loved; full of distinction, and power, and patience almost Oriental;—a thing, Joan Tregenza, worth a wilderness of 'harmonies' and 'impressions,' 'nocturnes' and 'notes,' smudges and audacities. But, I suppose, that is all gibberish to you?"

"''Iss, so it be," she admitted.

"Learn to love everything that is beautiful, my good child. But I think you do—unconsciously perhaps."

"I don't take much 'count of things."

"Yes—unconsciously. You have a cowslip there stuck in your frock, though where you got it from I can't imagine. The flower is a month too early."

"'Iss, 'tis. I found en in a lew, sunshiny plaace. Us have got a frame for growin' things under glass, an' it had bin put down 'pon top this cowslip, an' drawed en up."

"Will you give it to me?"

She did so, and he smelt it.

"D'you know that the green of the cowslip is the most beautiful green in all nature, Joan? Here, I have a flower too; we will exchange if you like."

He took a scrap of blackthorn bloom from his coat and

held it out to her; but she shrunk backwards, and he learnt something.

"Please, not that. Truly 'tis the dreadfulest wicked flower. Doan't 'e ax me to take en."

"Unlucky?"

"'Iss, fay! Him or her as first brings blackthorn in the house dies afore it blows again. Truth—solemn—us all knaws it down in these paarts. 'Tis a bewitched thing, a wicked plant, an' you can see it grawin' all humpetty-backed an' bent an' crooked. Wance, when a man killed hisself, they did use to bury en wheer roads met, an' put a blackthorn stake through en, an' it allus grawed arter; an' that's the worstest sort o' all."

"Dear, dear! I'm glad you told me, Joan. I will not wear it, nor shall you," he said, and flung it down and stamped on it very seriously.

The girl was gratified.

"I judge you'm a furriner, else you'd knawn 'bout the wickedness o' blackthorn."

"I am. Thank you very much. But for you, I should have gone home wearing it. That puts me in your debt, Joan."

"'Tain't nothin', awnly there's a many coorious Carnish things like that, an' coorious customs what some doan't hold with an' some does."

She sat down near the cliff edge, with her back to him, and he smiled to himself to find how quickly his mild manners and reserve had put the girl at her ease. She looked perfect that afternoon, and he yearned to begin painting her, but his scheme of action demanded time for its fulfilment and ultimate success. He let the little fearless chatterbox talk. Her voice was soft and musical as the cooing of a wood-dove, and the sweet, full notes chimed in striking contrast to her uncouth speech. But Joan's diction gave pleasure to the listener; it had freedom and wildness, and was almost wholly innocent of any petrifying educational influences.

Joan, for her part, felt at ease. The man was so polite, so humble, so small. He thanked her for her information most gratefully. Moreover, he evidently cared nothing about her or her looks. She felt perfectly safe, for it was easy to see that he thought only of the gorse.

"My faither's agin' such wise words an' sayin's," she babbled on, "but I dunnaw. They seems truth to me, an' to many as is cleverer than what I be. My mother b'lieved in 'em, an' Joe did, till faither turned en away from 'em. But when us plighted troth, I made en jine hands wi' me under a livin' spring o' water, though he said 'twas heathenish; awnly, somehow, I knawed 'twas a proper thing to do."

"I should like to hear more about these old customs some day," he said, as though Joan and he were to meet often in the future, "and I should be obliged to you for telling me about them, because I always delight in such matters."

She was quicker of mind than he thought, and rose, taking his last remark as a hint that he wished to be alone.

"Don't go, Joan, unless you must. I'm a very lonely man, and it is a great pleasure to me to hear you talk. Look here."

She approached him, and he showed her a pencil sketch now perched on the easel—a drawing considerably larger than that upon which he had been working when she arrived.

"This is a rough idea of my picture. It is going to be much larger, though, and I have sent all the way to London for a canvas on which to paint it."

"'Twill be a gert big picksher, then?"

"So big that I think I must try and get something into it besides the gorse. I want something or other in the middle, just for a change. What could I paint there?"

"I dunnaw."

"More do I. I wonder how that little white pony tethered yonder would do?"

Joan laughed.

"You'd never get the likes o' him to bide still for 'e."

"No, I'm afraid not; and I doubt if I'm clever enough to paint him either. You see, I'm only a beginner—not like these clever artists who can draw anything. Well, I must think:

to-morrow is Sunday.   I shall begin my big picture on Monday
if the weather keeps kind.   I shall paint here, in the open air.
And I will bring your ship, too, if you care to take the trouble
to come for it."

"'Iss; an' thank 'e, sir."

"Not at all.   I owe you thanks.   Just think if I had gone
home with that horrid blackthorn!"

He turned to his work as though she were no longer present,
and the girl prepared to depart.

"I'll bid you good arternoon now, sir," she said timidly.

He looked up with surprise.

"Haven't you gone, Joan?   I thought you had started.
Good-bye until Monday.   Remember, if it is cold or rainy, I
shall not be here."

The girl trotted off; and when she had gone, Barron drew
her from memory in the centre of his sketch; for the golden
glories of the gorse were destined to be no more than a frame
for something fairer.

CHAPTER V.

COLD COMFORT.

JOHN BARRON made other preparations for his picture beside those detailed to Joan Tregenza. He designed a large canvas, and proposed to paint it in the open air according to his custom. His health had improved, and the sustained splendour of the spring weather flattered hopes that, his model once won, the work he proposed would grow into an accomplished fact. There was no cottage where he might house his picture and materials within half a mile of Gorse Point, but a granite cow-byre rose considerably nearer at a corner of an upland field. Wind-worn and lichen-stained it stood, situate not more than two hundred yards from the spot on which Barron's picture was to be painted. A pathway to outlying farms cut the fields hard by the byre, and about it lay implements of husbandry: a chain harrow and a rusty plough. Black, tar-pitched double doors gave entrance to the shed, and light entered from a solitary window now roughly nailed up from the outside with boards. A pad-lock fastened the door, but by wrenching down the covering of the window Barron got sight of the interior. A smell of vermin and decay rose from the inner darkness; then, as his eyes focussed the gloom, he noted a dry, spacious chamber likely enough to answer his purpose. Brown litter of last year's fern filled one corner, and in it was marked a lair as of some medium-sized beast; elsewhere a few sacks with spades and picks, and a small pile of potatoes appeared; the roots were all sprouting feebly from white eyes, as though they knew spring held the world, though neither sunshine warmed them, nor soft earth aided their struggle for life. Here the man might well keep his canvas and other matters. Assuming that temporary possession of the shed was possible, his property would certainly be safe enough there, for artists are respected in and about Newlyn, and their needs considered when possible. A farm, known as Middle Hemyll, showed grey chimneys above the fields, half a mile distant, and after finding the shed, Barron proceeded thither to learn its ownership. The master of Middle Hemyll speedily enlightened him, and the visitor learnt that not only did he speak to the possessor of the cow-byre, but that Farmer Ford was a keen supporter of art, and would be happy to rent his outhouse for a moderate consideration.

"The land ban't under pasture now, an' the plaace ed'n much used just this minute, so you'm welcome if you mind to. My auld goat did live theer wance, but er's dead this long time. Maybe you seed the carcase of en outside? I'll have the byre cleared come to-morrer; an' if so be you wants winders in the roof, same as other paintin' gents, you'll have to put 'em theer wi' your awn money."

Barron explained that he only needed the shed as a store-house for his picture and tools.

"Just so—just so. Then you'll find a bwoy wi' the key theer Monday, an' all vitty; an' you can pay in advancement or arter, as you please to. Us'll say half a crown a week, if that'll soot 'e."

The listener produced half-a-sovereign, much to Farmer Ford's gratification, and asked that a lad or man might be found to return with him there and then to the shed.

"I am anxious to see the place, and have it in order before I go back to Newlyn," he explained. "I will pay you extra for the necessary labour, and it should not take above an hour."

"No more 'twill, an' I'll come 'long with 'e myself this minute," answered the other.

Getting a key to the padlock, and a big birch broom, he returned with Barron, and soon had the doors of the disused byre thrown open to the air.

"I shut en up when the auld goat went dead. Theer 'a used to lie in the corner, but now he'm outside, an' I doubt the piskeys, what they talks 'bout, be mighty savage wi' mo for not buryin' the beast, 'cause all fairies is 'dicted to goats, they do say, an' mighty fond o' the milk of 'em."

Farmer Ford soon cleared the place of potatoes, sacks, and tools. Then, taking his broom, he made a clean sweep of dust and dirt.

"Theer's a many more rats here than I knawed, seemin'ly," he said as he examined a sink in the stones of the floor, used for draining the stalls. "They come up here for sartain, an' runs out 'long the heydge to the mangel-wurzel mound, I lay."

Without, evidences of the vermin were clear enough. Long hardened tracks, patted down by many paws, ran this way and that, and the main rat thoroughfare extended, as the farmer foretold, to a great mound, where, stowed snugly in straw under earth, lay packed the remains of a mangel-wurzel crop. At one end the store had been opened and drawn upon for winter use, but a goodly pile of the great tawny globes still remained, small lemon-coloured leaves sprouting from them. Farmer Ford, however, viewed the treasure without satisfaction.

"Us killed a power o' sheep wi' they blarsted roots last winter," he said. "You'd never think now as the frost could touch 'em, but it did though, awin' to the wicked long winter. It got to 'em, sure 'nough, an' theer was frost in 'em when us gived 'em to the sheep, an' it rotted theer innards, poor twoads, an' they died, more'n a score."

Barron listened thoughtfully to these details, then pointed to an ugly sight beyond the wurzel mound.

"I should like that removed," he said.

It was the dead goat, withered to a mummy almost, with horns and hide intact, and a rat-way bored through the body of the beast under a tunnel of its ribs.

"Jimmery! to see what them varmints have done to en! But I'll bury what's left right on end; an' I'll stop the sink in the house, then you'll be free of 'em."

These things the farmer did, and presently departed, promising to revisit the spot ere long with some dogs and a ferret or two. So Barron was left master of the place. He found it dry, weather-proof, and well suited to his requirements in every respect. The concerns which he had ordered from London would be with him that night if all went well, and he decided that they should be conveyed to the byre at an early hour on Monday morning.

The next day was Sunday, and half a dozen men, with Barron and Murdoch among them, strolled into Brady's great white-washed studio to see and criticize his Academy picture, which was finished. Everybody declared that the artist had excelled himself in " The End of the Voyage." It represented a sweep of the rocky coast by the Lizard, a wide grey sand left naked by the tide, with the fringe of a heavy sea churning on it, and sea-fowl strutting here and there. In the foreground, half buried under tangles of brown weed, torn from the rocks by a past storm, lay a dead sailor, and a big herring-gull, with its head on one side, and a world of inquiry in its yellow eyes, was looking at him. Tremendous vigour marked the work, and only a Brady could have come safely through the difficulties which had been surmounted in its creation. Everybody sang praises, and Barron nodded warm approval, but said nothing until challenged.

" Now, find the faults, then tell me what's good," said the gigantic painter. He stood there, burly, hearty, physically splendid—the man of all others in that throng who might have been pointed to as the creator of the solemn grey picture before them.

" Leave fault-finding to Fleet Street," said Barron ; " let the critics tell you where you are wrong. I am no critic, but I know what a mountain of hard work went to this."

" That's all right, old man ; never mind the work—or me. Be impartial."

" Why should I ? To be impartial, as this world wags, is to be friendless. "

"Good Lord! d'you think I mind mauling? There's something wrong, or you wouldn't be so deucedly evasive. Out with it!"

"Well, your sailor's not dead."

Brady roared with laughter.

"Man! the poor divil's been in the water a week!"

"Not he. 'Tis a mistake in nine painted corpses out of ten. If you want to paint a drowned man, wait till you've seen one close. That sailor in the seaweed's asleep. Sleep is graceful, remember, death by drowning is generally ugly—stiff, stark, hideous, eyeless, fish-gnawed a week after the event. But what does it matter? You've painted a great picture. That sea, with the circular swirl, as each wave goes back into the belly of the next, is well done; and those lumps of spume fluttering above water-mark, that was finely noted. Easy to write down in print, but difficult as the fiend to paint. And the picture is full of wind, too. Your troubles are amply repaid, and I congratulate you. A man who could paint that will go as far as he likes."

The simple Brady forgot the powder in swallowing the jam. Barron had touched those things in his work which were precious to him. His impulsive nature took fire, and there was almost a quiver of emotion in his big voice as he answered—

"Damn it, you're a brick! I'd sooner hear you praise those lumps of sea-spume, racing over the sand there, than see my picture on the lines."

But sentiment was strange to John Barron's impersonal nature, and he froze.

"Another fault exists which probably nobody will tell you but me. Your seaweed's great, and you knew it by heart before you painted it—that I'll swear to; but your sleeper there would never lie in the line of it as you have him. Reflect: the sea must float the light weed after it could move him no more. He should be stogged in the sand nearer the sea."

Brady, however, contested this criticism, and so the talk

wore on until the men separated. But the Irishman called on Barron after midday dinner, and together they strolled through Newlyn towards the neighbouring village. Chance brought them face to face with two persons more vital to the narrative than themselves, and, pausing to chronicle the event of the meeting, we may leave the artists and follow those whom they encountered.

Grey Michael kept ashore on Sundays, and to-day, having come off the sea at dawn, was not again putting forth until next morning. He had attended meeting with his wife, his daughter, and his son; he had dined also, and was now walking over to Mousehole that he might bring some religious comfort to a sorely stricken Luke Gospeller—a young sheep but lately won to the fold, and who now lay at the point of death. Joan accompanied him, and upon the way they met John Barron and his companion. The girl blushed hotly, then chilled with a great disappointment, for Barron's eyes were on the sea. He was talking as he passed by, and he apparently saw neither her nor her Sunday gown, which circumstance was a sorrow to Joan. But in reality Barron missed nothing. He had shivered at her green dress and poor finery long before she reached him. Her garb ruffled his senses and left him wounded.

"There goes your beauty," laughed Brady. "How would you like to paint her in that frock, with those sinful blue flowers on her hat?"

"Nature must weep to see the bizarre carnival these people enjoy on the seventh day," answered the other. "Their duns and drabs, their russets and tawny tones of red and orange are of their environment, the proper skins for their bodies; but to think of that girl brightening the eyes of a hundred louts by virtue of those fine feathers! Dream of her in the stone age, clad in a petticoat torn from a wolf, with her straw-coloured hair to her waist and a necklace of shells or wild beasts' teeth between her breasts! And that splendid man—her father, I suppose— what a picture his broadcloth and soft black hat make of him— like the head of a patriarch stuck on a tailor's dummy!"

Meanwhile, ignorant of these startling criticisms, Mr. Tregenza and his daughter pursued their road, and presently stopped before a cottage in one of the cobble-paved alley-ways of Mousehole. A worn old woman opened the door and curtseyed to Grey Michael. He wished her good afternoon, then entered the cottage, first bidding Joan return in an hour. She had friends near at hand, and hurried off, glad to escape the sight of sickness and the prayers she knew that her father would presently deliver.

"How be Albert?" inquired the fisherman; and the widowed mother of the patient answered—

"Better, I do pray. 'Er was in the doldrums 'issterday, an' bad by night also, a-dwaling an' moaning gashly; but, the Lard be praised, he'm better in mind by now, an' I do think 'tis more along of Bible-readin' than all the doctor's traade * he've took. I read to en 'bout that theer bwoy, the awnly son o' his mother, and her a widder-wumman, an' how as the Lard brought en round arter he'd gone dead."

Grey Michael sniffed and made no comment.

"I'll see en an' put up a prayer or so," he said.

"An' the Lard'll reward 'e, Mr. Tregenza."

Young Albert Vallack greeted the visitor with even greater reverence than his mother had done. He and the old woman were Falmouth folks, and had drifted westerly upon the father's death, until chance anchored them in Newlyn. Now the lad— a dissolute youth enough, until sudden illness had frightened him to religion—was dying of consumption, and dying fast, though as yet he knew it not.

"'Tis handsome in you, a-comin' to see the likes o' me," said the patient, flushing with satisfaction. "You'm like the stickler at a wras'lin' match, Mr. Tregenza, sir; you sees fair play betwixt God an' man."

"So you'm better, Albert, your mother sez."

"'Iss, a bit. Theer's more kick an' sprawl † in me than theer have bin; an' I feels more hopeful like 'bout the future."

* *Doctor's traade,* physic.   † *Kick an' sprawl,* strength, vitality.

Self-righteousness in a new-fledged Luke Gospeller who had been of the fold but three months, and whose previous record was extremely unsatisfactory, irritated Grey Michael not a little.

"Bwoy!" he said loudly, "doan't 'e be deceived that way. 'Gird 'e wi' sackcloth, lament and howl; for the fierce anger o' the Lard is *not* turned back from us.' Three months o' righteousness is a purty bad set off 'gainst twenty years o' sin, an' it doan't become 'e to feel hopeful, I 'sure ye."

The sick man's colour paled, and a certain note as of triumph in his voice died out of it. His mother had left them, feeling that her presence might hinder conversation and lessen the comfort which Mr. Tregenza brought.

"I did ought to be chap-fall'n, I s'pose."

"'Iss, you did, my son, nobody more'n you. Maybe you'll live; maybe you'll die; but keep humble. I doan't wish to deceive 'e. Us abbun had time to make no certainty 'bout things. You'm in the Lard's hand, an' it becomes 'e to sing small, an' remember what your life's bin."

The other grew uneasy, and his voice faltered while he still fought for a happy eternity.

"I'd felt like 'twas all right arter what mother read."

"Not so. God's a just God 'fore everything. Theer ed'n no favourin' wi' Him. I hopes you'll live this many a day, Vallack; an' then, when your hour comes, you'll have piled up a tidy record an' can go wi' a certainty faacin' you. Seems you'm better, an' us at chapel's prayed hot an' strong to the Throne that you might be left to work out your salvation now your foot's 'pon the road."

"But if I dies, mister?"

"'The prayer of the righteous man availeth much,'" answered Grey Michael, evasively. "I be come," he added, "to read the Scriptures to 'e."

"You all prayed for me, sir?"

"'Iss, every man, but theer was no mincin' matters, Albert. Us was axin' for a miserable sinner—a lost sheep awnly just strayed back—an' we put it plain as that was so."

"'Twoer mighty kind o' the Luke Gosp'lers, sir."

"'Twas their dooty.   Now I be gwaine to read the Book."

"1 feels that uneasy now," whined the sufferer, in a voice where fear spoke instead of hope, "but I s'pose 'tis a sign o' graace I should be?"

"'Iss, 'tis.   I've comed to tell 'e the truth, for 'tis ill as a man should be blind to facts on what may be his last bed 'bove the airth.   Listen to this, my son; an' if theer's anything you doan't onderstand, ax me, an' I'll thraw light 'pon it."

He read, with loud, slow voice, the fifty-fifth chapter of Isaiah, and that glorious clarion of great promise gave Michael the lie and drowned his own religious opinions as thunder drowns the croaking of marsh frogs; but he knew it not.   The brighter burned his own shining light, the blacker the shadows it threw upon the future of all sinners.

As Tregenza finished and put down his Bible, the other spoke, and quoted eagerly—

"'Incline your ear, an' come unto Me; hear, an' your sawl shall live'!   Theer do seem a hope in that, if it ed'n awver-bold me thinkin' so?" he asked.

"That's like them Church o' Englanders, a-tearin' wan text away from t'others, an' readin' it accordin' as they pleases.   I'll expound it all to wance, as a godfearing man did ought to treat the Scriptures."

Grey Michael's exposition illustrated nothing beyond his own narrow intellectual limitations.   His cold cloud of words obscured the prophet's sunshine, and again the light went out of the dying man's face, leaving only alarm.   He trembled on the brink of the horrid truth; he heard it thinly veiled in the other's stern utterance; saw it looking from his hard, blue eyes.   After the sermon, silence followed, broken by Vallack, who coughed once and again, then raised himself, and braced his heart to the tremendous question that demanded answering.

"I wants your awn feelin' like, mister.   I must have it. I caan't sleep no more wi'out knawin' the best or worst.   You be the justest man ever I seed or heard tell on out the

Scriptures, an' I wants 'e to gimme your opinion like. S'pose you was the Judge, an' I comed afore 'e, an' the books was theer, and you'd read 'em, an' had to conclude 'pon 'em?"

The fisherman reflected. Vallack's proposition did not strike him as particularly grotesque. He felt it was a natural question, and he only regretted that it had been put, because, though he had driven more than one young man to righteousness along the path of terror, in this present case the truth came too late, save to add another horror to death. He believed in all sincerity that as surely as the young man before him presently died, so surely would he be damned, but he saw no particular object in stating the fact. Such intelligence might tell upon Vallack's physical condition—a thing of all others to be avoided; for Grey Michael held that the sufferer's only chance of a happy eternity was increased and lengthened opportunity in time.

"It ed'n for me to sit in the judgment seat, Albert. ' Vengeance is Mine, sayeth the Lord.' You must allus hold in mind that theer's mighty few saved alive, best o' times. Many be called, but few chosen. Men go down to the graave every second o' the day an' night, but if you could see the sawls a-streamin' away, thicker'n a cloud of starlings, you'd find a mass, black as a storm, went down-long, an' awnly just a summer cloud like o' the blessed riz up. Hell's bigger'n heaven; an' er's need to be, for heaven's like to be a lonely plaace when all's said. I won't speak no more 'bout the subjec'. 'Tis good fashion weather for 'e just now, an' us'll hope as you ban't gwaine to die for many a day."

"Say it out, mister; say it out. I knaws what you means. You reckons, if I gaws, I'm lost."

"My poor sawl, justice is justice; an' the Lard's all for justice, an' no less. Theer's no favourin' wi' Him, Albert."

" But mightn't He favour the whole bilin' of us, good 'n bad, 'cause He made us?"

" Surely not. Wheer's the justice o' that? If He done that, how'd the godly get their fair dues—eh? Be the righteous man to share God's heaven wi' publicans and sinners? That ed'n justice, anyhow. Don't fret, lad; tears won't mend bad years. Bide quiet, an' listen to me whiles I pray for 'e."

The man in the bed had grown very white; his eyes burnt wildly out of a shrunken face; and he gripped the sheets, and shivered in pure physical terror.

"I caan't die; I caan't die not yet," he groaned. "Pray to the Lard to keep me from dyin' yet awhile, mister. Ax en to give me just a li'l, li'l time, 'cause I'm that sorry for my scarlet sins."

Thereupon Michael knelt, clasped his hands so closely that the bent finger-joints grew white, raised his massive head upwards, and prayed with his eyes closed. The intercession for life ended, he rose up, shook Vallack by the hand, and so departed.

"Allus, when you've got the chance, bear the balm o' Gilead to a sinner's couch," he said to his daughter as they walked home. "'Tis the duty of man an' maid to spread the Truth, an' bring peace to the troubled, an' strength to the weak-hearted, an' rise up them that fall."

A week later Mr. Tregenza heard how Albert Vallack had burst a blood-vessel and died, fighting horribly with invisible terrors.

"Another sawl gone down in the pit," he said. "I reckon fewer an' fewer be chose every year, as the world do grow older an' riper for the last fires."

CHAPTER VI.

Joan found her sketch waiting for her the next day when she reached Gorse Point about eleven o'clock, and she also discovered John Barron with a large canvas before him. He had constructed his picture and already made many drawings for it. Now he knew exactly what he wanted, and he designed to paint Joan looking out at a distant sea, which would lie far behind the spectator of the picture. When she arrived, on a fine morning and mild, Barron rose from his camp-stool, lifted up a little canvas which stood framed at his side, and presented it to her. The sketch in oils of the *Anna* was cleverer than Joan could possibly know, but she took no small delight in it, and in the setting of rough deal brightly gilded.

"Sure 'tis truly good of 'e, sir!"

"You are more than welcome. Only let me say one word, Joan. Keep your picture hidden away until Joe comes back from sea and marries you. From what you tell me, your father might not like you to have this trifle, and I should be very sorry to annoy him."

"I waddun gwaine to show en," she confessed, "I shall store the picksher away, as you sez."

"You are wise. Now, look here—doesn't this promise to be a big affair? The gorse will be nearly as large as life; and I've been wondering ever so long what I shall put in the middle. And whatever do you think I've thought of?"

"I dunnaw. That white pony us saw, p'raps?"

"No; something much prettier. How would it do, d'you

think, if you stood here in front of the gorse just to fill up the
middle piece of the picture?"

"Oh no, no!　My faither——"

"You misunderstand, Joan.　I don't want a picture of *you*,
you know; I'm going to paint the gorse.　But if you just stood
here, you'd make a sort of contrast, with your brown frock.
Not a portrait at all, only just a figure to help the colour.
Besides, you mustn't think I'm an artist; I shouldn't go selling
the picture or hanging it up for everybody to stare at it.　I'm
certain your father wouldn't mind, and I'll tell him all about it
afterwards if you like."

She hesitated and reflected with trouble in her eyes, while
Barron quietly took the picture he had brought her, and
wrapped it up in a piece of paper.　His object was to remind
her, without appearing to do so, of her obligation to him; and
Joan was clever enough to take the hint, though not clever
enough to see that it was an intentional one.

"Would it be a long job, sir?" she asked at length.

"Yes, it would; because I'm a slow painter and rather
stupid.　But I should think it very, very kind of you.　I'm not
strong, you know, and I dare say this is the last picture I shall
ever paint."

"You ban't strong, sir?"

"Not at all."

She was silent, and a great sympathy rose in her girl's heart,
for frail health always made her sad. :

"You don't judge 'tis wrong, then, for a maiden to be
painted in a picksher?"

"Certainly not, Joan.　I should never suggest such a thing
to you if I thought it was in the least wrong.　I *know* it isn't
wrong."

"I seed you 'issterday," she said, changing the subject
suddenly; "but you dedn' see me—did 'e?"

"Yes, I did, and your father.　He is a grand-looking man.
By the way, Joan, I think I never told you my name.　I'm
called John.　That's short and simple—isn't it?"

" Mister Jan ? " she said.

" No, not ' mister '—just Jan," he answered, adopting her pronunciation. " I don't call you ' Miss ' Joan."

She looked at once uncomfortable and pleased.

" We must be friends," the man continued calmly, " now you have promised to let me put you here among the gorse bushes."

" Sure, I dunnaw 'bout the picksher, Mister Jan."

" Well, you would be doing me a great service. I want to paint you very much, and I think you will be kind."

He looked into her eyes with a steady, inquiring glance, and Joan experienced a new emotion. Joe had never looked like that, nor yet her father. She felt a will stronger than her own was busy with her inclinations. Volition remained free, and yet she doubted whether under any circumstances could she refuse his petition. As it happened, however, she already liked the man. He was so respectful and polite. Moreover, she felt sad to hear that he suffered in health. He would not ask her to do wrong, and she felt certain that she might trust him. A trembling wish to comply with his request already mastered her mind.

" You'm sure—gospel truth—theer ed'n no harm in it ? "

" Trust me."

In five minutes he had posed her as he wished, and was drawing, while every word he spoke put Joan more at her case. The spice of adventure and secrecy fired her, and she felt the spirit of romance in her blood, though she knew no name for it. Here was a secret delight knocking at the grey threshold of everyday life—an adventure which might last for many days.

Barron, to touch the woman in her if he could, harped upon her gown and the colour of it, on her shoes and sun-bonnet— on everything but herself. Presently he reaped his reward.

" Ban't you gwaine to paint my faace as well, Mister Jan ? "

" Yes, if I can. But your eyes are blue, and blue eyes are hard to paint well. Yours are so very blue, Joan. Didn't Joe ever tell you that ? "

"No; that's all fulishness."

"Nothing that's true is foolish. Now I'm going to make some little sketches of you, so as to learn something about you, like I learnt the gorse."

Barron drew rapidly, and Joan—ever ready to talk to a willing listener when her confidence was won—prattled on, turning the conversation as usual to the matters she loved. Upon her favourite subjects she dared not open her mouth at home, and even her lover refused to listen to the legends of the land; but they were part of the girl's life notwithstanding, drawn into her blood from her mother—a thousand times more real and precious than even the promised heaven of Luke Gospeldom, not to be wholly smothered at any time. Occasionally, indeed, uneasy fears that discussion of such concerns was absolutely sinful kept her dumb for a week; then the religious wave swept on, and Cornish folk-lore, with its splendour and romance, again filled her heart and bubbled from her lips. Her little stories pleased Barron mightily. Excitement heightened Joan's beauty. Her absolute innocence, at the age of seventeen, struck him as remarkable. It seemed curious that a child born in a cottage, where realities and facts are apt to roughly front boy and girl alike, should know so little. She was a beautiful, primitive creature, with strange store of picturesque fable in her mind; a treasury which brought colour and joy into life. So she prattled ancient "drolls" and fairy stories while the man painted.

Pure artistic interest filled Barron's brain at this season; not a shadow of passion made his pencil shaky, or his eye dim; and he began to learn the girl with as little emotion as he had learned the gorse. He asked her to unfasten the top button of her dress, that he might see the lines of her plump throat, and she complied without hesitation or ceasing from her chatter. He noted where the tan on her neck faded to white under her dress, and occupied himself with all the artistic problems she unconsciously spread before him; while she merely talked, garnered in his questions and comments on all she said, and found delight in the apparent interest and entertainment her conversation afforded him.

"I seed a maggotty-pie * comin' along this marnin'," she said. "Wan's bad an' a sign o' sorrer; but if you spits twice awver your left shoulder it doan't matter so much. But I be better off than many maidens, 'cause I be saint-protected like."

"That's interesting, Joan."

"Faither'd be mad if I let on 'bout it to him, so I doesn't. He doan't b'lieve much in dead saints, though Carnwall's full of 'em. Have 'e heard tell 'bout Saint Madern?"

"Ah, the saint of the well?"

"'Iss, an' the brook as runs by the Madern chapel."

"I sketched the little ruin of the baptistery some time ago."

"'Twas thot a deal of wance, an' the holy water theer was reckoned better for childern than any doctor's traade as ever was. My mother weer a Madern cheel; an' 'er ordained I should be tu, an' when faither was to sea, as fell out just 'pon the right day, mother took me up theer. That was my awn mother, as is dead. More folks b'lieved in the spring then than what do now, 'cause that was sebbenteen year agone. An' from bein' a puny cheel, I grawed a bonny wan arter dipping. But some liked the crick-stone better for li'l baabies than even the Madern Brook."

"Mên-an-tol that stone is called?"

"Maybe 'tis. Us knaws it as the crick-stone. Theer's a big hole in en, an' if a cheel was passed through nine times runnin', gwaine 'gainst the way of the sun every time, it made en as strong as a lion. An' 'tis good for grawn people tu, awnly folks is afeared to try now, 'cause t'others laugh at 'em. But I reckon the Madern Brook's holy water still. An' theer's wonnerful things said 'bout the crick-stones, an' long stones tu. A many of 'em stands round 'bout these paarts."

"D'you know Mên Scryfa—the stone with the writing on it? That's a famous long stone, up beyond Lanyon farmhouse."

"I've seed en, 'pon the heath. 'Tis butivul an' solemn an'

* *Maggotty-pie*, magpie.

still an' ancient, all aloan out theer in a croft to itself. I trapsed up-long wan day, an' got beside of en an' ate a pasty wi' Joe. But Joe chid me, an' said 'tweer a heathenish thing sticked theer by the Phœnicians, as comed for tin in Solomon's times."

"Don't you believe that, Joan. Mên Scyrfa marks the memory of a good Briton—one who knew King Arthur very likely. I love the old stones too. You are right to love them. They are landmarks in time, books from which we may read something of a far, fascinating past."

"'Iss; but I ded'n tell 'e all 'bout the Madern waters. The best day for 'em be the fust Sunday in May; an' come that, the mothers did use to gaw up to the chapel—dozens of 'em—wi' poor li'l baabies. They dipped 'em naked in the brook, an' 'twas just a miracle for rashes an' braggety legs, an' sich like. An', arterwards, the mothers made offerin's to the saint. 'Twas awnly the thot like, but folks reckoned the saint 'ud take the will for the act, 'cause poor people couldn' give a saint nothin' worth namin'."

Barron had heard of the votive offerings left by the faithful in past days at St. Madron's shrine, but felt somewhat surprised to find the practice dated back to a time so recent as Joan's infancy. He let her talk on, for the subject was evidently dear to the girl.

"And what did the mothers give the saint?"

"Why, rags mostly. Just a rag tored off a petticoat, or some sich thing. They hanged 'em up around about on the thorn bushes, to shaw as they'd 'a' done more for the good saint if they'd had the power. An' theer's another marvellous thing as washin' in thicky waters done: it kep' the fairies off—the bad fairies, I mean, 'cause theer'm good an' bad piskeys, same as good an' bad men folks."

"You believe in fairies, Joan?"

She looked at him shyly, but he had apparently asked for information, and was not in the least amused.

"I dunnaw. P'raps. 'Iss, I do, then. Many wiser'n me do b'lieve in 'em. You ax the tinners—them as works deep.

They knaws; they've 'card the knackers an' gathorns many a time, an' some's seen 'em. But the mine fairies be mostly wicked li'l humpetty-backed twoads as'll do harm if they can; an' the buccas is onkind to fishermen most times; an' 'tis said they used to bide in the shape of a cat by day. But theer be land fairies as is mighty good-hearted if a body behaves seemly."

"I believe in the fairies, too," said Barron, gravely; "but I've never seen one."

"Do 'e now, Mister Jan! Then I'm sure theer is sich things. I ne'er seed wan neither; but I'd love to. Some maids has vanished away an' dwelt 'mong 'em for many days, an' then comed home. Theer's Robin o' the Carn as had a maiden to work for en. You may have heard the tale?"

"No, never."

"'Tis a fine tale; an' the girl had a braave time 'mongst the li'l people till she disobeyed 'em an' found herself back 'mongst men-folk agin. But, in coorse, some of them—the piskeys, I mean—works for men-folk themselves. My gran'mother Chirgwin, when she was very auld, seed 'em a-threshin' corn in a barn up Drift. They was tiny fellers, wi' gert beards an' red faaces, an' they handled the flails cruel clever. Then, arter a bit, they done the threshin', an' was kickin' the short straw out the grain, which riz a gert dust; an' the piskeys all beginned sneezin'. An' my gran'mother, as was peepin' through the door unbeknown to 'em, forgot you must never speak to a piskey, an sez, 'God bless 'e, li'l men!'—'cause that's what us allus sez if a body sneezes. Then they all took fright, an' vanished away in the twinkle of a eye. Which must be true, 'cause my awn gran'mother tawld it. But they ded'n leave the farm, though nobody seed 'em agin, for arter that 'tis said as the cows gived a wonnerful shower o' milk, better'n ever was knawn before. An' I 'sure 'e I'd dearly like to be maiden to good piskeys, if they'd let me work for 'em."

"Ah, I'm certain you would suit them well, Joan, and they would be lucky to get you, I think; but I hope they won't go and carry you off until I've done with you, at any rate."

She laughed, and he bid her put down her hand from her eyes and rest. He had brought some oranges for her, but judged the friendship had gone far enough, and first decided not to produce them. Half-an-hour later, however, when the sitting was ended, he changed his mind.

"Can you come to-morrow, Joan? I am entirely in your hands, remember, and must consider your convenience always. In fact, I am your servant, and shall wait your pleasure at all times."

Joan felt proud, and rather important.

"I'll come at 'lebben o'clock to-morrer, but I doubt I caan't be here next day, Mister Jan."

"Thank you very much. To-morrow at eleven will do splendidly. By the way, I have an orange here—two, in fact. I thought we might be thirsty. Will you take one to eat going home?"

He held out the fruit, and she took it.

"My! What a butivul orange!"

"Good-bye until to-morrow, Joan; and thank you for your great kindness to a very friendless man. You'll never be sorry for it, I'm sure."

He bowed gravely, and took off his cap, then turned to his easel; and she blushed with a lively pleasure. She had seen men take off their hats to women, but no one had ever paid her that respect until then, and it seemed good to her. She marched off with her picture and her orange, but did not eat the fruit until out of sight of Gorse Point.

The man painting there already began to fill a space in Joan's thoughts. He knew so much, and yet was glad to learn from her. He never laughed or talked lightly. He put her in mind of her father for that reason; but then his heart was soft, and he loved Nature and beautiful things, and believed in fairies, and spoke no ill of anybody. Joan speculated as to how these meetings could be kept a secret, and came to the conclusion it would not be difficult to hide them. Then, reaching home, she hid her picture behind the pig-sty until opportunity offered for taking it indoors to her own bedroom unobserved.

As for John Barron, he felt kindly enough towards his model. He could hold himself with an iron hand when he pleased, and proposed that the growing friendship should ripen into a fine work of Art, and no more. But what might go to the making of the picture could not be foretold. He would certainly allow nothing to check inspiration, or stand between him and the very best he had power to achieve. No sacrifice could be too great for Art, and Barron, who was now awake and alive for an achievement, would, according to his rule, count nothing hard, nothing impossible that might add a grain of value to the work. His own skill and Joan's beauty were brought in contact, and he meant to do everything a man might do to make the result immortal. But the human instruments necessary to such work counted for nothing, and their personal prosperity or welfare would weigh no more with him than the future of the brushes which he might use, after he had done with them.

CHAPTER VII.

UNCLE CHIRGWIN.

Joan's first announcement upon the following morning was a regret that the sitting must be short.

"We'm mighty busy, come wan thing an' another," she said. "Mother's gwaine to Penzance wi' my brother to buy his seafarin' kit; an' Uncle Chirgwin, as keeps a farm up Drift, be comin' to dinner, which he ain't done for this long time; an' faither may be home tu so like as not, for the first bwoats be tackin' back from the islands a'ready."

"You shall stop just as short a time as you choose, Joan. It was very good of you to come at all under these circumstances," declared the artist.

"Us be fine an' busy when uncle comes down-long, an' partickler this time, 'cause theer've bin a difference of 'pinion 'bout —'bout a matter betwixt him and faither; but now he's wrote through the post to say as he'm comin', so 'tis all right, I s'pose; an' us'll have to give en a good dinner anyways."

"Of course you must," admitted Barron, working steadily the while.

"He'm a dear sawl, an' I likes en better'n anybody in the world, I think, 'cept faither. But Uncle Sampy's easier to please than faither, an' so humble as a beggar-man. An' I wants to make some cakes for en against tea-time, 'cause when he comes, he allus bides till candle-teening or later."

Presently the artist bade her rest for a short while, and her thoughts reverted to him and the picture.

"I hope as you'm feelin' strong an' no worser, Mister Jan," she said timidly.

He was puzzled for a moment, then recollected that he had mentioned his health to her.

"Thank you very much for asking, Joan. It was good and thoughtful. I am no worse—rather better if anything, now I come to think about it. Your Cornish air is kind to me; and when the sun shines I am happy."

"How be the picksher farin'?"

"I get on well, I think."

"'Tis 'mazin' clever of 'e, Mister Jan. An' you'll paint me wi' the fuzz all around?"

"That is what I hope to do; a harmony in brown and gold."

"You'll get my likeness tu, I s'pose, same as the photograph-man done it last winter to Penzance? Me an' Joe was took side by side, an' folks reckoned 'twas the moral of us, specially when the gen'leman painted Joe's hair black and mine yeller, for another shillin' cost."

"It must have been very excellent."

"'Iss, 'twas for sartain."

"What did Mr. Tregenza say of it?"

"Well, faither, he'm contrary to sich things, as I tawld 'e, Mister Jan. Faither said Joe'd better by a deal keep his money in his purse; but he let me have the picksher, an' 'tis nailed up in a li'l frame what Joe made at home in the parlour." She stopped a moment and sighed, then spoke again. "Faither's a wonnerful God-fearin' man, sure 'nough."

"Is he a God-loving man too, Joan?"

"I dunnaw. That ed'n 'sackly the same, I s'pose?"

"As different as fear and love. I'm not an atom frightened of God myself—no more than I am of you."

"Lard, Mister Jan!"

"Why should I be? You are not frightened of the air you breathe—yet that is part of God; you are not frightened of the gold gorse or the blue sky—yet they are part of God too.

God made you—you are part of God—a deliberate manifestation
of Him.   What's the use of being frightened?   You and I can
only know God by the shapes He takes—by the bluebells, and
the ferns, and the larks in the sky, and the rabbits, and wild
things."

His effort to inspire the girl with nature-worship, though
crudely cast in a fashion most likely to attract her, yet failed
just then, and failed ludicrously.   Her mind comprehended
barely enough to accept his idea in a sense suggested by her
acquaintance with fable, and when he instanced a rabbit as an
earthly manifestation of the Everlasting, she felt she could cap
the example from her own store of knowledge.

"I reckon I sees what you'm meanin', Mister Jan.   Theer's
things us calls witch-hares in these paarts up-long.   The
higher-quarter people have seed 'em 'fore now; nothin' but silver
bullets will kill 'em.   They goes loppettin' about down lawnly
lanes on moonlight nights, an' they draws folks arter 'em.   But
if you could kill wan of 'em, 'tis said as they'd turn into witches
theer an' then.   So you means that God A'mighty takes shaapes
sometimes same as they witches do, doan't 'e?"

"Not quite that, Joan.   What I want you to know is that
the great Being you call God is nearer to you here, on Gorse
Point, than in the Luke Gospellers' meeting-house, and He
takes greater delight in a bird's song than in all your father's
prayers and sermons put together.   That is because the great
Being taught the bird to sing Himself, but He never taught
your father to pray."

"I dunnaw 'sackly what you means, Mister Jan; but I
judges you ban't so religious-like as what faither is."

"Religion came from God to man, Joan, because man wanted
it, and couldn't get on comfortably without it; but theology—
if you know what that means—man invented for himself.
Religion is the light; theology is the candlestick.   Never
quarrel with any man's candlestick as long as you can see his
light burning bravely.   Mr. Tregenza thinks all men are
mistaken but the Luke Gospellers—so you told me.   But if

that is the case, what becomes of all your good Cornish saints?
They were not Luke Gospellers—at least, I don't think they
were."

Joan frowned over this tremendous problem, then dismissed
it for the pleasanter and simpler theme John Barron's last
remark suggested.

"Them saints was righteous men, anyhow—an' they worked
miracles tu, so it ban't no good sayin' they wasn't godly in
their ways, the whole boilin' of 'em. Theer's St. Piran, St.
Michael, St. Austell, St. Blazey, St. Buryan, St. Ives, St. Sennen,
St. Levan, an' a many more I could call home if I was to think.
Did 'e ever hear tell about St. Neot, Mister Jan?"

"No, Joan; I'm afraid I don't know much about him."

"Not 'bout they feesh?"

"Tell me, while you rest a minute or two."

"'Tis a holy story, an' true as any Bible tale, I should guess.
St. Neot had a well, an' wan day he seed three feesh a swimmin'
in it, an' he was mazed to knaw how they comed theer. So a
angel flew down an' tawld en that they was put theer for his
eatin', but he must never draw out more'n wan at a time.
Then he'd allus find three when he come again. An' so he did;
but wance he falled sick, an' his servant had to look arter his
vittles meantime. He was a man by the name of Barius, an'
he judged as maybe a change of eatin' might do the saint good.
So he goes an' takes two o' them feesh, 'stead o' wan, as the angel
said. An' he biled wan feesh an' fried t'other, an' took 'em to
St. Neot; an' when he seed what his man been 'bout, he was
flustered, I tell 'e. Then the saint up and done a marvellous
straange thing, for he flinged them feesh back in the well, just
as they was, and began praayin' to the Lard to forgive his man.
An' the feesh comed alive agin', and swimmed around, though
Barius had cleaned 'em, I s'pose, an' everything. Then the
chap just catched wan feesh proper, an' St. Neot ate en, and
grawed well by sundown. So he was a saint, anyways."

"You can't have a miracle without a saint, of course,
Joan?"

"Or else the Lard. But I'll hold in mind what you sez 'bout Him bein' hid in flowers an' birds an' sich like, 'cause that's a butivul thing to knaw."

"And in the stars and the sun and the moon, Joan; and in the winds and clouds. See how I've got on to-day! I don't think I ever did so much work in an hour before."

She looked and blushed to note her brown frock and shoes. "You've done a good deal more to them fuzzes than what you have done to me, seemin'ly," she said.

"That's because the gorse is always here and you are not. I work at the gorse morning after morning, when the sun is up, until my fingers ache. You'll see great changes in the picture of yourself soon, though."

But she was not satisfied—of course, misunderstanding the unfinished work.

"You musn't say anything yet, you know, Joan," added the artist, seeing her pouting lips.

"But—but you've drawed me as flat as a cheeld, an' I be round as a wummon, ban't I?" she said, holding out her hands that he might see her figure.

Her blue eyes were clouded, for she deemed that he had put an insult upon her budding womanhood. Barron showed no sign of his enjoyment, but explained as clearly as possible that she was looking at a thing wholly unfinished—indeed, scarce begun.

"You might as well grumble with me for not painting your fingers or your face, Joan. I told you I was a slow artist. Only be patient; I'm going to do all fitting honour to every scrap of you, if only you will let me."

Warmer words had come to his lips, but he did not suffer them to pass. Then the girl's beautiful face broke into a smile again.

"I be nigher eighteen than sebbenteen, you knaw, Mister Jan. But coourse, I hadn't no bizness to talk like that to 'e, 'cause what do I knaw 'bout sich things?"

"You shan't see the picture again till it is finished, Joan.

It was my fault for showing it to you like that, and you had every right to protest. Now you must go, for it's long past twelve o'clock."

"I'm afeared I caan't come to-morrer."

"As you please. I shall be here every day, ready and only too glad to see you."

"An'—an' you ban't cross wi' me for speakin' so rude, Mister Jan?"

"Cross, Joan? No, I'm never cross with anybody but myself. I couldn't be cross with my kind little friend if I tried to be."

He shook hands; it was the first occasion that he had done so, and she blushed. His hand was cold and thin, and she heard one of the bones in it give a little crack as he held her palm within his own for the briefest space of time. Then, as usual, the moment after he had said "Good-bye," he appeared to become absolutely unconscious of her presence, and returned to his picture.

Joan's mind dwelt much upon the artist after she had departed, and every train of reflection came back to the last words Barron spoke that morning. He had called her his kind little friend. It was very wonderful, Joan thought, and a statement not to be explained at all. Her stepmother's voice cut these pleasant memories sharply, and she returned home to find that Uncle Chirgwin had already arrived—a fact his old grey horse, tethered in the orchard, and his two-wheeled market-cart, drawn up in the side-lane, testified to before Mrs. Tregenza announced it.

"Out again, of coourse, just because you knawed I was to be drove off my blessed legs to-day. I'll tell your faither of 'e, so I will. Girls like you did ought to be chained 'long side theer work till 'tis done."

Uncle Chirgwin sat by the fireside with a placid, if bored, expression on his round face. His hands were folded on his stomach; his short legs were stuck out before him; his head was quite bald, his colour high, his grey eyes weak, though they had some laughter hidden in them. His double chin was shaved, but a very white bristle of stubbly whisker surrounded it, and ascended to where all that remained of his hair stuck, like two patches of cotton wool, above his ears. The old man wore a suit of grey tweed, and blinked benignly through a pair of spectacles. He had already heard enough of Mrs. Tregenza's troubles to last some time, and turned with pleasure to Joan as she entered. So, hearty indeed was the greeting, and a kiss which accompanied it, that his niece felt the displeasure which her uncle had recorded by post upon the occasion of her engagement to Mary Chirgwin's former sweetheart existed no more.

"My ivers! a braave, bowerly maid you'm grawin' sure 'nough! Joan'll be a wummon 'fore us can look round, mother."

"'Iss—an' a fine an' lazy wummon tu. I wish you could make her work like what Mary does up Drift."

"Well, I dunnaw. You see, there's all sorts of girls, same as plants an' 'osses an' cetera. Some's for work, some's for shaw. You 'specks a flower to be purty, but you don't blame a 'tater plant 'cause 'o ed'n particular butivul. Same wi' 'osses an' wi' girls. Joan's like that chinee plate 'pon the bracket, wi' the pickshers o' Saltash Burdge 'pon en, an' gold writin' under, an' Mary's like that pie-dish what you put in the ubben a while back. Wan's just eyeable, t'other's for use—oh?"

"Gwan! you'm jokin', Uncle Sampy!" said Joan.

"An' a poor joke tu, so 'tis. You'd turn any girl's 'ead wi' your stuff, Chirgwin. Wheer's the good of a fuzz-pole o' yeller hair an' a pair o' blue eyes stuck 'pon top of a idle, good-for-nothin' body? Maidens caan't live by looks in these paarts, an' they'll find theerselves in trouble mighty quick if they tries to."

Uncle Chirgwin instantly admitted that Mrs. Tregenza had the better of the argument. He was a simple man, with a soft heart and no brains worth naming. Most people laughed at him and loved him. As sure as he went to Penzance on market-day, he was cordially greeted and made much of and robbed.

People suspected that his shrewd, black-eyed niece, Mary, stood between him and absolute misfortune. She never let him go to market without her if she could help it; for on those infrequent occasions, when he jogged to town with his grey horse and cart alone, he always went with a great trust of the world in his heart, and endeavoured to conduct the sale of farm produce in the spirit of Christianity—which was magnificent, but not business. Mr. Chirgwin's simple theories had kept him a poor man; yet the discovery, often repeated, that his knowledge of human nature was bad, never embittered him, and he mildly persisted in a pernicious habit of trusting everybody until he found he could not; unlike his neighbours, who trusted nobody until they found that they could. The farmer had blazed with indignation when Joe Noy broke with Mary Chirgwin, because she would not become a Luke Gospeller. But that matter was now blown over; for the jilted girl, though the secret bitterness of her sorrow still bred much gall in her bosom, never paraded it or showed a shadow of it in her dark face. Uncle Sampy greatly admired Mary, and even feared her; but he loved Joan, for she was like her dead mother outwardly, and like himself in character—a right Chirgwin, loving sunshine and happiness, herself sunny and happy.

"'Pears I've comed the wrong day, Joan," he said presently, when Mrs. Tregenza's back was turned; "but now I be here you must do with me as you can."

"Mother's gwaine to town wi' Tom bimebye; then me an' you'll have a talk, uncle, wi'out nothin' to let us. You'm lookin' braave, me auld dear."

He liked a compliment, and anticipated pleasure from a quiet afternoon with his niece. She bustled about as usual to make up for lost time, and presently, when the cloth was laid, walked to the cottage door to see if her father's lugger was at its moorings or in sight. Meantime, Mrs. Tregenza, having brought forth dinner from the oven, called at the back door to her son in a voice harsh and shrill beyond customary measure, as became her exceptional tribulations.

"Come in, will 'e, an' ait your food, bwoy. Theer ed'n no call to kick out they boots agin' the pig's 'ouse because I be gwaine to buy new wans for 'e presently."

Fired by a word which she had heard from John Barron, that flowers became the house as well as the garden, Joan plucked an early sprig of pink ribe and some buds of wall-flower before returning to the kitchen. These she put in a jug of water and planted boldly upon the dinner-table as Mrs. Tregenza brought out a pie.

"Butivul, sure 'nough," said Mr. Chirgwin, drawing in his chair. His eye was on the pie-dish, but Joan thought he referred to her bouquet.

"Lard! what'll 'e do next? Take they things off the table to wance, Joan!"

"But Uncle Sampy sez they'm butivul," she pleaded.

"They'm pleasant," admitted Mr. Chirgwin, "but bloody-warriors * be out o' plaace 'pon the dinner-table, I was 'ludin' to this here. You do brown a 'tater to rights, mother."

Mrs. Tregenza's shepherd's pies had a reputation, and any-body eating of one without favourable comment was judged to have made a hole in his manners. Now she helped the steam-ing delicacy, and sighed as she sat down before her ample share.

"Lard knaws how I done it to-day! 'Tis just a enstance how some things comes nachrul to some people. You wants a light hand wi' herbs, an' to knaw your ubben. Get the brandy, Joan; uncle allus likes the edge off drinkin' water."

The Tregenzas were teetotalers, but a bottle of brandy for medicinal purposes occupied the corner of a certain cupboard.

"You puts it right, mother; 'tis just the sharpness I takes off. I can't drink no beer nowadays, though fond o' it, 'cause 'tis belly-vengeance stuff arter you gets past a certain time o' life. But I'd as soon have tea."

"That's bad to drink 'long wi' flesh," said Mrs. Tregenza. "Tea turns mayte leather-hard, an' plagues the stomach cruel, as I knaws to my cost."

* *Bloody-warrior*, wallflower.

They ate in silence awhile, then, having expressed and twice repeated a wish that Mary could be taught to make shepherd's pies after the rare fashion of his hostess, Mr. Chirgwin turned to Tom.

"So you'm off for a sailor bwoy, my lad?"

"'Iss, uncle, an' mother's gwaine to spend fi' puns o' money on my kit."

"By Golles! be she now? I lay you'll be smart an' vitty!"

"That he will!" said Joan.

But Mrs. Tregenza shook her head. "I did sadly want en to be a landsman an' 'prenticed to some good body in bizness. It's runnin' 'gainst dreams as I had 'fore the bwoy was born, an' the voice I heard speakin' by night arter I were churched by the Luke Gosp'lers. But you knaw Michael. What's dreams to him, nor yet voices?"

"The worst paart 'bout 'em, if I may say it, is that they'm so uncommon well acquainted like wi' theer awn virtues. I mean the Gosp'lers, an' all chapel-members likewise. It blunts my pleasure in a good man to find he knaws how good he is. Same as wan doesn't like to see a purty girl tossin' her head tu high."

"You caan't say no sich thing o' Michael, I'm sure," remonstrated Mrs. Tregenza, instantly; "he'm that modest wi' his righteousness as can be. I've knawn 'em say open in prayer, 'fore the whole chapel, as he's no better'n a crawlin' worm. An' if he's a worm, what's common folks like you an' me? Awnly Michael doan't seem to take 'count in voices an' dreams, but I knaws they'm sent a purpose, an' not for nort."

Mr. Chirgwin admitted his own ridiculous religious insignificance as contrasted with Grey Michael. Indeed the comparison, so little in his favour, amused him extremely. He sipped his brandy and water, and enjoyed a treacle-pudding which followed the pie. Then, when Joan was clearing up, and Mrs. Tregenza had departed to prepare for her visit to Penzance, Uncle Sampy began to puff out his cheeks, and blow, and frown, and look uneasily to the right and left—actions invariably performed when he contemplated certain monetary achievements of which he was only too fond. The sight of Mary's eyes upon him had often killed such indiscretions in the bud; but she was not present just then, so, with further furtive glances, he brought out his purse, opened it, and found a half-sovereign, which reposed alone in the splendour of a separate compartment. Uncle Chirgwin then beckoned to Tom, who had gone into the garden till his mother should be ready to start.

"Good speed to 'e, bwoy!" he said, "an' may the Lard watch over 'e by land an' sea. Take you this li'l piece o' money to buy what you've a mind to; an' knaw you've got a auld man's blessin' long wi' it."

"Mother," said Tom a minute later, "Uncle have gived me a bit o' gawld!"

She took the coin from him, and her eyes rested on it lovingly, while the outlines of her face grew softer, and she moistened her lips.

"First gawld's ever I had," commented Tom.

"You'm 'mazin' generous wi' your moneys, uncle, an' I thank 'e hearty for the bwoy. Mighty good of 'e—so much money to wance," said Thomasin, showing more gratification than she knew.

"I wants en to be thrifty," answered the old man, very wisely. "You knaws how hard it is to teach young people the worth o' money."

"Ay, an' some auld wans! Blest if I doan't think you'd give your head away if 'e could. But I'll take this here half-suvrin' for Tom. 'Tis a nest-egg he shall add to as he may."

Tom did not foresee this arrangement, and had something to say as he tramped off with his mother to town; but though he could do more with her, and get more out of her than anybody else in the world, money was a subject concerning which Mrs. Tregenza always had her way. She understood it, and loved it, and allowed no interference from anybody, Michael alone excepted. But he cared not much for money, and was well content to let his wife hold the purse; yet when he did occasionally demand an account, it was always forthcoming to the uttermost farthing, and he fully believed what other people told him, that Thomasin could make a sixpenny-piece go further than any other woman in Newlyn.

Mother and son presently departed; while Mr. Chirgwin took off his coat, lighted his pipe, and walked with Joan round about the orchard. He foretold great things for the plums, now in full flower; he poked the pigs with his stick, and spoke encouragingly of their future also. Then he discussed Joan's prospects, and gladdened her heart by telling her the past must be let alone, and need never be reverted to again.

"Mary's gettin' over it tu," he said; "leastways, I think she is. Her knaws wheer to look for comfort, bless her. Us must all keep friendly, for life's not long enough to do 'nough good in, I allus says, let alone the doin' o' bad."

Then he discussed Joe Noy, and Joan was startled to find, when she came to think seriously upon the subject, that though but a week and three days had passed since she bid her lover "good-bye," yet the picture of him in her mind already grew a trifle dim, and the prospect of his absence for a year held not the least sorrow in it for her.

Presently, after looking to his horse, Uncle Sampy hinted at forty winks, if the same would be quite convenient, and Joan, settling him with some approach to comfort upon a little horse-hair sofa in the parlour, turned her attention to the making of saffron cakes for tea.

CHAPTER VIII.

THE MAKING OF PROGRESS.

JOHN BARRON held strong theories about the importance of the mental condition when work was in hand. Once fairly engaged upon a picture, he painted very fast, laboured without cessation, and separated himself as far as might be from every outside influence. No new interests were suffered to intrude upon his mind; no distractions of any sort, intellectual or otherwise, were permitted to occupy even those leisure intervals which of necessity lay between the periods of his work. On the present occasion he merely fed and slept and dwelt solitary, shunning society of every sort, and spending as little time in Newlyn as possible. Fortunately for his achievement, the weather continued wonderfully fine, and each successive day brought like conditions of sunshine and colour, light and air. This circumstance enabled him to proceed rapidly, and another fact also contributed to progress; the temperature kept high, and the cow-byre, wherein Barron stored his implements and growing picture, proved so well-built and so snug withal, that on more than one occasion he spent the entire night there. Sweet brown bracken filled a manger, and of this he pulled down sufficient quantities to make, with railway rugs, an ample bed. The outdoor life appeared to suit his health well; some colour had come to his pale cheeks; he felt considerably stronger in body, and mentally invigorated by the strain of work now upon him.

But though he turned his back on his fellow-men, they sought him out, and rumours at length grew to a certainty that Barron was busy painting somewhere on the cliffs beyond

Mousehole. Everybody supposed he had abandoned his ambition to get a portrait of Joan Tregenza; but one man was in his confidence: Edmund Murdoch. The young artist had been useful to Barron. On many occasions he tramped out from Newlyn with additions to the scanty larder kept at the cowbyre. He would bring hard-boiled eggs, sandwiches, bottles of soda-water and whisky; and once he arrived at six o'clock in the morning with a pony-cart, in which was a little oil stove. Barron had confided in Murdoch, but begged he would let it be known that he courted no society for the present. As the work grew he spent more and more time upon it. He explained to his friend quite seriously that he was painting the gorse, but that Joan Tregenza had consented to fill a part of the picture— a statement which amused the younger artist not a little.

"But the gorse is extraordinary, I'll admit. You must have worked without ceasing. She will be exquisite. Where shall you get the blue for her eyes?"

"Out of the sky and the sea."

"Does the girl inspire you herself, John? I swear something has. This is going to be great."

"It's going to be true, that's all. No; Joan is a dear child; but her body's no more than a perfect casket to a commonplace little soul. She talks a great deal, and I like nothing better than to listen, for although what she says is naught, yet her manner of saying it does not lack charm. Her voice is wonderfully sweet—it comes from her throat like a wood-pigeon's— and education has not ruined her diction."

"She's as shy as any wood-pigeon too—we all know that; and you've done a clever thing to tame her."

"God forbid that I should tame her. We met and grew friendly as wild things both. She is a child of Nature; her mind is as pure as the sea. Moreover, Joan walks saint-guided. Folk-lore and your Cornish 'drolls' and other local twaddle does not appeal overmuch to me, as you know, yet the stories drop prettily from her lips, and I find pleasure in listening."

Murdoch whistled. "By Jove! I never heard you so

cnthusiastic, so positive, so personally alive and awake and interested. Don't fall in love with the girl before you know it."

To this warning Barron made a curious reply.

"Everything depends on my picture. You know my rule of life—to sacrifice all things to mood. I shall do so here. The best I can do must be done, whatever the cost."

A shadow almost sinister lay behind the utterance, yet young Murdoch could not fathom it. Barron spoke in his usual slow unimpassioned tones, and painted all the time; for the conversation took place on Gorse Point.

"Not sure if I quite understand you, old man," said Murdoch.

"It doesn't matter in the least if you don't, my dear fellow." His words were hardly civil, but the tone in which Barron spoke robbed the utterance of any offence. "All you need do," he continued, "is to keep silent, in the interests of Art and of Joan. I don't want her precious visits to me to get back to her father's ears, or they will cease; and I don't wish to do her a bad turn in her home, for I owe her a great debt of gratitude. If men ask what I'm doing, lie to them, and beg them not to disturb me, for the sake of Art. What a glint the east wind gives to colour! Yet this is hardly to be called an east wind, so soft and balmy does it keep."

"Well, you seem to be the better for your work, at any rate. You're getting absolutely fat. If Newlyn brings you health as well as fame, I hope you'll retract some of the many hard things you have said about it."

"It has brought me an interest, and for that, at any rate, I am grateful. Good-bye. I shall probably come down to-night, despite the fact that you have replenished my stores so handsomely."

Murdoch started homewards, and met Joan Tregenza upon the way. She had given Barron one further sitting after Uncle Chirgwin's call at Newlyn, but since the last occasion, and for a period of two days, chance prevented the girl from paying him another visit. Now she arrived, however, as early as half-past ten; and Murdoch, while he passed her on the hill from Mousehole, envied his friend the morning's work before him.

Joan was very hot and very apologetic upon her arrival.

"I began to fear you had forgotten me," the artist said.

But she was loud in her protestations to the contrary. "No, no, Mister Jan. I've fretted 'bout not comin' up like anything; ay, an' I've cried of a night, 'cause I thot you'd be reckoning I waddun comin' no more. But 'tweern't my doin', noways."

"You hadn't forgotten me?"

"Indeed, an' I hadn't. An' I'd be sorrerful if I thot you thot so."

She walked to the old position before the gorse, and fell naturally into it, speaking the while.

"'Tis this way: mother's been bad wi' faaceache arter my brother Tom went to sea wi' faither. An' mother grizzled an' worrited herself reg'lar ill, an' stopped in bed two days, an' kep' on whinin' 'bout what I was to do if she died, 'cause she s'posed she was gwaine to; but so soon as Tom comed off his first trip, mother cheered wonnerful, an' riz up to see to en, an hear tell 'bout how he fared on the water."

"Your head a wee bit higher, Joan. Well, I'm thankful to see you again. I was getting very, very lonely, I promise you. And the more I thought about the picture, the more unhappy I became. There's such a lot to do, and only such a clumsy hand to do it. The better I know you, Joan, the harder become the problems you set me. How am I going to get your soul looking out of your eyes, d'you think? How am I to make those who may see my picture some day—years after you and I are both dead and gone, Joan—fall in love with you?"

"I dunnaw, Mister Jan."

"Nor do I. How shall I make the picture so true that generations unborn will delight in the portrait, and deem it great and fine?"

"I dunnaw."

"And yet you deserve it, Joan, for I don't think God ever made anything prettier."

She blushed and looked softly at him, but took no alarm; for though such a compliment had never before been paid her, yet, as Barron spoke the words, slowly, critically, without enthusiasm or any expression of pleasure on his face, they had little power to alarm. He merely stated what he seemed to regard as a fact. There was almost a suggestion of irritation in his utterance, as though his model's rare beauty only increased his own artistic difficulties; and, perhaps, fearing from her smile that she found undue pleasure in his statement, he added to it—

"I don't say that to flatter you, Joan. I hate compliments, and never pay them. I told you, remember, that your wrists were a thought too big."

"You needn't be sayin' it awver an' awver, Mister Jan," she answered, her smile changing to a pout.

"But you wouldn't like me any more if I stopped telling you the truth. We have agreed to love what is true, and to worship Mother Nature because she always speaks the truth."

The girl made no answer, and he went on working for a few moments, then spoke again.

"I'm selfish, Joan, and think more of my picture than do I of my little model. Put down your arm and take a good rest. I tried holding my hand above my eyes yesterday to see how long I could do so without wearying myself. I found that three minutes was quite enough, but I have often kept you posed for five."

"It hurted my arm 'tween the shoulder an' elbow a li'l bit at first, but I've grawed used to it now."

"How ever shall I repay you, kind Joan, for all your trouble and your long walks and pretty stories?"

"I don't need no pay. If 'twas a matter o' payin', 'twould be a wrong thing to do, I reckon. There's auld Bascombe up to Paul—him wi' curls o' long hair an' gawld rings in 's ears. Gents pay en to taake his likeness; an' theer's girls make money so, more'n wan; but faither says 'tis a heathenish way of livin', an' not honest. An'—an' I'd never let nobody paint me else but you, Mister Jan, cause you'm different."

"Well, you make me a proud man, Joan. I'm afraid I must be a poor substitute for Joe."

He noticed she had never mentioned her sweetheart since their early interview, and wanted to ascertain of what nature was Joan's affection for the sailor. He did not yet dream how faint a thing poor Joe had shrunk to be in Joan's mind, or how the present episode in her life was dwarfing and dominating all others, present and past. Nor did the girl's answer to his remark enlighten him.

"In coourse you an' Joe's differ'nt as can be. You knaws everything seemin'ly an' be a gen'leman; Joe's only a seafarin' man, an' 'e doan't knaw much 'cept what he's larned from faither. But Joe used to say a sight more'n what you do for all that."

"I like to hear you talk, Joan. Perhaps Joe liked to hear himself talk. Most men do. But, you see, the things you have told me are pleasant to me, and they were not to Joe because he didn't believe in them. Don't look at me, Joan; look right away to the edge of the sea."

"You'm surprised like as I talks to ye, Mister Jan. Doan't ladies talk so free as what I do?"

"Other women talk, but they are very seldom in earnest like you, Joan. They don't believe half they say; they pretend and make believe—they've got to do so, poor things, because the world they live in is all built up on ancient foundations of great festering lies. The lies are carefully coated over and disinfected as much as possible and quite hidden out of sight; but everybody knows they are there—everybody knows the quaking foundations they tread upon. Civilization means universal civility, I suppose, Joan; and to be civil to everybody argues a great power of telling lies. People call it tact. But I don't like polite society myself, because my nose is sensitive, and I smell the stinking basis through all the pretty paint.

You and I, Joan, belong to Nature. She is not always civil, but you can trust her; she is seldom polite, but she never says what is not true."

" You talk as though 'e dedn' much like ladies an' gen'lemen, same as you be."

" I don't; and I'm not what you understand by ' a gentleman,' Joan. Gentlemen and ladies let me go among them and mix with them because I happen to have a great deal of money—thousands and thousands of pounds. That opens the door to their drawing-rooms, if I wanted to open it, but I don't. I've seen them, and gone about among them, and I'm sick of them. If a man wishes to know what polite society is, let him go into it as a very wealthy bachelor. I'm not ' a gentleman,' you know, Joan, fortunately."

" Surely, Mister Jan ! "

" No more than you're a lady. But I can try to be gentle and manly, which is better. You and I come from the same class, Joan—from the people. The only difference is that my father happened to make a huge fortune in London. Guess what he sold ? "

" I dunnaw."

" Fish—just plaice and flounders and herrings, and so forth. He sold them by tens of thousands. Your father sells them too. But what d'you think was the difference? Why, your father is an honest man; mine wasn't. The fishermen sold their fish, after they had had the trouble and danger of catching them, to my father; and then my father sold the fish again to the public. And the fishermen got too little, and the public paid too much, and so—I'm a very rich man to-day—the son of a thief."

" Mister Jan ! "

" Nobody ever called him a thief but me. He was a great light in this same polite society I speak of. He fed hundreds of fat people on the money that ought to have gone into the fishermen's pockets; and he died after eating too much salmon and cucumber at his own table. Poetic justice, you know. There are stained-glass windows up to his memory in two churches, and tons of good white marble were wasted when they made his grave. But he was a thief, just as surely as your father is an honest man; so you have the advantage of me, Joan. I really doubt if I'm respectable enough for you to know and trust."

"I'd trust 'e with anything, Mister Jan, 'cause you'm plain-spoken an' true."

"Don't be too sure—the son of a thief may have wrong ideas and lax principles. Many things not to be bought can easily be stolen."

Again he struck a sinister note, but this time on an ear wholly unable to appreciate or suspect it. Joan was occupied with Barron's startling scraps of biography, and, as usual, when he began talking in a way she could not understand, turned to her own thoughts. This sudden alteration of his position she took literally; it struck her in a happy light.

"If you'm not a gen'leman, then you wouldn' look down 'pon me, would 'e?"

"God forbid! I look up to you, Joan."

She was silent, trying to master this remarkable assertion. The artist stood no longer upon that lofty pedestal where she had placed him; but the change of attitude seemed to bring him a little closer, and Joan forgot the fall in contemplating the nearer approach.

"That's why I asked you not to call me 'Mister' Jan," Barron added, after a pause. "We are, you see, only different because I'm a man and you're a woman. Money merely makes a difference to outside things, like houses and clothes. But you've got possessions which no money can bring to me—a happy home and a lover coming back to you from the sea. Think what it must be to have nobody in the world to care whether you live or die. Why, I haven't a relation near enough to be even interested in all my money—there's loneliness for you!"

Joan felt full of a great pity, but could not tell how to

express it. Even her dull brains were not slow enough to credit his frank assertion that he and she were equals, but she accepted the statement in some degree, and now, with her mind wandering in his lonely existence, wondered if she might presume to express sympathy for him and proclaim herself his friend. She hesitated, for such friendship as hers, though it came hot from her little heart, seemed a ludicrous thing to offer this man. Every day of intercourse with him filled her more with wonder and with admiration; every day he occupied a wider place in her thoughts; and at that moment his utterances and his declaration of a want in life made him more human than ever to her, more easily to be comprehended, more within the reach of her understanding. And that was not a circumstance calculated to lessen her regard for him by any means. Until that day he had appeared a being far apart, whose interests and main threads of life belonged to another sphere; now he had deliberately come into her world and declared it his own.

The silence became painful to Joan, but she could not pluck up courage enough to tell the artist that she at least was a friend. Finally she spoke, feeling that he waited for her to do so, and her words led to the point, for she found, in his answer to them, that he took her good-will for granted.

"Ain't you got no uncles, nor nothin' o' that even, Mister Jan?"

He laughed and shook his head. "Not one, Joan — not anybody in all the world to think twice about me but you."

Her heart beat hard, and her breath quickened, but she did not speak.

Then Barron, putting down his brushes and beginning to load a pipe, that his next remark might not seem too serious, proceeded—

"I call you 'friend,' Joan, because I know you are one. And I want you to think of me sometimes when I am gone—will you?"

He went on filling his pipe, and then, looking suddenly into her eyes, saw there a light that was strange—a light that he

would have given his soul to put into paint; a light that Joe's
name never had kindled, and never could.

Joan wiped her hand across her mouth uneasily; then she
twisted her hands behind her back, like a school-child standing
in class, and made answer with her eyes on the ground.

"'Iss, I will, then, Mister Jan; an' maybe I couldn't help it
if I would."

He lighted his pipe carefully before answering. "Then I
shall be happy, Joan."

But while she grew rose-red at the boldness of her sudden
announcement, he took care neither to look at her nor to let
her know that he had realized the earnestness with which she
spoke. And when, ten minutes later, she had departed, he
mused speculatively on the course of their conversation, asking
himself what whim had led him to pretend to so much human
feeling and to lament his loneliness. This condition of his life
he loved above all others. No man, woman, or child had the
right to interfere with his selfish, impersonal existence, and he
gloried in the fact. But to the scraps of his life's history, which
he had spread before Joan in their absolute, cynical truth, he
had added this fiction of friendless loneliness, and it had worked
a wonder. He saw that he was growing to be much to her, and
the problem lying in his path rose again, as it had for a moment
when Murdoch warned him in jest against falling in love with
Joan Tregenza. Dim suspicions crossed his mind with greater
frequency, and being now a mere remorseless savage, hunting
to its completion a fine picture, he made no effort to shut their
shadows from his calculation. Everything which bore even
indirectly upon his work received its share of attention. To
mood must all sacrifices be made; and now a new mood began
to dawn in him. He knew it; he accepted it. He had not
sought it, but the thing was there, and Nature had sent it to
him. To shun it and fly from it meant a lie to his art; to open
his arms to it promised the destruction of a human unit. Barron
was not the man to hesitate between two such courses. If any
action could heighten his inspiration, add a glimmer of glory to

his picture, or bring a shadow more soul into the painted blue eyes of the subject, he held such action justified. For the present his mind was chaos on the subject, and he left the future to work itself out as chance might determine.

His painting was all he concerned himself with; and should Nature ultimately indicate that greater perfection might be achieved through worship and even sacrifice at her shrine, neither worship nor sacrifice would be withheld.

CHAPTER IX.

A WEDDING.

JOAN TREGENZA went home in a dream that day. She did not know where to begin thinking. "Mister Jan" had told her so many astounding things—and her own heart, too, had made bold utterances—concerning matters which she had crushed out of sight, with some shame and many secret blushes, until now. But, seen in the light of John Barron's revelations, this emotion which she had thrust so resolutely to the back of her mind could remain there no more. It arose, strong, rampant, and ridiculous—only, from her point of view, no humour distinguished it. This man, then, was like herself, made of the same flesh and blood, sprung from the people. That fact, though possessing absolutely no significance whatever in reality, struck Joan with great force. Her primitive instincts stretched a wide gulf between the thing called "gentlemen" and other men, which was the result of training from parents of the old-fashioned sort, whose world lay outside and behind the modern spirit; who had reached the highest development of their intelligence, and formed their opinions before the passing of the Education Act. Grey Michael naturally held the great ones of the earth as objects of pity from an eternal standpoint; but birth weighed with him, and in temporal concerns he treated his superiors with all respect and civility when rare chance brought him into contact with them. He viewed uneasily the last outcome of progress and the vastly increased facilities for instruction of the juvenile population. The age was sufficiently godless in his judgment, and he found that a Board-school education was the first nail in the coffin of every young man's faith,

Joan, therefore, allowing nothing for the value of riches, of education, of intellect, was content to accept Barron's own cynical statement in a spirit widely different from the speaker's. He had sneered at himself, just as he had sneered at his own dead father. But Joan missed all the bitterness of his speech. To her he was simply a wondrously honest man, who loved truth for itself, who could never utter anything not true, who held it no offence to speak truth even of the dead. Gentle or simple, he seemed infinitely superior to all men whom she had met with. And yet this beautiful nature walked through the world quite alone. He had asked her to remember him when he was gone; he had said that she was his friend. And he cared little for women—there was, perhaps, no other woman in the world he had called a friend.

Then the girl's heart fluttered at the presumption of her silly, soaring thoughts, and she glanced nervously to the right and to the left of the lonely road, as though fearful that some hidden eavesdropper might peep into her open mind. The magic spell was upon her. This little, pale, clever man, so quiet, so strange, so unlike anything else within her seventeen years of experience, had wrought Nature's vital miracle, and Joan, who until then believed herself in love with her sailor sweetheart, now stood aghast before the truth—stood bewildered between the tame and bloodless phantasy of her affection for Joe Noy and this wild, live reality. She looked far back into a past already dim, and remembered that she had told Joe many times how she loved him with all her heart. But the words were spoken before she knew that she possessed a heart at all. Yet Joe then formed no inconsiderable figure in life. She had looked forward to marriage with him as a comfortable and sufficient background for present existence; she had viewed Joe as a handsome, solid figure—a man well thought of, one who would give her a home with bigger rooms and better furniture in it than most fishermen's daughters might reasonably hope for. But this new blinding light was more than the memory of Joe could face uninjured.

He shrivelled and shrank in it. Like St. Michael's Mount, seen afar, through curtains of rain, Joe had once bulked large, towering, even grand; but under noonday sun, the great mass dwindles as a whole, though every detail becomes more apparent. And so with poor Joe Noy. Removed to a distance of a thousand miles though he was, Joan had never known him better, never realized the height, breadth, depth of him so acutely as she did now. The former ignorance in such a case had been bliss indeed, for whereunto her present acquired wisdom might point even she dared not consider.

Any other girl must have remained sufficiently alive to the enormous disparity every way between herself and the artist; and Joan grasped the difference, but from the wrong point of view. The man's delicacy of discernment, his wisdom, his love of the things which she loved, his fine feeling, his humility —all combined, in Joan's judgment, to place him far above herself, though she had not words to name the qualities; but whereas another lowly woman, reaching this point, must, if she possessed any mother-wit or knowledge of the world, have awakened to the danger and grown guarded, Joan, claiming little wit to speak of, and being an empty vessel so far as the knowledge of the world was concerned, saw no danger, and allowed her thoughts to run away with her in a direction wholly insane. This she did for two reasons : because she felt absolutely safe, and because she suspected that Nature, who was "Mister Jan's" god, had now come to be her god also. The man was very wise, and he hated everything which lacked truth; therefore he would always do what was right, and he would not be less true to her than he was to the world. Truth was his guiding star, and he had always found Nature true. Therefore why should not Joan find it true? Nature was talking to her now, and teaching her rapidly. She must be content to wait and learn.

The two men, Noy and Barron, fairly represented those opposite views of life each entertained, and Joan felt the new music wake a thousand sleeping echoes in her heart, while

the old grew more harsh and unlovely as she considered
it. Joe had so many opinions, and so little information;
"Mister Jan" knew everything, and asserted nothing save
what Nature had taught him. Joe was so self-righteous and
overbearing, so like her father, so convinced that Luke Gospeldom was the only gate to glory; "Mister Jan" had said there
was more of the everlasting God in a bluebell than the whole
of the Old Testament. He had declared that the smell of the
gorse and the sunshine on the deep sea were better things than
the incense and banners at St. Peter's; he had asserted that the
purring of kittens was sweeter to the Father of all than the
thunder of a mighty organ played in the noblest cathedral ever
made with hands. All these foolish and inconsequent com-
parisons, uttered thoughtlessly by Barron's lips while his mind
was on his picture, seemed very fine to Joan, and the finer
because she did not understand them. Again, Joe rarely
listened to her; this man always did, and he liked to hear her
talk—he had declared as much.

Her brains almost hurt Joan on her way back to the white
cottage that morning. They seemed so loaded; they lifted her
up high above the working-day world, and made her feel many
years older. Such reflections and ideas came to grown women,
doubtless, she thought. A great unrest arose from the shadows
of these varied speculations—a great unrest and disquiet, a
feeling of coming change, like the note in the air when the
swallows meet together in autumn, like the whisper of the
leaves on the high tops of the forest before rain. Her heart
was very full. She walked more slowly as the thoughts weighed
heavier; she went back to her room round-eyed and solemn,
wondering at many things—at the extension of her life's horizon, at the mental picture of Joe standing clearly out of the
mists, viewed from a woman's standpoint.

That day much serving awaited her, but, at every turn and
pause in the small affairs of her duty, Joan's mind swooped
back like a hawk to the easel on Gorse Point; and when it did
her cheeks flushed, and she turned to bend over sink or pig's-

trough, to hide the new fire that burned in her heart and lighted her eyes.

Mrs. Tregenza, who had suffered from neuralgia and profound depression of spirits upon Tom's departure to the sea, but who comforted herself, even in her darkest hour, by reflection that no lugger-boy ever joined the fishing fleet with such an equipment of new clothes as her son, was somewhat better and more cheerful now that the lad had made his first trip, and survived it. Moreover, Tom would be home again that night in all probability, and, since Michael was last ashore, the butcher from Paul had called and offered three shillings and sixpence more for the next pig to be killed than ever a Tregenza pig had fetched until that day. Life, therefore, held some prosperity in it, even for Thomasin.

After their dinner both women, the elder with a shawl muffled about her face, went down the road to Newlyn to see a sight. They stopped at George Trevennick's little house. It had a garden in front of it, with a short flagstaff erected thereon, and all looked neat, trim, and shipshape, as became the home of a retired Royal Navy man. A wedding was afoot, and Mr. Trevennick, who never lost an opportunity to display his rare store of bunting, had plentifully shaken out bright reds and yellows, blues and greens. The little flags fluttered in four streamers from the head of the flagstaff, and their colours looked harsh and crude until associated with the human interests they marked.

Already many children gazed with awe from the road, while a favoured few, including the Tregenzas, stood in Mr. Trevennick's garden, which was raised above the causeway. Great good-humour prevailed, together with some questionable jesting, and Joan heard the merriment with a sense of discomfort. They would talk like this when Joe came back to marry her; but the great day of a maid's life had lost its greatness for her now. The rough, good-natured fun grated on her nerves as it had never grated before, because, though she only guessed at the sly jokes of her elders, something told her that "Mister Jan" would have found no pleasure in such merriment. Mrs. Tregenza talked, Mr. Trevennick smoked, and Sally Trevennick, the old sailor's daughter, entertained the party, and had a word for all. She was not young, and not well-favoured, and unduly plump, but a sweet-hearted woman nevertheless, with a great love for the little children. This, indeed, presently appeared, for while the party waited, there happened a tragedy in the street which brought extreme sorrow to a pair of very small people. They had a big crab-shell full of dirt off the road, which they drew after them by a string, and in which they took no small pride and pleasure; but a young sailor, coming hastily round a corner, trampled upon the shell, smashed it, and passed laughing on. The infants, overwhelmed by this sudden disaster to their most cherished earthly possession, crushed to the earth by such blotting out of the sunshine of the day, lifted up their voices, and wept before the shattered ruins. One, the biggest, dropped the useless string, and put his face against the wall that his extreme grief might be hidden; but the smaller hesitated not to make his sorrows widely known. He bawled, then took a deep breath and bawled again. As the full extent of his loss was borne in upon him, he absolutely danced with access of frenzied grief; and everybody laughed but fat Sally Trevennick. Her black eyes grew clouded, and she went down into the road to bring comfort to the sufferers.

"Never mind, then; never mind, you bwoys; us'll get 'e another braave shell, so us will. Theer, theer, give awver an' come 'long wi' me an' see the flags. Theer's many bigger auld crab-shells wheer that comed from, I lay. Your faither'll get 'e another."

She took a hand of each babe and brought them into the garden, from which they could look down upon their fellows. Such exaltation naturally soothed their sufferings, and, amid many gasps and gurgles, they found a return to peace in the close contemplation of Mr. Trevennick's flagstaff and the discussion of a saffron pasty.

Presently the bridegroom and his young brother passed on

the way to church. Both looked the reverse of happy; both
wore their Sunday broadcloth, and both swung along as fast as
their legs would carry them. They were red hot, and going
five miles an hour; but, though Mousehole men, everybody in
Newlyn knew them, and they were forced to run the gauntlet
of much chaff.

"Time was when they did use to thrash a new-married
couple to bed," said Mr. Trevennick. "'Twas an amoosin'
carcumstance, an' I've 'elped at many; but them good auld
doin's is dyin' out fast."

Mrs. Tregenza was discussing the bridegroom's family.

"He be a poor Billy-be-damned sort o' feller, I've allus
heard, an' awnly a common tinner, though his faither wore a
grass cap'n at Levant Mine."

"But he's a steady chap," said Sally; "an' them in his awn
station sez he's reg'lar at church-goin', an' well thot 'pon by
everybody. 'Tedn' all young pairs as parson'll ax out, I can
tell 'e. He wants to knaw a bit fore 'e'll marry bwoys an
girls; but theer weren't no trouble 'bout Mark Taskes."

"Sure I'm glad to hear it, Sally, 'cause if he caan't do everything, everything won't be done. They Penns be a pauper lot
—him a fish-jouster as ain't so much as his awn donkey an'
cart; an' lame tu. Not that 'twas his awn fault, I s'pose, but
they do say a lame chap's never caught in a good trick notwith-
standin'."

"Here comes the weddeners!" said Joan; "but tedn' a very
braave shaw," she added. "They'm all a-foot, I do b'lieve."

"Aw, my dear sawl! look at that now!" cried Mrs. Tregenza.
"Walkin', ackshally walkin'. Well—well!"

The little bride advanced between her father and mother,
while relations and friends marched two and two behind. A
vision it was of age and youth, of bright spring flowers, of
spotless cotton and black broadcloth. A matron or two marched
in flaming colours; a few fishermen wore their blue jerseys
under their reefer jackets; the smaller children were led by
hand; and the whole party numbered twelve all told. Mr.

Penn looked up at the flags as he limped along, and a great delight broke out upon his face; the bride's mother beamed with satisfaction at a compliment not by any means expected, for the Penns were humble folk; and the bride blushed and stole a nervous peep at the display. Mr. Penn touched his hat to the party in the garden, and Mr. Trevennick, feeling the eye of the multitude upon him, loudly wished the wedding party well as it passed by.

"Good speed to 'e an' to thy maid, Bill Penn! May she live 'appy an' be a credit to all parties consarned!"

"Thank 'e—thank 'e, kindly, Mr. Trevennick. An' us takes it mighty favourable to see your butivul flags a hangin' out—mighty favourable, I 'sure 'e."

So the party tramped on, and ugly Sally looked after them with dim eyes; but Mrs. Tregenza's thin voice dried them.

"A bad come-along o't for a girl to walk 'pon sich a day. They did ought to 'a' got her a lift to her weddin', come what might."

"Maybe 'tis all wan to them poor dears. A coach an' four 'orses wouldn't make that cheel no better pleased. God bless her! did 'e look how she flickered up when she seed faither's flags a flyin'?"

"Theer's a right way an' a wrong o' doin' weddin's, Sarah, an' tedn' a question whether a girl's better pleased or no. It's all wan to a dead corpse how 'tis took to the yard; but theer's a wrong an' a right way o' buryin', same as o' marryin'."

"They'm savin' the money for the feed. Theer's gwaine to be a deal o' clome liftin' at Penn's cottage bimebye," said another of the party.

"No honeymoon neither, so I hear tell," added Mrs. Tregenza.

"But Taskes have brought flam-new furniture for his parlour they sez," declared the former speaker.

"Of coourse. Still no honeymoon 'tall! Who ever heard tell of sich a thing nowadays? I wouder they ban't 'shamed!"

"Less shame, Mrs. Tregenza, than trapsing off to Truro or somewheres an' wastin' their time and spendin' money they'll be wanting back agin 'fore Christmas," retorted Sally, with some warmth.

But Mrs. Tregenza only shook her head and sighed. "You speaks as a onmarried wummon, Sarah; but if you comed to be a bride, you'd sing different. No honeymoon's wrong, an' your faither'll tell the same."

Mr. Trevennick admitted that no honeymoon was bad. He went farther and declared the omission of such an institution to be unprincipled. He even said that had he known of this serious defect in the ceremonies he should certainly have abstained from lending the brightness of his bunting to them. Then he went to eye the flags from different points of view, while Sally, in a minority of one, turned to Joan.

"And what do you say?" she asked. "You'm 'mazin' quiet an' tongue-tied for you. I s'pose you'm thinkin' of the time when Joe Noy comes home? I lay you'll have a honeymoon, anyways."

"'Iss, that you may depend 'pon," said Mrs. Tregenza.

And Joan, who had in truth been thinking of her sweetheart's return, grew red, whereat they all laughed. But she felt secretly superior to every one of them, for the shrinking process began to extend beyond Joe now. A fortnight before, she had been much gratified by allusions to the future, and had felt herself an important individual enough. Then she would have shared her stepmother's pity at the poverty of the pageant which had just passed by. Now all the world was changed. Matrimony with Joe Noy or the thought of it brought no present delight to her, but the little bride who had just gone to her wedding filled Joan's thoughts. What was in that girl's heart? She greatly wondered. Did Milly Penn feel for long-legged Mark Taskes what Joan felt for "Mister Jan"? Was it possible that any other woman had ever experienced similar mysterious splendours of mind? She could not tell, but it seemed unlikely to her; it appeared improbable that an ordinary man had power to inspire another heart with such love magic as glorified her own.

Presently she departed with her stepmother, whereupon Sally Trevennick relieved her pent-up feelings.

"Thank the Lard that chitter-faaced wummon ed'n gwaine to the weddin', anyways! Us knaws she's a dear good sawl 'nough; but what wi' her sour voice, an' her sour way o' talkin' an' her sour 'pinions, she'm enough to set a rat-trap's teeth on edge."

CHAPTER X.

MOONLIGHT.

THAT evening Thomasin had another spasm of face-ache, and went to bed soon after drinking tea. Michael was due at home about ten o'clock or earlier, and Joan, having set out supper, made all ready and ascertained that her stepmother had gone to sleep, walked out to the pier-head, there to wait for Mr. Tregenza and Tom. Under moonlight, the returning luggers crept homewards, like inky silhouettes on a background of dull silver. Every moment added to the forest of masts anchored at the moorings outside the harbour; every minute another riding-light glimmered and another rowing-boat shot between the granite piers, to slide silently within the darkness under shore, as it left moonlit rings widening out behind at each dip of the oars. Joan sat down under the lighthouse and waited in the stillness for her father's boat. Yellow flashes, like fireflies, twinkled along through Newlyn, and above them the moon brought out square patches of silver-bright roof, seen through a blue night. Now and then a bell rang in the harbour and lights leapt here and there mingling red snakes and steamers of fire with the white moonbeams where they lay on still water. Then Joan knew the fish were being sold by auction, and she grew anxious for her father's return, fearing that prices might have fallen before he arrived. Great periods of silence lay between the ringings of the bell, and at such times faint laughter and voices floated out from shore, blocks chipped and rattled as sails came down, a concertina squeaked fitfully where it was played on a Norwegian ice-boat at the harbour quay. The tide was coming in, and Joan watched many lights reflected in the harbour, and wondered why the gold of them contrasted so ill with the silver from the moon.

Presently two men walked along to the pier-head. They smoked, looked at the sea, and did not notice her where she sat in shadow. One, the larger, wore knickerbockers, talked loudly, and looked a giant in the vague light; the other was muffled up in a big ulster, and Joan would not have recognized Barron had he not spoken; but he answered his friend, and then the girl's heart leapt to hear that quiet, unimpassioned voice. He spoke of matters which she did not understand, of pictures, light values, and all manner of puzzles set by Nature for the solution of art; but though his remarks mainly conveyed no meaning to her, yet he closed a sentence with words that made her happy and warmed her heart and left a precious memory behind them.

" Moonlight is a problem only less difficult than sunshine," he said to his friend. " Where are you going to get that? " and he pointed to the sea.

" It's been jolly well done all the same."

" Never. It is not to be done. You can suggest by a trick, but God defend us from tricks and sleight-of-hand in connection with the solemn business of painting pictures. Let us be true or nothing."

They walked away together, and Joan pondered over the last words. Truth seemed an eternal, [abiding passion with John Barron, and the contemplation of this idea gave her considerable pleasure. She did not know that a man may be at once true to his art and a liar to his fellows.

Presently her father returned with Tom, and the three walked home together. Grey Michael appeared quietly satisfied that his son was shaping well and showing courage and nerve. But he silenced the lad quickly enough when Tom began to talk with some gasconade concerning great deeds done westward of the Scilly Islands.

" 'Let another man praise thee, an' not thine awn mouth,'

my bwoy," said Mr. Tregenza. "It ban't the wave as makes most splash what gaws highest up the beach, mind. You get Joan to teach 'e how to peel 'taties, 'cause 'tis a job you made a tidy bawk of, not to mention no other. Keep your weather-eye liftin' an' your tongue still, then you'll do. An' mind— the bwoat's clean as a smelt by five o'clock to-morrow marnin', an' no later."

Tom, dashed by these base details, answered seaman fashion—

"Ay, ay, faither!"

Then they all tramped home, and the boy enjoyed the glories of a late supper, though he was half asleep before he had finished it.

CHAPTER XI.

THE KISS.

By half-past five o'clock, Mr. Tregenza's black lugger was off again in a grey dawn all tangled with gold on the eastern horizon.

His mother had given Tom an early breakfast at half-past four, and the youngster, agape and dim-eyed at first, speedily brightened up, for he had a willing listener, and poured a tale of moving incidents into Thomasin's proud but uneasy mind.

" Them Pritchards sez as they'll make a busker * of me, 'cause it blawed a bit 'issterday marnin', but 'twas all wan to me; and you abbun no call to fret yourself, nohow, mother, 'cause faither's 'lowed to be the best sailor in the fleet, an' theer ban't a better foul-weather boat sails from Newlyn than ourn."

He chattered on, larding his discourse with new words picked up aboard, and presently rolled off to get things ship-shape just as his father came down to breakfast.

When the men had gone, little remained to be done that day, and by half-past eight, about which hour Mrs. Tregenza went into the village that she might whine with a widow who had two boys in the fleet, Joan found herself free until the afternoon. She determined, therefore, to reach Gorse Point before the artist should arrive there, and set off accordingly.

Early though she was, she had but a short time to wait, for Barron appeared with his big canvas before ten o'clock. She thought he showed more pleasure than usual at the sight of

* *Busker*, a rare good fisherman.

her. Certainly he shook hands and congratulated her upon such early hours.

"This is an unexpected pleasure, Joan. You must have been up betimes indeed."

"'Iss fay; us took breakfus' by five, an' faither sailed by half-past. 'Tis busy times for fishin' folk when the mackerl begins shoalin'."

"I'm glad I came back to my den in the fields yonder, and didn't stop in Newlyn last night. You must see my little cow-byre some day or other, Joan. I've made it wonderfully snug. Farmer Ford is good enough to let me take possession of it for the present; and I've got food and drink stowed away, and a beautiful bed of sweet withered bracken. I sleep well there, and the dawn comes in and wakens me."

"You ban't feared o' piskeys nor nothin' in sich a lawnsome plaace?"

"No, no; the rats are rather intrusive, though."

"But they'm piskeys or spriggans so like's not! You see, the li'l people takes all manner o' shaapes, Mister Jan; an' they chaanges 'em tu, but every time they chaanges, they've got to alter into somethin' smaller than what they was before. An' so, in coourse of time, they do say they comes down into muryans an' sich like insects."

"Piskeys or no piskeys, I've caught several in a trap and killed them."

"They'm gashly things, rats, an' I shouldn't think as no good piskeys would turn into varmints like them."

"More should I. But something better than rats came to see me last night, Joan. Guess who it was."

"I dunnaw."

"Why, you came!"

"Me, Mister Jan! You must a bin dreamin'!"

"Yes, of course I was; but such a lovely dream, Joan. You see men who paint pictures, and love what is beautiful, and dream about beautiful things and beautiful people, see all sorts of visions sometimes. I have pictures in my head a thousand times more splendid than any I shall ever put upon canvas, because mere paint-brushes cannot do much even when they are in the cleverest hands ; but a man's brain is not bound down by material, mechanical matters. My brain made a picture of you last night—a picture that came and looked at me on my fern bed—a picture so real, so alive, that I could see it move and hear it laugh. You think that wonderful. It isn't, really, because my brain has done nothing but think of you now for nearly six weeks. My eye studies you, and stamps you upon my brain, then, when night comes, and no man works, and the world is dark and silent, my brain sets off on its own account and raises up a magic vision just to show me what you really are—how different to this poor daub here ! "

"Lard, Mister Jan ! I never heard tell of sich a coorious thing as that."

"And the pretty dream-Joan can talk almost as well as you can ! Why, last night, while I was half awake and half asleep, she put her hand upon my shoulder and said kind things, but I dared not move or kiss her hand at first for fear she would vanish if I did."

Joan laughed. "That is a funny story, sure 'nough," she said. "I 'spect 'twas awnly another fairy-body, arter all."

"No, it wasn't. She had your voice and your spirit in her ; and that picture which my brain painted for me was so much better than this thing my hand has painted that, in the morning, I was almost tempted to destroy it altogether. But I didn't."

"An' what did this here misty sort o' maid say to 'o ?"

"Strange things—strange things. Things I would give a great deal to hear you say. It seemed that you had come, Joan ; it seemed that you had purposely come from your little cottage on the cliff through the darkness before dawn. Why ? To share my loneliness, to brighten my poor shadowy life. Dreams are funny things, are they not ? What d'you think you said ? "

"Sure I dunnaw,"

" Why, you said that you were not going to leave me any more, that you believed in me, and that you had come to me because it was bad for a man to live all alone in the world. You said that you felt alone, too—without me. And it made me feel happy to hear you say that, though I knew, all the time, that it was not the real beautiful Joan who spoke to me."

Thereupon the girl asked a question which seemed to argue some sharpening of intelligence within her.

" An' when I spoke that, what did you say, Mister Jan?"

" I didn't say anything at all. I just took that sweet Joan-of-dreams into my arms and kissed her."

He was looking listlessly out over the sea as he spoke, and Joan felt thankful his eyes were turned away from her, for this wonderful dream incident made her grow hot all over. He seemed to divine by her silence that his answer to her question had not added to her happiness.

" I shouldn't have told you that, Joan, only you asked me. You see, in dreams we are real in some senses, though unreal in others. In dreams the savage part of us comes to the top, and Nature can whisper to us. She chooses night to do so, and often speaks to men in visions, because by day the voice of the world is in their ears, and they have no attention for any other. It was strange, too, that I should fancy such a thing—should imagine I was kissing you—because I never kissed a woman in my life."

But from her point of view this falsehood was not so alluring as he meant to make it sound.

" 'Twould be wrong to kiss any maiden, I reckon, onless you was tokened to her, or she were your awn sister."

" But, as we look at life, we're all brothers and sisters, Joan, with Nature for our mother. We agreed about that long ago."

He turned to his easel, and she went and stood where her feet had already made a brown mark on the grass.

" I seen you last night, but you dedn' see me," she said, changing the conversation with abruptness.

"Yes, I did," he answered—"sitting under the shadow of the lighthouse, waiting for Mr. Tregenza, I expect."

"An' you never took no note o' me!"

He put down his brushes, turned away from the picture before he had touched it, and went and lay near the edge of the cliff.

"Come here, Joan, and I will tell you why I didn't notice you, though I longed to do so. Come and sit down by me, and I'll explain why I seemed so rude."

She came slowly, and sat down some distance from him, putting her elbows on her knees and looking away to sea.

"'Tweern't kind," she said; "but when you'm with other folks, I s'pose you'm ashamed o' me, 'spite what you tawld me 'bout yourself."

"You mustn't say that, Joan, or you'll make me unhappy. Ashamed of you! Is it likely I'm ashamed of the only friend I've got in the world? No; I'm frightened of losing you. I'm selfish. I couldn't make you known to any other man, because I should be afraid you'd like him better than me, and then I should have no friend at all. So I wouldn't speak, and reveal my treasure to anybody else. I'm very fond of my friend, and very proud of her, and as greedy as a miser over his gold."

Joan took a long breath before this tremendous assertion. He had told her in so many words that he was fond of her, and he had mentioned it most casually, as a point long since decided. Here was the question which she had asked herself so often answered once for all. Her heart leapt at tidings of great joy; and as she looked up into his face, the man saw infinite wonder and delight in her own. Mind was adding beauty to flesh; and he, fast losing the artist's instinct before another, thought she had never looked so lovely as then.

"Oh, Mister Jan, you'm fond o' me!"

"Why, didn't you know it, Joan? Did it want my words to tell you so? Hadn't you guessed it?" He rose slowly, and approached his picture. "Oh, how I wish this was a little

more like my dream and like reality! I need inspiration, Joan.
I have reached a point beyond which I cannot go. My colours
are dead; my soul is dead! Something must happen to me, or
I shall never finish this."

"Ban't you so well as you was?"

"No, Joan, I'm not. A thing has come between me and my
happiness, between me and my picture. I know not what to
call it. Nature has sent it."

"Then 'tis right an' proper, I s'pose?"

"I suppose so; but it stops work. It makes my hand
shake and my heart throb fast and my brains grow hot."

"Can't 'e take no physic for 't?"

"Why, yes; but I hesitate." He turned to her, and went
close to her. "Let me look at you, Joan—close—very close—
so close that I can feel your breath. It was so easy to learn
the furze; it is so hard to learn you."

"Sure I've comed out butivul in the picksher."

"Not yet—not yet."

He put his hands on her shoulders, and looked into her eyes
until she grew nervous, and brushed her hand across her cheek.
Then, without a second's warning, he bent down and kissed
her on the mouth.

"Mister Jan! How could 'e! 'Tis wrong—wrong of 'e!
I'd never 'a' thot——"

She started from him, wild, alarmed, blushing hotly; and
he shook his head at her dismay, and answered very calmly,
very seriously—

"It was not wrong, Joan, or I should not have done it.
You heard me ask to whom I should pray for inspiration, and
Nature told me I must seek it from you. And I have."

"You shouldn't never 'a' done it. I trusted 'e so!"

"But I had to do it. Nature said, 'Kiss her, and you will
find what you want.' Do you understand that? I have
touched you, and I am awake and alive again. I have touched
you, Joan, and I am not hopeless and sad, but happy. Nature
thought of me, Joan, when she made you and brought you into

the world; and she thought of sweet Joan when she fashioned Jan.   Believe it.   You must believe it."

"You did ought to 'a' axed me."

"Listen.   Nature let you live quiet in the country—for me, Joan.   She let me live all lonely in the world—for you; only for you.   Can't you understand?"

"You did ought to 'a' axed me.   Kissing be wrong 'tween us.   You knaws it, Mister Jan."

"It is right and proper, and fair and beautiful," he said quietly.   "My heart sang when I kissed you, Joan; and so did yours.   D'you know why?   Because we are two halves of a whole.   Because the sunshine of your life would go out without me; because my life, which never had any sunshine in it until now, has been full of sunshine since I knew Joan."

"I dunnaw.   'Twadden a proper thing to do, seein' how I trusted 'e."

"We are children of Nature, Joan.   I always do what she tells me.   I can't help it.   I have obeyed her all my life.   She tells me to love you, Joan, and I do.   I'm very sorry.   I thought she had told you to love me; but I suppose I was wrong. Never mind this once.   Forgive me, Joan.   I'll even fight Nature rather than make you angry with me.   Let me finish my picture and go away.   Come.   I've no business to waste your precious time, though you have been so kind and generous with it.   Only I was tired and hopeless, and you came like a drink of wine to me, Joan; and I drank too much, I suppose."

He picked up his brushes, spoke in a sad minor key, and seemed crushed and weary.   The flash died from his face, and he looked older again.

Joan, the mistress of the situation, found it wholly bitter. She was bewildered; for affairs had proceeded with such rapidity.   He had declared frankly that he loved her, and yet had stopped there.   To her ideas it was impossible that a man should say as much as that to a woman and no more.   Love invariably meant ultimate union for life, Joan thought.   She could not easily imagine any other end to it.   The man talked about Nature as a little child talks of its mother. He had deemed himself entirely in the right; yet something—not Nature, she supposed—had told her that he was wrong. But who was she to judge him? Who was she to say where his conduct erred? He loved truth. It was not a lie to kiss a girl. He promised nothing. How could he promise anything or propose anything? Was she not another man's sweetheart? That, doubtless, had been the reason why he had said no more than that he loved her. To love her could be no sin. Nature had told him to; and God knew how she loved him now.

But she felt powerless to make it up again. A dark curtain seemed to have fallen between them. The old reserve, which had only melted away after many meetings, was upon him once more. He stood, as it seemed, on the former pedestal. A strange surging sensation filled her head—a sense of helpless fighting against a flood of unhappy affairs. All the new glory of life was suddenly tarnished through her own act, and she felt that things would never be as they had been.

She thought and thought. Then John Barron saw Joan's blue eyes begin to wink ominously, the corners of her bonny mouth drag down, and something bright twinkle over her cheek. He took no notice, and when he looked up again she had moved away, and was sitting on the grass crying bitterly, with her hands over her face. The sun was bright, a lark sang overhead. From adjacent inland fields came the jolt and clank of a plough, with a man's voice calling to his horses at the turns. The artist put down his palette and walked over to Joan.

"My dear—my dear," he said, "d'you know what's making you so unhappy?"

She sobbed on, and did not answer.

"I can tell you, I think. You don't quite know whether to believe me or not, Joan. That is very natural. Why should you believe me? And yet if you knew——"

She sat up, swallowed some of her tears, and smudged her face with her knuckles. He took a clean handkerchief from his pocket and handed it to her. It was cool and pleasant, and she went on crying a while, but tears which were comforting and different to the first stinging drops bred from a sudden, forlorn survey of life. He talked on, and his voice soothed her. He kept his distance, and presently, as her ruffled spirit grew calmer, his remarks assumed a brighter note.

"Has my poor little Lady of the Gorse forgiven me at last? She won't punish me any more, I know; and it is a very terrible punishment to see tears in her eyes."

Then Joan found her tongue again, and words to answer him, together with fluttering sighs that told the tears were ended.

"I dunnaw why for I cried, Mister Jan, but I seemed 'mazed like. I'm a stupid fool of a maid, I reckon, an' I s'pose 'tis auld-fashioned notions as I've got 'bout what be right an' wrong. But, coourse, you knaws better'n what I can; an' you'd do me no hurt, 'cause you loves me—you've said it; an'—an'— I love 'e, tu, Mister Jan, I 'sure 'e—better'n anything in all the world."

"Why, that's good, sweet news, Joan; and Nature told me the truth after all! We're bound to love one another. We cannot help it if we would."

He knew that her mind was full of the tangles of life, and that she wanted him to solve some of the riddles just then uppermost in her own existence. He felt that Joe was in her thoughts, and he easily divined her unuttered question as to why Nature had sent Joe before she had sent him. But though answers and explanations of her troubles were not likely to be difficult, he had no wish to make them, or to pursue the subject just then. Indeed, he bid Joan depart an hour before she need have done so. Her face was spoiled for that sitting, and matters had progressed up to the threshold of the barrier. Before this could be broken down, she must be made to feel that he was necessary to the happiness of her life; as he already felt that she was necessary to the completion of his picture. She loved him very dearly, and he, though such an emotion was not possible to his nature, could feel a substitute.

He had fairly stepped out of his impersonal shell into reality. Presently he would return to his shell again. For a moment a model had grown more to him than an achievement, and he told himself that he must obey Nature in order adequately to serve Art.

He picked up the handkerchief he had lent Joan, looked at the dampness of the tear-stains, and then spread it in the sun to dry.

CHAPTER XII.

JOAN WALKS HOME.

WHILE John Barron determined that a space of time extending over some days should now separate him from Joan, she, for her part, had scarce left Gorse Point after the conversation just chronicled, when there came a great longing in her heart to return thither. As she walked home, she viewed wearily the hours which lay between her and the following morning, when she might go back to him and see his face again. Time promised to drag for the next day and night. Already she framed in her mind the things her mouth should say to-morrow, and that almost before she was beyond sight of the man's easel. Her fears had vanished with her tears. The future was entirely in his hand now; for she had accepted his teaching, endeavoured to look at life with his eyes, made his God her own, so far as she had wit to discern what his God was. She accepted the situation with trust, and felt responsibility shifted on to "Mister Jan's" shoulders with infinite relief. He was very wise, and knew everything, and loved the truth. It is desirable to harp and harp upon this ever-recurring thought—the artist's grand love for truth—because all Joan's reflections on the subject terminated in the same conclusion. His sincerity begat absolute trust. And as John Barron and his words and thoughts filled the foreground of life for her, so, correspondingly, did the affairs of her home, with all the circumstances of existence in the old environment, peak and dwindle towards shadowy insignificance. Her father lost his majestic proportions; the Luke Gospellers became mere objects for compassion; the petty temporal interests and concerns of the passing hour henceforth appeared mere worthless affairs for the occupation and waste of time. "Mister Jan" loved her, and she loved him, and what else mattered? Past hours of unrest and wakefulness were forgotten; her tears washed the dead anxieties clean away; and the kiss which had caused them, though it scorched her lip when it fell there, was now set as a seal and a crowning glory to her life. He never kissed any other woman. That pledge of this rare man's affection had been won by the magic of love; and Joan welcomed Nature gladly, and called it God with a warm heart and thankful soul; for Nature had brought about this miracle. Her former religion worked no wonders, but only conveyed terror to her, and a comprehensive knowledge of hell. "Mister Jan" smiled at hell: therefore she could laugh at her old fears. How was it possible to hesitate between two such creeds? She did not do so; and upon final acceptation of the new, and secret rejection of the old, came a great peace to Joan's heart, with the whisper of many voices telling her that she had done rightly.

So the storm gave place to periods of calm and content, only clouded by a longing to be back with the artist again. He loved her. The voice of his love was the song of the spring weather, and the thrush echoed it and the early flowers wrote it on the hedgerows. God was everywhere to her open eyes. Everything that was beautiful, everything that was good, seemed to have been created for her delight during that homeward walk. She was mightily lifted up. Nature seemed so strong, so kind, such a guardian angel for a maiden. And the birds sang out that "Mister Jan" was Nature's priest, and could do no wrong, and that to obey Nature was the highest good.

From which reflection rose a hazy happiness—dim, beautiful, and indefinable as the twinkling gold upon the sea under the throne of the sun. Joan dwelt on the memory of the day which was now over for her, and upon the thought of morning hours which to-morrow would bring. But she looked no further, and backward she did not gaze at all. No thought of Joe Noy dimmed her mental delight, no shadowy cloud darkened the horizon then. All was bright, all perfect. Her mind seemed to be breaking its little case, as the butterfly bursts the chrysalis. Her life till then had been mere grub existence; now she could fly, and had seen the sun drawing the scent from flowers. Great ideas filled her soul, new emotions awoke; she was like a baby trying to utter the thing he has no word for. Her vocabulary broke down under the strain, and as she walked she gave thanks to Nature in a mere wordless song, like the lark, because she could not put her acknowledgment into language. And the great mother—to whom life is all in all, the living individual nothing—looked on at a world wakening from sleep, and viewed the loves of the flowers and the loves of the birds and beasts and fishes with concern as keen as the love in the blue eyes of Joan upon her homeward way.

Busy, indeed, at this vernal season is the mysterious nurse of God's little world. Her hands rest not from her labours. She works strange wonders on the waste—by magic of a million breaking buds, by burying of the dead, by wafting of subtle pollen-life from blossom to blossom. In cliffs above the green waters the young of her wild-fowl are already warm in sprouting feathers; neither will her samphires be forgotten in their dizzy habitations; and salt spray sprinkles her uncurling sea-ferns in caves and crannies where they grow. With satisfaction she views her porpoises rolling their fat sides into sunshine; she brings the sea-otter where it shall find food for its cubs; she leads the giant congers to drowned men; she pats the sleek head of the sad-eyed seal. Upon the wastes and uplands and in secret places she shows the father-hawk a leveret crouching in his form; she takes young rabbits to the new spring grass, the fox to the fowl, the fly to the spider, the blight to the bud. Her weakly nestlings fall from tree and cliff to perish, but unconcerned she beholds the death of them; her weasel sucks the grey bird's egg, yet no hand is raised against the thief, no voice comforts the screaming agony of the mother. With the van of her legions she passes, and the suffering stragglers cry in vain, for her concerns are not with them. She does no right, she works no evil; she is not cruel, neither shall we call her kind; human standards of conduct, human conceits in ethics, may not be applied to her, for she moves mysterious and outside them; she answers to no tribunal of her children.

CHAPTER XIII.

LONELY DAYS.

HAVING already learned from experience that hard work
quickens the flight of time, Joan, returning in happy mood
to her home, and with no trace of the past tears upon her
cheeks, surprised Mrs. Tregenza by a display of most unusual
energy and activity. She helped the butcher to get the pig
into a low cart, built expressly for the conveyance of such
unwieldy animals; she looked mournfully at her departing
companion, knowing that the morrow had nothing for him but
a knife, that he had eaten his last meal. And while Joan
listened to the farewell grunts of the fattest pig which had
ever adorned her father's sty, Mrs. Tregenza counted the money,
bit a piece here and there, and wondered if she could get
the next young porker from Uncle Chirgwin for even a lower
figure than the last.

The day which had worked such wonders for Joan's inner
life, and brought to her eyes a sort of tears unshed till then,
ended at last, and, for her, a sleepless night followed upon it.
Not until long past one o'clock in the morning did she lose
consciousness, and then the thoughts of the day broke loose
again in visions, taking upon themselves fantastic shapes, and
moving amid dream scenery of strange splendour. Now it was
her turn to conjure brain-pictures out of fevered thoughts, and
she woke at last with a start in the dawn, to see a faint light
painting the square of her bedroom window. Looking out, she
found the world dimly visible, a darker shadow through the
gloom, where the fishing-boats were gathering in the bay, the

lighthouse lamp still shining, stars twinkling overhead, absolute silence everywhere, and a cold bite about the air. The girl went back to bed again, but slept no more, and anon arose, dressed, set about morning duties, and, much to Mrs. Tregenza's astonishment, had the fire burning and the breakfast ready by the time her stepmother appeared.

"Aw jimmery!" Thomasin exclaimed, as Joan came in from the outhouse to find her warming cold hands at the fire, "I couldn't b'lieve my eyes at first, an' thot the piskey men had come to do us a turn, spite o' what faither sez. You've turned over a leaf seemin'ly. Workin' out o' core be a new game for you."

"I couldn' sleep for thinkin' 'bout—'bout the pig, an' wan thing an' 'nother."

"He's pork now, or nearly. You heard butcher promise me some nattlin's, dedn' 'e? You'd best walk up to Paul bimebye an' fetch 'em. 'Tis easier to call to mind other folk's promises than our awn. He said the same last pig-killin', an' it comed to nort."

Joan escaped soon after breakfast, and set off eagerly enough. She took a basket with her, and designed to call at Paul on the way home again. Moreover, she chose a longer route to Gorse Point than that through Mousehole; for her very regular habits of late had caused some comment in that village, and more than one acquaintance had asked her—half in jest, half in earnest—who it was she went to see up Mousehole hill. This had frightened Joan twice already; and to-day, for the first time, she took the longer route above Paul church-town. It brought her over fields near the cow-byre, where Barron spent much of his time, and kept his picture; and when she saw that her footpath must pass the door of the little house, a flutter quickened her pulses, and she branched away over the field, and proceeded to the cliffs through a gap in the hedge, some distance from the byre.

But as Joan came out upon the sward through the furzes, her heart sank in sight of loneliness. She was not early to-day, yet she had come earlier than " Mister Jan." The grey figure was invisible. There were marks on the turf, where his easel and camp-stool stood; there was the spot his feet were wont to press, and her own standing-point against the glimmering gorse; but that was all. She knew no reason for his delay. The weather was splendid, the day was warm, and he had never been so late before, within her recollection. Joan, much wondering, sat down to wait, with her eyes upon the sea, her ears alert for the first footstep, and her mind listening also. Time passed, and indefinite uneasiness grew into a fear; then that expanded and multiplied as her mind approached the problem of " Mister Jan's " non-appearance from a dozen different standpoints. Hope declared some private concern had kept him, and he would not be long in coming; fear inquired what unforeseen incident was likely to have risen since yesterday—asked the question and answered it a dozen different ways. The girl waited, walked here and there, scanned the footpath and the road, returned, sat down in patience, ate a cake she had brought, and so whiled the long minutes away. Fears grew as hour and half-hour passed— fears for him, not herself. The crowning despair did not touch her mind till later, and her first sorrow was a simple terror that harm had fallen upon the man. He had told her that he valued life but little, how at best no great length of days awaited him; and now she thought that, wandering about the cliffs by night, he might have met the death he did not fear. Then she remembered he was but a sick man always, with frail breathing parts; and her thoughts turned to the shed, and she pictured him lying ill there, unable to communicate with friends, perhaps waiting and praying long hours for her foot- fall, as she had been waiting and praying for his. Upon this most plausible possibility striking Joan, her heart beat hard below her breast and her cheeks grew white. She rose from her seat upon the cliff, turned her face to the cow-byre, and made a few quick steps in that direction. Then a vague flutter of sense, as of warning where no danger is visible, slowed her speed for a moment; but her heart was strung to action, and the strange new voice did not sound like Nature's, so she put it aside and let it drown into silence before the clamour of fear for "Mister Jan's" well-being. Indeed, the strange premonitory whisper excited a moment's anger in the girl that any distrust could shadow her love for such an one at such a time. She hated herself, held the thought a sin of her own commission, and sped onwards until she stood upon the northern side of the byre, in a shadow cast from it by the sun.

The place was padlocked, and at that sight Joan's spirits, though they rose in one direction, yet fell in another. One fear vanished, a second loomed the larger; for the padlock, while it indicated that the artist had left his lonely habitation for the time, did not explain his absence now, or dispel the possibilities of an accident or disaster. The tar-pitched double-door of the shed was fast, and offered no peep-hole; but Joan went round to the south side, where an aperture appeared, and where a little glass window had taken the place of the wooden shutters. Sunshine lighted the shed inside; she could see every detail of the chamber, and she photographed it on her mind with a quick glance. A big easel, with the life-size picture of herself upon it, stood in the middle of the shed, and a smaller easel appeared hard by. The artist's palettes, brushes, and colours littered a bench, and bottles and tumblers were scattered among them. Two pipes, which she had seen in his mouth, lay together upon a box on the floor, and beside them stood a tin of tobacco wrapped in yellow paper. A white umbrella and some sticks stood in one corner, and another she saw was filled by some railway-rugs spread over dried bracken. Two coats hung on nails in the wall, and above one of them was suspended a Panama hat, which Barron often wore when painting. Something moved suddenly, and, looking upon the stone floor, she saw a rat-trap with a live rat in it. The beast was running as far as it could this way and that, poking its nose up and trying the roof of its prison. She noticed its snout was raw from thrusting between the wire, and she wished she could get in to kill it.

She did not know that it was a mother rat, with young ones outside, squeaking faintly in the stack of mangel-wurzels ; she did not know, as it hopped round and round, that its beady eyes were glittering with a great agony, and that "Mister Jan's" God was powerless to break down a mere wire or two and save it.

Presently, worn and weary, Joan trudged back again, with no very happy mind. She found food for comfort in one reflection alone : the artist had made no special appointment for that day, and it might be that business, or an engagement at Newlyn, Penzance, or elsewhere was occupying his time. She felt it must be so, and tried hard to convince herself that he would surely be at the usual spot upon the morrow.

So, after fulfilling her mother's orders at Paul, she walked home unhappy ; and time, which had dragged yesterday, to-day stood still. Before night she had lived an age. The hours of darkness were endless. But her father's return furnished excuse for another morning of early rising ; and when Grey Michael and Tom had eaten, donned clean raiment, and returned to the sea, Joan, having seen them to the pier-head, did not go home, but hastened straight away for Gorse Point, and arrived there earlier than ever she had done before. There was something soothing to her troubled mind in being upon the spot sacred to him. Though he was not present, she seemed closer far to him on Gorse Point than anywhere else. His foot had marked the turf there ; his eye had mirrored the furzes a thousand times. She knew just where his shadow had fallen as he stood painting, and the spot upon which he was wont to lie by the cliff edge when came the time for rest. Beside this holy place she now sat herself, and waited with hope higher in the splendour of the morning. For sorrows, fears, and ills are always blackest when the sun has set ; and every man or woman can better face trouble on opening their eyes in a sunny dawn than after midnight has struck, a sad day left them weakened, and nothing wakes in the world but Care and themselves.

The morning wore away, and the old fears returned with greater force to chill her soul. The sun was burnishing the sea, and she watched Mousehole luggers putting out and dancing away through the gold. Under the cliffs the gulls wheeled with sad cries, and the long-necked cormorants hastened backwards and forwards, now flying fast and low over the water, now fishing here and there in couples. She saw them rear in the water as they dived, then go down head first, leaving a rippling circle, which widened out and vanished long before the fishers bobbed up again twenty yards further on. Time after time she watched them, speculating vaguely after each disappearance as to how long the bird would remain out of sight. Then she turned her face to the land, weary of waiting, weary of the bright sea and sky, and of the music of the gulls, and of life. She sat down again presently, and put her hand over her face and struggled with her thoughts. Manifold fears compassed her mind about; but one, not felt till then, rose now, a giant above the rest. Yesterday she had been all alarm for "Mister Jan;" to-day there came terror for herself. Something said, "He has gone; he has left you." Her brain, without any warning, framed the words and spoke them to her. It was as though a stranger had brought the news, and she rose up white and stricken at this fatal explanation of the artist's continued absence. She put the thought from her as she had put another; but it returned with pertinacity, and each time larger than before, until the fear filled all her mind and made her wild and desperate, under the conviction of a sudden, awful life-quake launched against her existence, to shatter all her new joy and dash the brimming cup of love from her lips.

Hours passed, and she grew somewhat faint and hollow every way—in head and heart and stomach. Her eyes ached, her brains were worn out with thinking. She felt old, her body was heavy, energy had died. The world changed, too. The gorse looked strange as the sun went round, the lark sang no more, the wind blew coldly, and the sea's gold was darkened by a rack of flying clouds, whose shadows fell purple and grey upon the waters. He had gone; he had left her. Perhaps she would never see him or hear of him again. Then the place grew hateful to her, and terrible as a grave. She dragged herself away, dizzy, weary, wretched; and not until halfway home again did she find power to steady her mind and control thought. Then the old alarm returned—that first fear which had pictured him dead, perhaps even now rolling over and over under the precipices, or hid for ever in a cranny of some dark cavern at the root of the cliffs, where high tides spouted and thundered, and battered the flesh off his bones against granite. She suffered terribly in mind upon that homeward journey. Her own light and darkness mattered nothing now, and her personal and selfish fears had vanished before she reached Newlyn. She was thinking how she could raise an alarm, how she should tell his friends, who possibly imagined "Mister Jan" safe and comfortable in the cow-byre. But who were his friends, and how might she approach them without such an action becoming known and getting talked about? Her misery was stamped on her face when she at last returned to the white cottage at three o'clock in the afternoon of that day; and Mrs. Tregenza saw it there.

"God save us! Wheer you bin to, an' what you bin 'bout? You'm so pasty an' round-eyed, as if you'd bin piskey-led somewheers. An' me worn to death wi' work."

"I went walkin' 'long the cliffs in the sun, an' forgot the time. Gimme somethin' t' ate, mother. I be hungry an' fainty like wi' gwaine tu far. I could hardly fetch home."

"You'm a queer twoad," said Thomasin, "an' I doan't knaw what's come over 'e of late days. 'Pears to me you'm hidin' summat from me; an' if I thot that, I'd mighty quick get faither to find out what 'twas, I can tell 'e."

Then she went off, and brought cold potatoes and dripping, with bread and salt, and a cup of milk.

CHAPTER XIV.

LESSONS LEARNED.

The lesson which he had set for Joan Tregenza's learning taught John Barron something also. Eight and forty hours he stayed in Newlyn, and was astounded to discover, during that period, what grip this girl had got upon his mind, how she had dragged him out of himself. His first thought was to escape all physical excitement and emotion by abandoning his picture almost upon the moment of its completion, and relinquishing his model too; but various considerations cried out against such a course. To go was to escape no difficulty, but to fly from the spoils of victory. The fruit only wanted plucking; and, through pleasure, he believed that he would proceed to speedy, easy, and triumphant completion of his work. No lasting compunction coloured the tenour of his thoughts. Once, indeed, upon the day when he returned to Gorse Point, and saw Joan again, some shadow of regret for her swept through his brain; but that and the issue of it will be detailed in their place.

Time went heavily for him while he kept away from Joan. He roamed listlessly here and there, and watched the weather-glass uneasily; for this abstention from work was a deliberate challenge to Providence to change sunshine for rain, and high temperature for low. Upon the third day, therefore, he returned at early morning to the picture in the shed. The greater part was finished, and the masses of gorse stood out strong, solid, and complete, with the slender brown figure before them. The face of it was very sweet, but to Barron it seemed as the face of a ghost, with no hot blood in its veins, no live interests in its eyes.

"'Tis the countenance of a nun," he said sneeringly to himself. "No fire, no love, no story—a sweet virgin page of life, innocent of history or of interest as a new-blown lily." The problem was difficult, and he had now quite convinced himself that solution depended on one course alone. "And why not?" he asked himself. "Why, when pleasures are offered, shall I refuse them? God knows, Nature is chary enough with her delights! She has sowed death in me—here, in my lungs. I shall bleed away my life some day, or die strangled, unless I anticipate the climax and choose another exit. Why not take what she throws to me in the mean time?"

He walked down to the Point, set up his easel, and waited, feeling that Joan had certainly made two pilgrimages since his last visit, and little doubting that she would come a third time.

Presently, indeed, she did, scarcely daring to raise her eyes, but flushing with great waves of joy when she saw him, and crying "Mister Jan!" in a triumphant ripple of music from a full heart.

Then the artist rose very boldly, and put his arms round her and looked into her face, while she nestled close to him, and shut her eyes with a sigh of sheer content and thankfulness. She had learned her lesson thoroughly enough: she felt she could not live without him now, and when he kissed her, she did not start from the caress, but opened her eyes and looked into his face with great yearning love.

"Oh, thank the good God you'm come back agin to me! To think it be awnly two li'l days! An' the time have seemed a hundred years. I thot 'e was lost, or dead, or killed, an' I seed 'e, when I slept, a-tossin' over down in the zawns,* where the sea roars an' makes the world shake. Oh, Mister Jan, an' I woke screamin', an' mother comed up, an' I near spoke your name, but not quite!"

* *Zawns, sea-caves.*

"You need not have feared for me, Joan, though I have been very miserable too, my little sweetheart; I have, indeed. I was overworked and worried and wretched, so I stopped in Newlyn; but being away from you has only taught me I cannot exist away from you. The time was long and dreary, and it would have been still worse had I known that you were unhappy."

"Wisht as a winnard * I was without 'e, Mister Jan. I be such a poor lass in brains, an' I could awnly think of trouble, 'cause I loved 'e so true. Tedn' like the same plaace when you'm away. Then I thot you'd gone right back to Lunnon, an' I judged my heart 'ud break for 'e, I did."

"Poor little blue-eyed woman! Could you really think I was such a brute?"

"'Twas awnly wan thot among many. I never thot so much afore in my life. An' I looked 'bout tu; an' I went up to the li'l byre, where your things was, an' peeped in en. But I seed nought of 'e, awnly a gashly auld rat in a trap. But 'e won't gaw aways like that agin, will 'e?"

"No, no. It was too bad."

"Coourse I knawed that if all was well with 'e, you'd 'a' done the right thing, but it 'peared as if the right thing couldn' be to leave me, Mister Jan—not now, now you be my world like; 'cause theer ed'n nothin' or nobody else in the world but you for me. 'Tis wicked, but 'tothers be all faded away; an' faither's nort, an' Joe's nort alongside o' you."

He did not answer, and began to paint. Joan's face was far short of looking its best; there were dark shadows under her eyes, and less colour than usual brightened her cheeks. He tried to work, but circumstances and his own feelings were alike against him. He was restless, and lacked patience, nor could his eye see colour aright. In half an hour he had spoilt not a little of what was already done. Then he took a palette-knife, made a clean sweep of much previous labour, and began again. But the music of her happy voice was in his blood

* *Winnard*, redwing.

to-day. The child had come out of the valley of sorrow, and she was boisterously happy, and her laughter made him wild. Mists gathered in his eyes, and his breath caught now and again. Passion fairly gripped him by the throat, till even the sound of his own voice was strange to him, and he felt his knees shake. He put down his brushes, turned from the picture and went to the cliff-edge, there flinging himself upon the grass.

" I cannot paint to-day, Joan; I'm too overjoyed at getting you back to me. My hand is not steady, and my Joan of paint and canvas seems worse and feebler than ever beside your flesh and blood. You don't know—you cannot guess how I have missed you."

" 'Iss fay, but I can, Mister Jan, if you felt same as what I done. 'Tweer cruel, cruel. But, then, you've got a many things, an' folks to fill up your time; I abbun got nothin' now but you."

" I expect Joe often thinks about you."

" I dunnaw. 'Tis awful wicked, but Joe, he gone clean out of my mind now. I thot I loved en, but I was a cheel then, an' I didn't 'sackly knaw what love was; now I do. 'Twadden what I felt for Joe Noy 'tall: 'tis what I feels for you, Mister Jan."

" Ah, I like to hear you say that. Nature has brought you to me, Joan, my little jewel; and she has brought Jan to you. You could not understand that last time I told you; now you can, and you do. We belong to each other—you and I—and to nobody else."

" I'd be well content to belong to 'e, Mister Jan. You'm my good fairy, I reckon. If I could work for 'e allus, an' see 'e an' 'ear 'e every day, I shouldn' want nothin' better'n that."

Then it was that the shade of a compunction and the shadow of a regret touched John Barron; and it cooled his hot blood for a brief moment, and he swore to himself he would try to paint her again as she was. He would fight Nature for once, and try if pure intellect was strong enough to get the face he wanted on to the canvas without the gratification of his flesh and blood. In which determination glimmered something almost approaching to self-sacrifice in such a man. He did not answer Joan's last remark, but rose and went to his picture, and she, thinking herself snubbed by his silence after her avowal, grew hot and uncomfortable.

"The weather is going to change, sweetheart," he said, allowing himself the luxury of affectionate words in the moment of his half-hearted struggle; "the weather-glass creeps back slowly. We must not waste time. Come, Joan; we are the children of Nature, but the slaves of Art. Let me try again."

But she, who had spoken in all innocence, and with a child's love, was pained that he should have taken no note of her speech. She was almost angry that he had power to conjure such words to her lips; and yet the anger vanished from her mind quickly enough, and her thoughts were all happy as she resumed her pose for him.

The past few days had vastly deepened and widened her mental horizon; and now Barron, for the first time, saw something of what he wanted in her eyes as she gazed away over the sea, and did not look at him as usual. There, sure enough, was the soul that he knew slept somewhere, but had never seen until then. And the sight of it came as a shock, and swept away his ugly-woven sophistries. He had told himself that Nature, through one channel only, would bring the mystery of hidden thought to Joan's blue eyes, and he had felt well satisfied to believe it was so; but now even the plea of Art could not excuse the thing which had grown within him of late, for experiences other than those he dreamed of had glorified the frank blue eyes, and brought mind into them. Now it only remained for him to paint them if he could. Not wholly untroubled, but never much more beautiful than upon that morning, Joan gazed over the remote sea. Then the thoughtful mood passed, and she laughed and babbled again, and the new-born beauty departed from her eyes for a season, and the warm blood raced through her veins, and she was all happiness. Meanwhile nothing came of his painting, and he was not sorry when she ended the ordeal.

"The bwoats be comin' back home-along, Mister Jan. I doan't mark faither's yet, but when 'tis wance in sight he'll be to Newlyn sooner'n me. So I'd best be gwaine, though it ed'n more than noon, I s'pose. An' my heart's a tidy sight lighter now than 'tweer 'issterday, indeed."

"I'm almost afraid to let you go, Joan."

She looked at him curiously, waiting for his bidding; but he seemed moody, and said no more.

"When be you comin' next?"

"To-morrow, and to-morrow, and to-morrow, my pearl above price. It is so hard, so very hard," he answered. "Fine or wet, I shall be here to-morrow, for I am not going back to Newlyn again till my work is done. Three more sittings, Joan, if you have enough patience."

"In coourse, Mister Jan."

She did not explain to him what difficulties daily grew in the way of her coming, how rumour was alive, and how her stepmother had threatened more than once to tell Grey Michael that his wayward daughter was growing a gadabout. Joan had explained away her roaming with a variety of more or less ingenious lies, and she always found her brain startlingly fertile where the artist and his picture were concerned. She felt little doubt that three more visits to Gorse Point might be achieved —ay, and thirty more if necessary. But afterwards? What would follow the painting of the picture? She asked herself the question as he kissed her, with a kiss that was almost rough, while he bid her go quickly; and the former reply to every doubt made answer. Her fears fled as usual before the invigorating spectacle of this sterling, truth-loving man. With him all the future remained, and with him only. Hers was the pleasant, passive task of obedience to one utterly trusted and passionately loved. Her fate lay hidden in his heart, as the fate of the clay lies hid in the brain of the potter.

And so home she went, walking in a sunshine of her own thoughts. The clouds were gone; they massed gloomily on the horizon of the past; but, looking forward, she saw no more of them. All time to come was at the disposition of the wisest man she had ever met. She did not know or guess at the battle which this same wise man had fought and lost under her eyes; she gathered nothing of the truth from his gloom, his silence, his changed voice, his sudden farewell. She did not know passion when she saw it, and the visible signs thereof told no tale to her.

CHAPTER XV.

STORM.

THAT night the change came, and the wind veered first to the south, then to the south-west. By morning, grey clouds hid the sky, and hourly grew darker and lower. As yet no rain fell, but the world had altered, and every light-value, from an artist's standpoint, was modified.

John Barron sat by his stove in the byre, made himself a cup of black tea, and presently, wrapped in a big mackintosh, walked out to Gorse Point. His picture he left, of course, at the shed, for painting was out of the question.

Nature, who had been smiling so pleasantly in sunshine these many days, now awoke in a grim, grey mood. The sea ran high, its white foam-caps and ridges fretting the rolling volume of it; the luggers fought their way out with buried noses and labouring hulls. Rain still held off, but it was coming quickly, and the furze and the young grasses panted for it on Gorse Point. Below the cliffs a wild spirit inhabited the sea-fowl, and they screamed and wheeled in many an aërial circle, now sliding with motionless, outstretched wing upon the gathering gale, now beating back against it, now dancing in a fleet below, and making music far away upon the foam. Over the beach the dry sand whipped round in whirls and eddies where wind-gusts caught it; the naked rocks thrust shining weed-covered heads out of a low tide, and the wet, white light of them glimmered raw through the grey tones of the atmosphere. Now and then a little cloud of dust would puff out from the cliff-face, where the wind dislodged a dry particle of stone or mould. Elsewhere, Barron saw the sure-rooted samphire, with tufts of sea-pink, innocent of flowers as yet; and sometimes little squeaking dabs of down might also be observed below, where infant gulls huddled together on the ledges outside their nests, and gazed upon a condition of things as yet beyond their experience.

Joan came presently, to find the artist looking out at the sea.

"You ban't gwaine to paint, I s'pose, 'cause o' this ugly fashion weather?" she said.

"No, sweetheart. All the gold has gone out of the world, and there is nothing left but lead and dross-colour. See how strange the green is under the grey, and note the thickness of the air. Everything is uncertain and dim upon the eye to-day; the sky is full of coming rain, and the sea is a wild harmony in grey and silver."

"'Iss, the cleeves be callin' this marnin'. 'Tis a sort o' whisper as falls 'pon a body's ear, an' it means that the high hills knaws the rain is nigh. An' they tell it wan to 'tother, an' moans it mournful over the valleys 'pon the wind. 'The storm be comin'; the storm be comin'!' they sez."

The south and west regions of distance blackened as they sat there on the cliff, and upon the sea separate heavy gusts of wind roughened up the hollows of the waves; which effect, seen from afar, flickered weirdly, like a sort of submarine lightning shivering white through dark water. Presently a cloud broke, showing a bank of paler grey behind, and misty silver arrows fell in broad bands of light upon the sea. They sped round each upon the last, like the spokes of a gigantic wheel trundling over the world; then the clouds huddled together again, and the gleam of brightness died.

"You'm wisht this marnin', Mister Jan. You abbun so much as two words for me. 'Tis 'cause you caan't paint your picksher, I reckon."

He sighed, and took her hand in his. "Don't think that, my Joan. Once I cared nothing for you, everything for my picture; now I care nothing for my picture, everything for you.   And the better I love you, the worse I paint you.   That's funny, isn't it?"

"'Iss, 'tis coorious.   But I'm sure you do draw me a mighty sight finer than I be.   'Tis wonnerful clever, an' theer edn' no call to be sad, for no man else could 'a' done better, I lay."

He did not answer, and still held her hand.   Then there came a harder breath of wind, with a sound of sob in it, while already over the distant sea swept separate grey curtains of rain.

"It's coming, Joan—the storm.   It's everywhere—in earth, and air, and water, and in my blood.   I am savage to-day, Joan—savage and thirsty.   What will be the end of it?"

He spoke wildly, like the weather.   She did not understand, but she felt his hand clench tightly over hers, and, looking at the white, thin fingers crooked round her wrist, they brought to her mind the twisted claws of a dead sea-gull she remembered to have found upon the beach.

"What will be the end of it, Joan?   Can't you answer me?"

"Doan't 'e, Mister Jan; you'm hurtin' my hand.   I s'pose as a sou'westerly gale be comin'.   Us knaws 'em well enough in these paarts.   Faither reckoned theer was dirty weather blawin' up 'fore he sailed.   He was away by daylight.   The gales do bring trouble to somebody most times."

"What will be the end of us, I mean?—not of the weather. The rain will come and the clouds will melt, and we know, as sure as God's in heaven, that we shall see sunshine and blue sky again.   But what about our storm, Joan—the storm of love that's burst in my heart for you?   What follows that?"

His question frightened her.   She had asked herself the same, and been well content to leave an answer to him.   Here was he faced with a like problem, and now inviting her to solve it.

"I dunnaw.   I thot such love never comed to an end, Mister Jan.   I thot 'tweer good to wear.   But—but how do I knaw if you doan't?"

"You trust me, Joan?"

" Why, who should I trust if 'tweern't you? I never knawed any person else 'cept faither as set such store by the truth. I doan't s'pose the cherrybims in heaven loves it more'n what you do."

" Here's the rain on tho back of the wind," he said.

A few heavy drops fell, cold as ice upon his burning face, and Joan laughed as sho held out her hand, on which a groat splash as big as a shilling had spread.

" That be wan of Tregagle's tears," she said ; " an' 'tis the voice of en as you can hear howlin' in the wind. He's allus a-bawlin' an' squealin', poor sawl ! But you can awnly hear en now an' again 'fore a storm, when the gale blaws his hollerin' this way."

" Who was Tregagle ? "

" He was a lawyer man wance, an' killed a-many wives, an' did a-many shameful deeds 'fore he went dead. Then, to Bodmin Court, theer comes a law case, an' they wanted Tregagle, an' a man said Tregagle was the awnly witness, an' another said he wadden. The second man up an' swore, ' If Tregagle saw it done, then I wish to God ho may rise from's graave and come this minute.' Then, sure enough, tho ghost of Tregagle 'peared in the court-house an' shawed the man was a liar. But they couldn' lay the ghost no more arter; an' it was a devil-ghost, which is the worstest kind ; an' it stuck close to thicky lyin' man an' wouldn' leave en nohow. But at last a white-witch bound the spirit, an' condemned it to empty out Dosmery Pool wi' a crogan wi' a hole in it. A crogan's a limpet-shell, which you mightn't knaw, Mister Jan. Tregagle, he done that purty quick, an' then he was at tho man again ; but a passon got the bettermost of en, an' tamed en wi' Scripture, till Tregagle was as gentle as a cheel. Then they set en to work again, an' bid en make a truss o' sand down in Gwenvor Cove, an' carry it 'pon his shoulder up to Carn Olva. Tregagle wore a braave time doin' that, I can 'sure 'e, but theer comed a gert frost wan winter, an' he got water from the brook an' poured it 'pon the truss o' sand, so it froze hard. Then he carried it up Carn Olva, an' then, bein' a free spirit agin, he flew off quicker'n lightning to that lyin' man to tear en to pieces this time. But by good chance, when Tregagle comed to en, the man weer carryin' a li'l baaby in's arms—a li'l cheel as had never done a single wicked act, bein' tu young—so Tregagle couldn' do no hurt. An' they caught en again, an' passon set en 'pon another job—to make a truss o' sand in Whitsand Bay wi'out usin' any fresh water. But Tregagle caan't never do that; so he cries bitter sometimes, an' howls; an' when 'e howls you knaw the storm's a-comin' to scatter the truss o' sand he's builded up."

Barron followed the legend with interest. Tregagle and his victim and the charm of the pure child that saved one from the other filled his thought, together with the event to which Fate was now relentlessly dragging him. He argued with himself a little; then the rain came down and the wind leapt like a lion over the edge of the land, and the man's blood boiled as he breathed ocean air.

"Us'll be wetted proper! I'll run for it, Mister Jan, an' you'd best to go up long to your li'l lew house. Wet's bad for 'e, I reckon."

"No," he said, "I can't let you go, Joan. Look over there. Another flood is going to burst, I think. Follow me quickly, quickly."

The rain came slanting over the gorse in earnest, but Joan hesitated and hung back. Louder than the wind, louder than the cry of the birds, than the howling of Tregagle, than the calling of the cleeves, spoke something. And it said, "Turn on the wing of the storm; fly before it, alone. Let this man walk in the teeth of the gale, if he will; but you, Joan Tregenza, follow the wind, and set your face to the east, where the sole brightness now left in the sky is shining."

Sheets of grey swept over them; the world was wet in an instant; a little mist of water splashed up two inches high off the ground; the gorse tossed and swayed its tough arms; the soa and the struggling craft upon it vanished like a dream; from the heart of the storm cried gulls, themselves invisible.

"Come, Joan; we shall be drowned."

He had wrapped her in a part of the mackintosh, and laughed as he fastened them both into it, and hugged her close to himself. But she broke away, greatly fearing, yet knowing not what she feared.

"I reckon I'd best run down fast. Indeed, an' I want to go."

"Go? Where? Where should you go? Come to me, Joan; you shall; you must. We two it will be, sweetheart—we two against the rain and the wind, and the world. Come! It will kill me to stand here, and you don't want that."

"But—— "

"Come, I say. Quicker and quicker! We two—only we two. Don't make me command you, my priceless treasure of a Joan. Come with me. You are mine now and always. Quicker and quicker, I say. God! what rain!"

Still she hesitated, and he grew angry.

"This is folly, madness. Where is your trust and belief? You don't trust, nor love, nor—— "

"Doan't 'e say that! Never say that! It edn' true. You'm all to me, an' you knaws it right well, an' I'll gaw to the world's end with 'e, I will—ay, an' trust 'e wi' my life!"

He moved away and she followed, hastening as he hastened. Unutterable desolation marked the spot. Life had vanished save only where sheep clustered under a bank with their tails to the weather, and where two long-legged lambs blinked their yellow eyes and bleated as the couple passed. Despite their haste, the man and the girl were very wet before reaching the shelter of the byre. Rain-water dribbled off his cap on to his hot face, and his feet were soaking. Joan was breathless with haste; her draggled skirts clung to her; and the struggle against the storm made her giddy.

So they reached the place of shelter; and the gale burst over it with a great, crowning yell of wind and hurtle of rain.

Then John Barron opened the byre door, and Joan Tregenza passed in before him, whereupon he followed and shut the door.

A loose slate clattered upon the roof, and from inside the byre it sounded like a hand tapping high above the artist's bed of brown fern—tapping some message which neither the man nor the girl could read—tapping, tapping, tapping tirelessly upon ears wholly deaf to it.

BOOK II.

NATURE.

CHAPTER I.

AN INTERVAL.

FOR a week the rain came down, and it blew hard from the west. Then the weather moderated, and there were intervals of brightness and mild, damp warmth, that brought a green veil trembling over the world like magic. The elms broke into a million buds, the pear trees were already past their prime of snowy blossom; the apple orchards blushed with rosy dawn of splendours to come. In the market gardens around and about Newlyn, plums were already setting; the wallflowers, which make a carpet of golden-brown beneath the fruit trees, were velvety with bloom; the raspberry canes, bent hoop-like in long rows, beautifully brightened the dark earth with young green; and new-born verdure likewise twinkled to the heart of the forests, to the stony nipples of the moor's vast, lonely bosom. So spring came, heralded by the thrush, riding free upon the wings of the western wind. And then followed a brief change, with more heavy rains and lower temperature.

The furzes on Gorse Point were a scented glory now—a nimbus of gold for the skull of the lofty cliff. Here John Barron and Joan Tregenza had met but twice since the beginning of the unsettled weather. For her this period was in a measure mysterious and strange. Centuries of experience appeared to separate her from the past, and, looking backwards, it seemed that infinite spaces of time already stretched between what had been, and what was. Not overmuch sorrow mingled with her reflections, though a leaven of it ran through all—a sense of loss, of sacrifice, of change, which flits, like the shadow of a summer cloud, even through the soul of the most deeply loving woman who ever opened her eyes to smile upon the first day-dawn of married life. But Joan's sorrow was no greater than that, and little unquiet or uneasiness went with it. She had his promises; from him they could but be absolute; and not a hundred attested ceremonies had left her heart more at ease. In fact, she believed that John Barron was presently going to marry her, and that when he vanished from Newlyn, she, as the better-loved part of himself, would vanish too. It was the old, stale falsehood which men have told a hundred thousand times; which men will go on telling and women believing, because it is the only lie which meets all requirements of the case, and answers its exact purpose effectively. Age cannot kill it, for experience is no part of the armour of the deceived, and Love and Trust have never stopped to think since the world began.

As for the artist, each day now saw him slipping more deeply, more comfortably back into the convolutions of his old subjective shell. He had been dragged out, not unwilling, by a giant passion, and he had sacrificed to it, sent it to sleep again, and so returned. He felt infinitely kind to Joan. A week after her visit to the byre, he, while sitting alone there, had turned her picture about on the easel, withdrawn its face from the wall, and studied his work. And looking, with restored critical faculty and cold blood, he loved the paint for itself, and deemed it very good. The storm was over, the transitory lightnings drowned lesser lights no more, and that steady beacon-flame of his life, which had been merged, not lost, in the fleeting blaze, now shone out again, steadfast and clear. Such a revulsion of feeling argued well for the completion of his picture, ill for the model of it.

They sat one day, as the weather grew more settled, beside a granite boulder, which studded the short turf at the extremity of Gorse Point, where it jutted above the sea. Joan, with her chin upon her hands, looked out upon the water as usual; Barron, lying on a railway rug, leant back and smoked his pipe, and studied her face with the old, keen, passionless eagerness of their earliest meetings.

" When'll 'e tell me, Jan love? When'll 'e tell me what 'e be gwaine to do? Us be wan now—you an' me—but the lines be all the lovin'est wife can p'int to in proof she *be* a wife. Couldn't us be axed out in church purty soon? "

He did not make immediate answer, but only longed for his easel. There, in her face, was the wistful, far-away expression he had sighed for; a measure of reflection had come to the little animal—her brains were awake, and her blue eyes had never looked like this before. Joan asked the question again, and Barron answered.

" The same matter was in my own mind, sweetheart. I am in a mighty hurry too, believe it. You are safe with your husband, Joan. You belong to me now, and you must trust the future with me. All that law demands to make us man and wife it shall have; and all religion clamours for as well, if that is a great matter to you. But not here—in this Newlyn. I think of you when I say that, Joan, for it matters nothing to me."

" 'Iss. I dunnaw what awful sayin's might go abroad. Things is all contrary to home as 'tis. Mother's guessed part, an' she tawld faither I weer gwaine daft, or else in love wi' some pusson else than Joe. An' faither was short an' sharp, an' took me out walkin', an' bid me bide at home an' give over trapsin' 'bout. An' 'e said as 'ow I was tokened to Joe Noy, an' bound by God A'mighty to wait for en if 'twas a score years. But if faither had knawed I weer never for Noy, he'd 'a' said more'n that. I ban't 'feared o' faither now I knaws you, Jan; but I be cruel 'feared o' bein' cussed, 'cause theer's times when cusses doan't fall to the ground, but sticks. 'Twouldn' be well for the likes o' you to have a ill-wished, awver-luked body for wife. An' if faither knawed 'bout you, then I lay, he'd do more'n speak. So like's not he'd strike me dead for't, bein' that religious in his way. But you must take me away, Jan, dear heart. I'm yourn now, an' you must go on lovin' me allus, 'cause theer'll never be nobody else to not now. I've chose you, an' gived 'e myself for your awn, an' I caan't do no more."

He listened to her delicious voice, and shut out the crude words as much as might be while he marked the music. He was thinking that if Joan had possessed a reasonable measure of intellect, a foundation for an education, he would have been satisfied to keep her about him during that probably limited number of years which must span his existence. But the gulf between them was too wide; and, as for the present position, he considered that no harm had been done which time would not remedy. Joan was not sufficiently intelligent to suffer long or much. She would forget quickly. She was very young. Her sailor must return before the end of the year. Then he began to think of money, and then sneered at himself. But, after all, it was natural that he should follow step by step upon the beaten track of similar events. "Better not attempt originality," he thought, "for the thing I have done is scarce capable of original treatment. I suppose the curtain always rings down on a cheque—either taken or spurned."

"So you think you can give them all up for poor me, Joan? Your home, your father, brother, mother—all?"

"I've gived up a sight more'n them, Jan. But my folks weern't hard to throw awver. 'Tis long since they was ought to me now. I gaws an 'comes from the cottage an' sez, all the time, 'This ban't home no more. Mister Jan's home be mine,' I sez to myself. An' each time as I breaks bread, an' sleeps, an' wakes, an' looks arter faither's clothes, I feels 'tis wan time nigher the last. They'll look back an' think what a snake 'twas they had 'bout the house, I s'pose. Mother'll whine an' say, 'Ah! 'er was a bitter weed, for sartain;' an' faither'll thunder till the crocks rattle an' bid none dare foul the air wi' my name no more. But I be wearyin' of 'e wi' my clackin', Jan, dear heart?"

"Not so, Joan—never think that. I could listen to you till doomsday. Only we must act now and talk presently. I know you're tired of the picture, and you were cross last time we met because I could speak of it; but I must for a moment more. It cries out to be finished. A few hours' good work and all's done. The weather steadies now and the glass is rising, so our sittings may begin in a day or two. Let me make one last, grand struggle. Then, if I fail, I shall fling the picture over this cliff, and my palette after it. So we will keep our secret a little longer. And, when the picture is made or marred, away we'll go, and by the time they miss you from your old home you will be halfway to your new one."

But she did not heed the latter part of his remarks, for her thoughts were occupied with what had gone before.

"'Pears, when all's said, you'd sooner have the picksher Joan than the real wan. 'Tis all the picksher, an' the picksher, an' the picksher."

This was not less than the truth; but, of course, he blamed her for so speaking, and said her words hurt him.

"'Tis this way," she said: "I've larned so much since I knawed 'e, an' I be like as if I was woke from a sleep. Things is all differ'nt now; but 'tis awnly my gert love for 'e as makes me 'feared sometimes 'cause life's too butivul to last. An' the picksher frights me more'n fancy, 'cause, seemin'ly, theer's two Joans, an' the picksher Joan's purtier than me. 'Er's me, but better'n me. 'Er's allus bright an' bonny; 'er's never crossed an' wisht; 'er 'olds 'er tongue an' doan't talk countrified same as me. Theer'll never be no tears nor trouble in 'er eyes; she'll bring 'e a name, and bide purty an'—an' I hates the picksher now, so I do."

Barron listened with considerable interest to these remarks. There was passion in Joan's voice as she concluded, and her emotion presently found relief in tears. She only uttered thoughts long in her mind, without for an instant guessing the grim truth or suspecting what his work was to the man; yet, things being as they were, she felt some real passing pain to find him devote so much thought to it. Before the storm his painting had sunk to insignificance, since then it began to grow into a great matter again; and Joan was honestly jealous of the attention the artist bestowed upon it now. If she had dared, she would have asked him to destroy it; but something told her he would refuse.   No fear for the future was mingled with this emotion.   Only his mighty interest in the work annoyed her. It was a natural, petty jealousy ; and when John Barron laughed at her and kissed her tears away, she laughed too, and felt a little ashamed, though none the less glad that she had spoken.

But while he flung jests at her anger, Barron felt secretly surprised to note the strides his Awdrey's mind was making. Much worth consideration appeared in her sudden attack upon the picture.   She had evidently been really reflecting, with coherence and lucidity.   That astonished him.   But still he answered with a laugh—

"Jealous, Joan !   Jealous of yourself—of the poor painted thing which has risen from the contents of small tubes smeared over a bit of canvas !   My funny little dear delight !   Will you always amuse me, I wonder ?   I hope you will.   Nobody else can.   Why, the gorse there will grumble next, and think I love my poor, daubed burlesque of its gold better than the thing itself.   If I find pleasure in the picture, how much the more must I love the soul of it ?   You see, I'm ambitious. You are quite the hardest thing I ever found to paint, and so I go on trying and trying.   Hard to win and hard to paint, Joan."

She stretched out her hands to him and shook her head. "Not hard to win, Jan.   Easy enough to win to you.   I ne'er seed the likes o' you in my small world.   Not hard to win, I wasn't."

"You won't refuse me a few more sittings, then, because you have become my precious wife ? "

"In coorse not.   An' I'm sorry I was cranky.   I dedn' mean what I said ezacally."

To-day, coming fresh to his ear after a week's interval, after many hours spent with cultured friends and acquaintances in Newlyn, Joan's rustic speech grated more painfully than usual. Once he had found pleasure in it; but he was not a Cornishman to love the sound of those venerable words which sprinkled Joan's utterances, and which have long since vanished from all vocabularies save those of the common people; and now her language began to get upon his nerves and jar them. He was tired of it. Often, while he painted, she had prattled, and he, occupied with his work, had heard nothing; but to-day he recognized the debt he owed, and listened patiently for a considerable time. Her deep expectancy irritated him too. He had anticipated that, however, and was aware that her trust and confidence in him were alike profound. Perhaps a shadow of fear, distrust, or uneasiness had pleased him better. He was snugly back in his tub of impersonality, from which he liked to view the fools' show drift pass. His last experiment in the actively objective had ruined a girl, and promised to produce a fine picture. And that was the end of it. No fellow-creature would ever share this cynic's barrel with him.

Presently Joan departed upon her long tramp home. She had gone to convey a message to one of Thomasin Tregenza's friends at Paul. And when the girl left him, with a promise to come at all costs upon the next sunny morning, Barron began to think about money again. He found that the larger the imaginary figures, the smaller shadow of discomfort clouded his thoughts. So he decided upon an act of princely generosity, as the result of which resolve peace returned, and an unruffled mind. For the musty conventionality of his conclusion, it merely served as a peg upon which to hang thoughts not necessary to set down here.

CHAPTER II.

THE PARTING.

JOAN had only told her lover a little of what happened in her home, when Thomasin broke her suspicions to Grey Michael. He had taken the matter very seriously indeed, delivered a stern homily, and commanded his daughter to read the Book of Ecclesiasticus through thrice.

"The gad-about is a vain thing and a mighty cause for stumblin'. You mind that, an' take better care hencefarrard to set a right example to other maids an' not lead 'em wrong. Theer shan't be no froward liver under this roof, Joan Tregenza; an' you, as be my awn darter, is the last I'd count to find wanderin'."

She lied as to particulars. She had no fear of her father now as a man, but hard words always hurt her, and superstition, though she was fast breaking from many forms of it under Barron's tuition, still chained her soul in some directions. Did her father know even a shadow of the truth, some dire and blasting prediction would probably result from it, and though personally he was little to her now, yet, as a mouthpiece of supernatural powers, he might bring blighting words upon her; for he walked with God. But Michael's God was Joan's no more. She had fled from that awful divinity to the more beautiful goddess of John Barron. She was kind and gentle, and the girl loved to hear her voice in the hum of the bees upon the gorse and see her face everywhere in the fair on-coming of spring. Nature, moreover, chimed harmoniously with the things her mother had taught Joan. She found room for all the old stories in this new creed. The dear saints fitted in with it, and their wonders and mysteries, and the comprehensive if vague knowledge that "God is Love." She believed she understood the truth about religion at last; and Nature smiled very sweetly at her and shared in the delight of the time. So she walked dreaming on towards the invisible door of her fool's paradise, and never guessed how near it was or what Nature would look like from the other side.

She still dwelt at the little home on the cliff, so unreal and shadowy now; she built cloud castles ablaze with happiness; she found falsehood not difficult, for her former absolute truthfulness deadened her step-mother's suspicion. Certain lies told at home enabled her to keep faith with the artist; and the weather also befriending him, three more sittings in speedy succession brought John Barron to the end of his labours. After Joan's exhibition of jealousy he was careful to say little about his work and affect no further interest in it. He let her chatter concerning the future, told her of his big house in London, and presently took care to drop hints from time to time that the habitation was by no means as yet ready to receive his bride. She always spoke on the assumption that when the picture was done he would leave for London and take her with him. She already imagined herself creeping off to join him at the station, sitting beside him in the train and then rolling away, past Marazion, into the great unfamiliar world which lay beyond. And he knew that no such thing would happen. He intended that Joan should become a pleasant memory, with the veil of distance and time over it to beautify what was already beautiful. He wanted to remember the music of her throbbing voice, and forget the words it used to utter. The living girl's part was played and ended. Their lives had crossed at right angles and would never meet again. "Nature makes a glorious present to Art, and I am privileged to execute the deed of gift," thought Barron; "that is the position in an epigram." He felt very grateful to Joan. He knew her arm must have ached often enough, but whether her heart would presently do so he hardly felt qualified to judge. The incidents of that stormy day might have been buried in time ten years, so faint was his recollection of them now. He remembered the matter with no greater concern than the image of the shivering negresses in the blue water at Tobago.

And so the picture, called " Joe's Ship," was finished, and while it fell far short of what Barron had hoped, yet he knew his work was great and the best thing he had done. A packing case for the canvas was already ordered, and he expected it upon the identical day that saw his farewell to Joan.

Bit by bit he had broken to her that it was not his intention to take her with him, but that he must go to his house alone and order things in readiness. Then he would come back and fetch her. And she had accepted the position and felt wondrous sad at the first meeting with Barron after the completion of the picture. It seemed as though a great link was broken between them, and she realized now what folly her dislike of his work had been.

" I wish I could take you right away with me, Joan, my little wife ; but a bachelor's house is a comfortless concern from a woman's point of view. You will hear from me in a day or two. You must call at the post-office in Penzance for letters, because I shall not send them to your home."

" You'll print out what you writes big, so's I doan't miss nort, won't 'e ? "

" I'll make the meaning as clear as possible, Joan."

" 'Tis wisht to think as theer'll be hunderds o' miles 'twixt us. I doan't know how I be gwaine to live the days out."

" Only a fortnight, remember."

" Fourteen whole days an' nights."

" Yes, indeed. It seems a terribly long time. You must comfort me, sweetheart, and tell me that they will be very quickly done with."

Joan laughed at this turning of the tables.

" I reckon a man's allus got a plenty things to make time pass for en. But 'tis different wi' a gal."

She trusted him as she trusted God to lift the sun out of the eastern sea next morning, and swing it in its solemn course over heaven. And because there was no fear of danger and no shadow of distrust upon her, Joan made a braver parting than her lover expected.

"Some men are coming to see my picture presently," he said very gently. "I expect my sweet Joan would like to be gone before they arrive."

She took the hint, braced her heart for the ordeal, and rose from where they had been sitting on Gorse Point. She looked dreamily a moment at the furzes and the place whereon she had stood so often, then turned to the man and came close and held up four little spring lilies which she had carried with her. Her voice grew unsteady, but she mastered it again and smiled at him.

"I brot these for 'e, dear Jan. Us calls 'em butter-an'-eggs, 'cause o' the colours, I s'pose. They'm awnly four li'l flowers. Will 'e keep 'em? An'—an' give me summat as I can knaw's just bin in your hand, will 'e? 'Tis foolishness, dear heart, but I'm thinkin' 'twould make the days a dinky bit shorter."

He took the gift, thought a moment, and gave her a little silver ring off his finger. Then he kissed her, pressed her close to him, and said "good-bye," asking God to bless her, and so forth.

With but a few tears rebelling against her determination, Joan prayed good upon his head, repaid the caress, begged him for his love to come quickly back again, then tore herself away, turned, and hastened off with her head held bravely up.

But the green fields swam and the sea danced for her a moment later; the world was all splashed and blotched and misty. "I'll be braave like him," she thought, smothering the great sobs and rubbing her knuckles into her eyes till she hurt them. But she could not stem the sorrow in a moment, and, climbing through a gap in the hedge, she sat down, where only ewes and lambs might see, and cried bitterly awhile. And so weeping, a sensation strange, vague, tremendous came into her being; and she knew not what it meant; but the mystery of it filled her with great awe. "'Tis God," she said to herself; "'tis God's Hand upon me. He've touched me; He've sealed me to dear, dear Jan. 'Tis a feelin' to bring happiness along with it, not sorrer." She battled with herself to read the wonder aright, and yet at the bottom of her heart was fear. Then physical sensations distracted her; she found her head was aching and her body feeling sick. Truly the girl had been through an ordeal that day, and so she explained her discomfort. "I be wivvery an' wisht along o' leavin' en," she said, "Oh, kind, good God A'mighty, as hears all, send en back to me, send en back to me very soon, for I caan't live wi'out en no more."

As for the man, he sighed when Joan disappeared, and the expiration of breath was short and sharp as the sound of a key in a lock. He had, in truth, turned the key upon a diary to be opened no more; for the sweetness of the closed chapter was embalmed in memory, blazoned on canvas. Yet bitterness of a sort lurked in his sigh, and the result of this sunken twinge at his heart appeared when Brady, Tarrant, and one or two other artists presently joined him. They saw their companion was perturbed, and found him plunged into a black, cynic fit more deeply than usual. He spared no subject, no individual, least of all himself.

Paul Tarrant—a Christian painter, already mentioned—was the first to find fault with Barron's picture. The rest had little but praise for it, and Brady, who grew madly enthusiastic, swore that "Joe's Ship" was the finest bit of work that ever went out of Cornwall. But Tarrant cherished a private grievance, and as his view of art and ethics made it possible for him, from his standpoint, to criticize the picture unfavourably in some respects, he did so. It happened that he had recently finished a curious work for the Academy—a painting called " The Good Shepherd." It represented a young labouring man, with a face of rare beauty, but little power, plodding homeward at evening time. Upon his arm he bore a lamb, and behind his head the sinking sun made a glorious nimbus.

Barron had seen this work, admired some of the painting, but bluntly sneered at the false sentiment and vulgar parade of religious conviction which, as he conceived, animated the whole. And now, the other man, in whose heart those contemptuous words still rankled, found his turn had come. He had bitterly resented Barron's sarcastic reference to those holy things which guided his life; there was something of feminine nature in him too; so he did not much regret the present opportunity.

"And you, Tarrant? This gives you scant pleasure—eh?" asked Barron.

"It is very wonderful painting, but there's nothing under the paint that I can see. Nothing but the canvas—in so far at least as the spectator is concerned. Every work of art must have a secret history only known to its creator."

"What the divil d'you mean, Paul?" asked Brady.

"You know what I mean well enough," answered Tarrant, coldly. "My views are not unfamiliar to any of you. Here is a thing without a soul—to me."

"God! you say that! You can look at those eyes and say that?"

"I admire the painting, but *cui bono?* Who is the better, the wiser? There is nothing under the paint."

"You are one of those who turn shadows into crosses, clouds into angels. Is it not so?" asked Barron, smiling; and the other fired at this allusion to his best-known picture.

"I am one of those who know that Art is the handmaid of God," he answered hotly. "I happen to believe in Jesus Christ, and I conceive that no picture is truly to be called great or worthy of any Christian's painting unless it possess some qualities calculated to ennoble the mind of those who behold it. Art is the noblest labour man can employ time upon. The thing comes from God; it is a talent only to be employed in the highest sense when devoted to His glory."

"Then what of heathen art? You let your religion distort your view of Nature. You sacrifice truth to a dogma. Nature has no ethics. You profess to paint facts, and paint them wrong. You are not a mystic; that we could understand and criticize accordingly. You try to run with the hare, and hunt with the hounds. You talk about truth, and paint things not true."

"From your standpoint possibly. Yours is the truth of naturalism; mine is the truth of Faith."

"If you are going to entrench yourself behind Faith, I have done, of course. Only don't go about saying, as you did just now, that Art is the noblest labour man can employ time upon. That's bosh, pure and simple. There are some occupations not so noble, that is all. Art is a heathen and always will be, and you missionary-men, with a paint-pot in one hand and a Bible in the other, are even worse than certain objectionable literary celebrities, whose novels reek of the 'new journalism' and the Sermon on the Mount—the ridiculous and sublime in tasteless combination. You missionaries, I say, sap the primitive strength of Art; you demoralize her. To dare to make Art pander to a passing creed is vile—worse than the spectacle of the Salvation Army trying to convert Buddhists. That I saw in India, and laughed. But we won't quarrel. You paint Faith's jewellery; I'll amuse myself with Truth's drabs and duns. The point of view is all. I depict pretty Joan Tregenza looking over the sea to catch a glimpse of her sweetheart's outward-bound ship. I paint her just as I saw her. There was no occasion to leave out or put in. I revelled in a mere direct transcript of Nature. You would have set her down by one of the old Cornish crosses praying to Christ to guard her man. And round her you would have wrought a world of idle significance. You would have twisted dogma into the flowers and grass-blades. The fact that the girl happened to be practically brainless and a Luke Gospeller would not have weighed with you a moment."

"I'm weary of the old cant about Nature," said Tarrant. "You're a naturalist and a materialist. That ends it. There is no possibility of argument between us."

"Would the man who painted that gorse cant?" burst out

Brady. "Damn it all, Tarrant, if a chap can teach us to paint perhaps he can teach us something else as well. Look at that gorse. That's the truth, won with many a wrestle and heartache, I'll swear. You know as well as I do what went to get that, and yet you say there's nothing behind the paint. That's cant if you like. And as to your religious spirit, what's the good of preaching sermons in paint, if the paint's false? We're on it now, and I'll say what I believe, which is that your 'Good Shepherd' is all wrong, apart from any question of sentiment at all. Your own party will probably say it's blasphemous, and I say it's ridiculous. You've painted a grand sky, and then ruined it with the subject. Did you ever see a man's head bang between you and a clear setting sun? Anyway, that figure of yours was never painted with a sunset behind him, I'll swear."

"You can't paint truth as you find it, and preach truth as you believe it on the same canvas, if you belong to any creed but mine," said Barron, calmly. "You build on the foundations of Art a series of temples to your religious convictions. You blaze Christianity on every canvas. I suppose that is natural in a man of your opinions, but to me it is as painful as the spectacle of advertisements of quack nostrums planted, as you shall see them, beside railway lines—here in a golden field of buttercups; here rising above young barley. Of course I don't presume to assert that your faith is a quack nostrum; only real art and religion won't run in double harness for you or anybody. They did once, but the world has passed beyond that point."

"Never," answered Tarrant. "We have proof of it. Souls have been saved by pictures. That is as certain as that God made the earth and everything on it."

"There again! Every word you speak only shows how difficult it is for us to exchange ideas. Why is it so positively certain that God made the earth and everything on it? To attribute man's origin direct to God is always, in my mind, the supreme proposition of human conceit. Did it need a God to manufacture you or me or Brady? I don't think so. Consider creation. I suppose if an ant could gauge the ingenuity of a steam-engine, he would attribute it without hesitation to God; but it happens that the steam-engine is the work of a creature— a being standing somewhere between God and the ant, but much nearer the latter than the former. You follow me? Even Tarrant will admit, for it is an article of his creed, that there exist many beings nearer to God than man. They have wings, he would tell us, and are eternal, immortal, everlasting."

"I see," said Brady; "you're going to say next that faulty concerns like this particular world are the work of minor intelligences. What rot you can talk at times, old man!"

"Yet is it an honour to God Almighty that we attribute the contents of this poor pill of a planet to Him? I think it would be an insult, if you ask me. Out of respect to the Everlasting, I would rather suppose that the earth, being by chance a concern too small for His present purposes, He tosses it, as we toss a dog a bone, to some ingenious archangel, with a theory. Then you enjoy the spectacle of that seraph about as busy over this notable world as a child with a mud-pie. The winged one sets to work with a will. A little pinch of life develops under his skilful manipulation; evolution takes its remorseless course through the wastes of Time until—behold! the apotheosis of the ape at last. Picture that well-meaning, but muddle-headed archangel's dismay at such a conclusion! All his theories and conceits—his splendid scheme of evolution and the rest—end in a mean but obstinate creature with conscious intelligence, and an absolute contempt and disregard for Nature. This poor Frankenstein of a cherub watches the worm he has produced defy him, refuse absolutely to obey his most fundamental postulates or accept his axioms. The fittest survive no more; these gregarious, new-born things presently form themselves into a pestilential society; they breed rubbish; they—— "

"Stop it, John," said Murdoch. "Now you're going too far. Look at Tarrant. He'd burn you over a slow fire for this if he could. Speak for yourself, at any rate, not for us,"

“I do,” answered the other, bitterly. “I speak for myself. I know what a poor, rotten cur I am, physically and mentally—not worth the bread I eat to keep me alive. And shall I dare say that the Almighty Father made me?”

“But what's the end of this philosophy of despair, old chap?” asked Brady; “what becomes of your worst of all possible planets?”

“The end? Dust and ashes. My unfortunate workman, having blundered on for certain millions of years tinkering and patching and improving his dismal colony, will give the thing up; and God will laugh and show him the mistakes and then blot the essay out, as a master runs his pen through the errors in a pupil's exercise. The earth grows cold at last, and the herds of humanity die, and the countless ages of agony and misery are over. Yes, the poor vermin perish to the last one; then their black tomb goes whirling on until it shall be allowed to meet another like itself, when a new sun shines in heaven, and space is the richer by one more star.”

“May God forgive you for your profanity, John Barron,” said Tarrant. “That He places in your hand such power, and suffers your brain to breed the devil's dung that fills it, is to me a mystery. May you live to learn your awful errors and regret them.”

He turned away, and two men followed him. Conversation among those who remained reverted to the picture; and presently all were gone, excepting only Barron, who had to wait and see his work packed.

Remorse will take strange shapes. His bitter tirade against his environment and himself was the direct result of this man's recent experiences. He knew himself for a mean knave in his dealings with an innocent girl, and the thought turned the aspect of all things into gall.

Solitude brought back a measure of peace. The picture was packed and started to Penzance railway-station, while Barron's tools also went by pony-cart back to his rooms in Newlyn. He was to leave upon the following morning with

Murdoch and others who were taking their work to the
exhibitions.

Now he looked round the cow-byre before locking it for the
last time and returning the key to Farmer Ford's boy, who
waited outside to receive it. "The chapter ended," he said to
himself—"the chapter which contains the best thing that ever I
did. Art happily rises above those misty abstractions which
the ignorant call right and wrong. She resembles Nature
herself there. Both demand their sacrifices. 'The white
martyrdom of self-denial, the red martyrdom of blood,' each
is a thousand times recorded in the history of painting, and
will be a thousand times again."

CHAPTER III.

So John Barron set forth, well content to believe that he
would never again visit Cornwall, and Joan called at the
Penzance post-office on the morning which followed his departure. Her geographical knowledge was scanty. Truro and
Plymouth, in her belief, lay somewhere upon the edge of the
world; and she scarcely imagined that London could be much
more remote.

But no letter awaited her, and life grew to be terribly
empty. For a week she struggled with herself to keep from the
post-office, and then, nothing doubting that her patience would
now be well rewarded, Joan marched off with confidence for the
treasure. But only a greater disappointment than the last
resulted; and she went home very sorrowful, building up
explanations of the silence, finding excuses for "Mister Jan."
The prefix to his name, which had dropped during their latter
intimacy, returned to her mind now the man was gone: as
"Mister Jan" she always thought about him and prayed
for him.

The days passed quickly, and when a fortnight stood
between herself and the last glimpse of her lover, Joan began
to grow very anxious. She wept through long nights now, and
her father, finding the girl changed, guessed she had a secret,
and told his wife to find it out. But it was some time before
Thomasin made any discovery; for Joan lied stoutly by day, and
prayed to God to pardon by night. She strove hard to follow
the teaching of the artist, to find joy in flowers and leaves, in

the spring music of birds, in the colour of the sea. But now she dimly guessed that it was love of him which went so far to make all things beautiful; that it was the magic and wisdom of his words which had gilded the world with gold and thrown new light upon the old familiar objects of life. Nature's organ was dumb now that the hands which played upon it so skilfully had passed far away. But she was loyal to her teacher; she remembered many things which he had said, and tried hard to feel as he felt; to put her hand in beautiful Mother Nature's, and walk with her and be at peace. Mister Jan would soon return; the fortnight was already past; each day as she rose she felt he might come to claim her before the evening.

And, meanwhile, other concerns occupied her thoughts. The voice which spoke to her after she bid John Barron "good-bye," had since then similarly sounded on the ear of her heart. Alike at high noon and in the silence of the night-watches it addressed her; and the mystery of it, taken with her other sorrows, began to affect her physically. For the first time in her life the girl felt ill in body. Her appetite failed, dawn found her sick and weary; her glass told her of a white, unhappy face, of eyes that were lighted from within and shone with strange thoughts. She was always listening now—listening for the new voice that she might hear the word it uttered. Her physical illness she hid with some cunning, and put a bright face upon life as far as she could do so before those of her home; but the task grew daily more difficult. Then, with a period of greatly increased bodily discomfort, Joan grew alarmed and turned to the kind God of "Mister Jan," and made great, tearful praying for a return of strength. Her petition was apparently granted, for the girl enjoyed some improvement of health and spirit. Whereupon she became fired with a notable thought, and determined to seek her patron saint where still she suspected his power held sway: at the little brook which tinkles along beside the ruins of St. Madron's Chapel in a fair coomb below the Cornish moorlands. The precious water, as Joan remembered, had brought strength and health to her when a baby; and now the girl longed to try its virtues again, and a great conviction grew upon her that the ancient saint never forgot his own little ones. Opportunity presently offered, and through the first misty grey of a morning in early April, she set out upon her long tramp from Newlyn through Madron to the ruined baptistery.

St. Madron, or Padern, lived in the sixth century somewhat earlier than Augustine. A Breton by birth, he laboured chiefly in Wales, established a monastery on Brito-Celtic lines in Cardiganshire, and became its bishop when a see was established in that district. He travelled far, visited Mount's Bay, and established the church of Madron, still sacred to his name; while doubtless the brook and chapel hard by were associated with him from the same period. In Scawen's time folks were wont to take their hurts thither on Corpus Christi Evening, drink of the water, deposit an offering, and repose upon the chapel floor till dawn. Then, drinking again, they departed whole, if faith sufficiently mighty had supported them. Norden remarks of the water that "its fame was great for the supposed vertue of healinge, which St. Maderne had thereunto infused; and maine votaries made anuale pilgrimages unto it." In connection with the custom of immersion here indicated, we find there obtained the equally venerable practice of hanging votive rags upon the thorn bushes round about the chapel. This conceit is ancient as Japan, and one not only in usage to this day amongst the Shintoists of that land, but likewise common throughout Northern Asia and, nearer home, in the Orkneys, in Scotland, in Ireland. Older far than Christianity are these customs; the megalithic monuments of the pagan witness similar practices in remote corners of the earth; rag-trees, burdened with the tattered offerings of the devout, yet stud the desert of Suez, and those who seek shall surely find some holy well or grave hard at hand in every case. To mark and examine the junction of these venerable fancies with Christian superstition is no part of our present purpose, but that ideas, pagan in their birth, have lent themselves with sufficient readiness to successive creeds, and been knit into the dogmas of each in turn, is certain enough. Thus, through Cornwall, the imaginings of wizard and wonder-worker in hoary time come, centuries later, to be the glory and special power of a saint. Such fantastic lore was definitely interdicted in King Edgar's reign, when "stone-worshippings, divinations, well-worshippings, and necromances" were proclaimed things heathen, and unhallowed; but with the advent of the Saint-Bishops from Wales, from Ireland, from Brittany, primitive superstitions were patched upon the new creed, and, to suit private purposes, the old giants of the Christian faith sanctified holy well and holy stone, posing by right divine as sure dispensers of the hidden virtue in stream and granite. But the roots of these fables burrow back to paganism. Hundreds of weakly infants were passed through the stone Mên-an-tol in the names of Saints; and hundreds had already been handed through it centuries before under like appeal to pagan deities.

Of Madron baptistery, now a picturesque ruin, it seems clear that until the Reformation regular worship and the service of baptism were therein celebrated. The place has mercifully escaped all restoration or renovation, and stands at this moment open to the sky in the slow hand of Time. A brook runs babbling outside, but the holy well, or colymbethra, is now dry, though it might easily be filled again. This interesting portion of the chapel remains intact, and the entrance to it lies upon the level of the floor, according to ancient custom, being so ordered that the adult to undergo baptism might step down into the water, and that not without dignity.

Hither came Joan. Her patchwork of faith and Nature-worship was a live thing to her now, and she found no difficulty in reconciling the sweet saint-stories heard in childhood from her dead mother's lips, with the beautiful and fair exposition of truth which "Mister Jan" found written large upon the world by Nature in spring-time.

It was half-past four o'clock when she trudged through

Madron to see the grey church and the little grey houses all sleeping under the grey sky. She plodded on up the hill past the gaunt workhouse which stands at the top of it; and what had seemed soft, sweet repose among the cottage homes, felt like cold death beneath these ashy walls. To Joan, the workhouse was a word of shame unutterable. Those among whom she lived would hurl the word against enemies as a prophecy of the utmost degradation. She shivered as she passed, and was sad, knowing that a whole world of poverty, failure, sorrow, regret, lay hidden in that cold, still pile. But the hand of sleep rested softly there; only a sick soul or two stirred, the paupers were the equal of princes till a hoarse bell brought them back out of blessed unconsciousness.

Bars of light streaked the east, and Joan, after stopping at the hill crest to see dawn open silver eyes on the sea, hastened inland through silent, dewy fields. Presently a fence and wall cut civilization from the wild land of the coomb, and the girl proceeded where grass-grown cart-ruts wound among furze and heather, and the silver coils of new-born bracken just beginning to peep up above the dead fern of last year. This hollow ran between undulations of ploughed land and meadow; no harrow clinked as yet; only the cows stood here and there above the dry patches on the dewy fields where they had lain their bodies in sleep. She saw their soft eyes and smelt the savour of their steaming breath. Presently the cart-ruts disappeared in fine grass, all be-diamonded, knobbed with heather, sprouting rusty-red, and sprinkled with tussocks of coarser grass whereon green blades sprang up above the bleached and sere dead ones. Rabbits flashed here and there, with little white scuts twinkling through the gorse; and then the birds woke up; a thrush sang low, sleepy notes in the heart of a whitethorn, and yellow-hammers piped their mournful calls from the furze. On Joan's left hand there now rose a clump of wind-worn beech trees, with brown spikes breaking to green, even where dead red leaves still clung to the parent branches. Beneath them ran a hedge of earth above a deep pool or two, fringed with young rushes, upright and

triumphant above the old dead ones. Everywhere Joan saw
life trampling and leaping, growing and laughing over the
ruins of things that had lived and died. It saddened her a
little. Did Nature forget so soon? Then she told herself that
kind Nature had loved them and gloried in them too; and now
she would presently bury all her dead children in beautiful
graves of new green. The mosses and marsh were lovely, and
the clear pools full of living creatures. But these things were
not saint-blessed and eternal. No spring fed these silent wells,
no holy man of old had ever smiled upon them.

A stepping-stone by a wall lay before her now; this she
crossed, heard the murmuring of the stream and hastened,
and presently stood beside it. Here were holy ground and
water; here were peace and a place to pray in. Forget-me-nots
looked up into eyes as blue as their own; and Joan smiled at
them, and drank of the ripples that ran at their roots. Grey
through the growing haze of green, a ruined wall showed close
to the girl. The blackthorns' blooms were faded around her;
the hawthorn was not yet powdered with white. She cast one
look to right and left before entering the chapel. A distant
view of the moorland rose to the sky, and the ragged edge
of the hills was marked by a gaunt engine-stack, denoting past
enterprise, triumphs long gone by and ruined hopes but recently
dead. Snug fox-covers of rhododendron swept up towards
the head of the coomb; and below, distant half a mile or more,
cottages already showed a glimmer of gold on their thatches,
where the increasing splendour of day brightened them, and
morning mists were raising jewelled arms. Then she passed
into the ruin through that narrow opening which marks the
door of it. The granite walls stood about the height of a
man's shoulder, and the chamber itself was small. Stone seats
ran round two sides of it; ivy and stone-worts and grasses
picked the mortar from the walls and clothed them, even as
emerald moss and lichens, black and gold, glorified each piece
of granite. A may-bush, tangled about a great ivy-tod, surmounted the western walls; furzes and heather and tall grasses

softened the jagged outlines of the ruin; and above a stone altar, at the east end of it, rose another whitethorn. At this season of the year the subsequent floral glories of the little chapel were only indicated. Young briars already thrust their soft points over the stone of the altar, and the first leaves of foxgloves were unfolding, with dandelions and docks, biting-stone-crop and ferns, ragged-robins and wild geraniums. These infant things softened no outline yet. The flat paving of the floor, where it yet remained, was bedded in grass; a little square incision upon the stone of the altar glimmered, full of water, and reflected the light from fleecy clouds which now climbed into heaven, bearing sunrise fires upward over a pale blue sky.

Here, under the circumambient, sparkling clearness, coolness, and silence, Joan stood, with strange medley of thoughts upon her soul. The saints and the fairies mingled there, with visions of Nature always smiling, with a vague shadow of one great God above the blue, but dim and very far away, and a nearer picture, which quickened her heart-beat—the picture of "Mister Jan." Here she felt herself at one with the world spread round her. The mother-eyes of a blackbird sitting upon her eggs in the ivy-tod kept their gold on Joan, but showed no fear; the young rabbits frisked at hand; a mole poked his snout and little paddle-paws out of the grass. All was peace and happiness, with the voice of good St. Madron murmuring love in his brooklet at hand.

Joan knelt down by the old altar, and bowed her head there, and prayed to Nature and to God. At first merely wordless prayers, full of passionate entreaty, rose to the throne; then utterance came in a wild, simple throng of petitions, and all her various knowledge, won from her mother and John Barron, found a place. Pan and Christ might each have heard and listened, for she called on the gods of earth and heaven from a heart that was full.

"Kind mother o' the flowers, doan't 'e forget a poor maiden what loves 'e so dear. I be sad an' sore-hearted, 'cause things is bad wi' me now Mister Jan's gone; an' I knaws as I've lied an' bin wicked 'bout Joe; but, kind mother, I awnly done what Mister Jan, as was wise an' loved me, bid. O God A'mighty, doan't 'E let on forget me, 'cause I've gived up all—all the li'l I had —for en, an' Nature made me as I be! O kind God, make me happy an' light-hearted an' strong agin, same as the li'l birds an' sich-like is happy an' strong. An' forgive me for all my sins, au' make me well for Mister Jan, an' clever for Mister Jan, so's I'll be a fine an' good wife to en. An' forgive me for lyin', 'cause what I done was Nature, 'cordin' to Mister Jan; an' Nature's kind to young things, 'cordin' to Mister Jan, an' I be young yet. An' make me a better lass, for I caan't a-bear to feel as I do; an' make me think o' the next world arter this wan. But, O dear God, make me well an' braave agin, for 'tis awful wisht for me wi'out Mister Jan; an' make Mister Jan strong too. I be all in a miz-maze, and doan't knaw wheer to turn, 'cept to Nature, dear Lard. O kind God A'mighty, lemme have my angel watchin' over me close, same as what mother used to say he did allus. An' bring Mister Jan back long very quick, 'cause I'm nothin' but sadness wi'out en. And, dear St. Madern, I ax 'e to bless me same as you done when—when I was a li'l baaby, 'cause I be gwaine to bathe in your brook, bein' a St. Madern cheel. O dear, good God o' all things, please to help me, an' look to me, 'cause I be very sad, an' I never done no harm to none; for Jesus Christ's sake. Amen."

Then she said the Lord's Prayer, because her mother had taught her that no human petition was ever heard unless accompanied by it. And it seemed as though the lark, winding upward with wide spiral to his song-throne in the sky, and tinkling thin music on the morning wind, was her messenger; which thought was beautiful to Joan, and made her heart glad.

Never had she looked fairer. Her blue eyes were misty; but the magic of prayer, the glory of speaking straight to the Father of all—call Him what she might—had nobly fortified her sinking spirit. Peace brooded in her soul then, and faith warmed her blood. She was sure her prayer would be answered; she was certain that her health and her loved one would both come back to her. And she stood by the altar and smiled at the golden morning, herself the fairest thing the sun shone upon.

Having peeped about her, Joan took off her clothes, placed them on the altar-stones, shook down her hair, and glided softly to the stream. At one point its waters caught the sunshine, and babbled over white sand between many budding spikes of wild parsley and young fronds of fern. Naked and beautiful the girl stood, her bright hair glinting to her waist, all rippled with the first red-gold of the morning; her body very white, save where the sun and western wind had browned both arms and neck; her form innocent as yet of the mystery hid for her in time. Joan's fair limbs spoke of blood not Cornish, of days far past, when a race of giants swept up from behind the North Sea to tread a new earth, and take wives of the little dark women of the land, abating the still prevalent nigrescence of the Celt with Saxon eyes and hair, adding their stature and their strength to races unborn. A sweet embodiment of all that was lovely and pure and fresh, she looked—a human incarnation of youth and springtime.

There was a pool deeper than the general shallowness of the stream which served for Joan's bath, and she entered there, where soft white sand made pleasant footing, where more forget-me-nots twinkled their turquoise about the margin, and where shining gorse towered like a sentinel above.

She suffered the holy water to flow over every inch of her body; and then, rubbing her white self red and glowing with the dead brake-fern of last year, and squeezing the water out of her hair, Joan quickly dressed again, and prepared to depart. She was about to leave a fragment torn from her skirt hanging by the chapel, but changed her mind; and getting a splinter of granite, rough-edged, she began to chip away a tress of her own bright hair, sawing it off upon the stone table as best she could. Like a fallen star it presently glimmered in the thorn-bush above St. Madron's altar, where she wound the little lock, presently to bring gold to the nests and joy to the heart of small feathered folk.

Joan walked home with the blood racing in her veins, roses on her cheeks, and the glory of hope in her eyes. Already she felt her prayers were being heard; already she was thanking God for heeding her cry, and St. Madron for the life-giving waters of his holy stream. Then, where finches chattered and fluttered forward, breakfasting together in pleasant company, a shadow and a swift, strong wing flashed across Joan's sight— and a hawk struck. The little people shrieked, a few grey feathers puffed here and there, and one spark of life was blown out that other sparks might shine the brighter; for presently Joan's kind "mother o' the flowers" watched the beaks of fledgeling hawks grow red; and the parent bird of prey's cold eyes brightened with satisfaction, as will every parent-eye brighten at the spectacle of baby-things eating wholesome food with hearty appetite.

The death of the small fowl clouded the pilgrim's thoughts, but only for a moment. Sentiment and emotion had passed; now she was eager with delicious physical hunger, and longing for her breakfast. The girl had not felt so well or so happy for a considerable time. Half her prayer, she told herself, was answered already; and the other half, relating to Mister Jan, would doubtless meet with similar merciful response ere many hours had flown.

So joyfully homeward, out of dreamland into a world of acts, Joan hastened.

CHAPTER IV.

A THOUSAND POUNDS.

A GLAD heart shortens the longest road, and Joan, whose return journey from the holy stream was, for the most part, down-hill, soon found herself back again in Penzance. The fire of devotion still actuated her movements, and she walked fearlessly, doubting nothing, to the post-office. There would be a letter to-day; she knew it; she felt it in her consciousness as a certainty. And when she asked for it, and mentioned her name, she put her hand out and waited until the sleepy-eyed clerk rummaged through a little pile of letters standing together, and tied with a separate string. She watched him slowly untie them and scan the addresses, grumbling as he did so. Then he came to the last of all, and read out—

"'Miss Joan Tregenza, Post-office, Penzance. To be left until called for.'"

"Mine, mine, sir! I knawed 'e'd have it! I knawed as the kind, good——"

Then she stopped and grew red, while the clerk looked at her curiously, and then yawned. "What's a draggle-tailed chit like her got to do with such a thing?" he wondered, and then spoke to Joan—

"Here you are; and you must sign this paper—it's a registered letter."

Joan, her hand shaking with excitement, wrote her name in brave round characters where he directed, thanked the man with a smile that softened him, and then hastened away.

The girl was faint with hunger and happiness before she

reached home. She did not dare to open the letter just then, but took it from her pocket a dozen times before she arrived at Newlyn, and feasted her eyes upon her own name, very beautifully and legibly printed. He had written it! His precious hand had held the pen, and formed each letter!

Deep, wordless thanks welled up in Joan's heart, for God was not very far away, after all. He had heard her prayer already, and answered it within an hour. No doubt it was easy for Him to grant such a little prayer. It could be nothing much to God that one small creature should enjoy such happiness; but what seemed wonderful was that He should have any time to listen at all—that He should have been able to turn from the mighty business of the great awakening world and give a thought to her.

"Sure 'twas the li'l lark as the good Lard heard, an' my asking as went up-long wi' en," said Joan to herself.

She found her father at home, and the family just about to take breakfast. Grey Michael had returned somewhat unexpectedly with a fine catch, and did not intend sailing again before the evening tide. A somewhat ominous silence greeted the girl—a silence which her father was the first to break.

"Ayte your food, my lass, an' then come in the garden 'long with me," he said. "I do want a word with 'e, an' things must be said which I've put off the sayin' of tu long. So be quick's you can."

But this sauce did not spoil the girl's enjoyment of her porridge and treacle. She ate heartily, and her happy humour seemed catching, at least so far as Tom was concerned. A bright colour warmed Joan's cheek; the cloud that had dimmed her eyes was there no longer; and more than once Mr. Tregenza looked at his wife inquiringly, for the tale she had been telling of Joan's recent moods and disorder was at variance with her present spirits and appetite. After breakfast she went to her room, while her father waited, and then it was that Joan snatched a moment to open John Barron's letter. There would be no time to read it then, she knew; that delicious task must take many hours of loving labour; but she wanted to count the pages and see "Mister Jan's" name at the end. She knew that crosses meant kisses, too. There might be crosses somewhere. So she opened the envelope in a fever of joyous excitement, being careful, however, not to tear a letter of the superscription. And from it there came a fat, folded pile of tissue-paper. Joan knew it was money, and flung it on her bed, and fumbled with sinking heart for something better. But there was nothing else—only ten pieces of tissue-paper. She remembered seeing her father with similar pieces, and her mother saying there was nothing like Bank of England notes. But they had been crumpled and dirty; these were snowy white. Each had a hundred pounds marked upon it; and Joan was aware that ten times a hundred is a thousand. But a thousand pounds possessed no more real meaning for her than a million of money does to the average man. She could not estimate its significance in the least, or gauge its possibilities. Only she knew that she would far rather have had a few words from "Mister Jan" than all the money in the world.

Mr. Tregenza's voice below broke in upon the girl's disappointment, and hastily hiding the money under some linen in a little chest of drawers, where the picture of Joe's ship was also concealed, she hurried to join her father. But the empty envelope, with her name printed on it, she put into her pocket that it might be near her.

Joan did not for an instant gather what meaning lay under this great gift of money, and to her the absence of a letter was no more than a passing sorrow. She read nothing between the lines of this silence; she only saw that he had not forgotten, and only thought that he perhaps imagined such vast sums of money would give her pleasure and make the waiting easier. What were bank-notes to Joan? What was life to her away from him? She sighed and fell back upon the thought of his wisdom and knowledge. He must be in the right to delay, because he was always in the right. A letter would presently come to explain why he had sent the money, and to treat of his return. The girl felt that she had much to thank God for, after all. He had sent her the letter; He had answered her prayer in His own way. It ill became her, she thought, to question more deeply. She must wait and be patient, however hard the waiting.

So thinking, she joined her father. Tom was away up the village; Mrs. Tregenza found plenty to occupy her mind and body indoors; Joan and Mr. Tregenza had the garden to themselves. He was silent until they reached the wicket; then, going through it, he led the way slowly up a hill which wound above the neighbouring stone-quarry, and as he walked he addressed Joan. She, weary enough already, prayed that her parent intended going no further than the summit of the hill; but, when he spoke, she forgot physical fatigue, for his manner was short and stern.

"Theer's things bein' hid 'twixt you an' me, darter, an' 'tis time you spoke up. Every parent's got some responsibility in the matter of his cheel's sawl; an' if theer's ought to knaw, 'tis I must hear it. 'The faither waketh for the darter when no man knaweth,' sez the Preacher, an' he never wrote nothin' truer. I've waked for you, Joan. 'Keep a sure watch over a shameless darter,' sez the Preacher agin ; but God forbid you'm that! Awnly you'm allus wool-gatherin', an' roamin', an' wastin' time. An' time wance squandered do never come agin. I hear tell this has been gwaine forrard since Joe went to sea. What's the matter with 'e? Say it out plain an' straight, an' now this minute!"

Joan had particularly prayed by the Madron altar that the Everlasting would keep her from telling of falsehoods. She remembered the fact as her father put his question, and she also recollected that John Barron had advised her to say nothing about their union until he returned to her. So she lied again, and that the more readily because Grey Michael's manner of asking his question put a reasonable answer into her head.

"I s'pose, as it might be I'm wisht 'cause of Joe Noy, faither."

"Then look 'e to it, an' let it cease. Joe's in the hand o' the Lard same as we be. He's got to work out his salvation in fear an' tremblin' same as us. Some do the Lard's work ashore, some afloat, some—sich as me—do it by land an' sea both. You doan't work Joe no good trapsing 'bout—here, theer, an' everywheers; an' you do yourself harm, 'cause it makes 'e oneasy an' restless. Mendin' holes an' washin' clothes, an' prayin' to the Lard to 'a' mercy on your sinful sawl's what you got to do; also learnin' to cook, 'gainst the time you'm a wife an' the mother o' childern, if God so wills. But this ban't no right way o' life for any wan, gentle or simple; so mend it. A gad-about, lazy female's hell-meat in any station. Theer's enough of 'em as 'tis—wi'in the edge of Carnwall, tu! What was you doin' this marnin'? Mother sez 'er heard you stirrin' 'fore the birds."

"I went out a long walk, to think, faither."

"What 'e want to think 'bout? Your plaace is to du, not to think. God'll think for 'e if 'e ax; an' the sooner you mind that an' call 'pon the A'mighty, the better, 'cause the devil's ready an' willin' to think for 'e tu. Read the Book more, an' look about 'e less. Man's eyes, and likewise maid's, is best 'pon the ground most times. Theer's no evil writ theer. The brain of man an' woman imagineth ill nearly allus. For why? 'Cause they looks about an' sees it. Evil comes in through the eyes of 'em. Evil's pasted large 'pon every dead wall in Newlyn. Read the Book—'tis all summed up in that. You've gotten a power o' your mother in 'e yet. Not but you've bin a good darter thus far, save for backslidin' in the past; but I saved your sawl then—thanks be to the voice o' God in me—an' I saved your mother's sawl, though theer was tidy wraslin' for her; an' I'll save yourn yet, if you'll do your paart."

Here Grey Michael paused and turned homewards, while Joan congratulated herself upon the fact that a conversation which promised to be difficult had ended so speedily and without misfortune. Then her father asked her another question,

"An' what's this I hear tell 'bout you bein' sick in body? You do look so well as ever I knawed 'e; but mother sez you'm that cranky with vittles as you never was afore, an' not yourself nohow."

"Ban't nothin', faither. 'Tis awver an' done. I ate tu much, or some sich thing, an' I be bonny well agin now."

"Doan't be thinkin', then. 'Tis all brain-sickness, I'll lay. I doan't want no doctor's traade in my 'ouse if us can keep it outside. The Lard's my doctor. Keep your sawl clean, an' the Lard'll watch your body. 'E's said as much. 'E knaws we'm poor, trashy worms; an' even a breath o' foul air'll take our lives, onless 'E be by to filter it. Faith's the awnly medicine worth usin'."

Joan remembered her morning bath, and felt comforted by this last reflection. Had she not already found the magic result? For a moment she thought of telling her father what she had done, but she changed her mind. Such faith as that would have brought nothing but wrath upon her.

While Mr. Tregenza improved the hour, and uttered various precepts for his daughter's help and guidance, Thomasin was occupied at home with grave thoughts respecting Joan. She more than suspected the truth from signs of indisposition full of meaning to a mother; but while duly mentioning the girl's indifferent health, Mrs. Tregenza did not dare to breathe the colour of her own explanation. She prayed to God in all honesty to prove her wrong, but her lynx eyes waited to read the truth she feared. If things were really so with Joan, then they could not be hid from her eyes much longer; and in the event of her suspicions proving correct, Mrs. Tregenza told herself, as a right Luke Gospeller, she must proclaim her horrid discovery, and let the perdition of her husband's daughter be generally made manifest. She knew so many were called, so few chosen. No girl had ever been more surely called than Joan. Her father's trumpet-tongue had thundered the ways of righteousness into her ears from her birth; but, after all, it began to look as though she was not chosen. The circumstance, of course, if proved, would rob her of every Luke Gospeller's regard. No weak pandering with sentiment and sin was permitted in that fold. And Mrs. Tregenza had little pity herself for unfortunate or mistaken women. Let a girl lose her character, and Thomasin usually refused to hear any plea of mercy from any source. Only once did she find extenuating circumstances—in a case where a ruined farmer's daughter brought an action for breach of promise, and won it, with heavy damages. But money acted in a peculiar way with this woman. It put her conscience and her judgment out of focus, softened the outlines of events, furnished excuses for unusual practices, gilded with a bright lining even the blackest cloud of wrong-doing. Where Mrs. Tregenza could see money, she could see light. Money made her charitable, broad-minded, even tolerant. She knew she loved it, and was careful to keep the fact out of Grey Michael's sight as far as possible. She held the purse, and he felt that it was in good hands, but cautioned her from time to time against the awful danger of letting a lust for this world's wealth come between the soul and God.

And now a course long indicated in Thomasin's mind was being by her pursued. Having convinced herself that under the present circumstances any step to found or dispel her fears concerning Joan would be just and proper, she took the exceptional one of searching the girl's little room while her step-daughter was out with Michael. Even as Mr. Tregenza turned to go homeward again, his wife stood in the midst of Joan's small sanctuary, and cast keen, inquiring eyes about her. She rarely visited the apartment, and had not been in it for six months. Now she came to set suspicion at rest, if possible, or confirm it. Her own secret opinion was that Joan had come to serious trouble with her superiors. In that case, letters, presents, or tokens had probably passed into her hands, and, if such existed, in this room they would be.

" God send as I'm makin' a mistake, an' shaan't find nothin 'tall," said Mrs. Tregenza to herself. And then she began her scrutiny.

CHAPTER V.

THE TRUTH.

THOMASIN saw that all things about Joan's room were neat, spotless, and in order. For one brief moment a sense of disquiet at the action before her touched the woman's heart and head; but duty alike to her husband and her step-daughter demanded the search, in her opinion. Should there be nothing to find, so much the better; if, on the other hand, matters affecting Joan's temporal and eternal welfare were here hidden, then they could not be uncovered too quickly. She looked first through the girl's wooden trunk, the key of which was in the lock, but little save a childish treasure or two rewarded Mrs. Tregenza here. In a broken desk, which had belonged to her mother, Joan kept a few Christmas cards and two silhouettes: one of Uncle Sampy of Drift, one of Mary Chirgwin. Here were also some cooking recipes copied in her mother's writing, an agate marble which Joan had found on Penzance beach, lavender tied up in a bag, and an odd toy that softened Thomasin's heart not a little as she picked it up and looked at it. The thing brought back to her memory a time four years earlier. It was a small, grotesque figure on wires, built up o' chestnuts and acorns, with a hazel-nut for its head and black pins stuck in for the eyes. She remembered Tom making it and giving it to Joan on her birthday. Then the memory of Joan's love for Tom from the time he was born came like a glow of sunshine into the mother's heart, and for a moment she was minded to relinquish her unpleasant task upon the spot; but she changed her intention again and proceeded. The box held little else save a parcel of old clothes tied up with rosemary in brown paper. These the woman surveyed curiously, and knew, without being told, that they had belonged to Joan's mother. For some reason the spectacle killed sentiment, and changed her mood.

She shut down the box, and then going to the chest of drawers, pulled out each compartment in turn. Nothing but Joan's apparel with her few brooches and trinkets appeared here, and the history of each and all was familiar to Mrs. Tregenza. But, on reaching the bottom drawer of the chest, she found it locked and the key absent. To continue her search, however, was not difficult. Nothing separated the drawers, and by removing that above the last, the contents of the lowest lay at her mercy. It was full of linen for the most part, but hidden at the bottom Thomasin made a discovery, and found certain matters which at once spoke of tremendous mystery and, to her mind, indicated the nature of it. First she came upon the little picture of Joe's ship in its rough gilded frame. This might be an innocent gift from some of the young men who had asked in the past to be allowed to paint Joan and received a curt negative from Grey Michael.

But the other discovery meant more. Pushing her hand about the drawer, she found a pile of paper, felt the crackle of it, and pulled it eagerly to the light. Then, and before she learned the grandeur of the sum, she was seized with a sudden palpitation, and sat down on Joan's bed. Her mouth grew full, as a hungry man's before a feast; her lips were wet; her hand shook as she opened and spread the notes. Then she counted them, and sat gasping like a landed fish. Thomasin had never seen so much money before in her life. A thousand pounds! Unlike Joan, to whom the sum conveyed no significance, Mrs. Tregenza could estimate it. Her mind reached that far, and the bank-notes, for her, lay within the estimation of avarice. Every snowy fragment meant a hundred pounds—a hundred sovereigns—two hundred ten-shilling pieces.

The first shock over-past, and long before she grew

sufficiently calm to associate the treasure with its possessor, Mrs. Tregenza began spending in her mind's eye. The points in house and garden, outhouse and sty, whereon money might be advantageously expended, rose up one after the other. Then she put aside eight hundred and fifty out of the grand total, and pictured herself taking it to the bank. She thought of a nest-egg that would "goody" against the time when Tom should grow into a man; she saw herself among the neighbours, pointed at, whispered of as a woman with hundreds and hundreds of pounds put by; she saw the rows of men sitting basking about in Newlyn, as their custom is when off the sea, and she heard them drop words of admiration at the sight of her.

Presently, however, this gilded vision vanished, and she began to connect the money with Joan. She solved the mystery then with a brutal directness which hit the mark in one direction—as to the source of the money—but went wide of it in some measure upon the subject of the girl. Thomasin held briefly that her step-daughter had fallen, and now, knowing her condition, had informed some man of it, with the result that from him came this unutterable gift. That the money made an enormous difference to Mrs. Tregenza's mental attitude must be confessed. She found herself fashioning absolute excuses for Joan. Girls so often came to ill through no fault of their own. The man must, at least, have been a gentleman to pay for his pleasure in four figures. Four figures! Here she stopped thinking in order to picture the vision of a unit followed by three ciphers. Then she marvelled as to what manner of man he was who could send a girl like Joan a thousand pounds. She never heard of such a price for the value received. Her respect for Joan began to increase when she realized that the money was hers. Probably there was even more where that came from.

"Anyway," she reflected, "it ban't no use cryin' ower spilt milk. What's done's done. An' a thousand pounds 'll go long ways to softenin' the road. She might travel up-long to Truro to my cousin, an' bide quiet theer till arter, an' no harm done, poor lass! When all's said, us knaws the Lard Hisself weer mighty easy wi' the likes o' she, an' worser wenches tu. But Michael—God A'mighty knaws he won't be easy. She'm a damned wummon, I s'pose, but she's got to live through 'er life here first, damned or saved; an' she's got a thousand pound to do't with. A terrible braave dollop o' money, sure 'nough. To think 'ow 'ard a man's got to work 'fore he earns even the leastest bit o' gawld!"

But her imagination centred upon Grey Michael now, and she almost forgot the bank-notes for a moment. She thought of his agony, and trembled for the result. He might strike Joan down and kill her. The man's anger against evil-doers was always a terrific thing; and he had no idea of the value of money. She hazarded guesses at the course he would pursue, and each idea was blacker than the last. Then Thomasin fell to wondering what Michael would be likely to do with the money. She sighed at this thought, and then she grew pale at the imaginary spectacle of her husband tearing the devil-sent notes to pieces, and scattering them over the cliff to the sea. This horrible possibility stung her to another train of ideas. Might it be within her power to win Joan's secret, share it, and keep it from the father? Her pluck, however, gave way when she looked a little deeper into the future. She would have done most things in her power for a thousand pounds, but she would not have dared any treachery to Michael. The woman put the notes together, and stroked them and listened to the rustle of them and rubbed her hard cheek with them Then, looking from the little window of Joan's garret, she saw the girl herself approaching with Mr. Tregenza. They were nearly home again, so Thomasin returned the money and the picture to their places in the chest of drawers, smoothed the bed where she had been sitting for half an hour, and went downstairs, still undetermined as to a course of action.

Before dinner was eaten, however, she had decided that her husband must know the truth. Even her desire towards the money cooled before the prospect of treachery to him. Fear had something to do with this decision, but the woman's own principles were strong. It is unlikely that in any case they would have broken down. She sent Joan on an errand to the village after the meal was ended; and upon her departure addressed her husband hurriedly—

"You said I was mazed to dinner, an' so I was. I've gotten bad news for 'e, Michael, touchin' Joan."

"No more o' that, mother!" he answered. "I've talked wi' her, an' said a word in season. She'm well in body, an' be gwaine to turn a new leaf, so theer's an end o' the matter."

"Tedn' so!" she declared. "I've bin in the gal's room, an' I've found—— But you bide here, an' I'll bring 'em to 'e. Hold yourself back, Michael, for us caan't say nothin' sure till us knaws the truth from Joan."

"She've tawld me the truth out a-walkin', an' I've shawed her the narrer path. What should you find?"

"Money—no li'l come-by-chance neither: more money than ever you or me seed in our born days afore or shall agin."

"You'm dreamin', wummon!" he said.

"God knaws I wishes it weer so," she answered, and went once more to Joan's room.

Grey Michael was walking up and down the kitchen when she returned, and Thomasin said nothing, but put money and picture upon the table. Her husband fought with himself a moment as it appeared, then seemed to pray awhile, standing still with his hand pressed over his eyes. Finally he sat himself down beside the things which Thomasin had brought.

"I'd no choice but to tell 'e," she said.

Grey Michael's eyes were on the picture, and utter astonishment appeared in them.

"Why, 'tis Joe Noy's ship! Us seed her off the islands outward bound. He might 'a' gived it her hisself, surely?"

"But t'other thing—the money. Count them notes. Noy never gived Joan them."

He spread the parcel, counted the money, and sat back thunderstruck.

"God in heaven! A thousan' pound! an' notes as never went through no dirty hands neither! What do it mean?"

"How should I tell what it means? I found the whole fortune hid beneath her smickets. Lard knaws how she comed by it! What have the likes o' she to give for money?"

"What do 'e mean by that?" he blazed out, rising to his feet and clenching his fists.

"Ax your darter. Do 'e think I'd dare to say a word onless I was sartain sure? You'd smash me, your awn wife, if I weer wrong, like enough. I ban't wrong. Joan's wi' cheel, or I never was. Maybe that thraws light on the money, maybe it doan't. I did pray as it might 'a' comed out to be her man at sea; but you'll find it weern't. God help 'e, Michael; my heart do bleed for 'e! Can 'e find it in 'e to be merciful, same as the Lard in like case, or——?"

He raised his hand to stop her. He was sitting back in his chair, with a face that had grown grey even to the skin, with eyes that looked out at nothing. There was a moment's silence, save for the tall clock in the corner; then Tregenza brushed beads of water off his forehead and dried his hand on his trousers. He raised his eyes to the roof and gripped his hands together on his chest, and slowly spoke a text which his wife had heard upon his lips before, but only at times of deep concern or emotion.

"'The Lard is King, be the people never so impatient; He sitteth between the cherubims, be the airth never so unquiet'!"

Few saw any particular meaning in this quotation applied in moments of stress, as Michael usually employed it; but to the man it was a supreme utterance, the last word to be spoken in the face of all the evil and wickedness of the world. Come what might, God still reigned in heaven.

He spoke aloud thus far, and afterwards, by the movement of his board and lip, Thomasin could see he was still talking or praying.

"Let the Lard lead 'e, husband, in this hard pass," she said. "'Vengeance is mine,' the Book sez."

He turned his eyes upon her. His brows were dragged down upon them; he had brushed his grey hair, like bristles, upright on his head; over the mighty wall of his forehead jagged crosslines were stamped, like the broken strata over a cliff-face.

"Ay, you say it. Vengeance be God's awn, an' mercy be God's awn. 'Tedn' for no man to meddle wi' them. Us caan't be ought but just. She'll have justice from me—no more'n that. 'Tis all wan now. Wanton or no wanton, she've flummoxed me this day. The giglet lied, an' said the thing that was not. She'm not o' the kingdom—the fust Tregenza as ever lied—the fust."

"God send it edn' as bad as it do look, master. 'Er carater belike ban't gone. S'pose as she'm married?"

"Hould your clack, wummon. I be thinkin'."

He was thinking, indeed. In the face of this discovery, the ghost of an idea which had haunted Grey Michael's mind more than once during the up-bringing of Joan returned, a greater and more pronounced shadow than ever before. The conviction carried truth stamped upon it from the standpoint of his present horrid knowledge. To an outsider his thought had appeared absolutely devilish, to the man himself it was as a buoy thrown to one drowning. The belief flooded his mind, swept him away, convinced him. Its nature presently appeared as he answered Thomasin. She was still thinking of the thousand pounds.

"Theer's no word in the Book agin' mercy, Michael. Joan's your awn darter—froward or not froward."

"You'm wrong theer," he said. He was now cool and quiet. "I did think so wance; I did tell her so when us walked not two hour agone. Now I sees differ'nt. She'm none o' my getting. She'm no Tregenza. Be nature—as made us Godfearin' to a man, to a wummon, to a cheel—gwaine to lie after generations 'pon generations? Look back at them as bred me, an' them as bred them—back, an' back, an' back. All Tregenzas was o' the Lard's harvest; an' should I, as feared God more'n any of em, an' fought for the Lard of Hosts 'fore I was higher'n this table—should I, Michael Tregenza, breed a damned sawl? The thot's comed black an' terrible 'pon my mind 'fore to-day; an' I've put en away from me, judgin' 'twas the devil. Now I knaw 'twas God spoke; now I knaw that her's no cheel o' mine. 'Who honoureth his faither shall 'a' joy o' his awn childern.' Shall I, as weer a pattern son, be cussed wi' a strumpet for a darter?"

"You'm speakin' a hard thing o' dead bones, then. The Chirgwins be upland folks o' long standin', knawn so far as the Land's End, an' up Drift, an' down Lizard likewise."

"She've lied to me," was his answer. "She've lied often-times; she'm false to whatever I did teach her; she've sawld herself—she've—— No more on it—no more on it, but awnly this: I call 'pon God A'mighty to bear witness she'm no Tregenza—never—never!"

"'Tweer her mother in the gal; but doan't 'e say more 'bout that, Michael. Poor, dear sawl, she'm dead an' gone, an' she loved 'e wi' all her 'eart, as I, what knawed her, can testify to."

"No more o' that," he said; "the gal's comin'. Thank God she ban't no cheel o' mine—thank God, as 'ave tawld me 'tedn' so. He whispered it, an' I put it away an' away. Now I knaws. You bide here, Thomasin Tregenza, and I'll speak what's fittin'."

Thus in one moment this hideous conviction was stamped upon the man's soul for life. He judged the dead mother by the daughter, and visited the child's sin upon the parent's memory. Any conclusion more monstrous, more directly opposed to every natural instinct, can hardly be conceived, but the man had been strangling natural instincts for fifty years. Only pride of family remained. There were but few Tregenzas left, and soon there would be none unless Tom carried on the name. Michael was the quintessence of the Tregenza spirit, the fruit of generations, the high-water mark. He stood on that giddy pinnacle which has religious mania for its precipice. To judge a dead woman was easier than to accept a wanton daughter.

Better an unfaithful wife than that any soul born of Tregenza blood should be lost. So he washed his hands of both, thanking God, who had launched the truth into his mind at last; and then he rose to his feet as Joan entered the room.

She stood for a moment in the doorway with her blue eyes fixed in amazement upon the kitchen table. Then she grew red to the roots of her hair, and came forward. There was almost a joy in her mind that the long story of falsehood must end at last. She did not fear her father now, and looked up into his face quite calmly as she approached the table.

"These be mine," she said. "Was it you, faither, as took 'em from wheer they was?"

"'Twas me, Joan," answered Mrs. Tregenza; "an' I judge the Lard led me."

The girl stood erect and scornful. "I'm glad you found them; now I can tell the truth."

"Truth!" thundered Michael; "truth! What do you knaw 'bout truth, darter o' Baal? Your life's a lie, your tongue's rotten in your mouth wi' lyin'. Never look in no honest faace again!"

"You'd do best to bide still while I tell 'e what this here means," said Joan, quietly. The man's rage alarmed her no more than the chatter of an angry bird. "I ban't no darter o' Baal, an' the money's come by honest. I've lied afore, but never shall again. An' I've let Joe go his ways thinkin' I loved en, which I doan't. I be tokened to a furriner from London, an' he's took me for his awn, an' he be gwaine to come down-long mighty soon an' take me away. But I couldn't tell 'e nothin' of that, 'cause he bid me keep my mouth shut. So theer."

"Took 'e for 'is awn! Wheer is he, then? Why be you here?"

"He'm comin', I tell 'e. He'm a true man, an' he shawed me what 'tis to love."

"Bought you, you damned harlot!"

She knew the word was vile, but a shred of John Barron's philosophy supported her.

"My awnly sin is I've lied to you, faither; an' you've no right to call me evil names."

"Never call me faither no more, lewd slut! I be no faither o' thine, nor never was. God A'mighty! A Treganza a wanton! I'd rather cut my hand off than b'lieve it so. It's this—this—blood-money—the price o' a damned sawl! No more lyin'. I knaw—I knaw. An' the picksher—the ship of a true man. It did ought to break your heart to see it if you had wan. A devil-spawned painting feller, in coourse. An' his black heart happy an' content 'cause he've sent this filth. You stare wi' your mother's eyes—you stare, an' stare!—Hell's yawning for 'e, wretched wummon, an' for him as bro't 'e to it!"

"He doan't believe in hell, no more doan't I," said Joan, calmly; "an' it ban't a faither's plaace to damn's awn flaish an' blood no way."

"Never name me thy faither no more! I ban't your faither, I tell 'e, an' I do never mean to see thy faace again. Go wheer you'm minded; but get o' gone from here. Tramp the broad road with the crowd—the narrer path's closed agin 'e. And this—this—let it burn same as him what sent it will."

He picked up the note nearest to him, crumpled it into a ball, and flung it upon the fire.

"Michael! Michael!" cried his wife, rushing forward. "For God's love, what be doin' of? The money ban't damned; the money's honest!"

But Joan did more than speak. As the gift flamed quickly up, then sunk to grey ash, a tempest of passion carried her out of herself. She trembled in her limbs, grew deadly pale, and flew at her father like a tigress. No evil word had ever crossed her lips till then, though they had echoed in her ears often enough. But now they jumped to her tongue, and she cursed Grey Michael, and tore the rest of the money out of his hand so quickly, that his intention of burning it was frustrated.

"It's mine—it's mine, blast you!" she screamed like a fury. "What right have you to burn it? It's mine—gived me by wan whose shoe you ban't worthy to latch! He's shawed me

what you be, an' the likes o' you, wi' your hell-fire, an' prayin',
an sour looks.   I ban't afeared o' you no more—none o' you.   I
be sick o' the smeech o' your God.   'Er's a poor thing alongside
o' mine an' Mister Jan's.   I'll gaw; I'll gaw so far away as ever
I can; an' I'll never call 'e my faither agin, s'elp me God!"

Mrs. Tregenza had thanked Providence under her breath
when Joan rescued the notes; but now, almost for the first time,
she realized that her own interest in this pile of money was as
nothing.   Every penny belonged to her step-daughter, and her
step-daughter evidently meant to keep it.   This discovery hit
her hard, and now the bitterness came forth in a flood of words
that tumbled each over the other, and stung like hornets as
they settled.

Grey Michael's broadside had roared harmlessly over Joan's
erect head; Thomasin's small shot did not miss the mark.
She was furious; her husband stood dumb; her virago tongue
screamed out the truth; and Joan, listening, knew that it was
the truth.

No matter what the elder woman said.   She missed no vile
word of them all.   She called Joan every name that chills the
ear of the fallen, and she explained the meaning of her expressions; she bid the girl take herself and the love-child
within her from out the sight of honest folks; she told her the
man had turned his back for ever, that only the ashy road of
the ruined remained for her to tread.   And that was how the
great news that Nature had looked upon her for a mother came
to Joan Tregenza.   Here was the riddle of the mysterious voice
unravelled; here was the secret of her physical sorrows made
clear.   She looked wildly from one to the other—from the man
to the woman; then she tottered a step away, clutching her
money and her little picture to her breast; and then she rolled
over, a huddled, senseless heap, upon the floor.

CHAPTER VI.

DRIFT.

WHEN Joan recovered consciousness, she found her head and neck wet, where her step-mother had flung cold water over her. Thomasin was at that moment burning a feather under her nose; but she stopped and withdrew it as the girl's eyes opened.

"Theer, now you'll be well by night. He've gone aboard. Best to change your gownd, for 'tis wetted. Then I'll tell 'e what er said. Can 'e get upstairs?"

Joan rose slowly, and went with swimming brain to her room. She still held her picture and her money. She took off her wet clothes, then sat down upon her bed to think; and as her mind grew clear, there crept through the gloomy shadows of the past tragedy a joy. It lightened her heart a moment, then vanished again, like the moon blotted suddenly from the sky by a rack of storm-cloud. Joan was full of the stupendous news. The shock of hearing her most unsuspected condition had indeed stricken her insensible, but it was the surprise of it as much as the dismay. Now she viewed the circumstance with uncertainty, not knowing the attitude "Mister Jan" would adopt towards it. She argued with herself long hours, and peace brooded over her at the end, for, as his cherished utterances passed in review before her memory, the sense and sum of them seemed to promise well. He would be very glad to share in the little life that was upon the way to earth. He always spoke kindly of children; he had called them the flower-buds in Nature's lap. Yes, he must be glad; and Nature would smile too. Nature knew what it was to be a mother, Joan told herself. She was in Nature's hands henceforth. But her blue eyes grew cold when she thought of the morning. So much for St. Madron and his holy water; so much for the good angels who her dead parent had told her were for ever stretching loving, invisible hands to guard and shield. "Mister Jan's be the awnly god," she thought, "an' he'm tu far aways to mind the likes o' we; so us must trust to the gert mother o' the flowers." She accepted the position with an open heart, then turned her thoughts to her loved one. Having now firmly convinced herself that her condition would bring him gratification, and draw them still nearer each to the other, Joan yearned unutterably for his presence. She puzzled her brains to know how she might communicate with him, how hasten his return. She remembered that he had once told her his surname, but she could not recollect it now. He had always been "Mister Jan" to her.

She went down to her supper in the course of the evening, and the great matter in her mind was for a while put aside before a present necessity. Action, she found, would be immediately required of her. Her father, before going from the kitchen after she had fainted, directed Thomasin to bid her never see his face again. She must depart, according to his direction, on the following day, for the thatched cottage upon the cliff could be her home no more.

"Theer weern't no time for talkin'; but I lay er'll sing differ'nt when next ashore. You bide quiet here till er's home agin. 'Tain't nachur to bid 's awn flaish an' blood go its ways like that. An', 'pears to me, as 'tedn' the law neither. But you bide till he'm back. I be sorry as I spawk so sharp, awnly you was that bowldacious that my dander brawk loose. Aw Jimmery! to think as you dedn' knaw you was cheeldin'!"

"'Twas hearin' so suddint like as made me come over fainty."

"Ayte hearty, then. An' mind henceforrard you'm feedin' an' drinkin' for two. Best get to bed so soon's you can. Us'll talk 'bout this coil in the marnin'."

" Us'll talk now. I be off by light. I edn' gwaine to stop
no more. Faither sez I ban't no cheel o' his, an' he doan't want
to soo my faace agen. Then he shaan't. I'll gaw to them as
won't be 'shamed o' me—my mother's people."

" Doan't 'e be in no tearin' hurry, Joan," said Mrs. Tregonza,
thinking of the money. " Let him — the chap—knaw fust
what's come along o' his carneying, an' maybe he'll marry 'e, as
you sez, right away. Bide wi' me till you tells en. Let en do
what's right an' soemly ; that's the shortest road—if he will."

" 'Iss, fay. He'm a true man. But I ban't gwaine to wait
for en in this 'ouse. To-morrow I'll send my box up Drift by
tho fust 'bus as belongs to start, an' walk myself, an' tell Uncle
Sampy all's there is to tell. He've got a heart in his breast,
an' I'll bide 'long wi' him till Mister Jan do come back."

" Wheer's he to now ? "

" To Lunnon. He've gone to make his house vitty for me."

" Well, best to get Uncle Chirgwin to write to en, onless
you'd like me to do it for 'e."

" No. He'll do what's right—a proper, braave man."

" An' 'mazin' rich seemin'ly ! For the Lard's love, if you'm
gwaine up Drift, take care o' all that blessed money. Doan't
say no word 'bout it till you'm in the farm, for theer's them—
the tinners out o' work an' sich—as 'ud knock 'e on the head for
half of it. To think as Michael burnt a hunderd pound ! Just
a flicker o' purpley fire, an' a hunderd pound gone ! 'Tis 'nough
to make a body rave ! "

The girl flushed, and something of her father's stern look
seemed reflected in her face.

" He stawl my money. No, I judge his word be truth.
He'm no faither o' mine, if the blood in the veins do count for
anything."

Joan went to bed abruptly on this remark, and lay awake
thinking and wondering through a long night—thinking what
she should say to Uncle Chirgwin ; wondering when " Mister
Jan " was coming back to her, and picturing his excitement at
her intelligence. In the morning she packed her box, ate her

breakfast, and then went into the village to find somebody who would carry her scanty luggage as far as Penzance. From there an omnibus ran through Drift, past Mr. Chirgwin's farmhouse door. Joan herself designed to walk, the distance by road from Newlyn being but trifling. It chanced that the girl met Billy Jago, he who in early spring had cut down an elm tree while John Barron watched. Him Joan knew, for he had worked on her uncle's farm for many years. Mr. Jago, who could be relied upon to do simple offices, undertook the task readily enough, and presently arrived with a wheelbarrow. He whined, as ever, about his physical sufferings, but drank a cup of tea with evident enjoyment; then fetched Joan's box from her room, and set off with it to meet the public vehicle. Her goods were to be left at Drift; and Joan herself started at an early hour, wishing to be at the farm before her property. She walked in the garden for the last time, marked the magic progress of spring, then took an unemotional leave of her step-mother.

"Theer cdu' no call to leave no message as I can see," said Joan, while she stood at the door. "He ban't my faither, he sez; so I'll take it for truth. But I'll ax you to kiss Tom for me. Us was allus good brother an' sister, whether or no, an' I loves en dearly."

" 'Iss, I knaw. He'll grizzle an' fret proper when he finds you'm gone. Good-bye to 'e. May the Lard forgive 'e, an' send your man 'long smart; an', for Heaven's sake, doan't lose them notes."

" They be safe stowed next to my skin. Uncle Sampy 'll look to them; an' you needn't be axin' God A'mighty to forgive me, 'cause I abbun done nothin' to want it. I be Nature's cheel now, an' I be in kindly hands. You caan't understand that, but I knaws what I knaws through bein' taught. Good-bye to 'e. Maybe us'll see each other bime-bye."

Joan held out her hand, and Mrs. Tregenza shook it. Then she stood and watched her step-daughter walk away into Newlyn. The day was cold and unpleasant, with high winds and driving mists. The village look greyer than usual; the boats were nearly all away; the gulls fluttered in the harbour, making their eternal music. Seawards, white horses flecked the leaden water, and a steamer hooted hoarsely, looming large under the low, sullen sky, as it approached the pier-heads. Presently a scat of heavy rain on a squall of wind shut out the harbour for a time. Mrs. Tregenza waited until Joan had disappeared, then went back to her kitchen, closed the door, sat in Grey Michael's great chair by the hearth, put her apron over her head, and wept. But the exact reason for her tears she could not have explained, for she did not know it. Mingled emotions possessed her. Disappointment had something to do with this present grief; sorrow for Joan was also responsible for it in a measure. That the girl should have asked her to kiss Tom was good, Thomasin thought, and the reflection moved her to further tears; while that Joan was going to put her money into the keeping of a simple old fool like Uncle Chirgwin seemed a highly pathetic circumstance to Mrs. Tregenza; indeed, the more she speculated upon it, the sadder it appeared.

Meanwhile Joan, leaving Newlyn and turning inland along the little lane which has St. Peter's Church and the Newlyn brook upon its right, escaped the wind and found herself walking through an emerald woodland world all wrapped in haze and rain. Past the smelting works, where purple smoke made wonderful colour in rising against the young green, over the brook, and under the avenue of great elms went Joan. Her heart ached this morning, and she thought of yesterday. It seemed as though a hundred years of experience had passed over her since she knelt by St. Madron's stone altar. She told herself bitterly how much wiser she was to-day, and so, thinking strange thoughts, tramped forward over Buryas Bridge, and faced the winding hill beyond. Then came doubts. Perhaps, after all, St. Madron had answered her prayer. Else why the underlying joy that now fringed her sorrows with happiness?

Drift is a place well-named, when seen, as then, grey through sad-coloured curtains of rain on the bare hilltop. But the orchard lands of the coomb below were fair, and many primroses twinkled in the soaking green of the tall hedge-banks. Joan splashed along through the mud, and presently a lump rose in her throat, born of thoughts. It had seemed nothing to leave the nest on the cliff, and she held her head high, and thanked God for a great deliverance. That was less than an hour ago, yet here, on the last hill to Drift, and within sight of the stone houses clustering at the summit, her head sank lower and lower, and it was not the rain which dimmed her eyes. She much doubted the value of further prayers now, yet every frantic hope and aspiration found its vent in a petition to her new god, as Joan mounted the hill. She prayed, because she could think of no other way to soothe her heart, but her mind was very weary and sad, not at the spectacle of the future, for that she knew was going to be fair enough, but at the vision of the past, at the years ended for ever, at the early pages of life closed, to be opened no more. A childhood, mostly quite happy, was over; she would probably visit the house wherein she was born never again. Yet even in her sorrow, the girl wondered why she should be sad.

Mr. Chirgwin's farm fronted the highway, and its grey stone face was separated therefrom by a small, and neat patch of garden. Below the house a gate opened into the farmyard, and Uncle Chirgwin's land chiefly sloped away into the coomb behind, though certain fields upon the opposite side of the high road also pertained to him. The farmhouse was time-stained, and the stone had taken some wealth of colour where black and golden lichens fretted it. The slates of the roof shone with wet, and reflected a streak of white light that now broke the clouds near the hidden sun. The drippings from the eaves had made a neat row of little regular holes among the crocuses in the garden. Tall jonquils also bent their heads there, heavy with water; and the white violets, which stood in patches upon either side of the front door, held each a raindrop glimmering within its cup. Japonica splashed one grey wall with crimson blossoms and young green leaves; but, for the rest, this house-front was quite bare. Joan saw Mary Chirgwin's neat hand in the snowy short blinds which crossed the upper windows; and she knew that the geraniums behind the diamond panes of the parlour were her uncle's care. They dwelt indoors, winter and summer, and their lanky, straggling limbs shut out much light.

The visitor did not go to the front door, whither a narrow path flanked with handsome masses of "Cornish diamonds," or quartz crystals, directly ran from the wicket, but entered at a larger gate which led into the farmyard. Here shippons ranged snugly on three sides of an open space, their venerable slates yellow with lichens; their thatches green with moss. In the centre of the yard a great manure heap made comfortable lying for pigs and poultry; while the farmhouse stretched back upon the fourth side. Another gate opened beyond it, and led to the land upon the sloping hill and the valley below. Joan passed a row of cream-pans, shining like frosted silver in the mist, then turned from the dripping world. The kitchen door was open, and revealed a large, low chamber, whose rafters were studded with orange-coloured hams, whose fireplace was vast and black save for a small wood fire filling but a quarter of the hearth. Grocer's almanacks brought brave colour to the walls, sharing the same with a big dresser, where the china made a play of reflected light from the windows. Above the lofty mantelpiece there hung an old fowling-piece, and a row of faded daguerreotypes, into most of which damp had eaten dull yellow patches. The mantel-shelf carried some rough stone-ware ornaments, an eight-day clock, a tobacco jar, and divers small utensils of polished tin. A big table covered with American cloth filled the centre of the kitchen, a low settle crossed the alcove of the window, and a leather screen, of four folds, and five feet high, surrounded Uncle Sampy's own roomy armchair in the chimney corner. Strips of cocoanut fibre lay upon the ground, but between them appeared the bare floor. It was paved with blue stone for the most part, though here and there a square of white broke the colour; and the latter patches had worn lower than the rest under many generations of hob-nailed boots. A faint odour of peat smoke was in the air, and the slight, stuffy smell of feathers.

A woman sat in the window as Joan entered. She had her back to the door, and not hearing the footfall, went on with her work, which was the plucking of a fowl. A cloth lay spread over the floor at her feet, and each moment the pile of feathers upon it increased as the plucker worked with rhythmic regularity, and sang to herself the while.

Mary Chirgwin was a dark, good-looking girl, with a face in which strong character appeared too prominently indicated to leave room for absolute beauty. But her features were regular, if swarthy; her eyes were splendid, and her brow, from which black hair was smoothly and plainly parted away, rose broad and low. There was nothing to mark kinship between the cousins, save that both held their heads finely, and possessed something of the same distinction of carriage. Mary was eight-and-twenty, and, whatever might be thought about her face, there could be but one opinion upon her feminine splendour of figure. Her broad chest produced a strange speaking and singing voice—mellow as Joan's, but far deeper in the notes. Mary gloried in congregational melodies, and those who had not before heard her contralto efforts at church on Sundays would often mistake her voice for a man's. She was dressed in print, with a big apron over-all; and her sleeves, turned up to her elbows, showed a pair of fine arms, perfect as to shape, but brown of colour as the woman's face.

Joan stood motionless, then her cousin looked round and started almost out of her chair at a sight so unexpected. But she composed herself again instantly, put down the semi-naked fowl, and came forward. They had not seen each other since the time when Joe Noy flung over Mary for Joan; and the latter, remembering this circumstance very well, had hoped she might escape from meeting her cousin until after some talk with Uncle Sampy. But Mary hid her emotion from Joan's sight, and they shook hands, and looked into one another's faces, each noting marked changes there since the last occasion of their meeting. The elder spoke first, and went straight to the past. It was her nature to have every connection and concern of life upon a definite and clear basis. She hated mystery, she disliked things hidden, she never allowed the relations between herself and any living being to stand otherwise than absolutely defined.

" You'm come, Joan, at last, though 'twas a soft day to choose. Listen to me, will 'e? Then us can let the past lie, same as us lets sleepin' dogs. I called 'pon God to blight your life, Joan Tregenza, when—— you knaw. I thot I weer gwaine to die, an' I read the cussin' psalm * agin you. 'Peared to me as you'd stawl the awnly thing as ever brot a bit o' brightness to my life. But that's all awver. Love weern't for me; I awnly dreamed it weer. An' I larned better an' didn't die; an' prayed to God a-many times to forgive that first prayer agin you. The likes o' you doan't know nort 'bout the grim side o' life, or what it is to lose the glory o' lovin'. But I doan't harbour no ill agin you no more."

" You'm good to hear, Polly, an' kind words is better'n food to me now. I'll tell 'e 'bout myself bime-bye. But I must speak to uncle fust. Things has happened."

" Nothin' wrong wi' your folks? "

" I ain't got no folks no more. But I'll tell 'e so soon's I've tawld Uncle Sampy."

" He'm in the croft somewheers. Better bide till dinner. Uncle'll be back by then."

" I caan't, Mary—not till I've spoke wi' en. I'll go long down Green Lane, then I shall meet en for sure. An' if a box o' mine comes by the 'bus, 'tis right."

" A box! Whatever is there in it, Joan? "

" All's I've gotten in the world—leastways nearly. Doan't ax me nothin' now. You'll knaw as soon as need be."

Without waiting for more words, Joan departed, hastened

* *The Cursing Psalm*, Psalm cix. If read by a wronged person before death, it was, and is sometimes yet, supposed to bring punishment upon the evil-doer.

through the gate on the inner wall of the farmyard, and walked along the steep hillside by a lane which wound muddily downwards to the grass lands, under high hazel hedges. New-born leaves dripped showers at every gust of the wind, then a gleam of wan sunlight brightened distant vistas of the way, while Joan heard the patter of a hundred hoofs in the mud, the bleat of lambs, the deeper answer of ewes, the barking of a shepherd's dog. Soon the cavalcade came into view—a flock of sheep first, a black and white dog, with a black and white pup which was learning his business, next, and Uncle Chirgwin himself bringing up the rear. The first sunshine of the day had found him out. It shone over his round red face, and twinkled in the dew on his white whiskers. He stumped along upon short, gaitered legs, but went not fast, and stayed at the steep shoulder of the hill, that his lambs might have rest and time to suck.

Mary Chirgwin meantime speculated on this sudden mystery of her cousin's arrival. She spread the cloth for dinner, bid her maid lay another place for Joan, and wondered much what manner of news she brought. There were changes in Joan's face since she last saw it—not changes which might have been attributed to the possession of Joe Noy, but an alteration of expression betokening thought, increased age, and experiences not wholly happy in their nature.

Joan had also marked the changes in Mary. These indications were clear enough, and filled her with sorrow. A river of tears will leave its bed marked upon a woman's face; and Joan, who had never thought overmuch of her cousin's sorrows until then, began to feel her heart fill, and run over with sudden sympathy. She asked herself what life would look like for her if "Mister Jan" changed his mind now and never came back again. That was how Mary felt, doubtless, when Joe Noy left her. Already Joan grew zealous in thought for Mary. She would teach her something of that sweet wisdom which was to support her own burden in the future; she would tell her about Nature—the "All Mother," as "Mister

Jan " called her once.   And, concerning Joe Noy, might it be
within the bounds of possibility, within the power of time to
bring these two together again?   The thought was golden to
Joan, and wholly occupied her mind until the sight of Uncle
Chirgwin, with his flock, brought her back to the present
moment and her own affairs.

CHAPTER VII.

A PROBLEM.

WHEN Mr. Chirgwin caught sight of Joan his astonishment knew no bounds, and his first thought was that something must be amiss. He stood in the roadway, a picture of surprise, and for a moment forgot both his sheep and lambs.

"My stars, Joan! Be it you, really? Whatever do 'e make at Drift, 'pon such a day as this? No evil news, I hope?"

"Uncle," she answered, "go slow a bit, an' listen to what I've got to say. You be a kind, good sawl as judges nobody, ban't you? And you love me 'cause your sister was my mother?"

"Surely, surely, Joan; an' I love you for yourself tu— nobody better in this world."

"You wouldn' go for to send me to hell-fire, would 'e?"

"God forbid, lass! Why, whatever be talkin' 'bout?"

"Uncle Sampy, faither's not my faither no more now. He've turned me out his house an' denied me. I ban't no darter of his henceforrard, an' he'm no faither o' mine. He don't mean never to look 'pon my faace agin, nor me 'pon his. The cottage edn' no home for me no more."

"Joan, gal alive! what talk be this?"

"'Tis gospel. I'm a damned wummon, 'cordin' to my faither as was."

"God A'mighty! You—paart a Chirgwin—as comed, o' wan side, from her as loved the Lard so dear, an', 'pon t'other, from him as feared so much! Never, Joan!"

"Uncle Sampy, I be in the fam'ly-way; an' faither's damned me, an' likewise the man as loves me, an' the cheel

I be gwaine to bring in the world. I've comed to hear you speak. Will you say the same? If you will, I'll pack off this instant moment."

The old man stood perfectly still, and his jaw went down while he breathed heavily; a world of amazement and piteous sorrow sat upon his face; his voice shook and whistled in the sound as he answered—

"Joan! My poor Joan! My awn gal, this be black news—black news. Thank God she'm not here to knaw—your mother."

"I've done no wrong, uncle; I ban't 'shamed o' it. He'm a true, good man, an' he'm comin' to marry me quick."

"Joe Noy?"

"No, no; not him. I thot I loved en well till Mister Jan comed an' opened my blind eyes, an' shawed me what love was. Mister Jan's a gen'leman—a furriner. He caan't live wi'out me no more; he's said as he caan't. An' I'm droopin' an' longin' for the sight o' en. An' I caan't bide in the streets, so I axes you to keep me till Mister Jan do come to fetch me. 1 find words hard to use to 'splain things, but his god's differ'nt to what the Luke Gosp'lers is, an' I lay 'tis differ'nt to yourn. But his god's mine anyways, an' I'm not afeared o' what I done, nor 'shamed to look folks in the faace. That's how 'tis, Uncle Sampy. 'Tis Nature, you mind, an' I be Nature's cheel now—wi' no faither nor mother but her."

The old man was snuffling, and a tear or two rolled down his red face, gathered the damp already there, and fell. He groaned to himself, then brought forth a big, red pocket-hand-kerchief, and wept outright, while Joan stood silently regarding him.

"I'd rather 'a' met death than this; I'd rather 'a' knawn you was coffined."

"Oh, if I could awnly 'splain!" she cried frantically—"if I awnly could find his words 'pon my tongue; but I caan't. They be hid down deep in me, an' by them I lives from day to day; but how can I make others see same as I see? I awnly brings sorrer 'pon sorrer now. Theer's nothin' left but him. If you could 'a' heard Mister Jan! *You* would understand, wi' your warm heart; but I caan't make 'e; I've no terrible braave butivul words! I'll go my ways, then. If any sawl had tawld me as I'd ever bring tears down your faace I'd never b'lieved 'em—never; but so I have, an' that's bitterness to me."

He took her by the hand and pressed it, then he put his arm round her and kissed her. His white bristles hurt, but Joan rejoiced exceedingly, and now it was her turn to shed tears.

"He'll come back—he'm a true man," she sobbed. "Theer ban't the likes o' Mister Jan in Carnwall; an'—an' if you knawed en you'd say no less. You'm the fust as have got to my heart since he went, an' he'd bless e' if he knawed."

"Come along with me, Joan," answered Uncle Chirgwin, straightening himself, and applying his big handkerchief to her face. "God send the man'll be 'longside 'e right soon, as you sez. Till he do come, you shaan't leave me no more. Drift's home for you while you'm pleased to bide theer. An' I'll see your faither presently, though I wish 'twas any other man."

"I knawed you was allus the same; I knawed you'd take me in. An' Mister Jan shall knaw. An' he'll love you for't when he do."

"Come an' see me put the ewes an' lambs in the croft; then us'll go to dinner, an' I'll hear you tell me all 'bout en."

He tried hard to put a hopeful face upon the position, and, himself as simple as a child, presently found Joan's story not hopeless at all. He seemed, indeed, to catch some of her spirit as she proceeded and painted the manifold glories of " Mister Jan " in the best language at her command. To love Nature was no sin ; Mr. Chirgwin himself did so ; and as for the money, instead of reading the truth of it, he told himself very wisely that the giver of a sum so tremendous must at least be in earnest. The amount astounded him. Fired by Joan's words—for as he played the ready listener her eloquence increased—he fell to thinking as she thought, and even speaking hopefully. The old farmer's reflections merely echoed his own simple trust in men and had best not been uttered, for they raised Joan's spirits to a futile height. But he caught the contagion from her, and spoke with sanguine words of the future, and even prayed Joan that, if wealth and a noble position awaited her, she would endeavour to brighten the lives of the poor, as became a good Cornishwoman. This she solemnly promised, and they built castles in the air—two children together. His sheep driven to their new pasture, Uncle Chirgwin led the way home, and listened as he walked to Joan's story. She quite convinced him before he reached his kitchen door—partly because he was very well content to be convinced, partly because he could honestly imagine no man base enough to betray this particular blue-eyed child.

Mr. Chirgwin's extremely unworldly review of the position was balm to Joan. Her heart grew warm again, and the old man's philosophy brightened her face, as the sun, now making a great clearness after rain, brightened the face of the land. But the recollection of Mary Chirgwin sobered her uncle not a little. How she would take this tremendous intelligence he failed to guess remotely. Opportunity to impart it occurred sooner than he expected, for Joan's box had just arrived. During dinner the old man explained that his niece was to be a visitor at Drift for a term of uncertain duration; and after the meal, when Joan disappeared to unpack her box and make tidy a little apple-room, which was now vacant and at her service, Uncle Chirgwin had speech with Mary. He braced himself to the trying task, waited until the kitchen was empty of those among his servants who ate at his table, and then replied to the question which his niece promptly put.

"What do this mean, Uncle Sampy? What's come o' Joan that she do drop in 'pon us like this here, wi' never a word to say she was comin'?"

"Polly," he answered, "your cousin Joan has seen sore trouble, in a manner o' speakin', an' you'd best to knaw fust as last. Us must be large-minded 'bout a thing like this. She'm tokened to a gen'leman from Lunnon."

"What! An' him—Joe Noy?"

"To be plain wi' you, Polly, she've thrawed en over. Listen 'fore you speaks. 'Twas a match o' Michael Tregenza's makin', I reckon, an', so like's not, Joe weern't any more heart-struck than Joan. I finds it hard to feel as I ought to Grey Michael, more shame to me. But Joan's falled in love wi' a gen'leman, an' he with her, an' he'm comin' any mornin' to fetch 'er—an'—an'—you must be tawld—'tis time as he did come. An' he've sent Joan a thousand pound o' paper money to show as 'e means the right thing."

But the woman's mind had not followed these last facts. Her face was white to the lips; her hands were shaking. She put her head down upon them as she sat by the fire, and a groan which no power could strangle broke from her deep bosom. She spoke, and regretted her words a moment later.

"Oh, my God! An' he brawk wi' me for the likes o' she!"

"Theer, theer, lass Mary; doan't 'e—doan't 'e. You've hid your tears that cunnin'; but my old eyes has seen the marks this many day, an' sorrered for 'e. 'Tis a hard matter viewed from the point what you looks 'pon it; but I knaws you, my awn good gal; I knaws your Saviour's done a 'mazin' deal to hold you up. An' 'twon't be for long, 'cause the man'll come for her mighty soon seemin'ly. Can 'e faace it, the Lard helpin'? Poor Joan's bin kicked out the house by her faither. I do *not* like en—never did. What do 'e say? She doan't count it no sin, mind you; an' doan't look for no reprovin', 'cause the gen'leman have taught her terrible coorious ideas; but 'tis just this: we'm all sinners—eh, Polly? An' us caan't say 'sactly what size a sin do look to God A'mighty's eye. An' us have got the Lard's way o' handlin' sich like troubles writ out clear —eh? Eh, Polly? He dedn' preach no sermon at the time neither."

The old man prattled on, setting out the position in the most favourable light to Joan that seemed possible to him. But his listener was one no longer. She had forgotten her cousin and the present circumstances, for her thoughts were with a sailor at sea. One tremendous moment of savage joy gripped her heart, but the primitive passion perished in its birth-pang, and left her cold and faint and ashamed. She wondered from what unknown, unscoured corner of her soul the vile thing came. It died on the instant, but the corpse fouled her thoughts and tainted them, and made her feel faint again. The irony of chance burst like a storm on the woman, and mazes of tangled thoughts made her brain whirl in a chaos of bewilderment. She sat motionless, her face dark, set, and much mystery in her wonderful eyes, while Mr. Chirgwin, with shaking head and scriptural quotation and tears, babbled on, pleading for Joan with all his strength. Mary heard little of what he said. She was occupied with facts, and asking herself her duty. From the storm in her mind arose a clear question at last, and she could not answer it. The point had appeared unimportant to anybody but Mary Chirgwin, but no question of conduct ever looked trivial to her. At least the doubt was definite, and afforded mental occupation. She wondered now whether it was well or possible that she and Joan could live together under the same roof. Why such a problem had arisen, she knew not; but it stood in the path, a fact to be dealt with. Her heart told her that Joan and her uncle alike erred in the supposition that the girl's seducer would ever return. She read the great gift of money as Thomasin had read it—rightly; and the thought of living with Joan was at first horrible to her.

Mr. Chirgwin talked, and Mary reflected. Then she rose to leave the room.

"'Tis tu gert a thing for me to say—no wummon was ever plaaced like what I be now. I do mean to see passon at Sancreed, uncle. He'll knaw what's right for me. If he bids me stay, I'll stay. 'Tis the thot o' Joe Noy maddens me. My head'll burst if I think any more. I'll go to passon."

"'Whether you'll stay,' Polly? Why shouldn't 'e stay? Surely it do——"

"Doan't 'e talk no more 'tall, uncle. You caan't knaw what this is to me; you doan't understan' a wummon faaced wi' a coil like this here. Joe—Joe, as loved 'er, I s'pose, different to what 'e did me. An' she, when his back weer turned—an'—an'—me—God help me—as never could do less than love en through all! "

She was gone before he had time to answer, but he realized her mighty agony of mind, and stood dumb and frightened before it. Then a thought came concerning Joan, and he felt that, at all costs, he must speak to Mary again before she went out. Mr. Chirgwin waited quietly at the stair-foot until she came down. The turmoil was in her eyes still, but she spoke calmly and listened to him when he replied.

"Doan't 'e say nuthin' to Joan, Unclo Sampy. I be gwaine to larn my duty, as is hidden from me. An' my duty I will do."

"An' so you allus have, Polly, since you was a grawed gal; an' God knaws it. But—do 'e think as you could, in a manner o' speakin' hide names from passon? Ban't no call to tell what's fallen out to other folks. Joan—eh, Polly? Might 'e speak in a parable like—same as Scripture—wi'out namin' no names? For Joan's sake, Mary—eh?"

She was silent a full minute, then answered slowly, "I see what you mean. I hadn' thot o' she just then. Iss, fay, you'm right theer. Ban't no work o' mine to tell 'bout her."

She hesitated, and the old man spoke again.

"I s'pose that a bit o' prayer wouldn' shaw light on it, eh, Polly, wi'out gwaine to Sancreed? The Lard knaws your fix better'n what any words 'ud put it clear to passon. An' theer's yourself tu. 'Pears to me, axin' your pardon, for you'm clever'n what I am, that 'tedn' a tale what you can put out 'fore any other body 'sactly—even a holy man like him."

She saw at once that it was not. Her custom had been to get the kind-hearted old clergyman of her parish church to soothe the doubts and perplexities which not seldom rose within her strenuous mind. And, before this great, crushing problem, with the pretext of the one difficulty which had tumbled uppermost from the chaos, and so been grasped as a reality, she had naturally turned to her guide and friend. But, as her uncle spoke, she saw that in truth this matter could not be laid naked before any man. Another's hidden life was involved; another's secret must come out if all was told; and Mary's sense of justice warned her that this could not be. She had taken her own mighty grief to the little parsonage at Sancreed, and a kindly counsellor, who knew sorrow at first hand, helped her upon the road that henceforth looked so lonely and so long; but this present trial, though it tore the old wounds open, must be borne alone. She saw as much, and turned and went upstairs again to her chamber.

"Think of her kindly," said Uncle Chirgwin, as Mary left him without more words. "She'm so young an' ignorant o' the gert world, Polly. An' if the worst falls, which God forbid, 'tis her as'll suffer most, not we."

"Us have all got to suffer an' suffer this side our graaves," she said, mounting wearily.

"So young an' purty as she be—the moral o' her mother. I doan't knaw—'tis sich a wonnerful world—but them blue eyes— them round blue eyes couldn't do a thing as was wrong afore God as wan might fancy," he said aloud, not knowing she was out of earshot. Then he heaved a sigh, returned to the kitchen, and presently departed to the fields.

CHAPTER VIII.

WAITING FOR "MISTER JAN."

WITH searching of heart, Mary Chirgwin spent time during that afternoon. In one room Joan, happier than she had been for many days, set out her few possessions, boldly hung the picture of Joe Noy's ship upon the wall and gazed at it with affection, for it spoke of the painter, not the sailor, to her; while in a chamber hard by Mary solved the problem of the day, coming at her conclusion with great struggle of mind and clashing of arguments. She resolved at last to abide at Drift with her uncle and with Joan. The reason for those events now crowding upon her life was hidden from her; and why Providence saw fit to awaken or mightily intensify the sorrows which time was lulling to sleep, she could not divine. She accepted her position, none the less, doubted nothing but that the secret hidden in these matters would some day be explained, and, according to her custom, before the approach of all mundane events and circumstances affecting herself, viewed the present trial as Heaven-sent to purify and strengthen. So your religious egotists are ever wont to read into the great waves of chance, as here and there a ripple from them sets their own little vessels shaking, as here and there some splash of foam or puff of wind strikes the nutshell which floats their lives, a personal, deliberate intervention, an event designed by the Everlasting to test their powers, ripen their characters, equip their souls for eternity.

At teatime the cousins met again, and Uncle Chirgwin, returning from his affairs, was rejoiced to learn Mary's decision. No outward sign marked her struggle. She was calm, even stately, with the natural distinction which physically appeared in her bearing and carriage. She chilled Joan a little, but not with intention. Yet Joan was bold for her love, and spoke no less than the truth when she asserted that she viewed her position without shame and without remorse. She spoke of it openly, fearlessly, and kept Uncle Chirgwin on thorns between the cold silence of his elder niece and the garrulous chatter of the younger. The saint was so stern, the sinner so happy and so perfectly impressed with her own innocence; which latter fact Mary too saw clearly, and it instantly solved half the problem in her mind. Joan had obviously been sent to Drift that the Truth might reach her heart. She came a heathen from the outer darkness of sin, with vain babbling on her lips and a mind empty. She called herself " Nature's child," and the theatric thunders of Luke Gospeldom had never taught her that she was God's. Here, then, was one to be brought into the fold with all possible despatch, and Mary, who loved religious battle, braced herself to the task while silently listening to Joan, that she might the better learn what manner of spiritual attack would best meet this sorry case.

Uncle Chirgwin took charge of his niece's bank-notes, and, after some persuasion, consented to accept the weekly sum of three shillings and sixpence from Joan. He made many objections to any such arrangement, but the girl overruled them, declaring absolutely that she would not stop at Drift, even until her future husband's return, unless the payment of money was accepted from her. It bred a secret joy in Joan to feel that " Mister Jan's " wealth now enabled her to enjoy an independence which even Mary could not share. She much desired to give more money, but Uncle Sampy fixed the sum at three shillings and sixpence weekly, and would take no more. This wealth was viewed with very considerable loathing by Mary Chirgwin, and she criticized her uncle's decision unfavourably; but he accepted the owner's view, arguing that it was only justice to all parties so to do, until facts proved whether Joan was mistaken. The notes did not

cause him uneasiness—at any rate, during this stage of affairs—
and he took them to Penzance upon the occasion of his next
visit. Mr. Chirgwin's lawyer saw to the safe bestowal of the
money, and when she heard that her nine hundred pounds
would produce about five and twenty every year, and yet not
decrease the while, Joan was much astonished.

Meantime John Barron neither came to fetch her, nor sent
any writing to tell of the causes for his delay. The girl was
fruitful of new reasons for his silence, and then grew a black
fear which answered all doubts and, by its reasonableness,
terrified her. Perhaps "Mister Jan" was ill—too ill even to
write. He had but little strength—that she knew—and few
friends—of this Joan was also aware, for he had told her so.
Yet, surely, there were those, if only his servants, who might
have written to bid her hasten. A line—a single word—and
she would get into the train and stop in it until she saw
"London" written on a board at a station. Then she would
leap out and find him, and get to his heart and warm it,
and kiss life back to his body, light to his grey eyes. So
thinking, time dragged, and as the novelty of the new life
abated and wore thin, Joan's spirits wavered until long and
longer intervals of gloomy sadness marked the duration of each
day for her. But she was young, and hope yet held revels in
her heart when the mood favoured, when the wind was soft,
the sun bright, and Mother Nature seemed close and kind, as
often happened. Joan worked, too, helping Mary and the
maids, but after a wayward manner of her own. There was
no counting upon her, and she loved better to be with her
uncle, abroad upon the land, or by herself, hidden in the
orchard, in the fruit garden, and in the secret places of the
coomb.

She had her favourite spots, for as yet that great overwhelming regard for the old stone crosses, which came to her
afterwards, had not grown into a live passion. Her present
pilgrimages were short, her shrines those of Nature's building.
Much she loved the arm of an ancient apple tree hid in the

very heart of the orchard. A great gnarled limb bent abruptly out, grew long and low, and was propped at a distance of three yards from the parent tree. Midway between the stem and support, a crooked elbow of the bough made a pleasant seat for Joan ; and here, when life at the farm looked more sad than common, she came and sometimes sat long hours. Her perch raised her above a velvet, scented sea of wallflowers, which ran in regular waves beneath the apple trees under murmuring of many bees. The blossom above Joan's head was all a lace-work of rose and cream ; and the sun painted glorious russet harmonies below, glinted magically in the green and white above, turned the grey lichens, which clustered on the weather side of the trunks and boughs, to silver. The glory of life here always heartened Joan. She felt the immortality of Nature, who, from naked earth and barren boughs, thus at the sun's smile splendidly awakened and teemed and overflowed with bewildering, inexhaustible, luxuriance. Not seldom this aspect of her mother's infinite wealth touched her blood, and a strange sensation as of very lust of life made her wild. At such times she would pick the green things and tear them, and watch the colourless life ooze from their wounds ; she would gather blossoms and scatter them against the wind, break buds open and pluck their hearts out, fill her mouth with sorrel and young grass-shoots, and feel the cool saps of them upon her palate. And sometimes her mother frightened her, for the dim clouds hid beneath the horizon of maternity were moving now and their colour was dark. Nature had as many moods as Joan, and often looked distant and terrible. Poor little blue-eyed " sister of the sun and moon " ! She likened herself so bravely to the other children of her mother—to the stars ; to the fair birch trees, where emerald showers now twinkled down over silver stems ; to the uncurling fronds of the fern ; to the little trout in the coomb-stream ;—and yet she was not content as they were.

"Her's good, so good ; but oh ! if her was a bit nigher—if I could sit in her lap an' feel her arms around me an' thread the daisies into chains like when I was a li'l maid ! But I be a grawed wummon now—and yet can't feel it so—not yet. Her'll hold my hand, maybe, an' lead me 'pon the road past pain an' sorrow. I can trust her, 'cause Mister Jan did say as Nature never lies—never."

So the girl's thoughts wandered on a day when she sat upon the bough, and brought a shower of pale petals down with every movement. But as yet only the shadows of shadows clouded her mind when she thought about herself. It was the loneliness brought real care—the loneliness and the waiting.

She spent time, too, in Uncle Chirgwin's old walled garden, a place which went for little in the traffic of the farm, though every year its owner was wont to count upon certain few baskets of choice fruit as an addition to his income, and every year his hopes were blighted. For the walls, whereon his peaches and nectarines grew had stood through generations, their red brickwork was much fretted by time, and the interstices between the bricks made snug homes for a variety of insects. Joan once listened to her uncle upon this subject, and henceforth chose to make his scanty fruit her special care.

"'Tis like this," he explained, "an' specially wi' the necter'ns. The moment they graws a shade, an' long afore they stone, them dratted li'l auld sow-pigs * falls 'pon 'em cruel. Then they gives awver an' waits theer time till the ripenin'; an', blame me, but the varmints do allus knaw just a day 'fore I does when things be ready, an' they eats the peaches an' necter'ns by night, gouging 'em shameful, same as if you'd done it wi' your nails.' Tis a terrible coorious wall for sow-pigs, likewise for snails; an' I be allus a-gwaine to have en repaired an' pointed, yet somehow 'tedn' done. But your sharp eyes'll be a sight o' use wi' creepin' things. 'Tis a reg'lar Noah's Ark o' a wall, to be sure; not but what I lay theer's five pound worth o' stone fruit 'pon it most years if 'twas let bide."

Joan enjoyed watching the peaches grow. First they peeped

* *Sow-pigs*, wood-lice.

like pearls from the dried frills of their blossoms; then they
expanded and cast off the encumbrance of dead petals, and
nestled against the red bricks that sucked up sunshine, and
held if for them when the sun had gone. She found the garden
wall was a whole busy world, and, taught by her vanished
master, she took interest in all that dwelt thereon. But the
snails and woodlice she slew ruthlessly that her uncle might
presently be the richer.

Mary Chirgwin discovered that the task of reforming her
cousin was like to be lengthy and arduous. There appeared
no foundations upon which to work, and while the certainty of
Barron's return still remained with Joan as a vital guide to
conduct, no other gospel than that which he had taught found
her a listener. She refused to go to church, to Mary's chagrin
and Uncle Sampy's sorrow; but he explained the matter
correctly, and indeed found a clue to most of Joan's actions at
this season. Mary saw the old man's growing love for the new
arrival, and a smaller mind might have sunk to jealousy quickly
enough under such circumstances, but she, deeply concerned
with Joan's eternal welfare, rose above temporal details. At
the same time her uncle's mild and tolerant attitude caused
her pain.

"As to church-gwaine," he said, on a Sunday morning when
he and his elder niece had driven off to Sancreed as usual,
leaving Joan in the orchard, "she've larned to look 'pon it
from a Luke Gosp'ler's pint o' view. Doan't you fret, Polly.
Let her bide. 'Twill come o' itself bime-bye wan o 'these
Sundays. Poor tiby lamb! Christ's a watchin' of her, Polly.
An' if this here gen'leman, by the name o' Mister Jan, doan't
come——"

"You make me daft!" she interrupted, with impatience.
"D'you mean as you ever thot he would?"

"I hopes. Theer's sich a 'mazin' deal o' good hid in human
nature. Mayhap he'm wrastlin' wi' his sawl to this hour. An'
the Lard do allus fight 'pon the side o' conscience. 'Iss fay,
some'ow I do think he'll come."

Mary said no more. She was quite positive that her cousin and her uncle were alike mistaken, but she saw that until the hard truth forced itself upon Joan, the girl would follow her present road. It was not that Joan lacked goodness and sweetness; but, in Mary's opinion, she took a wrong-headed course upon the one vital subject of her own salvation. Mary fought with herself to love Joan, and the battle now was only hard when Joe Noy came within the scope of her thoughts. She banished him as much as she could, but it never grew easy to do so, and the complex problems bred of reflection on this theme maddened her. She had always loved the sailor, and that affection thrust away as deadly sin when he left her for another, could not be wholly strangled now.

Time hung heavily and more heavily with Joan at Drift; but the hope of the ignorant and trustful dies very hard, and that faith which is bred of absolute love has a hundred lives. The girl walked into Penzance every second day, and hope blazed brightly on the road to the post-office, then sank a little deeper into the hidden places of her heart as she plodded empty-handed back to Drift.

Slowly, and so gradually that she herself knew it not, her thoughts grew something less occupied with John Barron, something more concerned about herself. For all the world was full of happy mothers now. One " Brindle "—a knot-cow of repute— dropped a fine bull-calf in a croft hard by the orchard, and Joan looked into Brindle's solemn eyes after the event, and learned. She marvelled to see the little brown calf stand on his shaking legs within an hour of his birth; then his mother licked him lovingly, while Uncle Chirgwin himself drew off her " buzzy milk." There was another mother in a disused pigsty. There Joan found a red-and-white tortoiseshell cat with four blind, squeaking atoms beside her, and as the cat rolled over, and the atoms sucked life, Joan saw her shining eyes, aforetime so bright and hard, full of a new strange light, like the cloud that glimmers over the fires of an opal. The cat's green orbs were full of mystery: of pain past, of joy present. So again Joan learned. But a black tragedy blotted out that happy family in the pigsty, and death, in the shape of Amos Bartlett, Mr. Chirgwin's head man, fell upon them. Then the farmer found that his niece could be angry. One morning Joan met the mother cat running wildly here and there, with a world of misery in its cry; while a moment afterwards she came upon the kittens in a duck-pond. Mr. Bartlett was present, and explained—

"Them chets had to go, missy. 'Tis a auld word, an' it ban't wise to take no count of sayings like that : ' May chets bad luck begets.' You've heard tell o' that? Never let live no kittens born in May. They theer dead chets comed May Day."

"You'm a cruel devil !" she said hotly. "How'd you like for your two li'l childern to be thrawed in the water, May or no May? Look at thicky cat, breakin' her heart, poor twoad !"

Mr. Bartlett was justly angry that Joan could dare to thus class his priceless twins with a litter of dead kittens, and he said more than was desirable, ramming home a truth, and that coarsely.

"Theer's plenty more wheer them comed from, I lay. Nachur's so free, you see—tu free like sometimes. Ban't no dearth o' chets or childern as I've heard on. They comes unaxed, an' unwanted tu. You might 'a' heard tell o' some sich p'raps?"

She grew hot, and shook with passion at this sudden new aspect of affairs. Here was a standpoint from which nobody had viewed her before. Worse—far worse than her father's rage or Uncle Chirgwin's tears was this. Amos Bartlett represented the world's attitude. The world would not be angry with her, or cry for her; it would merely laugh and pass on, like Mr. Bartlett. So Joan learned yet again; and the new knowledge cowed her for full eight-and-forty hours. But the eyes of the mothers had taught Joan something of the secret of pain, and a thread of gravity ran henceforth through all thoughts concerning the future. She much marvelled that "Mister Jan"

had never touched upon this leaf in the book. Beauty was
what he invariably talked about, and he found beauty hidden
in many a strange matter too; but not in pain. That was
because he suffered himself sometimes, Joan suspected. And
yet, to her, pain, though she had never felt it, seemed not
wholly hideous. She surprised herself mightily by the depths
of her own thoughts now. She seemed to stand upon the brink
of deep matters guessing dimly at things hidden. Then her
moods would break again from the clouds to brightness. Hot
sunshine on her cheek always raised her young spirits, and her
health, now excellent, threw joy into life despite the ever-
present anxiety.

Then came a meeting which roused interest and brought
very genuine delight with it.

It happened upon a fine Sunday afternoon, when Joan was
walking through the fields on the farm—those which extended
southwards—that she reached a stile where granite blocks lay
lengthwise, like the rungs of a ladder, between two uprights.
Here she stopped awhile, and sat her down, and looked out over
the promise of fine hay. The undulating green expanse was
studded with the black knobs of ribwort plantain and gemmed
with buttercups, which here were dotted like sparks of fire,
here massed in broad bunches and sheets of colour. The wind
swept over the field, and its course was marked by sudden
flecks and ripples of transient, sheeny light, paler and brighter
than the mass of the herbage. Then a figure appeared afar off,
following the course of the footpath where it wound through the
gold of the flowers and the silver of the bending grasses. It
approached, resolved itself into a fisher-boy, and presently
proved to be Tom Tregenza. Joan ran forward to meet him as
soon as the short figure, with its exaggerated nautical roll,
became known to her. She kissed her half-brother warmly, and
he hugged her and showed great delight at the meeting, for he
loved Joan well.

" I've stealed away, 'cause I was just burstin' to get sight of
'e again, Joan. Faither's home, an' I comed off for a walk,

creepin' round here, an' hopin' as we'd meet. 'Tis mighty wisht
to home now you'm gone, I can tell 'e. I've got a sore head
yet along o' you."

"G'wan, bwoy ! Why should 'e ? "

"'Iss fay ! 'Twas like this. When us comed back from sea
wan mornin' a week arter you'd gone, I ups an' sez, ''Tis
'bout as lively as bad feesh ashore now Joan bain't here.' I
dedn' knaw faither was in the doorway when I said it, 'cause
he'd gived out you was never to be named no more. But mother
seed on, an' sez to me, 'Shut your mouth.' An', not knawin'
faither was be'ind me, I ups agin an' sez, ' Why caan't I, as be
her awn brother, see Joan anyway, an' hear tell what 'tis she've
done? I lay as it bain't no mighty harm neither, 'cause Joan's
true Tregenza ! ' "

" Good Lard !   An' faither heard 'e ? "

"'Iss, an' next minute I knawed it. He blazed an' roared,
'an' comed over an' bummed my head 'pon the ear-hole—a buster
as might killed some lads. My ivers ! I seed stars 'nough to
fill a new sky, Joan, an' I went down tail over nose. I doubt
theer's nobody in Newlyn what can hit like faither. But I got
up agin an' sot mighty still, and faither sez, ' She as was here
ban't no Tregenza, nor my darter, nor nothin' to none under my
hellings * no more—never more, mark that ! ' Then mother
thrawed her apern over her faace an' hollered, 'cause I'd got
such a welt, an' faither walked out in the garden. I was for
axin' mother then, but reckoned not for fear as he might be
listenin' agin. But I knawed you was up Drift, 'cause I heard
mother say that much; an' now I've sot eyes on you agin ; an'
I know you'll tell me what's wrong wi' you, an' if I can do
anything for 'e I will, sink or swim."

"Faither's a cruel beast, an' he'll come to a bad end, Tom,
'spite of they Gosp'lers. He'm all wrong an' doan't knaw
nothin' 'tall 'bout God. I do knaw what I knaw. Theer's
more o' God in that gert shine o' buttercups 'pon the grass than
in all them whey-faced chapel-folks put together."

* *Hellings*, roof.

"My stars, Joan!"

"'Tis truth, an' you'll find 'tis some day, same as what I have."

"I doan't see how any lad be gwaine to get to heaven myself," said Tom, gloomily. "Us had a mining cap'n from Camborne preach this marnin', an', by Golles! 'tweer like sittin' tu near a gert red 'ot fire. Her rubbed it in, I tell 'e, same as you rubs salt into a hake. Faither said 'twas braave talk. But you, Joan, what's wrong with 'e, what have you done?"

"I ain't done no wrong, Tom, an' you can take my word for 't."

"Do 'e reckon you'm damned, like what faither sez?"

"Never! I doan't care a grain o' wheat what faither sez. What I done weern't no sin, 'cause him, as be wiser an' cleverer an' better every way than any man in Carnwall, said 'tweern't; an' he knawed. I've heard wise things said, an' I've minded some an' forgot others. None can damn folks but God, when all's done, an' He's the last as would, for God do love even the creeping, gashly worms under a turned stone tu well to damn 'em. Much more humans. I be a Nature's cheel, an' doan't b'lieve in no devil an' no hell-fire 'tall."

"I wish I was a Nature's cheel, then!"

Joan flung down a little bouquet of starry stitchworts she had gathered upon the way and turned very earnestly to Tom.

"You *be*—you *be* a Nature's cheel. Us all be, but awnly a few knaws it."

Tom laughed at this idea mightily. "Well, I'll slip back-long, Joan; an' if I be a Nature's cheel, I be; but I guess I'll keep it a secret. If I tawld faither I dedn' b'lieve in no auld devil, I guess he'd hurry me into next world so's I might see for myself I were out o' reckoning."

They walked a little way together. Then Tom grew frightened and stopped his companion.

"Guess you'd best to be turnin'. Folks is 'bout everywheer

in the fields, bein' Sunday, an' if it got back to faither as I'd
seed you, he'd make me hop."

"D'you like the sea still, Tom?"

"Doan't I just! Better'n better; an' I be grawin' smart,
'cause I heard faither tell mother so when I was in the wash-
'ouse an' they thot I wasn't. Faither said as I'd got a hawk's
eye for moorin's or what not. An' I licked the bwoy on Pratt's
bwoat a fortnight agone. A lot o' men seed me do 't. I hopes
I'll hit so hard as faither hisself one day, when I'm grawed.
Good-bye, sister Joan. I'll see 'e agin when I can, an' bring up
a feesh maybe. Doan't say nothin' 'bout me to them at the
farm, else it may get back."

So Tom marched off, speculating as to what particular lie
would best meet the case if cross-questioning awaited him on
his return, and Joan watched the thick-set little figure very
lovingly until it was out of sight.

CHAPTER IX.

MEADOWSWEETS.

JUNE came. The wallflowers were long plucked or dead, the last snows of apple-blossom had vanished away, and the fruit was setting well. The wood-lice were already ruining the young nectarines. "They spiles 'em in the growth, an' scores 'em wi' their wicked li'l teeth; then, come August, an' they ripens, they'll begin again. But the peaches they won't touch, now, 'cause of the fur 'pon 'em. Awnly they'll make up for't when the things is ready for eatin'." So Uncle Sampy explained the position to Joan. He, good man, had fulfilled his promise to see Michael Tregenza. It happened that a load of oarweed was wanted on the farm, and Mr. Chirgwin, instead of sending one of the hands with horse and cart to Newlyn, according to his custom when seaweed was needed, went himself. His elder niece expostulated with him, and explained that such a trip would be interpreted to mean straitened circumstances on the farm; but her uncle was not proud, and when he explained that his real object was an opportunity to speak with Joan's father, Mary said no more.

Screwing courage to the sticking point, therefore, the old man went down to Newlyn on a morning when Joan was not by to question his movements. Fortune favoured him. Michael had landed at daylight, and would sail again at dusk. The fisherman listened patiently; but Mr. Chirgwin's inconsequent and sentimental conversation sounded as tinkling brass upon his ear. Both argued the question upon religious grounds, but from an entirely different standpoint. Michael was not at the trouble to talk much, for his visitor seemed scarce worthy of powder and shot. He explained that he deemed it damnation to hold unnecessary converse with sinners; that, by her act, Joan had raised eternal barriers between herself and those of her own home, and, indeed, all chosen people; that he had walked in the light from the dawn of his days until the present time, and could not imperil the souls of his wife, his son, and himself by any further communion with one, in his judgment, lost beyond faintest possibility of redemption. Uncle Chirgwin listened with open mouth to these sentiments. He longed to relate how Joan had repented of her offence, how she had thrown herself upon the Lord, and found peace and forgiveness. No such thing could be recorded, however, and he felt himself at a disadvantage. He prayed for mercy on her behalf; but mercy was a luxury Grey Michael deemed beyond the reach of man. He showed absolutely no emotion upon the subject, and his chill unconcern quenched the farmer's ardour. Mr. Chirgwin mourned mightily that he held not a stronger case. Joan had tied his hands—at any rate, for the present. If she would only come round, accept the truth, and abandon her present attitude, then he knew that he would fight like a giant for her, and that, with right upon his side, he would surely prevail. His last words upon the subject shadowed this conviction.

"Please God, time may soften 'e, Tregenza; an', maybe, soften Joan tu. Her heart's warm yet, an' the truth will find its plaace theer in the Lard's awn time; but you—I doubt 'tedn' in you to change."

"Never, till wrong be right!"

"You makes me sorry for 'e, Tregenza."

"Weep for yourself, Sampson Chirgwin. You'm that contented—an' the contented sawl be allus farthest from God, if you awnly knawed it. Wheer's your fear an' tremblin', too? I've never seed 'e afeared or shaken 'fore the throne 'o the Most High in your life. But I 'sure 'e, thee'll come to it."

"An' you say that! You'm 'mazin' blind, Tregenza, for all you walk in the light! The light's dazed 'e, I'm thinkin', same as birds a-breakin' theer wings 'gainst lighthouse glasses.

You sez you be a worm twenty times a day, an' yet you'm proud enough for Satan purty nigh. If you'm a worm, why doan't 'e act like a worm, an' be humble-minded? 'Tis the li'l childern gets into heaven. You'm stiff-necked, Michael Tregenza. I sez it respectful an' in sorrer; but 'tis true."

"I hope the Lard won't lay thy sin to thy charge, my poor sawl," answered the fisherman, with perfect indifference. "You —you dares to speak agin' me! I wish I could give 'e a hand an' drag 'e a li'l higher up the ladder o' righteousness, Chirgwin; but you'm o' them as caan't dance, or else won't, not if God A'mighty's Self piped to 'e. Go your ways, an' knaw you'm in the prayers of a man whose prayers be heard."

"Then pray for Joan. If you'm so cocksure you gets a hearin' 'fore us church-folks, 'tis your fust duty to plead for her."

"It was," he said. "Now it is too late. I've sweated for her, an' wrastled wi' principalities an' powers for her, an' filled the night watches by sea an' shore wi' gert agonies o' prayer for her. But 'tweern't to be. Her name's writ in the big Book o' Death, not the small Book o' Life. David prayed hard till that cheel, got wrong side the blanket, died. Then he washed his face an' ate his meat. 'Twas like that wi' me. Joan's dead now. 'Let the dead bury theer dead.'"

"'Tis awful to hear 'e, Tregenza."

"The truth's a awful thing, Chirgwin, but a lie is awfuller still. 'Tis the common fate to be lost. You, an' sich as you, caan't grasp the truth 'bout that. Heaven's no need to be a big plaace—theer edn' gwaine to be no crowdin' theer. 'Tis hell as'll fill space wi' its roominess."

"I be gwaine," answered Mr. Chirgwin. "Us have talked three hour by the clock, an' us ain't gotten wan thot in common. I trusts in Christ; you trusts in yourself. Time'll shaw which was right. You damn the world; I wouldn't damn a dew-snail.* I awnly sez again, 'May you live to see all the pints you'm wrong.' An' if you do, 'twill be a tidy big prospect."

* Dew-snail, a slug.

They exchanged some further remarks in a similar strain. Then Tom informed Uncle Chirgwin that his cart, with a full load of oarweed, was waiting at the door. Whereupon the old man got his hat, loaded his pipe, wished Thomasin good-bye, and drove sorrowfully away. Mrs. Tregenza had secretly inquired after Joan's health and wealth. That the first was excellent, the second carefully put away in a lawyer's hands, caused her satisfaction. She told Mr. Chirgwin to make Joan write out a will.

"You never knaws," she said. "God keep the gal, but they do die now an' agin. 'Tweer better she wrote about the money 'cordin' to a lawyer's way. And say, for the Lard's love, not to leave it to Michael. So well light a fire wi' it as that. He bawled out as the money had lit a fire a'ready when I touched 'pon it to en—a fire as was gwaine to burn through eternity; but Michael's not like a human. His ideas 'pon affairs is all pure Bible. You and me caan't grasp hold o' all he says. An' the money's done no wrong. So you'll drop in Joan's ear as it might be worldly-wise to save trouble by sayin' what should be done if anything ill falled 'pon her—eh?"

Uncle Chirgwin promised that he would do so; and Mrs. Tregenza felt a weight off her mind which had distressed it for some while. She was thinking of Tom, of course. She knew that Joan loved him; and though the prospect of his ever coming by a penny of the money appeared slender, yet to know that he might be in a will, named for hundreds of pounds, was a shadowy sort of joy to her.

That night Joan's uncle told the girl of his afternoon's work, and she expressed some sorrow that he should have thus exerted himself on her behalf.

"Faither's dirt beside the likes of you," she said. "'Twas wastin' good time to talk to en. An' I wouldn't go back to Newlyn, you mind, if he was to ax me 'pon his knees. I'm a poor fool of a gal, but I knaws enough to laugh at the ignorance o' faither an' that fiddle-faaced crowd to the Luke Gospel chapel."

"Doan't o' be bitter, Joan. Us all makes mistakes, an' bad's the best o' human creatures. Your faither will chaange, sure as I'm a livin' man, some day. God ban't gwaine to let en go down to 's graave wi' sich a 'mazin' number o' wrong opinions. Else think o' the wakin' t'other side! 'Iss, it caan't be. Why, as 'tis, if he died sudden, he'd go marchin' into heaven as bold as brass, an' bang up to the right hand o' the throne! Theer's a situation for a body! An' the awk'ardness o' havin' to step forrard an' tell en to take a back plaace! No, no; the man'll be humbled, sure, 'fore his journey's end. Theer's Everlasting eyes 'pon en, think as you may."

"I never think at all about him," declared Joan, "an' I ban't gwaine to. He won't change, an' I never wants en to. I've got you to love me an' to love; an' I'm—I'm waitin' for wan as be gold to faither's dross."

She sighed as she spoke.

"Waitin' for en still?"

"Ay, for Mister Jan. It caan't be no gert length o' time now. I s'pose days go quicker up Lunnon town than wi' us."

"Joan, my dovey, 'tis idle. Even I sees it now. I did think wi' you fust as he was a true man. I caan't no more. I wish I could."

A month before Joan would have flashed into anger at such a speech as this, but now she did not answer. Young love is fertile in imagination. She had found a thousand glories in John Barron, and, when he left her, had woven a thousand explanations for his delayed return. Now invention grew dull; enthusiasm waned; her confidence was shaken, though she denied the fact, even to herself, as a sort of treachery. But there is no standing still in time. The remorseless fact of his non-return extended over weeks and months.

Mr. Chirgwin saw her silence, noted the little quiver of her mouth as he declared his own loss of faith, stroked the hand she thrust dumbly into his, and felt her silence hurt his heart.

Presently Joan spoke. "I've got none to b'lieve in en no more, then—not wan now—not even you. Whiles you stuck up for en, I felt braave 'bout his comin'; now—now Mister Jan have awnly got me to say a word for en. An' you doan't think he'm a true man no more, then, uncle?"

"Lassie, I wish to God as I did. Time's time. Why ban't he here?"

"I doan't dare think this be the end, uncle. I'm feared to look forrard now. If it do wance come 'pon me as he've gone, 'twill drive me mad, I knaws."

"No; never; not if you'd awnly turn your faace the right way. Theer's oceans o' comfort an' love waitin' for 'e, gal. You did belong to a hard world, as I knaws who have just comed from speech wi' your faither; but 'twas a world o' clean eatin' an' dressin' and livin'—a God-fearin' world, leadin' up'ards on a narrer, ugly road, but a safe road, I s'pose. An' you left it. You'll say I be harsh, but my heart do bleed for 'e, Joan. If you'd awnly drop this talk 'bout Nature, as none of us understands, an' turn to the living Christ, as all can understand. That's wheer rest lies for 'e, nowheers else. You'm like Eve in the garden. She was kindiddled an' did eat, an' lost eternal life, an' had to quit Eden. An' 'tis forbidden fruit as you've ate, not knawin' 'twas sich. Nature doan't label her pisins, worse luck?"

"Eve? No, I bain't no Eve. She had Adam."

There was a world of sorrow in the words, and the hopeless ring in them startled Uncle Sampy, for it denoted greater changes in the girl's mind than he thought existed. She seemed nearer to the truth. It cut his heart to see her suffering; but he thanked Heaven that the inevitable knowledge was coming, and prayed it might be the first step towards peace. He was silent with his thoughts, and Joan spoke again, repeating her last words.

"'Iss; Eve had Adam to put his arm around her an' kiss her wet eyes. He were more to her than what the garden was, I'll lay—or God either. That's the bitter black God o' my faither. What for did He let the snake in the garden 'tall, if He really loved them fust, poor fools? Why dedn' He put they flamin' angels theer sooner. 'Twas the snake they should 'a' watched an' kep' out."

Tho farmer looked at her with round terrified eyes. Sho had never echoed Barron's sentiments to such a horrified listener.

"Doan't, for pity's sake, Joan! The wickedness of it! Him as taught you to think such frightful thoughts tried to ruin your sawl so well as your body. Oh, if you'd awnly up an' say, 'That man was wrong, an' I'll forget en an' turn to the Saviour.'"

"You caan't understan'. I do put ugly bits o' thot afore 'e, but if you'd heard him as opened my eyes, you'd knaw tedn' ugly taken altogether. I knaws so much, but caan't speak it out. Us done no sin, an' I ban't shamed to look the sun in tho faace, nor you. An' he *will* come—he will—if theer's a kind God in heaven he'll come back to me. If 'e doan't, then I'll say that faither's God's the right wan."

"Doan't 'e put on a bold front, Joan gal. Theer's things tu deep for the likes o' us. You ban't prayin' right, I reckon. Theer's a voice hid in you. Listen to that. Nature's spawk to 'e, an' now 'er's dumb. Listen to t'other, lassie. Nature do guide beasts an' birds an' the poor herbs o' the field; but you— you listen to t'other. You'll never be happy no more till you awns 'twas a sad mistake, an' do ax in tho right plaace for pardon."

"I want no pardon," she said. "I have done no wrong, I tell 'e. Wheer's justice to? 'Cause the man do bide away, I be wicked; if he comed back to-morrow an' married me—what then? I be sinless in the matter of it, an' Nature do knaw it, an' God do knaw it."

But her breast heaved and her eyes were wet with unshed tears. Uncle Chirgwin, her solitary trust and stand-by, had drifted away too. His hope was dead, and she could not revive it. He had never spoken so strongly before, but now he was taking up Mary's line of action, and had ranged himself against her. It almost seemed to Joan that he reflected in a meek, diluted fashion, as the moon turns tho sun's golden fire to silver, something of what he must have heard that afternoon from her father. This defection acted definitely on the girl's temperament. She fought fear, hardened her heart against doubt, cast suspicion far away as treason to " Mister Jan," and gave to hope a new lease of life. She would be patient for his sake, she would trust in him still. There was something grand in the loneliness, she told herself. He would know perhaps one day of her great patient faith and love. And the trial would make her brain and heart bigger, and better fit her for the position of wife to him. The struggle was fought by her with that courage which lies beyond man's comprehension. She looked at the world with bright eyes when there was necessity for facing it; she exhausted her ingenuity in schemes for communicating with John Barron. If he only knew! She felt that even had absence darkened his affection for her, yet, most surely, the thought of the baby must tempt him back again. Thus, with sustained bravery and ignorance, she left her hand in Nature's, and her faith, rising gloriously above the doubt of the time, trusted that majestic heaen goddess with her little destiny.

Fate played another prank upon her not long afterwards and thrust into her hands a possible means of access to John Barron. A favourite resort of Joan's was the brook which ran down the valley beneath Drift and Sancreed. The little stream wound through a fair coomb between orchards, meadows, wastes of fern and heather. At this season of the year the valley was very lonely, and a certain spot beside the stream often tempted Joan by reason of its comfort and its peace. From here, sitting on a granite boulder, clothed in soft green mosses, and having a shape into which human limbs might fit easily, the girl could see much that was fair. The meadows were all sprinkled with the silver-mauve of cuckoo-flowers—Shakespeare's " lady's smock ; " the hills sloped upwards under oaken saplings as yet too young for the stripping; the valley stretched winding landward beneath Sancreed ; and far away extended the Cornish moors, dotted with man's mining enterprises, chiefly deserted. There Ding-Dong raised its gaunt engine-stack, and,

distant though it was, Joan's sharp eyes could see the rusty arm
of iron stretching forth from the brickwork, motionless, not
worth the removing. Close at hand, where the stream wandered
babbling at her feet, the whole glory of new-born June shone
in blossoms and grasses where the world of the stream-side sent
forth a warm living smell. The wildness of the upland moors
stretched down into the valleys below them. There glimmered
blue-green patches of bracken, speckled with the red and white
hides of calves which fed and scampered dew-lap deep; and the
fern was all silvered with light where the sunshine brightened
its polished leaves. The stream wound through the midst
bedecked and adorned with purple bugle flowers, bridged with
dog-roses and honeysuckles, in festoons, in bunches and in
sprays, crowned with scented gorse, fringed with yellow irises
which splashed flaming reflections where the brook widened and
slowed into shallow little backwaters. Flags and cresses
framed the margins; meadowsweets made the air fragrant
above, and granite boulders fretted the water's crystal, their
foundations hidden in dark weeds. Sunshine danced on every
tiny cascade and threw stars and twinkling flashes of reflected
light upward from the brown pools on to the banks. Everything was upon a miniature scale, even to the trout which lived
in the stream, flashed their dim shadows under its waters
leapt into the air after the flies, set little clouds of sand
shimmering as they darted up and down, or, when surprised,
wriggled away into favourite holes and hiding places beneath
the banks and trailing weeds. Ling and wortleberry, too, were
moorland visitors in the valley, and the bog-heather already
budded.

Here was one of the many favourite resting-places of Joan,
and hither she came on a sunny morning at the wish of another
person.

Uncle Sampy had set his niece a task, and the object of
her present visit was no mere dawdling and thinking while
perched upon the granite throne above the meadowsweets.
This fact a basket and a three-pronged fork indicated. Her

uncle deemed himself an authority on simples, and possessed much information, mostly erroneous, concerning the properties of wild herbs and flowers. A decoction of hemp agrimony he at all times considered a most valuable bitter tonic; and the flesh-coloured flowers of this plant grew pretty freely on their long green stems by the stream-side in the valley. The time of blossoming was not yet come, but Joan knew the dull leaf of the herb well enough, and, that found, she could easily dig up the root, wherein its virtue dwelt. But before starting on her search, the girl rested awhile where the serrated foliage and creamy blossom of the meadowsweets laced and fringed the granite of her couch.

And, as she sat there, her eye taking in the happy valley, her brain reading into the luxuriant life of nature some strange new thoughts hidden until lately, she became suddenly conscious of a phenomenon beyond her power to immediately explain or understand. It drove the hemp agrimony quite out of her head, and, when the mystery came to be explained, filled Joan's mind with the memory of her own sad affairs. First, and repeatedly, there glimmered a gossamer over the stream, falling into the water and as often rising again; then above the film of light flashed another, rising abruptly golden into the sunshine. Not for a moment or two did she discover the flashing thing was a fly-rod, but presently the man who held it appeared below her at a bend of the stream. He was clad much like the artists, and it made the blood flush hot to her cheek as she thought he might be one. Young men sometimes fished the brook for the fingerling trout it contained. They were small, but sweet, and the catching of them with a fly was difficult work in a stream so overhung with tangles of bine and briar, so densely planted in the wider reaches with rushes, water-hemlock and lesser weeds. This fisherman, at any rate, found successful sport beyond his power to achieve. He flogged away, but hung his fly clear of the stream at every second cast, and deceived not the smallest troutlet of them all. The young man, after the manner of those anglers classified as " chuck and chance it," worked his clumsy way towards Joan's chair on the granite boulder. Motionless she sat, and her drab attire and faded sun-bonnet harmonized so well with the tones around it— the grey of the stones, the lights of the river, the masses of the meadowsweet—that while noting a broad and sparkling stickle winding away beneath her, the angler missed the girl herself. This stickle spread, with an oily tremor and white under-current full of air pearls, from a waterfall where the foot of Joan's throne fretted the stream. Below it the waters slowed and ran smoothly into dark brown shadows, being here marked by the wrinkled lines of their currents and splashed with the sky's reflected blue.

An ideal spot for a trout it doubtless was, and the sportsman exercised unusual care in his approach, crouching along the bank and finally creeping, bent double, within casting distance. Then, as he freed his fly, he saw Joan, like a queen of the pool, reigning motionless and silent. She suddenly moved, and no fish was now likely to rise within the visual radius of her action. Thereupon the angler in the man cursed; the artist in him drew a short, sharp breath. He scrambled to his feet and looked again upon a beautiful picture. The plump, baby freshness of Joan's face had vanished indeed; but, in her seated position, no tangible suggestion of a hidden life was thrust upon the spectator's view. He only saw a wondrously pretty woman in a charming attitude amidst objects which enhanced her beauty by their own. She seemed a trifle pale for a cottage girl, but her mouth was scarlet and dewy as ripe wood-straw-berries; her eyes were just of that colour where the blue sky above was reflected and changed to a slightly darker shade by the pools of the brook. She sat with her hands folded in her lap, and looked straight at the sportsman with a frank interest which surprised him. He was a modest lad, but the sudden presentment of an object so lovely woke his pluck, and he fished ostentatiously to Joan's very feet, suspecting that the absurdity of the action would not be apparent to her. She watched the morsel of feather and fur dragged across the water after the fantastic fashion of the " chuck and chance it " angler, and he, when her eyes were on the water, kept his own fast upon her face.

Both man and woman were profoundly anxious each to hear the other's voice, but neither felt brave enough to speak first. Then the artist's ingenuity found a means, and Joan presently saw his fly stick fast upon the side of the stream where she sat. The thing was caught at the seed-head of a rush within reach of Joan's hand, and while this incident appeared absolutely accidental, yet it was not so, for the artist had long been endeavouring to get fast somewhere hard by Joan. Now, finding his manœuvre accomplished, he made but the feeblest efforts to loosen the fly, then raised his hat and accosted her.

" Might I trouble you to set my line clear? Ashamed to ask such a thing, but it would be awfully kind. Oh, thank you, thank you. Take care of your fingers! The hook is very sharp."

Joan got the fly free in a moment, and then, to Harry Murdoch's gratification, addressed him. The young fellow was Edmund Murdoch's cousin, and at present dwelt in Newlyn with the elder artist, already mentioned as John Barron's friend.

" May I make so bold as to ax if you do knaw a paintin' gen'leman by name o'—o' Mister Jan? Leastways, that's wan on's names, but I never can call home the other, though ho tawld me wance. He was here last early spring-time, an' painted a gert picture of me up 'pon top the hill they call Gorse Point."

" Lucky devil," thought the artist, but though he knew something of Barron and his work, and had heard that Barron painted when at Newlyn, he did not associate these facts with the girl before him.

" He'm in Lunnon so far's I know," she continued.

Harry Murdoch had to look hard at Joan before answering, and he delayed a while with an expression of deep thought upon his face. At length he spoke.

" No, I cannot say that I have heard of him or the picture.

But perhaps some of the men in Newlyn will know. He was lucky to get you to paint. I wish you would let me try."

She shook her head impatiently. "No, no. He done it 'cause—'cause he just wanted a livin' thing to fill up a bit o' his canvas. 'Tweern't for shaw or for folks to see; he done it for pleasure. An' I wants to knaw wheer he lives, 'cause he might think I be in Newlyn still; but I ban't. I'm livin' up Drift along wi' Mr. Chirgwin; an' I wish he could knaw it."

"He was called 'Mister John'? Well, I'll see what I can do to find out anything about him. And your name?"

"Joan Tregenza. If you'll be so good as to put a question round 'mongst the painting gen'leman, I'd thank 'e kindly."

"Then I certainly will; and on Saturday next I'll come here again to tell you if I have heard anything. Will you come?"

"'Iss, fay; an' thank you, sir."

So he passed slowly forward, and she sat a full hour after he had left her building new castles on the old crumbling foundations. It was even in her mind to pray, to pray with her whole heart and soul; but chaos had settled like a storm upon her beliefs. She did not know where to pray to now; yet to-day Hope once more glimmered like a lighthouse lamp through the dreary darkness. So she turned her eyes to that radiance and waited for next Saturday to come.

Then she set about grubbing up roots of hemp agrimony where they grew. She was almost happy, and whistled gently to herself as she filled her little basket.

That night Edmund Murdoch heard his cousin's story, and explained that "Mister Jan" was doubtless John Barron.

"I'm owing the beggar a letter. I'll write to-morrow."

"Was it a good picture?"

"I should say that few better ever went out of Newlyn. Is the model as pretty as ever?"

Young Harry raved of the vision that Joan had presented among the meadowsweets.

"Well, I suppose he wouldn't mind her knowing where he lives; but he's such a queer devil that I'll write and ask him first. We shall hear in a couple of days. I can tell him her address, at any rate; then he may write direct to her, if he cares to."

CHAPTER X.

TWO LETTERS.

Four days elapsed, and then Edmund Murdoch received an answer to his letter. He had written at length upon various affairs, and his friend did no less.

> "No. 6, Melbury Gardens, S.W.,
> "8 June, 189—.

" DEAR MURDOCH,

" Your long screed gave me some pleasure and killed half-an-hour. You relate the even course of your days since my departure from Cornwall, and I envy the good health and happy contentment of mind which your note indicates. I gained no slight benefit from my visit to the West Country, and it had doubtless carried me bravely through this summer but for an unfortunate event. A sharp cold, which settled on my chest, has laid me low for some length of time, though I am now as well again as I shall ever be. So much for facing the night air in evening dress. Nature has no patience with our idiotic conventions, and hates man's shirt-front and woman's bare bosom alike when displayed, as is our imbecile custom, at the most dangerous hours in the twenty-four. My doctors are for sending me away, and I shall probably follow their advice presently. But the end is not very far off.

" I rejoice that you have sucked in something of my spirit, and are trying to get at the heart of rocks and sea before you paint them. Men waste so much time poking about in art galleries, like the blind moles they mostly are, and forget that Nature's art gallery is open every day at sunrise. Dwell much

in the air; glean the secrets of dawns; listen when the white
rain whispers over woodland; translate the tinkle of summer
seas where they kiss your rocky shores. Get behind the sunset;
think not of what colours you will mix when you try to paint
it, but let the pageant sink into your soul like a song. Do not
drag your art everywhere. Forget it sometimes, and develop
your individuality. You have learned to draw tolerably; now
learn to think. Believe me, the painting people do not think
enough.

"Truly, I am content to die in the face of the folly I read
and see around me. Know you what certain obscure writers
are now about in magazines? They are vindicating the cosmic
forces, whitewashing Mother Nature after Huxley's Romanes
lecture! He told the truth, and Nature loved him for it; but
now come hysterical religious ciphers who squeak boldly forth
in print that Nature is the mother of altruism, that self-sacrifice
is her first law! One genius observes that 'tis their cruelty
and selfishness have arrested the progress of the tiger and the
ape! Poor Nature! Never a word of shot-guns in all this
drivel, of course. Cruelty and selfishness! Qualities purely
and solely human—qualities resulting from conscious intelligence alone. You and I are selfish, not the ape; you and I are
cruel, not the tiger. He at least learns Nature's lesson, and
obeys her dictates; we never do, and never shall. A plague
upon these fools with their drivel, built on theologic rubbish
heaps. They would prostitute the very founts of reason, and
make Nature's eternal circle fit the little squares of their own
faiths. Man! I tell you that the root of human misery might
be pulled out and destroyed to-morrow like the fang of a
decayed tooth, if only Reason could kill these weeds of falsehood
which choke civilization and strangle religion. But the world's
' doors ' have all got 'faith' (or pretend to it); the world's
thinkers are mere shadows moving about in the background of
active affairs. They only write and talk. Action is the sole
way of chaining a nation's mind.

"Your Churchman is active enough; hence the spread of

that poison which keeps human reason stunted, impotent, anæmic. Take Liberty—the cursed *ignis fatuus* our dear poets have shrieked for, our preachers have prayed for, our patriots have perished for through all time. In pursuit of this rainbow-gold more blood and brains have been wasted than would have sufficed to make a nation. And yet a breath from Reason blows the thing to tatters, as an uprising wind annihilates a fog. Freedom is an attribute of the Eternal, and creation cannot share it with Him, any more than it can share His throne with Him. ' The liberty of the subject ! ' A contradiction in terms. Banish this unutterable folly of freedom, and control the breeding of human flesh as we control the output of beef and mutton. Then the face of the world will alter. Millions of money is annually spent in order that mindless humanity, congenital lunatics and madmen, may be fed and housed and kept alive. Their existences are to themselves less pleasurable than that of the beasts; they are a source of agony to those who have borne them ; but they live to old age, and devour tons of good food, while wholesome intellects starve in the gutters of every big city. Banish this cant of freedom. The lightning in heaven is not free; the stars are not free ; Nature herself is the created slave of the Great Will—and *we* prattle about liberty. Let the State look to it and practise these lessons Nature has taught and still preaches patiently to deaf ears. Let it be as penal to bring life into the world without permission from authority as it is to put life out of the world. Let the begetting of paupers be a crime ; let the health and happiness of the community rise higher than the satisfaction of individuals ; let the self-denial practised by the reasonable few be made a legal necessity to the unreasonable many. Let the blighted, the malformed, the brainless, go back to the earth from which they came. Let the world of humanity be cleansed and sweetened and purified as Nature cleanses and sweetens and purifies her own kingdom. She removes her failures ; we put ours under glass and treat them like hot-house flowers, That is called humanity. It is the mad leading the mad. . . . But why waste your time? Nature will have the last word; Reason must win in the end. A genius, at once thinker and doer, will some day appear and set the world right, at a happy moment when the din of theologists is out of its ears. We want a new practical religion, for Christianity, distorted and twisted through the centuries into its present outworn, effete, ignoble shape, is a mere political force or a money-making machine, according to the genius of the country which professes it. The golden key of the founder, which is lost, may be found again, but I think it never will be."

[Here the man elaborated his opinions. They were like himself—a medley, a farrago, wherein acerbity, acuteness, and a mind naturally philosophic were stranded in the arid deserts of a pessimism bred partly from his own decaying physical circumstances, and partly from recognition of his own wasted time.]

"I do not suppose that I shall paint any more. I had my Cornish picture brought from its packing-case and framed, and supported on a great easel at the foot of my bed while I was stricken down last month. Mistress Joan eyed me curiously from under her hand, and through the night-watches, while my man snored in the next chamber and I tossed with great unrest, the girl seemed to live and move and smile at me under the flicker of the night-lamp. Everybody is pleased to say that 'Joe's Ship' seems good to them. I have it now in the studio and contrasted it yesterday with my bathing negresses from Tobago. I think I like it better. It is difficult to read the soul in black faces, especially when the models are freezing to death as mine were. But there is something near to soul in this painted Joan—more I doubt than the living reality would be found to possess to-day. She was a good girl, all the same, and I am gratified to hear she did not quite forget me. I have written to her at the address you mention. They pester me to send the picture somewhere, and to stop their importunities— especially the women—I have promised to let the thing go to the Institute in the autumn. I shall doubtless change my mind before the time comes.

"My life slowly but surely dwindles to that mere battle with Death which your consumptive wages at the finish. I fancy Biskra will see my bones later in the year. The R.A. took not less than six months off my waning days this spring. Thank God they hung Brady as he deserved. Perhaps twenty good works I saw—'the rest is silence.'

"Yours, while I remain,

"JOHN BARRON."

It was true that the artist had written another letter addressed to Joan Tregenza at Drift. He had written it first—written it hurriedly, wildly on the spur of the moment. But after the completion of his communication to Murdoch, the mood of the man changed. He had coldly read again the former epistle, and altered his mind concerning it. Barron wanted Joan back again sometimes, if life dragged more than usual, but pens and paper generally modified his desire when he got that far towards calling her to him. Her memory tickled him pleasantly, and whiled away time. He framed the various sketches he had made of her and suffered thought to occupy itself with her as with no other woman who had entered his life. But the day on which he wrote to Murdoch was a good one with him. He felt stronger and better able to suck pleasure out of living than he had for a month.

"When I whistle she will come," he thought to himself. "Perhaps there would be some pleasure in taking her to Biskra presently. I will wait, at any rate, until nearer the last scene. She would be pretty to look at when I'm dying. Yes, she shall close my eyes some day, if she likes. That's a pleasant thought—for me."

So the letter to Murdoch was sent forth, but the letter to Joan, containing some poetic thoughts on Nature, a pathetic description of Barron's enfeebled state, and an appeal to her to join him that they might part no more on this side of the grave, was torn up. He laughed at the trouble he had wasted, then pondered pleasantly on the picture which Murdoch had drawn of Joan ruling the kingdom of the meadowsweets, and of her eager question concerning " Mister Jan."

"Strange," he reflected, " that her mediocre intelligence should have clung to a man so outwardly mean as myself. If I thought that she had remembered half I said when I was with her, or had made a single attempt to practise the gospel I preached so finely, I would have her back again to-morrow, and be proud of her too. But it can't be. She was such an absolute fool. No, I much fear she only desires to find out what has become of the goose who laid the big golden egg. Or if she doesn't, perhaps her God-fearing father and mother do."

Which conclusion is not uninteresting, for it illustrates the usual failure of materialism to gauge those mental possibilities which lie hidden even within the humblest and worst equipped intelligences. John Barron was an able man in some respects, but his knowledge of Joan Tregenza had taught him nothing concerning her character and its latent powers of development.

CHAPTER XI.

DISENCHANTMENT.

With summer, Nature, proceeding on her busy way, approached again the annual phenomena of seed-time and harvest. To Joan, as spring had brought with it a world of mothers, so the subsequent season filled Nature with babies; and, in the light of all this new-born life, the mothers suffered a change. Now, sorrow-guided, did Joan begin to read under the face of things, "to get behind the sunset," as Barron had said in his letter to Murdoch; to realize a little of the secret hidden in green leaves and swelling fruits and ripening grain; to observe the presence of mystery, though she could not translate more than an occasional manifestation thereof. She found much matter for wonder and for fear. Visible Nature had grown to be a curtain, behind which raged eternal struggles for life. Every leaf sheltered a tragedy, every bough was a battle-field. The awful frailty of existence began to dawn upon Joan Tregenza, and the discovery left her helpless, lonely, longing for new gods. She knew not where to turn. Any brightness from any source had been welcome then.

Disenchantment came with the second visit of the artist to the stream. There young Murdoch had met her, and told her that "Mister Jan" was going to write her a letter. Upon which she had sung glad songs in a sunlit world, and amazed Mary and Uncle Chirgwin alike by the exhibition of a sudden and profound happiness. But the longed-for letter never came. Weeks passed by; the truth rolled up over her life at last, and, as a world seen in a blaze of sunshine only dazzles

us and conceals its facts under too much light, but reveals the
same clear-cut and distinct at dawn or early twilight, so now
Joan's eyes, obscured no more by the blinding promise of
great joy, began to see her world as it was, her future as it
would be.

Strange thoughts came to her on an evening when she
stood by the door of the kitchen at Drift, waiting for the cart
to return from market. It was a cool, grey gloaming, wreathed
in diaphanous mists born of past rain. These rendered every
outline of tree and building vague and immense. Where Joan
stood, the peace of the time was broken only by a gentle
dripping from the leaves of a great laurel by the gate which
led from the farmyard to the fields. Below it moist ground
was stamped with the trident impress of many fowls' feet; and
now and then a feather sidled down from the heart of the ever-
green, where poultry, black and white and spangled, were
settling to roost. A subdued clucking and fluttering marked
their hidden perches; then came showers of raindrops from
the shining leaves as a bird mounted to a higher branch; after
which silence fell again.

And Joan found all hope fairly dead at last. There and
then, in the misty evening-tide, the fact fell on the ear of her
heart, as though one had spoken it; and henceforth she dated
disenchantment from that hour. The whole pageant of her
romance, with the knightly figure of the painter that filled its
foreground, shrivelled to a scroll no bigger than a curled, dead
leaf—sere, wasted, ghostly, and light enough to be washed
away on a tear, borne away upon a sigh.

Then there followed for her prodigious transformations in
the panorama of Nature. Seen from the standpoint of his
great overwhelming lie to her, the philosophy which this man
had professed changed in its appearance, and that mightily.
He had used his cleverness like a net to trap her, and now,
though she could not prove his words untrue, save in one particular, yet that crowning act of faithlessness much tended to
vitiate all the beauties of imagination which had gone before it,

They were lilies grown from a dung-heap. Looking back in the new cold side-light, her life came out clearly, with all the colour gone from it and the remorseless details distinct. And in this survey Nature dwindled to a minor deity, a goddess with moods as many and whims as wild as a woman's. She was unstable, it seemed to Joan then; the immemorial solidity and splendour of her had departed; her eyes were not fixed on Heaven any more, nor did peace any longer rest within them—they were frightened, terrified, and their wild and furtive glances followed one Shadow, reflected one Shape. It stood waiting at the end of all her avenues; it peered from the heart of her forests; it wandered on her heaths and moors; it lay under the stones in her rivers; it stalked her seashores, floated on her waves, rode upon her lightning, hid in her four winds;—and the Shadow's name was Death. Joan stood face to face with it at last, and gazed round-eyed at a revelation.

She was saddened to find her own story told by Nature in so many allegories—painted upon the garden, set forth in waste places, fashioned by humble weeds, reflected in the small, brief lives of unconsidered creatures. Now she imagined herself an ill-shaped apple in the orchard, which the mother of all had neglected; it was crumpled up on one side, twisted out of its fair, full beauty, ruined by some wicked influence—a failure. Now she was a fly, caught by the gold spider who set his web shaking to deceive. Now she was a little bird, singing one moment, the next crawling dazed and shaking under the paw of a cat. Why should Nature make the strong her favourites, and be so cruel to the weak? That seemed an ungodly thing to Joan. She had only reached this point. She had no inkling of the great cleansing process which removes the dross, the eternal competition from which only the cleanest and sweetest and best come forth first. She saw the battle, indeed, but did not understand the meaning of it any more than the rest of the world which, in the words of the weakling Barron, beneath the emblems of a false humanity, keeps its weeds under hot-house glasses, and, out of mercy to futile individuals, does

terribly wrong its communities. Our cleansing processes are
only valuable so far as they go hand in hand with Nature, and
where the folly of many fools rejects the wisdom of the wise,
there Nature has her certain revenge sooner or later. The sins
of the State are visited on the children of the State; and those
who repeal laws which Science, walking hand in hand with
Nature, has advocated; those who refuse laws which Science,
Nature-taught, urges upon Power, do not, indeed, suffer themselves, but commit thousands of others to suffering. So false
sentiment in effect poisons the blood-springs of a nation.
Religion leads to these disasters, and any religion answerable
for gigantic human follies is either false or most falsely
comprehended.

Her uncle still tarried, and Joan, weary of waiting, betook
herself and her sorrows to the old garden, there to view a
spectacle which she never tired of. She watched the evening
primroses, saw their green bud-cases spring open, and the soft,
yellow leaves tremble out like butterflies new come from the
chrysalis. She loved these little lemon-coloured lamps, that
twinkled anew at every sundown in the green twilight of the
garden. She knew their eyes would watch through the night,
and that their reward would be death. Many shrivelled
fragments marked the old blossoms on the long stems, but
the crowns of each still put out new buds, and every dusk saw
the wakening of fresh blossoms, heedless of their dead sisters
below.

"They was killed 'cause they looked at the sun," thought
Joan. "I suppose the moon be theer mistress, an' they should
not chaange their god. Yet it do seem hard like to be scorched
to death for lookin' upward."

What she saw now typified in a dead flower was her own
case under a new symbol; but the girl wasted no anger on the
man who had played with her to make a holiday pleasant, on
that mock sun whose light now turned to darkness. Her mind
was occupied entirely with pity for herself. And that fact
probably promised to be a sure first step to peace. The lonely

void of her life must be filled, else Joan was like to go mad; and the filling, left to Faith, might yet be happily accomplished. For Faith, if no more than a "worm with diamond eyes," yet has eyes of diamonds, and rainbows are the arches of her shape. Faith is fair, and a very heart-companion to those who know her and love her courts; and Joan, of all others, was best endowed by disposition and instinct for the possession of her. Faith had slept in the girl's heart since her mother died; but, sleeping, had grown, and now waited in all strength to be called to a great task. The void was at its deepest just now; the lowest note of Joan's soul had sounded; the facts of her ruin and desertion were fully accepted at last; and such knowledge served even to turn the growing mother in her sour for a time. Maternal instinct stood still just a little while at this point in the girl's inner life; then, when all things whirled away to chaos; on this night, when nothing remained sure for her but death; in her hour of ultimate, unutterable weakness and at the dawn of blank despair, came one last plea from Uncle Chirgwin. Mary had given up talking, fairly wearied out, and convinced that to waste more words on Joan would be a culpable disposal of time; but Mr. Chirgwin blundered doggedly on with the humility of a worm and the obstinacy of a friendly dog. He hammered at the portals of Joan's spiritual being with admirable pertinacity; and at length he had his reward. Faith in something is an absolute and vital essential to the welfare of every woman, and Joan Tregenza was no exception to the rule.

It fell out, on the night of her uncle's weekly visit to market, that Joan had just left the garden, when she heard the clatter of the spring cart. It drew up at the kitchen door, and Mary alighted with Mr. Chirgwin. The baskets that had started laden with eggs, butter, and other produce came back empty, save for a few brown paper parcels. Exceptional prices had ruled in the market-place that day, so Mr. Chirgwin and his niece returned home in excellent temper.

They all met at supper, together with those farm-servants

who took their meals at their master's table. Then the labourers and the women-workers withdrew; Mary sat down to a little sewing before bedtime; and Mr. Chirgwin smoked his pipe and looked at Joan. He noticed that the weather reflected much upon her moods. She was more than usually silent to-night, despite the bright news from market.

Presently Mary put on the kettle, and brought out a bottle of rum. Her uncle had taken his nightcap of spirit and water from her hand for nearly ten years, and the little duty of preparing it was dear to her. She also made cups of tea for Joan and herself. Mary often blamed herself for this luxury, and only allowed it on the night that ended those arduous duties proper to market-day. While thus employed, both she and Uncle Sampy tried to draw Joan out of her gloomy silence.

"Theer's to be a braave sight o' singin' down to Penzance come next week, Joan. Lunnon folks, they tell me, wi' names a foot tall stuck 'pon the hoardings. Us thot 'twould be a pleasin' kind o' junketin' to go an' listen. Not but entertainments o' singin' by night be mighty exciting to the blood. Awnly just for wance, Polly reckoned it might do us all good. An' Polly knaws what's singin' an' what edn' so well as any lass. The riders * be comin' likewise, though maybe that's tu wild an' savage amoosment for quiet folks."

"You an' Polly go an' listen to the singin', then. 'Tedn' for the likes o' me." Then Joan turned to her cousin, who was pouring tea out of a little pot which held two cups and no more. "Let me have the last nine drops, Polly; they'm good for the heartache, an' mine's more'n common sore to-night."

Mary sighed, opened her mouth to preach a sermon, but shut it without a word. She drained the teapot into Joan's cup, and then, from a bright mood for her, relapsed into cold silence. Uncle Chirgwin, however, prattled on about the concert until his elder niece finished her tea and went to bed. Then he put down his pipe, took a pull at his drink, and began to talk hurriedly to Joan.

* *The riders*, a circus.

"I bin an' got a wonnerful fine notion this day, driving home-long, Joan; an' it's comed back an' back that importuneous that I lay it's truth, an' sent for me to remember. D'you knaw that since you come to Drift us have prospered uncommon? 'Iss, us have. The winter dedn' give no mighty promise, nor yet the spring, till you comed. Then the Lard smiled 'pon Drift. Look at the hay what's gwaine to be cut, God willin', next week. I never seed nothin' more butivul thick underneath in all my days. A rare aftermath tu, I'll warrant. 'Tis so all around. The wheat's kernin' somethin' cruel fine—I awnly wish theer was more of it—an' the sheep an' cattle's in braave kelter like-wise. Then the orchard do promise no worse. I never seed such a shaw of russets an' of quarantines 'pon they old trees afore."

"'Tis a fine, fair season."

"Why, so I say—a 'mazin' summer thus far—but what's the reason o't? That's the poser as an answer comed to in the cart a-drivin' home. You'm the reason! You mind when good Saint Levan walked through the fields that the grass grawed the greener for his tread, an' many days arter, when he'd gone dead years an' years, the corn allus comed richest 'long the path what he trod. An' 'tis the same here, 'cause God's eye be on you, Joan Tregenza, an' His eye caan't be fixed 'pon no spot wi'out brightening all around. You mind me, that's solemn truth. The Lard's watchin' over you—watchin' double tides as the sailors say—an' so this bit o' airth's smilin', from the herb o' the field to the biggest trees as graws. He'm watchin' over Drift for your sake, my girl, an' the farm prospers along o' the gert goodness o' the watchin' Lard. 'Iss, fay, He fills all things livin' with plenshousness, an' fats the root an' swells the corn 'cause He'm breathin' sweet over the land—'cause He'm waitin' an' watchin' for you, Joan."

"He'm watchin' all of us, I s'pose—just to catch the trippin' footstep, like what faither sez. He abbun no call to worry no more 'bout me, I reckon. I be Nature's awn cheel, I be; an' my mother's turnin' hard too—like a cat, as purrs to 'e wan moment

an' sclows 'e the next. My day's done. I've chose wrong, an'
must abide by it. But 'tis along o' bein' sich a li'l fool. Nature
pushes the weak to the wall. I've seed that much o' late days.
I was born to have my heart broke, I s'pose. 'Tedn' nothin'
very straange."

"I judge your angel do cry gert tears when you lets on like
that, my Joan. Oh, gal, why don't 'e give ear to me, as have
lived fifty an' more winters in the world than what you have?
Why caan't 'e taste an' try what the Lard is? Drabbit this
nonsense 'bout Nature! As if you was a fitcher, or an 'awk or
an owl! Caan't 'e see what a draggle-tail, low-minded pass all
this be bringin' 'e to? Yet you'm a thinkin' creature an' abbun
done no worse than scores o' folks who be tanklin' 'pon harps
afore the throne o' God this blessed minute. You chose wrong:
you said so, an' I was glad to hear 'e, for you never 'lowed even
that much till this night. What then? Everybody chooses
wrong wan time or another. Some allus goes for it, like the
bud-pickers to the red-currant bushes; some slips here an' theer,
an' do straightway right 'emselves—right 'emselves again an'
again. The best life be just a slippin' up an' rightin' over an'
over, till a man dies. You've slipped young, an' maybe theer's
half a cent'ry o' years waitin' for 'e to get 'pon the right road;
yet you sez you must abide by what you've done. Think how
it do stand. You've forgived him as wronged 'e, an' caan't the
Lard forgive as easy as you can? He forgived you 'fore you
was born. I lay the Luke Gosp'lers never told 'e that braave
fact, 'cause they doan't knaw it theerselves. 'Tis like this:
your man did take plain Nature for God, an' he did talk foolishness 'bout finding Him in the scent o' flowers, the hum o' bees
an' sich-like. Mayhap Nature's a good working god for a selfish
man, but she edn' wan for a maid, as you knaws by now. Then
your faither—his God do sit everlasting alongside hell-mouth,
an' do laugh an' girn to see all the world a-walkin' in, same as
the beasts walked in the Ark. Theer's another picksher of a
God for 'e; but mark this, gal, they be lying prophets—lying
prophets both! You've tried the wan, and found it left your

heart hollow like, an' you've tried t'other, an' found that left it
no better filled. Now try Christ, will 'e? Just try. Doan't
keep Him, as is allus busy, a-waitin' your whims no more. Try
Christ, Joan dearie, an' you'll feel what you've never felt yet.
I knaw, as put my 'and in His when 'twas plump an' young as
yourn. An' He holds it yet, now 'tis shrivelled an' crooked wi'
rheumatics. He holds it. 'Iss, He do."

The old man put out his hand to Joan as he spoke, and she
took it between her own and kissed it.

"You'm very good," she said, "an' you'm wise 'cause you'm
auld an' have seen many years. I prayed to Saint Madern to
hear 'me not long since, an' I bathed in his waters, an' went
home happy. But awnly the birds an' the rabbits heard me.
An' next day faither turned me out o' his house an' counted me
numbered for hell."

"Saints be very well, but 'tedn' in 'cordance with what
we'm tawld nowadays—to pray to any but the Lard direct."

He pleaded long and patiently, humbly praying for the
religion which had lightened his own road. The thought of his
vast experience, and the spectacle of his own blameless and
simple life as she reviewed it, made Joan relent at last. The
great loneliness of her heart yearned for something to fill it.
Man had failed her, saints had failed her; Nature had turned
cold; and Uncle Sampy held out a great promise.

"Ban't no sort o' use, I'm thinkin'," she said at last; "but if
you'm that set 'pon it I'll do your wish. I owe you that, an'
more'n that. 'Iss, I'll come along wi' you an' Mary to Sancreed
church next Sunday. 'Tis li'l enough to do for wan as have
done so much for me."

"Thank God!" he said earnestly. "That's good news to be
sure, bless your purty eyes! An' doan't 'e go a-tremblin' an'
fearin', you mind, like to meetin'. 'Tedn' no ways like that.
Just love o' the Lard an' moosic an' holy thots from passon, an'
not more hell-fire than keeps a body healthy-minded an' awake.
My ivers! I could a'most sing an' dance myself now—an' arter

my day's work tu—to think as you'll sit alongside o' me in church come Sunday ! "

Joan smiled at his enthusiasm on her behalf, then kissed him and went to bed; while the old man, mixing up his prayers, his last pipe and his final glass of spirits, according to his custom, sat the fire out while he drank deeper and prayed harder than usual in the light of his triumph.

"Polly couldn't do it, not for all her brains an' godliness," he murmured to himself; "yet 'twas given to an auld simple sawl like me! An' I have! I've led her slap-bang into the hand o' the Lard, an' the rest be His business. No man's done a better day's work in Carnwall to-day than what I have—that's sure ! "

CHAPTER XII.

FROM JOE.

Since her visit to the church at Newlyn, Joan had been in no place of worship save the chapel of the Luke Gospellers. What might be the nature of the service before her she did not know, nor did she care; but the girl kept her promise, and drove in the market-cart to Sancreed with her uncle and cousin when Sunday came. The little church lay bowered in its grove of sycamores, and, around it, a golden-green concourse of quivering shadows cooled those who had walked or driven from Drift—an outlying portion of the parish—approached through lanes innocent of all shade. Mr. Chirgwin put up the horse, and presently joined his nieces in church. Then Joan saw him under interesting and novel conditions. He wore glasses with gold rims; he covered his bald head with a little velvet cap; at the appointed time he took a wooden plate and carried it round for money. Mary found the old man's places for him, and sang in a way that fairly astounded Joan. The enormous satisfaction brought to herself by these vocal efforts was apparent. Her soul appeared mightily lifted up. She amused chance visitors to the church; but the regular congregation liked to hear Mary; and Joan, seeing the comfort her cousin sucked from singing, wished she had heart to join. That, however, she wholly lacked. Moreover, the words were strange to her.

The quiet service, brightened by music, dragged its slow length murmuringly along. The sermon, delivered by a visitor, was not of a sort to hold Joan, and, indeed, could hardly be expected to attract many in such a congregation. The preacher had lately been reading old Cornish history, and overcome by the startling fact that the far West of England—Cornwall and Devon—were Christian long before Augustine saw Kent, dwelt upon the matter after a very instructive fashion in ears unlikely to benefit from such knowledge. That the Cornu-British bishops preached Christ while yet Sussex, Wessex, Hampshire and other districts worshipped Woden, Freya, the Queen of Heaven, the Thunder God, and various deities whose altars were set up after the Conquest, did not interest Joan for one, or Mr. Chirgwin for another. But the girl woke up at the mention of Irish and Welsh and Breton saints. Pleasant to hear was the utterance of names which she had loved once, but of late almost forgotten. They came back now, and, the service having tuned her heart to softness, she welcomed them gladly as friends returned from afar. For the rest, the Litany it was which roused Joan to deepest interest, and opened her mind to new impressions. Here was a prayer, gigantic in length, universal, all-embracing, catholic beyond the compass of anything her thoughts had heretofore conceived. From the Queen upon her throne to Joan herself; from the bishops, the princes, and the Lords of the Council, to Uncle Chirgwin and his fruits of the earth, that astounding petition ranged with equal vigour and earnestness. Nothing was too high, nothing was too low for it; all the world was named, and the people cried for a hearing or for mercy between each supplication and each prayer. The overwhelming majesty of such praying impressed Joan much; as, indeed, it impresses all who come adult thereto and do not associate it with their childhood, with weary hours dragging interminably out, with sleepy buzz of voices, with sore knees or a breaking back, with yawnings stifled, with devices for passing time, with the longed-for sunshine stealing inch by inch eastwards on the church walls.

"A power o' larnin' in a small head-piece," commented Uncle Sampy as he drove home, with the girls sitting side by side on his left. "A braave ch'ice o' words an' a easy knowledge o' the saints as weern't picked up in a day. 'Tis well to hear a furriner now an' again. They do widen the grasp of a man's mind, looking 'pon things from a chaanged point o' view. Not as us could be 'spected to be Latiners, yet I seem 'tis very well to listen to it as chance offers. 'Tis something to knaw 'twas Latin, an' that did I, though I doubt some o' the good neighbours couldn' tell it for what 'twas, by no means."

Joan said little about the service, but she praised the Litany from her own peculiar attitude towards it.

"That be fine prayin'," she said, " with nobody forgot, an' all in black print, so's wance said 'tedn' lost."

After dinner, when Mary had gone to see a friend, and the farm people were dawdling abroad till evening milking-time, Joan made her uncle read the service through again. This he did comfortably between the whiffs of his pipe, and Joan answered the responses, cooing them in her sweet voice as softly as the red and blue pigeons crooned on the roof outside. Drift was asleep under a hot blaze of afternoon sunshine. Sometimes a child's keen voice in the road cut the drowsy silence and came to Joan's ears, where she sat, in the best parlour with Uncle Sampy; sometimes slow wheels rumbled up the hill towards Buryan. Other sounds there were none. The old people slept within their cottages after the extra baked meats of Sunday's dinner; many of the young paired, and walked where pathways ran over meadows and through yellowing wheat; while others, more gregarious and unattached, had tramped away to Penzance to join the parade by the sea, and meet their friends from the shops.

Anon nailed boots stamped up the little pathway to Drift farmhouse, and Tom Tregenza appeared. To-day he entered fearlessly, for he came upon an errand from his father. He kissed Joan, and shook hands with Uncle Sampy. Then he said—

" 'Tis a letter as I've brought for Joan."

The girl's heart beat hard, and the blood rushing from her cheeks, left them white. But the letter only came from Joe Noy, and it is certain that Mr. Tregenza would have forwarded no other. Excitement died, and was painfully renewed, in a

fresh direction, when Joan realized from whom the missive
came, and thought about its writer. He had long been a stranger
to her mind, and now he seemed suddenly to re-enter it—like a
stranger.

"I can stay for a bit of tea so long as I be back by chapel-
time," explained Tom.

"An' so you shall, my son. Run 'e out o' doors an' amoose
yourself where you mind to; awnly don't ope the li'l linhay in
the Brook Croft, 'cause auld bull's fastened up theer, an' his
temper's gettin' more'n more out o' hand."

So Tom departed, and Uncle Chirgwin read Joan's letter
aloud to her. It came from Santa Rosalia, and contained not
much news, but plenty of affection, and some religious sentiments
bred from the writer's foreign environment. Joe Noy would be
back in England again before the end of the year.

Joan was reduced to tears by this communication. She
refused to be comforted, and, indeed, the position was beyond
Uncle Chirgwin's power to brighten. The letter had come at a
bad moment, and that calm and repose which almost appeared
to be softening Joan's sorrows, now spread speedy wings and
departed, leaving her wholly forlorn. Curtains might be falling
behind her, but curtains were also rising in front. She had
looked forward vaguely, and now the position was suddenly
defined by the arrival of Joe's letter, with all its future phases
clear-cut, cold and terrible.

"My baaby's comin' just then. An' that's what'll fall 'pon
his ear fust thing. Oh, if us could awnly tell en afore he comes
so he might knaw 'tis all chaanged! 'Twould be easier for en,
lovin' me that keen. He'd grawed to be a shadder of a man in
my mind; but now I sees en real flaish'n blood again; an'
maybe—maybe he'll seek me out an' kill me for what's done."

"I do creem to hear 'e, gal! No, no; Joe Noy's a God-fearin'
sawl."

"If he'd forgive me fust, I'd so soon he killed me as not.
Sam Martin killed Widow Garth's gal 'cause she was ontrue
to en; an' a-many said 'twas wrong to hang the chap to Bodmin

arter. Death's my deserts, same as Ann Garth; an' she got it: an' I doan't care how soon I do. None wants me no more, nor what I'm breedin' neither. I'd die now, an' smilin', if 'tweern't for next world."

"Cuss the letter!" said Uncle Sampy, getting red in the face. "Cuss it, I says, for gwaine an' turnin' up just this day! A fortnight later you could 'a' looked on it wi' quiet mind an' knawed wheer to turn; to-day it's just bin an' undone what was done. Not but what 'tis as butivul a letter as ever comed off the sea; but if theer'd awnly been time to 'stablish 'e 'fore it comed! Now you've turned your back 'pon the Household o' Faith just as arms was being stretched out that lovin'."

"Faith won't undo what I've done, nor yet make my wicked-ness fall lighter for Joe. Yes, 'twas wicked, wicked, wicked. I knaw it now."

Mary and Tom came in from different directions about this time. The latter had regaled himself with a peep at "auld bull," heard the terrific snorting of his nostrils, and observed how he bellowed mightily at durance on such an afternoon. Tea being finished, the boy started homewards with a basket of fresh eggs and butter, a pound of cream, and some early apples of a sort used for cider, but yet equal to the making of a pie.

"As for the butter, 'tis Joan's churnin'," said Mary; "but you'd best not to tell your faither that, else, so like's not, he'll pitch it into the sea. If us could send en a pound o' charity, I doubt he'd be better for't."

"Faither's a holy man, whatever else he be," said Tom, stoutly. "He doan't want for no good qualities like, 'cause what he doan't knaw 'bout God edn' worth knawin'."

Mary laughed. It was a feat she seldom performed, and the sound of her amusement lacked joy.

"Well, us won't argue 'bout en. You'm right to say that. Be the basket too heavy for 'e?"

"No! not likely. Have 'e ever seed my fore-arm, Polly?"

"Never. I will another time. Best be gwaine, else you'll be late for chapel."

So Tom marched off, and Mary, returning to the house, heard of Joan's letter.

The old gusts of misery, sorrow, indignation, rose in her heart again then, but faintly, like the dying flutter of winds that have blown themselves out. She tried to find a way of bringing comfort to her cousin, but failed. Joan had retired, and refused consolation.

The glory of splendid summer hours passed away; the long twilight sank to darkness; the opal lights in the west at last died under the silver of the moon. And then, like a child weary with crying, Joan slept; while Mary, creeping a third time to see and speak with her, departed silently. But she did not sleep; and her wakefulness was fortunate, for long after eleven o'clock came a noisy summons at the outer door. Looking from her room, which faced the front of the house, the woman saw Tom, with his full basket, standing clearly defined below. The world of the weald and meadows shimmered silvery in dew and moonlight. Infinite silence reigned. Then the boy's small, indignant voice broke it.

"You'll have to let me in, I reckon. Blamed if I doan't think you was right 'bout faither, arter all."

The reason for Tom's return may be briefly told. He had taken his basket home, and got it safely under cover to his mother. Then, after chapel, Grey Michael went into the village, and Thomasin had an opportunity to ask some of those questions she was burning to put.

"An' how be Joan?" she began.

"Wisht an' drawed thin 'bout the faace seemin'ly. An' Joe's letter just made her cry fit to bust her eyes, 'stead o' cheerin' of her like."

"Poor lass! I dedn' expect nothin' differ'nt. I've most a mind to go up Drift an' see her—for a reason I've thot upon. Did Joan say anythin' 'bout a last will an' testament to 'e?"

"No, nothin' 'bout anything worth namin'. But Polly had a deal to say. Her wished her could send faither a pound o' charity 'stead o' butter."

"Her dared!"

At that moment Mr. Tregenza returned to supper, and soon afterwards his son went to bed. The lad had not been asleep half-an-hour before Grey Michael came across the basket from Drift. Two minutes later Tom heard the thunder of his father's voice.

"Tom, you come down here, an' be sharp about it!"

The boy tumbled out of bed instantly, and went down to the kitchen in his night-shirt and trousers. Michael Tregenza was standing by the table. Upon it appeared the basket from Drift, stored with cream, butter, eggs, and apples. Thomasin sat in the low chair by the fire, with her apron over her face, and that was always a bad sign, as Tom knew.

"What day be this, bwoy?" began Michael.

"The Lard's, faither."

"Ay, the Lard's awn day, though you've forgot it, seemin'ly."

"No, I abbun, faither."

"Doan't 'e answer me 'cept I tells you to. Where did these things come from?"

"Drift, faither. Uncle Sampy bid me bring 'em with his respects."

"Did you tell en 'twas breakin' the commandments?"

"No, faither."

"Why didn't 'e? You knawed it yourself?"

"'Iss, faither; but uncle's a ancient man, an' I guessed he knawed so well as me, an' I reckoned 'twould be sauce for such as me to say anything to a auld, grey body like him."

"Sinners is all colours an' ages. Another time doan't you do what's wrong, whether 'tis auld or young as tempts 'e to't. You'm a Luke Gosp'ler, an' it edn' being a shinin' light 'tall to go wrong just because wan, as did ought to knaw wiser an' doan't, tells 'e to. Now you can lace on your boots, as soon as you'm minded to, an' trapse up Drift with that theer basket an' all in it. 'Twon't harm godless folks to wake 'em an' faace 'em with theer wrong-doing. An' I lay you'll remember another time."

Tom, knowing that words would be utterly wasted, went back to his attic, dressed, and started. He had the satisfaction of eating apples in the moonlight, and of posing as a bitterly wronged boy at Drift when Mary came down, lighted a candle, and let him into the house.

Uncle Chirgwin also appeared, and criticised in a sleepy voice, while Tom drank cider and ate a big slice of bread and bacon.

"A terrible Old Testament man, your faither, sure 'nough," said Uncle Chirgwin. "Be you gwaine to stop the night 'long o' us or no?"

"Not me! I got to be in the bwoat 'fore half-past five to-morror marnin'."

"This marnin' 'tis," said Mary, "or will be in a few minutes. An' you can tell your faither what I said 'bout charity, if you like. I sez it again, an' it won't hurt en to knaw."

"But it might hurt me to tell. The less said soonest mended wi' faither."

Tom departed, the lighter for his basket. He flung a stone at a hare, listened to the jarring of a night-hawk, and finally returned home about one o'clock. Both his parents were awaiting him, and the boy saw that his mother had been enduring some trouble on his behalf.

"Mind, my son, hencefarrard that the sabbath is the Lard thy God's. You may have done others a good turn besides yourself this night."

"What did they say, Tom?" asked his mother.

"They wasn't best pleased. They said a hard sayin' I'd better not to say agin," answered the boy, heavy with sleep.

"Let it be. Us doan't want to hear it. Get you to bed. An', mind, the bwoat at the steps by half-past five to-morror."

"Ay, ay, faither."

Then Tom vanished, his parents went to their rest, and the cottage on the cliff slept within the music of the sea, its thatch all silver-bright under a summer moon.

CHAPTER XIII.

A BARGAIN FOR MRS. TREGENZA.

To the superficial eye dead hopes leave ugly traces; viewed more inquiringly, the cryptic significance of them appears, and that is often beautiful. Joan's soul looked out of her blue eyes now. Seen thoughtfully, her beauty was refined and exalted to an exquisite perfection; but the unintelligent observer had simply pronounced her pale and thin. The event which first promised to destroy the new-spun gossamers of a religious faith, and break them even on the day of their creation, in reality acted otherwise. For Joan, Joe's letter was like a window opening upon a hopeless dawn; and her helplessness before this spectacle of the future threw the girl upon religion—not as a sure rock in the storm of her life, but as a straw to the hand of the drowning. The world had nothing else left in it for her. She, to whom sunshine and happiness were the breath of life; she who had envied butterflies their joyous being, now stood before a future all uphill and grey, lonely and loveless. As yet but the dawn of affection for the unborn child lightened her mind. Thought upon that subject went hand in hand with fear of pain. And now, in her dark hours, Joan happily did not turn to feed upon her own heart, but fled from it. For distraction she read the four Gospels feverishly day by day, and she prayed long to the Lord of them by night.

Mary helped her in an earnest, cheerless fashion, and before her cousin's solicitude, Joan's eyes opened to another thought: the old friendship between Mary and Joe Noy. It had wakened once, on her first arrival at Drift, then slept again till now.

She was troubled to see the other woman's apparent indifference, and she formed plans to bring these two together again. The act of getting away from herself and thinking for others brought some comfort to her heart, and seemed to rise indirectly out of her reading.

The Christianity of Drift was old-fashioned, and reflected the Founder. No distractions rose between Joan and the story. She took it at first hand, escaping thus from those petty follies and fooleries which blight and fog the real issues to-day. She sucked her new faith pure. A noble rule of conduct lay before her; she dimly discerned something of its force; and unselfishness appeared in her, proving that she had read aright. As for the dogma, she opened her arms to that very readily, because it was beautiful and promised so much. Faith's votaries never turn critical eyes upon the foundations of her gorgeous fabric; their sight is fixed aloft on the rainbow towers and pinnacles, upon the golden fanes. And yet this man-born structure of Theology, with aisles and pillars fretting and crumbling under the hand of reason, needs such eternal propping, restoring, and repairing that priestly masons and hod-carriers are solely occupied with it. They grapple and fight for the poor shadows of dogma by which they live, and, so engaged, the spirit and substance of religion is by them too often lost. None of the Christian Churches can ever be overcrowded with men who possess brain-power worthy the name. Mediocrity and ignorance may starve, but talent and any new nostrum to strangle reason and keep the rot from the fabric will always open their coffers and win their temporal remarks.

Joan truly found the dogma more grateful and comforting than anything else within her experience; and the apparition of a living God, who had saved her with His own life's blood before she was born, appeared too beautiful and sufficing to be less than true. Her eyes, shut so long, seemed opening at last. With errors that signify nothing, she drew to herself great truths that matter much, and are vital to elevated conduct. She thought of other people and looked at them as one wakened from sleep. And, similarly, she looked at Nature, to find that even her vanished lover had not taught her all. There were truths below the formulæ of his worship; there were secrets deeper than his intellectual plummet had ever sounded. Without understanding it, Joan yet knew that a change had come to pass in material things. Sunshine on the deep sea hid more matters for wonder than John Barron had taught or known. Once only as yet had she caught a glimpse of Nature's beating heart; and that was upon the occasion of her visit to St. Madron's Chapel. She was lifted up then for a magic hour; but the lurid end of that day looked clearer afterwards than ever the dewy dawn of it. Nature had smiled, mutely and dumbly, at her sufferings for long months since then. But now added knowledge certainly grew, and from a matrix mightier than the love of Nature or of man was Joan's new life born. It embraced a new sight, new senses, ambitions, fears, and hopes.

Joan went to church at every opportunity. Faith seemed so easy and, soon, so necessary. Secret prayer became a real happiness to be approached with joy. To own to sins was as satisfactory as casting down a heavy burden at a journey's end; to confess them to God was to know that they were forgiven. There were not many clouds in her religious sky. While Mary's religion, bounded by her own capabilities, was exhibited against a background of gloom, which never absolutely vanished save in moments of rare exaltation, Joan's new-found faith, contrariwise, took upon itself an aspect of sunshine. Her clouds were made beautiful by the new light; they did not darken it. Mary's grey Cornish mind kept sentiment out of sight. She lived with clear eyes always focussing reality as it appeared to her. Heaven was indeed a pleasanter eternal fact than hell; yet the place of torment existed on Bible authority; and it was idle to suppose it existed for nothing. Grasping eternity as a truth, she occupied herself in strenuous preparation; which preparation took the form of good works and personal self-denial. Joan belonged to an order of emotional creatures widely different. She loved the beautiful for its own

sake, kept her face to the sun when it shone, shivered and shut
up like a scarlet pimpernel if bad weather was abroad.   And
now a chastened sunshine, daily growing stronger, shot through
the present clouds, painted beauty on their fringes, and lighted
the darkness of their recesses, so that even the secrets of suffering were fitfully revealed.   Joan grasped at new thoughts, the
outcome of her new road.

Nature presently seemed of a nobler face, and certain immemorial achievements of man also flashed out in the side-light of
the new convictions; as objects, themselves inconsiderable, will
suddenly develop unsuspected splendours from change of standpoint in the beholder. The magic of that Christianity, which
Joan now received directly from her Bible, wrought and embroidered a new significance into many things. And it worked
upon none as upon the old stone crosses—some perfect still, some
ruined as to arm or shaft, some quite worn and gnawed by time
from their original semblance. These plentifully dotted her
native land. Them she had always loved, but now they
appeared marvellously transfigured, and the soul hid in their
granite beamed through it. Supposing the true menhirs to be
but ruined crosses also, Joan shed over them no scantier affection
than upon the less venerable Brito-Celtic records of Christianity.
Bid so to do, and prompted also by her inclination, the girl was
wont to take walks of some extent for her health's sake; and
these had an object now. As her dead mother's legends came
back to her memory, and knit Nature to her new Saviour, so
the weather-beaten stones brought Him likewise nearer, marked
the goal of precious daily pilgrimages, and filled a sad young
life with friends.

Returning from a visit to Tremethick Cross, where it stands
upon a little mound above the St. Just road, Joan heard a thin
and well-known voice before she saw the speaker. It was Mrs.
Tregenza, who had walked over to drink tea and satisfy herself
on sundry points respecting her step-daughter.

"Oh, my Guy Faux, Polly!" she said upon arriving, "I'm
in a reg'lar take to be here, though I knaws Michael's t'other

side the islands, an' won't fetch home 'fore marnin'. I've comed 'cause I couldn't keep from it no more. How's her doin', poor tibby lamb? wi' all them piles o' money tu. Not that money did ought to make a differ'nce; but it do, an' that's the truth, an' it edn' no good sayin' it doan't. What a world to be sure! An' that letter from Noy? I knaw you was fond of en likewise in your time. The sadness of it! Just think o' that mariner comin' home 'pon top o' this mishap!"

Mary winced and answered coldly that the world was full of mishaps and of sadness.

"The man must faace sorrer, same as what us all have got to, Mrs. Tregenza. Some gets more, some gets less, as the sparks fly up'ard. Joe Noy's got religion tu."

Mary spoke the last words with some bitterness, which she noted too late, and set against herself for a sin.

"Oh, my dear sawl," said Mrs. Tregenza, looking round nervously, as though she feared the shadow of her husband might be listening, "Luke Gosp'ling's a mighty uncomfortable business, though I lay Tregenza'd most kill me if he heard the word. 'Tedn' stomachable to all, an' I doubts whether 'twill be a chain strong enough to hold Joe Noy, when he comes back an' meets this coil. 'Tis a kicklish business, an' I wish 'twas awver. Joe's a fiery feller when he reckons he's wronged; an' there ban't no balm to *this* hurt in Gosp'ling, take it as you will. I tell you, in your ear awnly, that Luke Gosp'lers graw reg'lar ferocious-like along o' the wickedness o' the airth. Take Michael, as walks wi' the Lard, same as Moses done; an' the more he do, the ferociouser he do get. Religion! He stinks o' religion worse than ever Newlyn stinks o' feesh; he goes in fear o' God to the marrow in his bones; an' yet 'tis uncomfortable now and then to live wi' sich a righteous member. Theer's a hardness along of it. Luke Gosp'ling doan't soften the heart of en."

"It should," said Mary.

"An' so it should; but he says the world's no plaace for softness. He'm a terror to the evil-doer, an' he'm a terror to the righteous-doer, an' to hisself no less, I reckon—an' to God

A'mighty tu, so like's not. The friends of en be as feared of en as his foes be. An' that's awful wisht, 'cause he goes an' comes purty nigh alone. The Gosp'lers be like fry flyin' this way an' that 'fore a school o' macker'l, when Michael's among 'em. Even minister, he do shrivel a inch or two 'longside o' Michael. I've seen en wras'lin' wi' the Word same as Jacob wras'led wi' the angel. An' yet why? Theer's a man chosen for glory this five-an'-forty years; an' he knaws it so well as I do, or any wan."

"He knaws nothin' o' the sort. The best abbun no right to say it," declared Mary.

Then Mrs. Tregenza fired up, for she resented any criticism on this subject other than her own.

"An' why not, Polly Chirgwin? Who's a right to doubt it? Not you, I reckon. Ban't your place to judge a man as walks wi' God like Moses done. If Michael edn' saved, then theer's no sawl saved 'pon land or sea. You talk—a young maiden! His sawl was bleedin' an' his hands raw a-batterin' the gate o' heaven 'fore you was born, Polly—ay, an' he'd got the bettermost o' the devil wance for all 'fore you was conceived in the womb; you mind that."

"Us caan't get the bettermost o' the devil wance for all," said Mary, changing the issue—"no, not no more'n us can wash our skin clean wance for all. But you an' me thinks differ'nt, an' allus shall, Mrs. Tregenza."

"'Iss; though I s'pose 'tis the same devil as takes back-slidin' church or chapel folks. Let that bide now. Wheer's Joan to? I've got to thank 'e kindly for lookin' arter Tom t'other Sunday night. 'Tis things like that makes religion un-comfortable. But you gived the bwoy some tidy belly-timber in the small hours o' day, an' he comed home dog-tired, but none the worse. An' thank 'e for they apples an' cream an' eggs, which I'm sorry they had sich poor speed. A butivul basket as hurt me to the heart to paart with. But I wasn't asked. No offence, I hope, 'bout it? Maybe uncle forgot 'twas the Lard's Day?"

"He'm the last ever to do that."

Joan entered at this point in the conversation, and betrayed some slight emotion as her step-mother kissed her. It was nearly five months since they had met, and Mary now departed, leaving them to discuss Joan's physical condition.

"I be doin' clever," said Joan; "never felt righter in body."

Mrs. Tregenza poured forth good advice, and after a lengthy conversation, came to a secret ambition and broached it with caution.

"I called to mind some baaby's things—shoes, clouts, frocks, an' sich-like—as I've got snug in lavender to home. They was all flam-new for Tom, an' I judged I'd have further use for 'em, but never did. Theer they be, even to a furry-cloth, as none doan't ever use nowadays, though my mother did, an' thot well on't. So I did tu. 'Tis just a bit o' crimson-red tailor's cloth to cover the soft plaace 'pon a li'l baaby's head 'fore the bones of en graw together. An' I reckon 'tis better to have it than not. I seem you'd do wise to take the whole kit; an' you'm that well-to-do that 'twouldn' be worth thinkin' 'bout. 'Twould be cheaper'n a shop; an' theer's everything a royal duke's cheel could want; an' a butivul robe wi' lace-work cut 'pon it, an' li'l bits o' ribbon to tie in the arm-holes Sundays. They'm vitty clothes."

Joan's eyes softened to a misty dreaminess before this aspect of the time to come. She had thought so little about the baby and all matters pertaining thereto, that every day now brought with it mental novelty and a fresh view of that experience stored for her in the future.

"'Iss; I do mind they things when Tom was in 'em. What be the value in money?"

Mrs. Tregenza answered shyly, and almost respectfully, "Well, 'tis so difficult to say, not bein' a reg'lar seller o' things. They cost, wi'out the robe, as was a gift from Mrs. Blight, more'n five pound."

"Take ten pound, then. I'll tell uncle."

Thomasin's red tongue-tip crept along her lips, and her bright eyes blinked, but conscience was too strong.

"No, no; a sight too much—too much by half. I'll let 'e have the lot for a fi'-pun' note. An' I'd like it to be a new one, if 'tis the same to you."

Joan agreed to this, and ten minutes afterwards Mr. Chirgwin was opening his cash-box and handing Thomasin the snowy, crackling fragment she desired.

"'Tis the fust bit o' money ever I kept unbeknawnst to Michael," she said; "an', 'pon me life, Chirgwin, I be a'most 'feared on't."

"You'll soon get awver that," declared Uncle Sampy. "I'll send the trap home with 'e, an' you can look out the frippery; an' you might send a nice split hake back-along with it, if you've got the likes of sich a thing gwaine beggin' to be ate."

Presently Mrs. Tregenza drove away, and Joan went to her room to think. Magic effects had risen from the spectacle of the well-remembered face, from the sound of the sharp, high voice. A new sensation grew out of them for Joan. Home rose like a vision, with the sighing of the sea, the crying of the gulls, the musical rattle of blocks in the bay, the clink, clink of the picks in the quarry, the occasional thunder of a blast. Many scents were with her—the odour of tar and twine and stores, the smell of drying fish. She saw the low cliffs, all gemmed at this season with moon-flowers—the great white convolvulus which twinkled there. A red and purple fuchsia in the garden had blossomed also. She could see the bees climbing into its drooping bells. She remembered their music, as it murmured drowsily from dead and gone summers, and sounded sweeter than the song of the bees at Drift. She heard the tinkle of a stream outside the cottage, where it ran under the hedge through a shute, and emptied itself into a great half-barrel; and then, turning her thoughts to the house, her own attic, with the view of St. Michael's Mount and the bay, appeared in her mind's eye. Every detail arose distinctly, even to the glass scent-bottle on the mantelpiece, and the coloured print of John Wesley being rescued in his childhood from a burning house. These and kindred memories made a live picture to

Joan's eyes. For the first time since she had left her home, the girl found in her heart a desire to return to it. She awoke next morning with the old recollections increased and multiplied; and the sensation bred from continued contemplation was the sensation of a loss.

BOOK III.

CHANCE.

CHAPTER I.

OF THE CROSSES.

THE significance of the ancient crosses in Joan Tregenza's
latest phase of mental growth becomes much finer after learning
somewhat more concerning them than she could ever know,
and the ephemeral life of one unhappy woman, viewed from
these granite records of Brito-Celtic pagan and Christian faith,
examined in its relation to these hoary splinters of stone, grows
an object of some pathetic interest. Such memorials of the past
as are here indicated vary mightily in age. The Christian
monuments are not older than the fifth century, but many have
been proved palimpsests, and rise on pagan foundations dating
from a time far more ancient than their own. The relics are
divided into two classes by antiquaries: Inscribed Pillar Stones
and Crosses. The former occur throughout the Celtic divisions
of Great Britain, the earliest examples being marked with the
Chi Rho monogram. They are of sepulchral significance, as
their inscriptions indicate. The plainer crosses denoted bound-
aries of sanctuary or were raised promiscuously where men and
women passed or congregated, their object being to encourage
devotion, and lead human thoughts heavenward. Upon many
of them will be found the pre-Norman figure of Christ in a
loose tunic, His head erect and His body unbent, after the
Byzantine fashion. The mediæval mode of carving a crucifix
representing the dead Christ is of much later date, and may
not be observed as occurring before the twelfth century. Of
the sculptured crosses only a few are inscribed. They served
a purpose similar to the pillar stones, and the ornament upon
them is, as a rule, a bad imitation of those interlaced or key
patterns found upon Irish examples.

Moro than three hundred erect crosses of various kinds exist within tho confines of Cornwall. In churchyards and by streams they stand; they have even been discovered wrought into the fabric of the churches themselves. The brown moor likewise knows them, for they stud its wildernesses and rise at tho meeting of many lonely roads; while elsewhere, villages hold them in their hearts, and the emblems appear daily before the sight of generation upon generation. In hedges they are also to be seen, and in fields. Many have been rescued from base uses; and all have stood through centuries as the sign and testimony of primitive Cornish faith, even as St. Piran's white cross on a black ground, the first banner of Cornwall, bore aloft the same symbol in days when the present emblem, with its fifteen bezants and its motto, "One and All," was not dimly dreamed of.

These ancient crosses now rose like grey sentinels on the grey life of Joan Tregenza. At Drift she was happily placed amongst them; many, not necessary to name separately, lay within the limit of her daily wanderings, and her superstitious nature, working with tho new-born faith, wove precious mystery into them. Much she loved the more remote and lonely stones, for beside them, hidden from the world's eye, she could pray. Those others about which circled human lives attracted her less frequently. To her the crosses were sentient creatures above the fret of Time, eternally watching human affairs. The dawn of art as shown in early religious sculpture generally amuses an ignorant mind, but to Joan the little shirted figures of her new Saviour, which opened blind eyes on the stones she loved, were matter for interest rather than amusement. They did by no means repel her, despite tho superficial hideousness of them; indeed, with a sort of intuition, Joan told herself that human hands had fashioned them somewhere in the dawn of the world when yet her Lord's blood was newly shed, at a time before men had learned skill to make beautiful things.

Once, beside the foot of the cross which stood in Sancreed

churchyard wall,* between two tree trunks under a dome of leaves, the girl found growing a spotted persicaria, and the force of the discovery at such a spot was great to her. Familiar with the legend of the purple mark on every leaf of the plant, nothing doubting it had aforetime grown at the foot of the true cross and there been splashed with the blood of her Master, Joan accepted the old story that henceforth the weed was granted this proud livery and badge. And now, finding it here, the fable revived with added truth and conviction; the legend of the persicaria was as true to her as that other of the Lord's resurrection from death. Thus her views of Nature suffered some approach to debasement in a new direction, but this degradation, so to call it, brought mighty comfort to her soul, daily rounded the ragged edges of life, woke merciful trust and belief in a promised life of bliss beyond the grave, and embroidered thereupon a patchwork, not unbeautiful, built of fairy folk-lore, saintly story, and venerable myth. Her credulous nature accepted right and left; anything that harboured a promise or was lovely or wonderful in itself found acceptance; and Joan read into the very pulses of the summer world the truth as she now understood it. Cornwall suddenly became a new Holy Land to the girl. Here the circumstances of life chimed with those recorded in the New Testament, and it was an easy mental achievement to transplant her Saviour from a historical environment into her own. She pictured Him as walking amid Uncle Chirgwin's ripening corn; she saw Him place His hands on the heads of the little children at cottage doors; she imagined Him standing upon one of the luggers in Newlyn Harbour, with the gulls floating round His head, and the fishermen listening to His utterance.

The growing mother-instincts in Joan also developed about this season and leapt from comparative quiescence into activity. They may indeed be recorded as having arisen within

* This fine sculptured cross has, since these events, been placed within the said churchyard, by the influence of Mr. Arthur G. Langdon, the greatest living authority on the subject of Cornish crosses.

her after a manner not less sudden than had the new faith itself, which was exhibited to you as blossoming with an abruptness almost violent, because it thus occurred. Most channels of thought now led Joan to her unborn infant, and there came at length an occasion upon which she prayed for the first time that the child might be justified in its existence.

This petition was raised where, in the past, she had uttered one widely different: at the altar-stone in the ruined baptistery of St. Madron. Thither, on a day in early August, Joan travelled, by short cuts over fields which brought the chapel within reach of Drift. The scene had changed from that of her former visit, and summer was keeping the promises of spring. Yellow stars of biting stone-crop covered the walls of the ruin; the fruit of the blackthorn was growing purple, of the hawthorn, red; the lesser dodder crept, like pink lace-work, over furze and heather; bright-eyed euphrasy and sweet wild thyme were murmured over by many bees; at the altar's foot grew brake fern and towering foxgloves; while upon the sacred stone itself brambles laid their fruit, a few ripe blackberries shining from clusters of red and green. Seeding grasses and docks likewise flourished within the little chapel, and ragged robins and dandelions brought the best beauty they had Amongst which matters, hid in loneliness, to the sound of that hymn of life which rises in a whisper from all earth at summer noon, Joan prayed for her baby that it might not be born in vain.

CHAPTER II.

HOME.

Amongst the varied ambitions now manifested by Joan was one already hinted at—one which increased to the displacement of smaller interests: she much desired to see again her home, if but for the space of an hour. The days and weeks of an unusually smiling summer brought autumn, and with it the cutting of ripe grain; but the bustle and custom of harvest failed to draw Joan amongst her kind. Human life faded somewhat, even to the verge of unreality with her. Silence fell upon her, and a gravity of demeanour which was new to the beholders. Uncle Chirgwin and Mary were alike puzzled at this sign, and, misunderstanding the nature of the change, feared that the girl's spiritual development must be meeting unseen opposition. Whims and moods were proper to her condition, so the farmer maintained, but the fancy of eternally sequestering herself, the conceit of regarding as friends those ancient stones of the moor and cross-roads, was beyond his power to appreciate. To Mary such conduct presented even greater elements of mystery. Yet the fact faced them, and the crosses came in time to be one of the few subjects which Joan cared to talk upon. Even then it was to her uncle alone she opened her heart concerning them, for Mary never unlocked the inner nature of her cousin.

"I got names o' my awn for each of 'em," Joan confessed, "an' I seem they do knaw my comin' an' my secrets an' my troubles. They teach me the force o' keepin' my mouth shut; an' much mixin' wi' other folks arter the silence o' the stones 'mazes me—men an' wummen do chatter so."

"An' so did you, lassie, an' weern't none the worse. Us doan't hear your purty voice enough now."

"'Tis better thinkin' than talkin', Uncle Sampy. I abbun nort to talk 'bout, you see, but a power o' things to think of. Th'auld stones speaks to me solemn, though they caan't talk. They'm wise, voiceless things, an' brings God closer. An' me, an' all the world o' grass an' flowers, an' the li'l chirruping griggans,* do 'pear so young beside 'em. But they'm big an' kind. They warm my heart somethin' braave; an' they let the grey mosses cling to 'em, an' the dinky blue butterflies open an' shut their wings 'pon 'em, an' the bramble climb around their arms. They've tawld me a many good things; an' fust as I must be humbler in my bearin'. Wance I said I'd forgive faither, an' I thot 'twas a fair thing to say; now I awnly wants en to forgive me an' let me come to my time wi' no man's anger hot agin me. If I could win just a peep o' home. I may never see it no more arter, 'cause things might fall out bad wi' me."

"'Tis nachrul as you harp on it; an', blame me, if I secs why you shouldn' go down-long. Us might ride in the cart so far, an' no harm done."

"Ay, do 'e come, theer's a dear sawl—just to look upon the plaace."

"As for that, if us goes, us must see the matter through, an' give your faither the chance to do what's right by 'e."

"He'll not change; but still I'd have en hear me tell I'm in sorrer for the ill I brot 'pon his name."

"Ay, facks! 'Tis a wise word an' a right. Us'll go this very arternoon. You get a odd pound or so o' scald cream, an' I'll see to a basket o' fruit wi' some o' they scoured necterns, as ban't no good for sellin', but eats so well as t'others. 'Iss, us'll go so soon as dinner be swallowed. Wishes doan't run in a body's head for nothin'."

Uncle Chirgwin's old market-cart, with the grey horse and the squeaking wheel, rattled off to Newlyn some two hours later,

* Grasshoppers.

and the ordeal, longed for at a distance, towered tremendous
and less beautiful at nearer approach. When they started,
Joan had hoped that her father might be at home; as they
neared Newlyn she felt a growing relief in the reflection that
his presence ashore was exceedingly improbable. Her anxieties
were forgotten for a few moments at sight of the well-known
outlines of the hills above the village. Now arrish-mows
glimmered in the pale-gilded stubbles of the fields; the orchards
gleamed with promise; the foliage of the elms was at its darkest
before the golden dawn of autumn. Well-remembered sights
arose on Joan's eyes with the music proper to them; then came
the smell of the sea and the jolting of the cart going over
rough stones. Narrow, steep streets and sharp corners had to
be traversed, not only with caution, but at a speed which easily
placed Joan within the focus of many glances. Then troubles
and humiliation of a sort wholly unexpected burst suddenly upon
her, bringing the girl's mind rudely back from dreams born of
·the familiar scene. Newlyn women bobbed about their cottage
doors with hum and stir, and every gossip's mouth was full of
news at this entry. Doors and windows filled with curious
heads and bright eyes; there was some laughter in the air;
fishermen got up with sidelong looks from the old masts or low
walls whereon, during hours of leisure, they sat in rows and
smoked. Joan, all aflame, prayed Uncle Chirgwin to hasten,
which he did to the best of his power; but their progress was
of necessity slow, and local curiosity enjoyed full scope and
play. Tears came to the girl's eyes long before the village
was traversed; then, through a mist of them, she saw a hand
stretched to meet her own, and heard a voice which rang kindly
on her ears. It was Sally Trevennick, who faced the spiteful
laughter without flinching, and said a few loud, friendly
words, though, indeed, her well-meant support brought scant
comfort with it for the victim.

"Lard sakes, Joan! doan't 'e take on so at them buzzin'
fooles! 'Tedn' the trouble, 'tis the money makes 'em clatter.
Bah! Wheer's the wan of them black-browed gals as 'alf the

sum wouldn' buy? You keep a bold faace, an' don't let 'em see
as their sniggerin's aught more to 'e than dog-barking."

"Us'll be theer in a minute," added Mr. Chirgwin, "an' I'll
drive back agin by Mouz'le; then you'll 'scape they she-cats.
I never thot as you'd a-got to stand that dressin' down in a
plaace what's knawed you an' yours these many years."

Joan asked Sally Trevennick whether she could say if Grey
Michael was on the water, and she felt very genuine thankfulness on learning that Sally believed so. Two minutes later
the spring-cart reached level ground above the sea, then,
whipping up his horse, Uncle Sampy increased the pace, and
very quickly Joan found herself at the door of home.

Thomasin was within, and, hearing the sound of wheels
cease before the cottage, came forth to learn who had arrived.
Her surprise was only equalled by her alarm at sight of Joan
and the farmer. So frightened, indeed, did she appear, that
both the new-comers supposed Mr. Tregenza must be within.
Such, however, was not the case, and Joan's step-mother
explained the nature of her fears.

"He'm to sea, but the whole world do knaw you be come,
I'll lay; and he'll knaw tu. Sure as death some long-tongued
female will babble it to en 'fore he's off the quay. Then
what?"

"'Tedn' your fault anyways," declared Uncle Sampy.
"Joan's wisht an' sad to see home agin, as was right an'
proper; an' in her present way she've got to be humoured.
So I've brot her, an' what blame comes o't my shoulders is
more'n broad enough to carry. I wish, for my paart, as
Michael was home, so I might faace en when Joan says what
her've comed to say. I be gwaine to Penzance now, 'pon a
matter of business, an' I'll come back here in an hour or so an'
drink a dish o' tea along with you 'fore we staarts."

He drove away immediately, and for a while Joan was left
with Mrs. Tregenza. The latter's curiosity presently soothed
her fears, and almost the first thing she began to talk about
was the 'will and testament' which she had long since urged

upon her step-daughter. But the girl, moving about in the well-known orchard, had no attention for anything but the sights, sounds, and scents around her. Silently and not unhappily she basked in old sensations renewed, and they filled her heart. Meanwhile Thomasin kept up a buzz of conversation concerning Joan's money and Joan's future.

"Touchin' that bit o' writin'. Do 'e see to it, soas; 'tis awnly wisdom. There's allus a fear wi' the fust, specially in the case o' a pin-tail built lass like you be. An' if you was took—which God forbid!—theer'd be that mort o' money to come to Michael, him bein' your faither—that is, s'pose the cheel was took tu, which God forbid likewise. An' he'd burn it —every note—I mean Michael. Now, if you was to name Tom —just in case o' accidents? He'm of your awn blood by's faither."

"But my baaby must be fust."

"In coourse 'er must. 'Tis lawful an' right. Love children do come as sweet an' innercent on to the airth as them born o' wedlock—purty sawls. 'Tis the fashion to apprentice 'em to theer faithers mostly, an' they be a sort o' poor cousins o' the rightful fam'ly; but your li'l wan—well, theer edn' gwaine to be any 'poor cousin' talk 'bout en, if it do live. But I was talkin' o' the will."

"I've writ it out all fair in ink, 'cordin' as Uncle Chirgwin advised," said Joan. "Fust comes my cheel, then Tom. Uncle sez theer ban't no call to name others. I wanted hisself to take a half on it; but he said theer weren't no need, an' he wouldn't nohow."

"Quite right," declared Thomasin. "'Iss, fay! He be a plain dealer an' a righteous man."

Joan's thoughts meanwhile were mainly concerned with her surroundings, and when she had walked thrice about the garden, visited the pigs, peeped into the tool-house to smell the paint and twine, noted the ripening plums and a promising little crop of beets coming on in the field beyond, she went indoors. There a pair of Michael's tall sea-boots stood in the chimney-corner, with a small pair of Tom's beside them; the old, well-remembered crockery shone from the dresser; geraniums and begonias filled the window; on a basket at the right of the fireside stood a small blue plate with gold lettering upon it, and a picture of Saltash Bridge in the middle. The legend ran—" *A Present for a Good Girl.*" It was a gift from her father to Joan on her tenth birthday. She picked it up, polished it, and asked for a piece of paper to wrap it in, designing to carry the trifle away with her.

Every old nook and corner had been visited by the time that Uncle Chirgwin returned. Then all sat down to eat and drink; and the taste of the tea went still further to quicken Joan's memory.

Mrs. Tregenza gave them such information as suggested itself to her during the progress of the meal. She was chiefly concerned about her son.

"Cruel 'ard worked he be, sure 'nough," she murmured. "'Tis contrary to reason a boy can graw when he's made to sweat as Tom be. An' short for his age as 'tis. But butivul broad, an' 'mazin' strong, an' a fine sight to see en ate his food. Then the Gosp'lers—well, they'm cold friends to the young. A bwoy like him caan't feel religion in his blood same as grawed folks."

"Small blame to en," said Joan, promptly. "Let en go to church an' hear proper holy ministers in black an' white gownds an' proper words set down in print, same as what I do."

"I'd a'most as soon not have my flaish creep down the spine 'pon Sundays," confessed Thomasin; "but Michael's Michael, an' so all's said."

Uncle Chirgwin went to smoke a pipe and water his horse at this juncture; but he returned within less than ten minutes.

"It's blowin'," he said, "an' the fust skew o' grey rain's breakin' over the sea. I knawed 'twas comin' by my corns. The bwoats is sailin' back tu—a frothin' in proper ower the lumpy water."

"Then you'd best be movin'," said Mrs. Tregenza. "I judged bad-fashioned weather was comin' tu, when, I touched the string o' seaweed as hangs by the winder. 'Tis clammy to the hand. God save us!" she continued, turning from the door; "theer's ourn at the moorin's! They've been driv' back 'fore us counted 'pon seein' 'em by the promise of storm. Get you gone, for the love o' the Lard; an' go Mouz'le way, else you'll run on top o' Michael for sure!"

"Bain't no odds if us do. Joan had a mind to," answered the farmer.

But Joan spoke for herself. She explained that she now wished to depart without seeing her father if possible.

It was, however, too late to escape a meeting. Even as the twain bade Mrs. Tregenza a hasty farewell, heavy feet sounded on the cobbles at the cottage door, and a moment later Tregenza entered. His oilskins were wet and shiny; half a dozen herrings, threaded through the gills on a string, hung from his right hand.

CHAPTER III.

"THE LORD IS KING."

Michael Tregenza instantly observed Joan where she sat by the window, and, seeing her, stood still. The fish fell from his hand, and went slithering in a heap on the stone floor. There was a silence so great that all could hear a patter of drops from the fisherman's oilskins as the water rolled to the ground. At the same moment gusts of rising wind shook the casement, and bleared the glass in it with rain. Joan, as she rose and stood near Mr. Chirgwin, heard her heart thump, and felt the blood leap. Then she nerved herself, came a little forward, and spoke before her father had time to do so. He had now turned his gaze from her, and was looking at the farmer.

"Faither," she said very gently—"faither dearie, forgive me. I begs it so hard; 'tis the thing I wants most. I feared to see 'e, but you was sent off the waters that I might. I comed in tremblin' an' sorrer to see where I've lived most all my days. I'm that differ'nt now to what I was. Uncle Sampy 'll tell 'e. I know I'm a sinful, wicked wummon, an' I'm heart-broke day an' night for the shame I've brot 'pon my folks. I'll trouble 'e no more if 'e will awnly say the word. Please, please, faither, forgive!"

She stood without moving, as did he. Uncle Chirgwin watched silently. Mrs. Tregenza made some stir at the fire to conceal her anxiety. No relenting glimmer softened either the steel of Grey Michael's eyes or one line in his great face. The furrows knotted between his eyebrows and at the corners of his eyes. His sou'wester still covered his head. At his mouth

was a down-drawing, as of disgust before some offensive sight
or smell, and the hand which had held the fish was clenched.
He swallowed, and found speech hard. Then Joan spoke again.

"Uncle's forgived me, an' Mary, an' Tom, an' mother here.
Caan't 'e—caan't 'e, faither? My road's that hard."

Then he answered, his words bursting out of his lips sharply,
painfully at first, rolling as usual in his mighty chest-voice
afterwards. The man twisted Scripture to his narrow purposes
according to Luke Gospel usage.

"Forgive? Who can forgive but the Lard; an' what is man
that he should forgive them the A'mighty's damned? 'Tis the
sinner's bleat an' whine for forgiveness what's crackin' the ear o'
God whensoever 'tis bent 'pon airth. Ain't your religion taught
you that—you, Sampson Chirgwin? If not, 'tis a brawken
reed, man. Get you gone, you faggot, you an' this here white-
haired sawl as is foolin' you an' holdin' converse wi' the outcast
o' Heaven. I ban't no faither o' yourn, thank God, as shawed
me I weern't—never, never. Gaw! Gaw, both of 'e. My God!
the sight of 'e do sicken me as I stand in the same air. You—
an auld man—touchin' her an' her devil-sent, filthy moneys!
'Twas a' evil day, Sampson Chirgwin, when I fust seed them
o' your blood—an ill hour, an' you drives it red-hot into my
brain with your actions. Bad, bad you be—bad as that lyin',
false, lost sinner theer—a-draggin' out your cant o' forgiveness,
an' foolin' a damned sawl wi' falsehoods. *You* knaws wheer
she'm gwaine; an' your squeakin', time-servin' passon knaws;
an' you both tells her differ'nt !"

"Out on 'e, stone-hearted wretch o' a man!" began Uncle
Chirgwin, in a small voice, shaking with anger.

But the fisherman had not said his last word, and roared the
other down. Grey Michael's self-control was less than usual;
his face had grown very red, and surcharged veins showed black
on the unwrinkled sides of his forehead.

"No more—not a word. Get you gone, an' never agin set
foot 'pon this here draxel.* Never—never, none o' the Chirgwin

* *Draxel*, threshold.

breed. Gaw! or auld as you be, I'll force 'e! God's on the side o' right!"

Hereupon Joan, not judging correctly of the black storm signs on her father's face, or the force of the voice now grating into a shriek as passion tumbled to flood, prayed yet again for that pardon which her parent was powerless to grant. The boon denied grew precious in her eyes. She wept and importuned, falling on her knees to him.

"God can do it—God can do it, faither. Please—please, for the sake o' the God as leads you, forgive. O God in heaven, make en forgive me—'tis all I wants!

But a religious delirium gripped Tregenza, and poisoned the blood in him. His breast rose, his fists clenched, his mouth was dragged sideways, and his under-lip shook. A damned soul, looking up with wild eyes into his, was all he saw—the very offscouring and filth of human nature—hell-tinder, to touch which in kindness was to risk his own salvation.

"Gaw—gaw! Else the Lard'll make me His weapon. He's whisperin'—He's whisperin'!"

There was something horribly akin to genuine madness in the frenzy of this utterance. Mrs. Tregenza screamed; Joan struggled to her feet in some terror, and her head swam. She turned to get her hat from the dresser-ledge, and as she did so the little blue plate, tied up in paper beside it, fell and broke, like the link of a snapping chain. Grey Michael was making a snorting in his nostrils, and his head seemed to grow lower on his shoulders. Then Mr. Chirgwin found his opportunity, and spoke.

"I've heard you, an' it ban't human nature to knuckle down dumb, so I be gwaine to speak, an' you can mind or not, as you please."

He flung his old hat upon the ground, and walked without fear close beside the fisherman, who towered above him.

"God be with 'e, I sez, for you need En fine an' bad for sartain—worse 'n that poor, 'mazed lamb shakin' theer. You talk o' the ways o' God to men, an' knaw no more 'bout 'em

than the feesh what you draw from the sea! You'm choustin'
yourself cruel wi' your self-righteousness—take it from me.
You'm saved, be you? *You* be gwaine to heaven, are 'e?
Who tawld 'e so, Michael Tregenza? Did God A'mighty send
a flyin' angel to tell 'e a purpose? Look in your heart, man,
an' see how much o' Christ be in it! Christ, I tell 'e—Christ
—Christ—Jesus Christ. 'Tis *Him* as 'll smuggle us all into
heaven—not your psalm-smitin', knock-me-down, ten-command-
ment, cussin' God. I'm grawin' very auld, an' I knaw what I
knaw. Your God's a *Devil*, fisherman—a graspin', cruel Devil;
an' them the Devil saves is damned. 'Tis Christ as you've
turned your stiff back 'pon—Christ as'll let this poor lass into
heaven afore ever you gets theer! You ban't in sight o' the
gates o' pearl, not you, for all your cold prayers. You'm young
in well-doin'; an' tis a 'ard road you'll fetch home by, I'll
swear; an' 'tis more 'n granite the Lard 'll use to make your
heart bleed. He'll break you, Tregenza—you, so bold, as looks
dry-eyed 'pon the sun, an' reckons your throne'll wan day be
as bright. He'll break you, an' bring you to your knees, an'
that 'fore your grey hairs be turned, as mine, to white. Oh,
Christ Jesus, look You at this blind sawl, an' give en somethin'
better to lay hold 'pon than his poor bally-muck o' religion
what's nort but a gert livin' lie!"

Uncle Chirgwin seemed mightily transfigured as he spoke.
The words came without an effort, but he uttered them with
pauses, and in a loud voice not lacking solemnity. His head
shook, yet he stood firm and motionless upon his feet; and he
made his points with a gesture, often repeated, of his open
right hand.

As for Tregenza, the man listened through all, though he
heard but little. His head was full of blood; there was a
weight on his tongue, striking it silent, and forcing his mouth
open at the same moment. The world looked red as he saw it;
his limbs were not bearing him stiffly. Thomasin had her eye
upon him, for she was quite prepared to throw over her previous
statements, and support her husband against an attack so

astounding and unexpected. And the more so that he had not himself hurled an immediate and crushing answer.

Meantime the old farmer's sudden fires died within him; he shrank to his true self, and the voice in which he now spoke seemed that of another man.

"Give heed to what I've said to 'e, Michael, an' be humble afore the Lard, same as your darter be. Go in fear, as you be for ever biddin' all flaish to go. Never say no sawl's lost while you give all power to the Maker o' sawls. Go in fear, I sez, else theer'll come a whirlwind o' God-sent sorrer to strike wheer your heart's desire be rooted. 'Tis allus so—allus——"

Tom entered upon these words, and Uncle Chirgwin's eyes dropping upon him as he spoke, his utterance sounded like a prophecy. So the boy's mother read it, and with a half-sob, half-shriek, she turned in all the frenzy of sudden maternal wrath. Her sharp tongue dropped mere vituperation, but did so with boundless vigour, and the woman's torrent of unbridled curses and threats swept that scene of storm to its close. Joan went first from the door, while Mr. Chirgwin, picking up his hat and buttoning his coat, retreated after her before the volume of Thomasin's virago attack. Tom stood open-mouthed and silent, dumbfounded at the tremendous spectacle of his mother's rage, and his father's stricken silence. Then, as Mrs. Tregenza slammed the door and wept, her husband sank slowly down with something strangely like terror in his eyes. The man, in truth, had just passed through a physical crisis of alarming nature. He sat in his easy chair now, removed his hat, and wiped the perspiration from his forehead with hands that shook. It was not what he had heard or beheld that woke alarm in a spirit which had never known it till then, but what he had felt; a horror which crowded down upon every sense, gripped his volition with unseen hands, blinded him, stopped his ears, held his limbs, stirred his brains into a whirling waste. He knew now that in his moment of passion he had stood upon the very brink of some terrific, shattering evil, possibly of death itself. Body or brain, or both, had passed through a great, unknown danger; and now, dazed and for the time much aged, he looked about him with slow eyes—mastered the situation, and realized the incident was ended.

"'The Lard'—'the Lard is King,'" he said, and stopped a moment. Then he slowly rose to his feet, and in the old voice, though it shook and slurred somewhat upon his tongue, spoke that text which served him in all occasions of unusual stress and significance. "'The Lard is King, be the people never so impatient; He sitteth between the cherubims, be the airth never so unquiet!'"

Then he sat again, and long remained motionless with his face buried in his hands.

Meantime the old horse dragged Uncle Chirgwin and his niece away along the level road to Mousehole. Joan was wrapped in a tarpaulin, and they proceeded silently awhile under cold rains, which swept up from a leaden south over the sea. The wind blew strong, tore green leaves from the hedges, and chimed with the thoughts of the man and his niece.

"How did you come to speak so big an' braave, Uncle Sampy? I couldn' say no more to en, for the lights rose up in my throat an' choked me; but you swelled out somethin' grand to see, an' spawk as no man ever yet spawk to faither afore."

"''Twas put in me to say; I doan't knaw how ever I done it, but my tongue weern't my awn for the time. Pull that thing tighter about 'e. This rain would go through a barn door."

At the steep hill rising from Mousehole to Paul, Uncle Chirgwin got out and walked, while the horse, with his shoulders to the collar, plodded forward. Then down the road came the labouring man, Billy Jago, mentioned aforetime as one who had worked for Mr. Chirgwin in the past. He touched his hat to his old master, and greeted him with respect and regard. For a moment the farmer also stopped. No false sentiment tied Billy's tongue, and he spoke of matters personal to those before him, having first mournfully described his own state of health.

" But theer, us gaws down to the tomb to make way for the new-born ; an' I hopes theer's a braave bwoy under your belt, young leddy. I do say, an' swear tu, that the butivulest things in all wild nachur be a ship in full sail an' a wummon in the fam'ly-way. Ban't nothin' to beat ' em. An' I'll say it here, 'pon this spot, though the rain's bitin' into my bones like teeth. So long to 'e, maaster, an' good cheeldin' to 'e, miss ! "

The man rolled with loutish gait down the hill ; the darkness gathered ; the wind whistled through high hedges on the left ; Farmer Chirgwin made some sounds of encouragement to his horse, which moved onwards ; and Joan thought with curious interest of those things that Billy Jago had said.

" 'Tis strange us met that poor, croony antic at sich a moment," mused Uncle Sampy. " The words of en jag sore 'pon a body's mind, comin' arter what's in our thots like."

" Maybe 'tis paart o' the queerness o' things as us should fall 'pon en now," answered Joan.

Then, through a stormy gloaming, they returned in sadness to the high lands of Drift.

CHAPTER IV.

A GLEN-ADER.

"A NEW broom sweeps clean, but 'tis the auld wan as is good for corners," said Uncle Chirgwin, when, with his nieces, he sat beside the kitchen fire that night and discussed the events of the day. "By which I means," he added, " that these new-fangled ways of approaching the A'mighty may go to branch and trunk, an' make a clean sweep o' evil, but they leaves the root o' pride stickin' in a man's sawl. T'is the auld broom as Christ brought in the world as routs into the dark corners like nothin' else."

"I be glad you spawk to en," said Mary. " Seed sawed do bring forth fruit in a 'mazin' way."

"I reckoned he'd 'a' smote me, but he dedn'. He just turned rosy red an' stood glazin' at me as if I was a ghost."

"I never see en look like that afore," declared Joan ; "he 'peared to be afeared. But the door's shut 'gainst me now. I caan't do no more'n I have done. He'll never forgive."

"As to that, Joan, I won't say. You bide quiet till the seed sprouts. I lay now as you'll hear tell about your faither, an' maybe get a message from en, 'fore the year's a month older."

With which hopeful prediction Uncle Chirgwin ended the discussion.

That night the circular storm, which had died away at dark, turned upon itself, and the wind moaned at window latches and down chimneys, prophesying autumn. Dawn broke on a drenched grey world, but the storm had clean passed, and at noon the grey brightened to silver and burnt to gold when the sun came out. The wind wore to the west and on to north-west; the weather settled down, and days of a rare late summer pursued their even way.

A fortnight passed, and the farmer's belief that Grey Michael would communicate with his daughter began to waver.

"Pharaoh's a soft-'earted twoad to this wan," he declared gloomily. "It do beat me to picksher sich a man. I've piped to en hot an' strong, as Joan knaws, but he ban't gwaine to dance 'tall seemin'ly. Poor sawl! When the hand o' the Lard do fall, God send 'twon't crush en all in all. 'Saved'—*him*—dear, dear!"

"The likes of Tregenza be saved 'pon St. Tibb's Eve,* I reckon, an' no sooner," answered Mary, scornfully. Then she modified her fiery statement according to her custom, for the woman's zeal always had first call upon her tongue, and her judgment usually took off the edge of every harsh statement immediately upon its utterance. "Leastways 'tis hard to see how sich bowldashious standin' up in the eye o' God should prosper. But us can be saved even from our awn selves, I s'pose. So Tregenza have got his chance along o' the best."

Joan never resented the outspoken criticisms on her parent. She listened, but rarely joined the discussion. The whole matter speedily sank to a position of insignificance. Her own mind was clear, and the dead-lock only cut off one more outer interest and reduced Life's existing influences to a smaller field. She drew more and more into herself, slipped more and more from out the routine life of Drift. She became self-centred, and when her body was not absent, as happened upon most fine days, her mind abstracted itself to extreme limits. She grew shy of fellow-creatures, found no day happy of which a part had not been spent beside a cross, showed a gradual indifference to the services of the Church, which not long since had attracted her so strongly and braced the foundations of her soul. There came at last a black Sunday when Joan refused to accompany Mary and the farmer to morning worship at Sancreed. She

* *St. Tibb's Eve,* equivalent to the "Greek Calends."

made no excuse, but designed a pilgrimage of more than usual length, and having driven as far as the church with her uncle and cousin, left them there and walked on her way. Even the fascinations of a harvest festival failed to charm her; and the spectacle of fat roots, mighty marrows, yellow corn and red apples on the window ledges; of grapes and tomatoes, flowers and loaves upon the altar, pulpit, and font, did not appeal over-much to Joan—a fact perhaps surprising.

With a plump pasty in her pocket, and one of Uncle Chirgwin's walking-sticks to help her footsteps, Joan went on her way, passed the Wesleyan chapel of Sancreed, and then maintained a reasonably direct line to her destination by short cuts and field paths. She intended to visit Mên Scryfa, that famous "long stone" which stands away in a moor croft beyond Lanyon. She knew that it was no right cross, but she remembered it well, having visited the monument fre-quently in the past. It was holy with infinite age, and the writing upon it fascinated her, as a mystery fascinates most of us. The words, "*Rialobrani Cunovali fili*," which probably mark the fact that Rialobran, son of Cunoval, some Brito-Celtic chieftain of old, lies buried not far distant, meant nothing to Joan; but the old grey-headed stone—perhaps the loneliest in all Cornwall—was pleasant to her thoughts, and she trudged forward gladly with her eyes open for all the beauties of a smiling world.

Summer clouds, sunny-hearted and towering against the blue, dropped immense shadows on the glimmering gold of much stubble, and on the wastes of the moor rising above them. In the corn-fields, visible now that the crops were cut and gathered into mows, stood little grey-green islands—a mark distinctive of Cornish husbandry. Here grew cow-cabbages in rank luxuriance on mounds of manure which would be presently scattered over the exhausted land. The little oases in the deserts of the fields were too familiar to arrest Joan's eye. She merely glanced at the garnered wheat and thought what a brief time the arrish geese, stuffing themselves in the stubble, had yet to live. A solemn, splendid peace held the country-side, and hardly a soul was abroad where the road led upwards to wild moor and waste. Sometimes a group of calves crowding under the shady side of hedges regarded Joan with youthful interest; sometimes, in a distant coomb-bottom, where black-berries grew, little sunbonnets bobbed above the fern, and a child's shrill voice came clear to her upon the wind. But the loneliness grew, and, anon, turning from her way awhile, the traveller sat on the grey crown of Trengwainton Carn to rest and look at the wide world.

From the little tor, over undulations of broad light and blue shadow, Joan could see afar to Buryan's lofty tower, to Paul above the sea, to Sancreed's sycamores, and to Drift beyond them. Wild sweeps of fell and field faded on the sight to those dim and remote hues of distance only visible upon days of exceeding aerial brilliancy. Immediately beneath the eminence subtended ragged expanses of rainbow coloured heath and furze and fern, spotted with small fir trees which showed blue against the tones of the moor. The heather's pink clearly contrasted with the paler shades of the ling, and an additional silvery twinkle of light inhabited the latter plant—its cause, last year's dead white branches and twigs, still scattered through the living foliage and flower. Out of a myriad bells that wild world spoke, and the murmur of the heath came as the murmur of a wise voice to the ear on which it fell. There was a soul in the day; it lived, and Joan looked into the eyes of a glorious, conscious entity, herself a little part of the space-filling whole.

Presently, refreshed by brief rest, the pilgrim journeyed on over a road which climbs the moor above deep fox-covers of rhododendron, already mentioned as visible from Madron chapel. The way dipped presently, crossed a rivulet and mounted again past the famous cromlech of Lanyon. But Joan passed the quoit unheeding, and kept upon flint roads through Lanyon farm, where its irregular buildings stretch across the hill-crest. She saw the stacks roped strangely in nets with heavy stones to secure them against winter gales; she observed the various familiar objects of Drift repeated on a greater scale; then, going downhill yet again, Joan struck up the course of another stream and passed steadily over broad, granite-dotted tangles of whin, heather, and rank grasses to her destination. Here the heath was blasted and scarred with summer fires. Great patches of the waste had been eaten naked by past flames, and Mên-an-tol —the " crickstone "—past which she progressed, stood with its lesser granite pillars in a dark bed of scorched earth and blackened furze-stems stripped bare by the fire. She stood in a wide, desolate cup of the Cornish moor. To the south Ding-Dong Mine reared its shattered chimney stack; towards the north-west Carn Galvas—that rock-piled fastness of dead giants—reared a grey head against the blue. A curlew piped; a lizard rustled into a tussock of grass where pink bog-heather and seeding cotton grasses gemmed the sodden ground; a dragon-fly from the marsh stayed a moment upon Mên-an-tol, and the jewel of his eyes was as a little world holding all the colours of the larger.

Joan, keeping her way to where Carn Galvas rose over the next ridge, walked another few hundred yards, crossed a disused road, climbed a stony bank, and then stood in the little croft sacred to Mên Scryfa. At the centre, above a land almost barren save for stunted heath and wind-beaten fern, it rose—a tall monolith of rough and irregular shape. The bare black earth, in which shone quartz crystals, stretched at hand in squares; from these raw spaces turf had been cut, to be subsequently burnt for manure; and it stood hard by, stacked in a row of beat-burrows or little piles of over-lapping pieces, the cut side out. Near the famous old stone itself, surmounting a barrow-like tumulus, grew stunted bracken; and here Joan presently sat down full of happiness in that her pilgrimage had been achieved. The granite pillar of Mên Scryfa was crested with that fine yellow-grey lichen which finds life on exposed stones; upon the windward side clung a few atoms of golden growth, and its rude carved inscription straggled down the northern face. The monument rose sheer above black corpses of crooked

furze—for fire had swept this region also—adding not a little to
the prevailing sobriety of it, and only the elemental splendour
of weather, and the canopy of blue and gold beneath which
spread this desolation, rendered it less than mournful. From
under these circumstances imagination, as though rebelling
against the conditions of sunshine and summer then main-
taining, leapt to picture Mên Scryfa under the black screaming
of winter storm or rising darkly upon deep snows; casting a
transitory shadow over a waste ghastly blue under flashes
of lightning, or throbbing to its deep roots when thunder
roared over the moor, and the levin hissed unseen into quag
and fen.

The double crown of Carn Galvas fronted Joan as she presently sat with her back resting against the stone; and a
medley of the old thoughts rose not unwelcome in her mind.
Giant mythology seemed a true thing in sight of these vast
regular piles of granite; and the thought of the kind simple
monsters who had raised that carn led to musings on the
" little people." Her mind brooded over the fairies and their
strange ways with young human mothers. She remembered
the stories of changelings, and vowed to herself that her own
babe should never be out of sight. These reflections found no
adverse criticism in faith. The Bible held its giants; and if
no fairies were mentioned therein, she had read nothing aimed
against them. Presently she prayed for the coming child. Her
soul went with the words; and they were addressed with
vagueness, as became her vague thoughts, half to Mên Scryfa,
half to God, all in the name of Christ.

Going home again, after noon, Joan found a glen-ader,*
which circumstance is here mentioned to illustrate the conflict-
ing nature of those many forces still active in her mind. That
they should have co-existed and not destroyed each other is the
point of most peculiarity. But it seemed for a moment as

---

* *Glen-ader*, the cast skin of an adder. Once accounted a powerful
amulet, and still sometimes secretly preserved by the ignorant, as sailors
treasure a caul.

though the girl had intellectually passed at least that form of superstition embraced by coveted possession of a glen-ader; for, upon finding the thing lying extended like a snake's ghost, she hesitated before picking it up. The old tradition, however, sucked in from a credulous parent with much similar folly at a time when the mind accepts impressions most readily, was too strong for Joan. Qualms she had, and some whisper at the bottom of her mind was heard with a clearness sufficient to make her uncomfortable, but reason held a feeble citadel at best within her. The whisper died, memory spoke of the notable value which wise men through long past years had placed upon this charm; and in the face of the future, it seemed wicked to reject a thing of such proven efficacy. So she picked up the adder's slough, designing to sew it upon a piece of flannel and henceforth wear it against her skin until her baby should be born. But she determined to tell neither Mary nor her uncle, though she did not stop to ask why secrecy thus commended itself to her.

That evening Mary came primed from church-going with grave admonition. Mr. Chirgwin was tearful, and hinted at his own sorrow arising from Joan's backsliding; but Mary did not mince language, and spoke what she thought.

"You'm wrong, an' you knaw you'm wrong," she said. "The crosses be very well, an' coorious, butivul things to see 'pon the land tu, but they'm poor food to a body's sawl. They caan't shaw wheer you'm out; they caan't lead 'e right."

"'Iss, they can, then, an' they do," declared Joan. "The more I bide along wi' 'em, the better I feel an' the nearer to God A'mighty, so theer! They'm allus the same, an' they puts thots in my head that's good to think; an' I must go my ways, Polly, same as you go yours."

When night came, Joan slept within the mystic circumference of the glen-ader; and that she derived a growing measure of mental satisfaction from its embrace is unquestionable.

CHAPTER V.

" COME TO ME!"

A SPACE of time six weeks in duration may be hastily dismissed
as producing no alteration in Joan's method of thought and life.
It swept her swiftly through shortening days and the last of
the summer weather to the climax of her fortunes. As the
season waned she kept nearer home, going not much further
than Tremathick Cross on the St. Just road, or to that relic
already mentioned as lying outside Sancreed churchyard. These,
in time, she associated as much with her child as with herself.
The baby had now taken its natural place in her mind, and she
prayed every day that it might presently forgive her for bringing it into the world at all. Not unhappy, with her beauty
still a startling fact, Joan mused away long hours at the feet
of her granite friends through the waning splendours of many
an autumn noon. Then, within the brief space of two weeks,
a period of weather almost unexampled in the memory of the
oldest agriculturists drew to its close.

That mighty rains must surely come all knew, but none
foretold their tremendous volume, or foresaw the havoc, ruin,
and destruction to follow upon their outpouring. Meantime,
with late September, the leaves began to hustle early to earth
under great winds. Rain fell at times, but not heavily at first,
and a thirsty world drank open-mouthed through deep sun-
cracks in field and moor and dried-up marsh. But bedraggled
autumn's robes were soon washed colourless; the heath turned
pallid before it faded to sere brown; rotten banks of decaying
leaves rose high under the hedges. There was no dry, crisp

whirl of gold on the wind, but a sodden condition gradually over-
spread the land. The earth grew drunken with the later rains,
and could hold no more. The end of October saw the last of the
purple and crimson, the tawny browns and royal yellows. Only
beeches, their wet leaves, by many shades inferior to their
customary splendour at this season, still retained much foliage.
The trees put on their winter shapes unduly early. The world
was dark, and sweated fungus. Uncouth children of the earth,
whose hour is that which sees the leaf fall, sprang into short-
lived being. Black goblins and grey, white goblins and brown,
spread weird life abroad. With fleshy gills, squat and lean, fat
and thin, bursting through the grass in companies and circles,
lurking livid, gigantic and alone on the trunks of forest trees,
gemming the rotten bough with crimson, twinkling like topaz
on the crooked stems of the furze, battening upon death, rising
into transitory vigour from the rack and rot of a festering earth,
—they flourished.

Heavy mists stretched their draperies over the high lands;
and exhalations from the corpse of the summer hung bluish
under the rain in the valleys. One night a full moon shone
clearly, and through the ambient light ominous sheets and
splashes of silver glimmered in the low fields. Here they
had slowly and silently spread into existence, their birth hidden under the mists, their significance marked by none but
anxious farmers. All men hoped that the full moon would
bring cessation of this rainfall; but another grey dawn faced
them on the morrow, and a thousand busy rills murmured and
babbled down the lanes round Drift. Here and there unsuspected springs burst their hidden chambers, and swept by steep
courses over the green grass to join these main waters, which
now raced through the valley. The light of day was heavy,
and pressed upon the sight. It acted like a telescope in the
intervals of no rain, and brought distant objects into strange
distinctness. The weather was much too warm even for western
Cornwall. A few leaves still hung on the crown of the apple
trees, and such scanty peach and nectarine foliage as yet

remained was green. The red currants flaunted a gold leaf or two, and the remaining leaves of the black currant were purple after his fashion. Joan marvelled to see sundry of her favourites thrusting forth tokens of spring almost before autumn was ended. Lilac buds swelled to bursting; a peony pushed many pink points upward through the brown ruins of the past; bulbs were growing rapidly; Nature had forgotten winter for once, as it seemed. Thus the sodden, sunless, steaming days followed each on the last until farming folk began to grow grave before a steady increase of water on the land. Much hay stood in danger, and some ricks had been already ruined. Many theories were rife, Uncle Chirgwin's being, upon the whole, the most fatuous.

"'Tis a thunder-planet," he told his nieces, "an' till us have a rousing storm o' crooked forks an' heavy thunder this rain'll go on fallin'. But not so much as a flap o' the collybran * do us get, for all the heat o' the air. I should knaw, if any, for I be out turnin' night into day, an' markin' the water in the valley every evenin' long after dark now. I'm fearin' graave for the big stack; an' theer's three paarts o' last year's hay beside, an' two tidy li'l mows of the aftermath. So sure's the waters do rise another foot and a half, 'tis 'good-bye' to the whole boilin'. Not but 'twill be a miracle for the stream to get much higher. The moor's burstin' wi' rain, but the coffins † do hold it up, I s'pose, an' keep it aloft. A penn'orth o' frost now would save a pound of produce from wan end o' Carnwall to t'other."

Joan spent many long days in the house at this time, and practised an unskilful needle, while her thoughts wandered far and near through the sullen weather to this old cross and that. Then came a night of rainless darkness, through which past accumulations of water still thundered. Nature rested for some hours before her final, shattering deluge; but the brief peace was more tremendous than rain or wind, for a mighty foreboding

* *Collybran*, sheet lightning.
† *Coffins*, ancient mining excavations.

permeated it, and all men felt the end was not yet, though none could say why they feared the silence more than storm.

It happened upon this black night that Joan was alone in the kitchen. Supper had been but a scrambling meal, and her uncle, with Amos Bartlett and all the men on the farm, were now somewhere in the valley under the darkness fighting for the hay with rising water. Where Mary was just then Joan did not know. Her thoughts were occupied with her own affairs, and in the oppressive silence she sat watching some little moving threadlike concerns which hung in a row through a crack below the mantel-piece above the open fire. They were the tails of mice which often here congregated nigh the warmth and sat in a row, themselves invisible. The tails moved, and Joan noted some shorter tails beside long ones, telling of infant vermin at their mothers' sides. In the silence she could hear the squeaking of them, and now and then she talked to them very softly.

"Thank God, you li'l mice, as you abbun got no brains in your heads, an' no call to look far in the future. I lay you'm happier than us, wi' nort to fear 'bout 'cept crumbs, an' a low snug spot to live in."

Thus she stumbled on the lowest note of pessimism : that conscious intelligence is a supreme mistake. But the significance of her idea she knew not.

Then Joan rose up, shivered with a sudden sense of chill, stamped her feet, and caused the row of tails below the mantel to vanish.

"Goose-flaish down the spine do mean as theer's feet walkin' 'pon my graave, I s'pose," she thought, as a heavy knock at the front door interrupted her reflections.

Hastening to open it, Joan found the postman—a rare visitor at Drift. He handed her a letter, and prepared to depart immediately.

"I'm grievous afeared o' Buryas Bridge to-night," he said. When I comed over, two hour back, the water was above the arches, an', so like's not, I won't get 'cross 'tall if it's riz higher. An' somethin' cruel's comin', I'll lay my life, 'fore maruin'. This pitch-black silence be worse than the noise o' the rain."

He vanished down the hill, and, returning to the kitchen, Joan lighted a candle and examined the letter. A fit of trembling shook the girl to the hidden seat of her soul as she did so for her own name greeted her, in neat printed letters akin to those on the superscription of another letter she had received in the past. From John Barron it was that this communication came, and the reception of it begot a wild chaos of mind which now carried Joan headlong backward. Images swept through her brain with the bewildering rapidity and brilliance of lightning flashes; she was whirled and tossed on a flood of thoughts. A single, sad-eyed figure retained permanency, and rose clear and separated itself from this phantasmagorial procession of personages and events wending through her mind. They dissolved each into the other; they stretched the circumstances of eight short months into an eternity; they crowded the solemn aisles of time past with shadows of those emotions which had reigned over the dead spring-time of the year, and were themselves long dead.

Thus she stood for a space of vast apparent duration, but in reality most brief. That trifling standpoint in time needed for a dream or for the brain-picture of his past which dominates the mind of the drowning, was all that had sped with Joan. Then, shaking herself clear of thought, she found her candle, which burnt dim when first lighted, was only now melting the wax and rising to its full flame. A mist of damp had long hung on the inner walls of the kitchen at Drift, begotten not of faulty building, but by the peculiar condition of the atmosphere; and as the candle flickered up in a chamber dark save for its light, and the subdued glow of a low fire, Joan noticed how the gathering moisture on the walls had coalesced, run into drops and fallen, streaking the misty grey with bright bars and networks, silvery as the slime of snails.

With shaking hand, she set the candle upon a table, dropped

into a chair beside it, and opened her letter. For a moment the page with its large printed characters danced before her eyes, then they steadied, and she was able to read. Like a message from one long dead came the words; and in truth, though the writer lived, he wrote upon the threshold of the grave. John Barron had put into force his project, which was, as may be remembered, to write to Joan when the end of his journey came in sight. The words were carefully chosen, for he remembered her sympathy with suffering and her extensive ignorance. He wrote in simple language therefore, and dwelt on his own helpless condition, exaggerating it to some extent.

"No. 6, Melbury Gardens, London.

"MY OWN DEAR LOVE,

"What can I say to make you know what has kept me away from you? There is but one word, and that is my poor sick and suffering body. I wrote to you and tore up what I wrote, for I loved you too much to ask you to come and share my sad life. It was very, very awful, to be away, and know you were waiting and waiting for Jan; yet I could not come because Mother Nature was so hard. Then I went far away, and hoped you had forgotten me. Doctors made me go to a place over the sea, where tall palm trees grew up out of a dry yellow desert; but my poor lungs were too sick to get well again, and I came home to die. Yes, sweetheart, you will forgive me for all when you know poor lonely Jan will soon be gone. He cannot live much longer, and he is so weak now that he has no more power to fight against the love of Joan.

"For your own good, dear one, I made myself keep away and hid myself from you. Now the little life left to me cries out by night and by day for you. Joan, my own true love, I cannot die until I have seen you again. Come to me, Joan love, if you do not hate me! Come to me! Come, and close my eyes, and let poor Jan have the one face that he loves quite near him at the end. Even your picture has gone; for they came when I was away and took it and put it in a place with many others for people to see. And all men and women say it is the best picture. I shall be dead before they send it back to me. So now I have nothing but the thoughts of my Joan. Oh, come to me, my love, if you can. It will not be for long, and when Jan lies under the ground all that he has is yours. I have fought so hard to keep from you, and from praying you to come to me, but I can fight no more. My home is named at the top of this letter. You have but to enter the train for London, and stop in it until it gets to the end of its journey. My servant shall wait each day for your coming. I can write no more; I can only pray to the God we both love to bring you to me. And if you come, or do not, I shall have the same great true love for you. I will die alone rather than trouble you to come if you have forgotten me, and not forgiven me for keeping silence. God bless you, my only love.   "JAN."

This feeble stuff rang like a clarion on the ear of the reader, for he who had written it knew how best to strike, how best to appeal with overwhelming force to Joan Tregenza. Her mind plunged straight into the struggle, and the billows of the storm, sweeping aside lesser obstructions, were soon beating against the new-built ramparts of faith. The rush of thought which had coursed through her brains before reading the letter now made the task of deciding upon it easier. Indeed, it can hardly be said that any real doubt from first to last assailed Joan's decision. Faith did not crumble, but, at a second glance, appeared to her wholly compatible with obedience to this demand. There was an electric force in every word of the letter. It proved Mister Jan's wondrous nobility of character, his unselfishness, his love. He had suffered too, had longed eternally for her, had denied himself out of consideration for her future happiness, had struggled with his love, and only broken down and given way to it in the shadow of death. Grief shook Joan upon this thought, but joy was uppermost. The long months of weary suffering faded from her recollection as nocturnal mists vanish at the touch of the sun's first fire. She had no power to analyze the position or reflect upon the various courses of action the man might have taken to spare her so much agony. She accepted his bald utterance word for word, as he knew she would. Every inclination and desire swept her towards him now. His cry of suffering; his love, his loneliness; her duty as it stood blazoned upon her mind ten minutes after reading his letter; the child to be born within two months;—all these considerations united to establish Joan's mind at this juncture.

"Come to me!" Those were the words echoing within her heart, and her soul cried upon Christ to shorten time that she might reach him the sooner. Before the world was next awake she would be upon her way; before another night fell "Mister Jan's" arms would be round her. The long, dreary nightmare had ended for her at last. Then came tears of bitter remorse, for she saw how his love had never left her, how he had been true as steel; while she, misled by appearances, had lost faith and lapsed into forgetfulness. A wild, unreasoning yearning, superior to time and space, got hold upon her. "Come to me!" "Come to me!" sounded in Joan's ears in the live voice she had loved and lost and found again. An hour's delay, a minute's, a moment's, seemed a crime. Yet delay there must be, but the tension and terrific excitement of her whole being at this period demanded some immediate outlet in action. She wanted to talk to Uncle Chirgwin, and she desired instant information upon the subject of her journey. First she thought of seeking the farmer in the valley; then it struck her, the hour being not later than eight o'clock, that by going into Penzance, she might learn at what time the morning train departed to London.

Out of doors it was inky black, very silent, very oppressive. Joan called Mary twice before departing, but received no answer. Indeed, the house was empty, though she did not know it. Finally, thrusting the letter into her bosom, taking her hat and cloak from a nail in the kitchen, and putting on a pair of walking shoes, the girl went abroad. Her present medley of thoughts begot a state of exceeding nervous excitation. For the letter touched the two poles of extreme happiness and utmost possible sorrow. "Mister Jan" was calling her to him indeed, but only calling her that she might see him die. Careless of her steps, soothed unconsciously by rapid motion, she walked from the farm, her mind full of joy and grief; and the night, silent no longer for her, was full of a voice crying, "Come to me, Joan, love! Come!"

CHAPTER VI.

THE FLOOD.

In the coomb beneath Drift, flashing as though red-hot from a theatre of unutterable blackness, certain figures, flame-lighted, flickered hurriedly this way and that about a dark and monstrous pile which rose in their midst. From the adjacent hill, superstitious watchers might have supposed that they beheld some demoniac throng newly burst out of the bowels of earth and to be presently re-engulfed; but seen nearer, the toiling creatures, fighting with all their hearts and souls to save a haystack from flood, had merely excited human interest and commiseration. Farmer Chirgwin and his men were girt, as to the legs, in old-fashioned hay-bands; some held torches, while others toiled with ropes to anchor the giant rick against the gathering waters. There was no immediate fear, for the pile still stood a clear foot above the stream on a gentle undulation distant nearly two yards from the present boundary of the swollen river. But, on the landward side, another danger threatened, because in that quarter the meadow sank in a slight hollow which had now changed to a lake fed by a brisk rivulet from the main river. The great rick thus stood almost insulated, and much further uprising of the flood would place it in a position not to be approached by man without danger. Above the stack, distant about five and twenty yards, stood a couple of stout pollarded willows, and by these Uncle Sampy had decided to moor his hay, trusting that they might hold the great mass of it secure, even though the threatened flood swept away its foundations.

Seven figures worked amain, and to them approached an eighth, appearing from the darkness, skirting the lake and splashing through the streamlet which fed it. Mary Chirgwin it was who now arrived—a grotesque figure with her gown and petticoats fastened high and wearing on her legs a pair of her uncle's leather gaiters. Mary had been up to the farm for more rope, but the clothes-line was all that she could find, and with this she now returned. Already three ropes had been passed round the rick and made fast to the willows, but none amongst them were of great stoutness, nor had they been tied at an elevation best calculated to resist a possible strain. Amos Bartlett took the line from Mary and set to work with many assistants; while the farmer himself, waving a torch and stumping hither and thither, now directed Bartlett, now encouraged two men who worked with all their might at the cutting of a trench from the lake in order that this dangerous body of water might be drained back to the main stream. The flame-light danced in many a flash and splash over the smooth surface of the face of the lake. Indeed, it reflected like a glass at present, for no wind fretted it, neither did a drop of rain fall. Intense, watchful silence held that hour. The squash of men's feet in the mud, the soft swirl of the water, the cry of voices alone disturbed the night.

"God be praised! I do think 'tis 'bating," cried the farmer presently.

He ran every few minutes to the water and examined a stake hammered into it a foot from the edge. It seemed, as far as might be judged by such fitful light and rough measurement, that the river had sunk an inch or two, but it was running in undulations, and what its muddy mass had lost in volume was gained in speed. The water chattered and hissed; and Amos Bartlett, who next made a survey, declared that the flood had by no means waned, but rather risen. Then, the last ropes being disposed to the best advantage, all joined the labourers who were digging. Twenty minutes later, however, and before the trench was more than three parts finished, there came a tremendous change. Turning hastily to the river, Bartlett uttered a shout of alarm and called for light. He had approached the tell-tale stake, and suddenly, before he reached it, found his feet in the water. The river was rising with fierce rapidity at last, and five minutes later began to lick at the edge of the hayrick and churn along with a strange hidden force and devil in it. The pace increased with the volume, and told of some prodigious outburst on the moor. The uncanny silence of the swelling water as it slipped downward was a curious feature of it in this phase. Chirgwin and his men huddled together at the side of the rick. Then Bartlett held up his hand and spoke.

"Hark 'e, all! 'Tis comin' now, by God!"

They kept silence and listened with straining ears and frightened eyes, fire-rimmed by the flickering torch-light. A sound floated from afar—a sound not unmelodious but singular, beyond power of language to express—a whisper of sinister significance to him who knew its meaning, of sheer mystery to all others. A murmur filled the air, a murmur of undefined noises still far distant. They might have been human; they might have arisen from the flight and terror of beasts, from the movement of vast bodies, from the reverberations of remote music. Earth or heaven might have bred them, or the upper chambers of the air midway between. They spoke of terrific energies, of outpourings of force, of elemental chaos come again, of a crown of unimagined horror set upon the night.

All listened fearfully while the solemn cadences crept on their ears, fascinated them like a syren song, wakened wild dread of tribulations and terrors unknown till now. It was indeed a sound but seldom heard and wholly unfamiliar to those beside the stack save one.

"'Tis the callin' o' the cleeves," said Uncle Chirgwin.

"Nay, man, I heard the like once when a lad. 'Tis a live, ragin' storm comed off the sea, an' tearin' ower the airth like a legion out o' hell! 'Tis the flood-gates o' God opened you'm hearin'! Ay, an' the four winds at each other's throats, an' a outburst o' all the springs 'pon the hills! 'Tis death an' ruin for the whole country-side as be yelling up-long now. An' 'tis comin' faster'n thot."

As Bartlett spoke the voice of the tempest grew rapidly nearer. All mystery faded out of it, and its murmuring changed to a hoarse rattle. Thunder growled a bass to the shriek of coming winds, and a flash of distant lightning bridged the head of the coomb with a crooked snake of fire.

"Us'd best to get 'pon high land out o' this," shouted Bartlett. "All as men can do us have done. The hay's in the hand o' Providence, but I wouldn't be perched on top o' that stack not for di'monds, all the same."

A cry fell on their ears. Mary had turned and found the way to higher ground already cut off. The lake was rising under their eyes, and that in spite of the fact that the waters had already reached the trench cut for them and now tumbled in a torrent back to the parent stream. Escape in this direction was clearly impossible. It only remained to wade through the head of the lake and that without a moment's delay. Mary herself, holding a torch, went first through water above her knees and the men hastily followed, Uncle Chirgwin coming last, and being nearly carried off his short legs as he turned to view the rick. Once through the water all were in safety, for the meadow sloped steeply upwards. An increasing play of lightning made the torches useless, and they were dropped, while the party pressed close beneath an overhanging hedge which ran along the upper boundary of the meadow. From this vantage ground they beheld a spectacle unexampled in the memory of any among them.

Yelling, like some incarnate and insane manifestation of all the elements massed in one, the hurricane launched itself upon that valley. As a wall the wind heralded the water, while forked lightnings, flaming above both, tore the black darkness into jagged rags and lighted a chaos of yellow, foaming wave which battled with livid front straight down the heart of the coomb. The swollen river was lost in the torrent of it, and the hiss of the rain was drowned by its sound.

So Nature's full, hollowed hand ran over, lightning-lighted, to the organ music of the thunder; but for these horror-stricken watchers the majestic phenomena sweeping before them held no splendour and prompted no admiration. They only saw ruin tearing at the roots of the land; they only imagined drowned beasts floating before them belly upwards, scattered hay hurried to the sea, wasted crops, a million tons of precious soil torn off the fields, orchards desolated, bridges and roads destroyed. For them misery stared out of the lightning, and starvation rode upon the flood. The roar of water, answering the thunder above it, was to their ears Earth groaning against the rod, and right well they realized that the pale torrent was drowning those summer labours which represented money and food for the on-coming of long winter months. They stared, silent and dumb, under the rain. They knew that the kernel of near a year's toil was riding away upon that raging water; that the higher meadows, held absolutely safe, were now immersed; that the flood tumbling under the blue fire most surely held sheep and cattle in its depths; that tons of upland hay swam upon it; that, like enough, dead men also turned and twisted there in a last mad journey to the sea.

A passing belief that their labours might save the stack sprung up in the breast of one alone. Uncle Chirgwin trusted Providence and his hempen ropes and clothes-line; but it was a childish hope, and, gazing open-mouthed upon that swelling, hurtling cataract of roaring water, none shared it. An almost continuous mist of livid light crossed and recrossed, festooned and cut by its own crinkled sources, revealed the progress of the flood, and, heedless of themselves, the farmer and his men watched the fate of the stack, now rising very pale of hue above the water, seen through shining curtains of rain. First the torrent tumbled and rose about it, and then a sudden tremor and turning of the mass told that the rick had floated. As it twisted, the weak ropes receiving the strain in turn, snapped one after another; then the great stack moved solemnly forward, stuck fast, moved again, lost its centre of gravity, and foundered like a ship. Under the lightning they saw it heave upward upon one side, plunge forward against the torrent which had swept its base from beneath it, and vanish. Uncle Sampy heaved a bitter groan.

"Dear God, that sich things can be in a Christian land!" he cried. "All gone—this year, an' last, an' the aftermath; an' Lard He knaws what be doin' in the valley bottom. I wish the light may strike me dead wheer I stand; for I be a blot afore Him, else I'd never be made to suffer like this here. Awnly if any man among 'e will up an' tell me what I've done, I'll thank en."

"'Tis the land as have sinned, not you," said Mary. "This reaches more'n us o' Drift. Come your ways an' get out o' these clothes, else you'll catch your death. Follow to the house, all of 'e," she cried to the rest. "Theer ban't no more for us to do till marnin' light."

"If ever it do come," groaned the man Bartlett. "So like's not the end o' the world be here; an' I'd be fust to hollo it, awnly theer's more water than fire here when all's said; an' the airth's to be burned, not drowned."

"Let a come when a will now," gasped an aged man as the drenched party moved slowly away upward to the farm. "Our ears be tuned to the trump o' God, for nort—no, not the screech o' horns blawed by all the angels in heaven—could be awfuller than the tantarra o' this gert tempest. I, Gaffer Polglaze, be the auldest piece up Drift, but I never heard tell o' no sich noise let alone havin' my awn ears flattened wi' it."

They climbed the steep lane to the farm, and the wind began to drown the more distant roar of the water. Rain fell more heavily than before and the full heart of the storm crashed and flamed over their heads as Drift was reached.

Dawn trembled out upon a tremendous chapter of disasters, still fresh in the memory of many who witnessed it. A grey, sullen morning, with sky-glimpses of blue, hastily shown and greedily hidden, broke over Western Cornwall and uncovered the handiwork of a flood more savage in its fury and far-reaching in its effects than man's memory could parallel—a flood which

already shrunk fast backwards from its own havoc. To describe
a single one of those valleys through which small rivers usually
ran to the sea, is to describe them all. Thus the torrent which
raved down the coomb beneath Drift and swept Uncle Chirgwin's massive hayrick with it like a child's toy-boat, had also
uprooted acres of gooseberry bushes and raspberry canes, torn
apple trees from the ground, laid waste extensive tracts of
produce and carried ripening roots by thousands into the sea.
Beneath the orchards, as the flood subsided, there appeared
great tracts of nakedness where banks of stone had been torn
out of the land and scattered upon it; dead beasts stuck jammed
in the low forks of trees; swine, sheep, and calves appeared,
cast up in fantastic places, strangled by the water; sandy
wastes, stripped of every living leaf and blade, ran like banks
where no banks formerly existed, and here and there from their
midst stuck out naked boughs of upturned trees, fragments of
man's contrivances, or the legs of dead beasts. Looking up the
coomb, desolation was writ large, and the utmost margins of the
flood, clearly recorded on branch and bough, where rubbish
which had floated to the fringe of the flood, was caught and
hung aloft.

Below, as the waters gained volume and force, Buryas
Bridge, an ancient structure of three arches, beneath which
the trout-stream peacefully babbled under ordinary conditions,
was swept headlong away, and the houses hard by flooded;
while the greatest disasters had fallen on these orchards
lying lowest in the valley. Indeed, the nearer the flood
approached Newlyn the more tremendous had been the ravage
wrought by it. The orchards of Talcarne valley were ruined
as though artillery had swept them, and of the lesser crops
scarce any at all remained. Then, bursting down Street-
an-nowan, as that lane is called, the waters running high where
their courses narrowed, swamped sundry cottages and leapt like
a wolf on the low-lying portion of Newlyn. Here it burst
through the alleys and narrow passages; drowned the basements
of many tenements, isolated cottages, stores and granaries,

threatened nearly a hundred lives startled from sleep by its assault.

Then, under the raging weather and in that babel of angry waters, brave deeds were done by the fisher-folk, who chanced to be ashore. Grave personal risks were hazarded by many a man in that turbid flood, and not a few women and children were rescued with utmost danger to their saviour's lives. Yet the petty rivalry of split and riven creeds actuated not a few even at that time of peril, and while life was allowed sacred and no man turned a deaf ear to the cry of woman or child, with property the case was altered, and the sects lifted not a finger each to help the other in the saving of furniture and effects.

Newlyn furnished but one theatre of a desolation which covered wide regions. At Penzance, the Laregan river flooded all the low lands as it swept with prodigious cataracts to the sea; mighty lakes stretched between Penzance and Gulval; the brooklets of Ponsandine and Coombe, swollen to torrents, bore crushing destruction upon the valleys through which they fell. Bleu Bridge, with its ancient inscribed "long stone," was swept into the bed of the Ponsandine; and here, as in other low-lying lands, many tons of hay were torn from their foundations and set adrift. At Churchtown the rainfall precipitated off the slopes of Castle-an-dinas, begot vast torrents which, upon their roaring way, tore the very heart out of steep and stony lanes, flooded farmyards, ploughed up miles of hillside, leapt the wall of the cemetery below and spread yellow fingers among the graves.

Three hundred tons of rain fell to the acre in the immediate tract of that terrible storm, and the world of misery, loss and suffering poured forth upon the humble dwellers of the land only came to be estimated in its bitter magnitude during the course of the winter which followed.

Ashore it was not immediately known whether any loss of human life had added crowning horror to catastrophe, but evil news came quickly over the sea. Mourning fell upon Mousehole for the crews of two among its fisher fleet who were lost that night upon the way towards Plymouth waters to join the herring fishery; and Newlyn heard the wail of a robbed mother.

At Drift the farmhouse was found to hold a mystery soon after the day had broken. Joan Tregenza, whose condition rendered it impossible for her to actively assist at the struggle in the coomb, did not retire early on the previous night, as her family supposed, and Mary, entering her room at breakfast-time, found it empty. There was no sign of the girl, and no indication of anything which could explain her absence.

CHAPTER VII.

OUT OF THE DEEP.

AT the dawn of the day which followed upon the great storm, while yet the sea ran high and the gale died hard, many tumbling luggers, some maimed, began to dot the wind-torn waters of Mount's Bay. The tide was out, but within the shelter of the shore which rose between Newlyn and the course of the wind, the returning boats found safety at their accustomed anchorage; and as one by one they made the little roads, as boat after boat came ashore from the fleet, tears, hysteric screams, and deep-voiced thanks to the Almighty arose from the crowd of men and women massed at the extremity of Newlyn pier beneath the lighthouse. Cheers and many a shake of hand greeted every party as, weary-eyed and worn, it landed and climbed the slippery steps. From such moments even those still in the shadow of fear plucked a little courage and brightened hopes. Then each of the returned fishermen, with his own clinging to him, set face homewards—a rejoicing stream of little separate processions, every one heralding a saved life. There crept thus inland wives smiling through dead tears; old mothers hobbling beside their bearded sons; young mothers pouring blessing on proud fisher-boys; sweethearts, withered ancients, daughters, sons, little children. Sad beyond power of thought were the hearts of all as they had hastened to the pier-head at early morning light; now the sorrowful still remained there, but those who came away rejoiced, for none returned without their treasure.

Thomasin stood with many another care-stricken soul, but

her fears grew greater as the delay increased, for the Tregenza
lugger was big and fast, yet many boats of less fame had
already come home. All the fishermen told the same story.
Bursting out of an ominous peace, the storm had fallen suddenly
upon them when westward of the Scilly Islands. One or two
were believed to have made neighbouring ports in the isles, but
the fleet was driven before the gale, and had experienced those
grave hazards reserved for small vessels in a heavy sea. That
all had weathered the night seemed a circumstance too happy
to hope for, but Newlyn hearts rose high as boat after boat
came back in safety. Then a dozen men hastened to Mrs.
Tregenza with the good news that her husband's boat was in
sight.

"She've lost her mizzen by the looks on it," said a fisherman; "an' that's more'n good reason for her bein' 'mong the
last to make home."

But Thomasin's hysterical joy was cut short by the most
unexpected appearance of Mary Chirgwin on the pier. She had
visited the white cottage to find it locked up and empty; she
had then joined the concourse at the pier-head, feeling certain
that the Tregenza's boat must still be at sea; and she now
added her congratulations to the rest, then told Mrs. Tregenza
her news.

"I be comed to knaw if you've heard or seen anything o'
Joan. 'Tis 'mazin' straange, but her've gone, like a dream, an'
us caan't find a sign of her. What wi' she an' terrible doin's
'pon the land last night, uncle's 'bout beside hisself. Us left
her in the kitchen, an' when we comed back from tryin' to save
the hay, she was nowheer. Of coourse, us thot she'd gone to
her bed. But she weern't, an' this mornin' we doan't see a
atom of her, but finds a envelope empty 'pon the kitchen floor.
'Twas addressed to Joan, an' comed from Lunnon."

"Aw jimmary! She've gone to en arter all, then—an' in
her state!"

"The floods was out, you see. Her might have marched off
to Penzance to larn 'bout the manner o' gwaine to Lunnon,

an' bin stopped in home-comin'; or her might have slept in Penzance to catch a early train away."

"'Iss, or her might 'a' got in the water, poor lamb!" said Thomasin, who never left the dark side of a position unconsidered.

Mary's face showed that the same idea had struck her.

"God grant 'tedn' nothin' like that, though maybe 'twould be better than t'other. Us caan't say she've run away, but I thot I'd tell 'e how things is, so's you could spread it abroad that she'm lost. Maybe us'll hear somethin' 'fore the day's much aulder. I be gwaine to Penzance now, an' I'll let 'e knaw if theer's anything to tell. Good-bye, an' I be glad all's well wi' your husband, though I don't hold wi' his 'pinions."

But Mrs. Tregenza did not answer. Her eyes were fixed on the lugger which had now got to its anchorage, and looked strange and unnatural, shorn of its lesser mast. She saw the moorings dragged up; and a few minutes later the boat, which had rolled and tumbled at them all night, was baled. Thereupon men took their seats in her, and began to row towards the harbour. It seemed that Grey Michael was steering, and his crew clearly pulled very weak and short, for their strength was spent.

Then, as they came between the arms of the harbour, as they shipped oars and glided to the steps, Tregenza's hybrid yellow dog, who accompanied the fisherman in all his goings, jumped ashore barking, and galloped up the slippery steps with joy; while, at the same moment, a woman's sharp cry cut the air like a knife, and two wild eyes looked down into the boat.

"Wheer'm the bwoy, Michael? Oh, my good God, wheer'm Tom?"

Everybody strained silently to hear the answer, but though the fisherman looked up, he made no reply. The boat steadied, and one after another the men in her went ashore, Tregenza mounting the steps last. His wife broke the silence. Only a hushed murmur of thankfulness had greeted the other men, for their faces showed a tragedy. They regarded their leader fearfully, and there was something more than death in their eyes.

"Wheer'm the bwoy—Tom? For the love of God, speak, caan't 'e? Why be you all dumb an' glazin' that awful!" cried the woman, knowing the truth before she heard it.

Then she listened to the elder Pritchard, who whispered to his wife, and so fell into a great convulsion of raving, dry-eyed sorrow.

"Oh, my bwoy! Drownded—my awn li'l precious Tom! God 'a' mercy! Dead! Then let me die tu!"

She gave vent to extravagant and savage grief after the manner of her kind. She would have torn her hair, and thrown herself off the quay but for kindly hands which restrained.

"God rot you, an' blast you, an' burn you up!" she screamed, shaking her fists at the sea. "I knawed this would be the end. I dreamed it 'fore 'e was born. Doan't 'e hold me back, you poor fools. Let me gaw an' bury myself in the same graave along wi' en. My Tom! my Tom! I awnly had but wan—awnly wan, an' now——"

She wailed and wrung her hands, while rough voices filled her ears with such comfort as words could bring to her.

"Rest easy; bide at peace, dear sawl." "'Tis the Lard's doin', mother; an' the li'l bwoy's better off now." "Take it calm, my poor, good creature." "Try an' bring tears to your eyes, theer's a dear wummon."

Tears finally came to her relief, and she wept and moaned while friends supported her, looking with wonder upon Michael, her husband. He stood aloof with the men about him. But never a word he spoke to his wife or any other. His eyes dilated, and had lost their steady, forward glance, though a mad misery lighted them with flashes that came and went; his face was a very burrow of time, seared and trenched with pits and wrinkles. His hat was gone, his hair blew wild, the strong set of his mouth had vanished; his head, usually held so high, hung forward on a shrunken neck.

The brothers Pritchard told their story as a party conducted

Thomasin back to her home. For the moment Grey Michael stood irresolute and alone, save for his dog, which ran round him.

"Us was tackin' when it fust began to blaw, an' all bustlin' 'bout in the dark, when the mainsail went lerrickin' 'cross, an' knocked the poor dam bwoy owerboard into as ugly a rage o' water as ever I seed. Tom had his sea-boots on, an' every sawl 'pon the boat knawed 'twas all up as soon as we lost en. We shawed a light, an' tumbled 'bout for quarter o' an hour, wi' the weather gettin' wicked. Then comed a scat as mighty near thrawed us 'pon our beam-ends, an' took the mizzen 'long wi' it. 'Tis terrible bad luck sure 'nough, for never a tidier bwoy wont feeshin'; but theer's worse to tell 'e. Look at that gert, good man, Tregenza. Oh, my God, my blood do creem when I think on't!"

The man stopped, and his brother took up the story.

'Twas afterwards, when us had weathered the worst an' was tryin' to fetch home. Michael falled forward on's faace arter the bwoy was drownded; an' us had to do all for the bwoat wi'out en. But he comed to bime-bye, an' didn't take on much, awnly kept so dumb as a adder. Not a word did er say till marnin' light; then a 'orrible thing fell 'pon en. You knaw that yaller dog as sails wi' us most times? He turned 'pon en sudden an' sez, 'Praise God! praise the Lard o' hosts, my sons, here's Tom; here's my lad as us thot weer drownded!' Then he kissed that beast, an' it licked his faace, an' he cried—that iron sawl cried like a wummon! Then he thundered out as the crew was to give God the praise, an' said the man as weern't on's knees in a twinklin' should be thrawed out the bwoat to Jonah's whale. God's truth! I never seed nothin' so awful as skipper's eyes 'pon airth! Then er calmed down, an' the back of en grawed humpetty, an' his head falled a bit forrard, an' he sat strokin' of the dog. Arter that, when us seed Newlyn, it 'peared to bring en to his senses a bit, an' he knawed Tom was drownded. He rambled in his speech awhile; then grawed mute again, wi' a new look in his eyes, as though he'd grawed so auld as history in a single night. Theer he do stand bedoled wi' all manner o' airthly sufferin', poor creature. Him wi' all his righteousness behind on tu ! But the thinkin' paarts of en be drownded wheer his bwoy was, an' I lay theer ban't no druggister, nor doctor neither, as'll bring 'em back to en."

"Look at that now!" exclaimed another man. "See who's a-talkin' to Tregenza! If that ban't terrible coorious! 'Tis Billy Jago, the softy !"

Billy was indeed addressing Grey Michael, and getting an answer to his remarks. The labourer's brains might be addled, but they still contained sane patches. He had heard of the fisherman's loss, and now touched his hat and expressed regret.

"Ay, the young be snatched, same as a buildin' craw do pick sprigs o' green wood for her nest an' leave the dead twig bide. Here I be, rotten an' coffin-ripe any time this two year, yet I'm passed awver for that braave young youth. An' how is it wi' you, Mr. Tregenza? I s'pose the Lard do look to His awn in such a pass ?"

Grey Michael regarded the speaker a moment, and then made answer—

"I be that sleepy, my son, an' hungry wi' it. 'Iss, fay! I could eat a gert raw dog-fish, an' think it no sin. See to this, but doan't say nothin' 'bout it. The bwoat went down wi' all hands, an' us flinged a bottle to Bucca for en to wash ashore wi' the news. But it never comed. For why? 'Cause that damnation devil bringed the bottle 'gainst the rocks, an' our message was washed away for mermaids to read an' laugh at; an' them grass-green splinters o' glass, as held the last cry o' drownin' men—why, li'l childern plays wi' 'em now 'pon the sand. 'Sing to the Lard, ye that gaw down to the sea.' An' I'll sing—trust me for that—but I must eat first. I speaks to you, Billy, 'cause you be wan o' God's chosen fools."

He stopped abruptly, pressed his hand over his forehead, said that he must break the news to his wife, and then walked slowly down the quay. The manner of his locomotion had wholly changed, and he moved like one whose life was a failure,

Meantime Jago, full of the great discovery, hastened to the Pritchards and other men who were now following Grey Michael at a distance. Them he told that the fisherman had taken leave of his senses—that he had actually called Billy himself one of God's chosen fools.

Several more boats had come in, and, as it was certainly known that some had taken refuge at Scilly, those vitally interested in the few remaining vessels withdrew from the quay, comforting each other and putting a hopeful face on the position. Grey Michael followed his wife home. As yet she had not learned of his state; but, although his conduct on returning was somewhat singular, no word which fell now from him spoke clearly of a disordered mind. He clamoured first for food, and, while he ate, gave a clear, if callous, account of his son's death and the lugger's danger. Having eaten, he went to his bedroom, dragged off his boots, flung himself down, and was soon sleeping heavily; while Thomasin, marvelling at his stolidity, and resenting it not a little, gave way to utter grief. During an interval between storms of tears the woman put on a black gown, then went to her work.

The day had now advanced. On seeing her again downstairs, two or three friends, including the Pritchards, entered the house and asked anxiously after Michael, without, however, stating the nature of their fears. She answered querulously that the man was asleep, and showed no more sorrow than a brute beast. She was very red-eyed and bedraggled. Every utterance was an excuse for a fresh outburst of weeping. Her breast heaved; her hands moved spasmodically; her nerves were in extreme tension, and she could not stay long in one place. Seeing that she was nearly light-headed with much grief, and hoping that her husband's disorder would vanish after his slumber was ended, her friends forbore to hint at what had happened to him. They comforted her to the best of their power; then, knowing that long hours of bitter sorrow must surely pass over the mother's head before such suffering could grow less, departed one by one, leaving her at last alone. She moved restlessly about from room to room, carrying in one hand a photograph of Tom, in the other a handkerchief. Now and then she sat down, looked at the picture, and wept anew. She tried to eat some supper presently, but could not. It is seldom a sudden loss strikes home so speedily as had her tribulation sunk into Thomasin Tregenza's soul. She drank some brandy and water which a friend had poured out for her and left standing on the mantel-shelf. Then she went up to bed—a stricken ruin of the woman who had risen from it in the morning. Her husband still slept; and Thomasin, her grief being of a nature which required spectators for its fullest and most soothing expression, felt irritated alike with him, and with those friends who had all departed and, from the best motives, left her thus. She flung herself into bed, and anger obscured her misery—anger with her husband. His heavy breathing worked her to a frenzy at last, and she sat up, took him by the shoulder, and tried to shake him.

"Wake up, for God's sake, an' speak to me, caan't 'e? You 'eat an' drink an' sleep like a gert hog—you new-come from your awnly son's drownin'! Oh, Christ, caan't 'e think o' me, as have lived a hunderd cruel years since you went to sleep? Ain't you got a word for me? An' you, as had your sawl centred 'pon en—how comes it you can—— "

She stopped abruptly, for he lay motionless, and made no sort of response to her shrill complaining. She had yet to learn the cause; she had yet to know that Michael had drifted beyond the reach of all further mental suffering whatsoever. No religious anxieties, no mundane trials, none of the million lesser carking troubles that fret the sane brain and stamp care on the face of conscious intelligence, would plague him more. Henceforth he was dead to the changes and chances of human life.

At midnight there came the awful waking. Thomasin slept at last, and slumbered dream-tossed in a shadow-world of fantastic troubles. Then a sound roused her—the sound of a voice speaking loudly, breaking off to laugh, and speaking again. The voice she knew, but the laugh she had never heard. She started up and listened. It was her husband who had wakened her.

"'Ow do it go, then? Lard! my memory be like a fishin' net, as holds the gert things an' lets the little uns creep through. 'Twas a braave song as faither singed, though maybe for God-fearers it ban't a likely song."

Then the bed trembled and the man reared up violently and roared out an order in such words as he had never used till then.

"Port! Port your God-damned helm if you don't want 'em to sink us!"

Thomasin, of whose presence her husband appeared unconscious, crept trembling from the bed. Then his voice changed, and he whispered—

"Port, my sons, 'cause of that 'pon the waters. Caan't 'e see—they bubbles a-glimmerin' on the foam? That's the last life o' my li'l Tom; an' the foam-wreath's put theer by God's awn right hand to mark the plaace. He'm saved, if 'twasn't that down at the bottom o' the sea a man be twenty fathom nearer hell than them as lies in graaves ashore. But let en wait for the last trump as 'll rip the deep oceans. An' the feesh—damn 'em—if I thot they'd nose Tom, by God, I'd catch every feesh as ever swum! But shall feesh be 'lowed to eat what's had a everlasting sawl in it? God forbid. He'm theer, I doubt, wi' seaweed round en, an' sea-maids a-cryin' awver his li'l white faace an' keepin' the crabs away. Hell take crabs—they'd 'a' ate Christ 'Isself if so be He'd falled in the water. Pearls—pearls—pearls is on Tom, an' the sea-creatures gives what they can, 'cause they knaw as he'd a grawed to be a man an' theer master. God bless 'em; they gives the best they can, 'cause they knawed how us loved en. 'The awnly son o' his mother.' Well, well, sleep's better'n medicine; but no sleepin' this weather if us wants to make home again. Steady! 'Tis freshenin' fast!"

He was busy about some matter, and she heard him breathing in the darkness and stirring himself. Thomasin, her heart near standing still before this awful discovery, hesitated between stopping and flying from the room before he should discover her. But she felt no fear of the man himself, and, bracing her nerves, struck a light. It showed Grey Michael sitting up, and evidently under the impression he was at sea. He grasped the bed-head as a tiller, and peered anxiously ahead.

"Theer's light shawin' forward!" he cried.

Then he laughed, and Thomasin saw his face was but the caricature of what it had been, with all the iron lines blotted out, and a strange, feeble expression about eyes and mouth. He nodded his head, looked up at the ceiling from time to time, and presently began to sing.

It was the old rhyme he had been trying to recollect, and it now came, tossed uppermost in the mind-quake which had shattered his intellect, buried matters of moment and flung to the surface long-hidden events and words of his youth.

> "'Bucca's a churnin' the waves of the sea;
> Bucca's a darkenin' the sky wi' his frown;
> His voice is the roll o' the thunder.
> The lightnin' do shaw us the land on our lee,
> An' do point to the plaace wheer our bodies shall drown
> When the bwoat gaws down from under.'

"Ha, ha, ha, missis! So you'm aboard, eh? Well, 'tis a funny picksher you makes, an' if tweern't murder an' hell-fire to do it, blamed if I wouldn't thraw 'e out the ship. 'Thou mad'st him lower than the angels,' but not much lower, I'm thinkin'. 'Tis all play an' no work wi' them. They ought to take a back seat 'fore the likes o' us. They abbun no devil at theer tails all time. 'But I'll tame the auld devil afore very long. If I caan't wi' my feests, I will wi' my tongue!'"

Thomasin Tregenza scuffled into her clothes while he babbled. Then, bidding him sleep in a shaking voice, putting out the candle, and taking the matches with her, she fled into

the night to rouse her neighbours and summon a doctor. She
forgot **all** her other troubles before this overwhelming tragedy.
And the man drivelled on in the dark, concerning himself for
the most part **with those interests which** had occupied his life
when he was a boy.

CHAPTER VIII.

THE DESTINATION OF JOAN.

MARY Chirgwin did not return to Newlyn after making inquiries at Penzance. There, indeed, she learned one fact which might prove important, but the possibilities to be read from it were various. Joan had been at the Penzance railway station, and chance made Mary question the identical porter who had studied the time-table for her cousin.

" She was anxious 'bout the Lunnon trains, an' tawld me she was travellin' up to town to-morrow," explained the man. " I weer 'pon the look-out this marnin', but she dedn' come again."

" What time did you see her last night ? "

" 'Bout nine or earlier. I mind the time 'cause the storm burst not so very long arter, an' I wondered if the gal had got to her home."

" No, she didn't. Might she have gone by any other train ? "

" She might, but I'm everywheers, an' 'ted'n likely as I shouldn't have seed her."

This much Mary heard, and then went home. Her news made Mr. Chirgwin very anxious, for supposing that Joan had returned from Penzance on the previous evening, or attempted to do so, it was probable that she had been in the lowest part of the valley, at or near Buryas Bridge, about the time of the flood. The waters still ran high, but Uncle Sampy sent out search parties through the afternoon of that day, and himself plodded not a few miles in the lower part of the coomb.

Meantime the truth may be stated. On the night of the storm, Joan had gone to Penzance, ascertained the first train which she might catch next day, and then returned as quickly as she could towards Drift. But at Buryas Bridge she remembered that her uncle was in the coomb with the farm hands, and would possibly be there all night. It was necessary that he should know her intentions and direct her in several particulars. A vehicle must also be ordered, for Joan would have to leave the farm at a very early hour. Strung to a tension of nerves above all power of fatigue, in a whirl of excitement, and wholly heedless of the mysterious nocturnal conditions around her, Joan determined to seek Uncle Sampy directly, and with that intention, instead of climbing the hill to Drift and so placing herself in a position of safety, passed the smithy and cots which lie by Buryas Bridge and prepared to ascend the coomb in this fashion and so reach her friends the quicker. She knew her road blindfold, but was quite ignorant of the altered character of the stream. Joan had not, however, travelled above a quarter of a mile through the orchard lands when she began to realize the difficulties. Once well out of the orchards, she believed that the meadows would offer an easier path, and thus, buried in her own thoughts, proceeded with many stumblings and splashings over the wet grasses and earth under a darkness that made progress very slow despite her familiarity with the way.

Then it was that, deep hidden in the night and all alone, where the stream ran into a pool above big boulders which banked it, at the spot, indeed, where she had reigned over the milky meadowsweets seated on a granite throne, the vibrating thread of Joan Tregenza's little life was sharply severed, and she died with none to see or hear in that tumult of rising waters which splashed and gurgled and rose on the skirts of the coming storm. A pathway ran here at the edge of the river, and the girl stepped upon it to find the swollen current suddenly up to her knees. Bewildered, she turned, slipped, turned again, and then, under the impression that she faced towards the meadow-bank, put up her hands to grapple safety, set her foot forward, and in a moment was drowning. Distant not half a mile, fighting like giants to save a thing far less precious than this life, toiled Uncle Sampy and his men. Had silence prevailed amongst them, the single cry which echoed up the valley might well have reached their ears; but all laboured amain, and Joan was at that moment the last thought in the minds of any among them.

So she died, for the gathering waters soon beat out her life and silenced her feeble struggle to save it. A short agony ended the nine months of experience through which Joan's existence has been followed; her fires were quenched, and that most roughly; her fears, hopes, sorrows, joys, were all swept away, and Nature stood, defeated by herself, to see a young life strangled on the threshold of motherhood, and an infant drowned so near to birth that its small heart had already begun to beat.

. Two men, tramping through the desolation of the ruined valley at Uncle Chirgwin's command, discovered Joan's body. The elder was Amos Bartlett, and he fell back a step at the spectacle with a sorrowful oath on his lips; the younger searcher turned white and showed fear. The dead girl lay on her back, so left by the water. Her dress had been caught between two great boulders near the pool of her drowning, and the flood had caused her no injury.

"God's goodness! how comes she here?" cried Bartlett. "Oh, but this'll be black news—black news; an' her brother drowned at sea likewise! Theer's a hidden meanin' in it, I lay, if us awnly knawed."

The lad who accompanied Bartlett was shaking, and did not dare to look at the still figure at their feet. Amos therefore bade him use his legs, hasten to the farm, break the news, and despatch a couple of men to the coomb.

"I can pull up a hurdle an' wattle it with withys meantime," he said; "for 'tis allus well to have work for the hand in such a pass as this. Ban't no good for me to sit an' look at her, poor fond wummon."

He busied himself with the hurdle accordingly, and when two of the hands presently came down from Drift, they found their burden ready for them.

The old, silent man called Gaffer Polglaze found sufficient excitement in the tragedy to loosen a tongue which seldom wagged. He spat on his hands and rubbed them together before seizing his end of the hurdle. Then he spoke.

"My stars! to see master when he heard! He rolled all about as if he was drunk. An' yet 'tis the bestest thing as could fall 'pon the gal. Er was lookin' for the cheel in a month or so, they do say. Poor sawl!—so cold as a quilkin * now, and the unborn baaby tu."

Then Mr. Bartlett answered, "The poor lamb was fine an' emperent to me 'bout a matter o' drownin' chets in the spring. Yet here she'm drowned herself, sure 'nough. Well, well, God's will be done."

"'Tis coorious, to be sure, how bazzomy † a corpse do get 'bout the faace arter a water death," said the first speaker, regarding the dead with frank interest.

"Her eyes do make me wimbly-wambly in the stomach," declared the second labourer. "When you've done talkin', Gaffer Polglaze, us'll go up-long, an' the sooner the better. Butivul eyes, tu, they was—wance," he continued. "Sky-colour, an' no less. What I'm wonderin' is as to however she comed here 'tall."

"Piskey-led, I'll warrant 'e," said the ancient.

"Nay, man-led, which is worse. You mind that printed envelope I found in the kitchen. 'Twas a dark doin' of some annointed vellun as brot her in trouble. Ay, an' if I could do en a graave hurt, I would, Chapel-member or no Chapel-member."

"He'm away," commented Bartlett. "'Tedn' no call for you nor yet to meddle wi' the devil's awn business. The man'll

---

* *Quilkin,* a frog.   † *Bazzomy,* blue or livid.

roast for't when his time do come. You'd best to take your coats off an' cover this poor clay, lest the wummen should catch a sight an' go soundin'."

They did as he bid them, and Mr. Bartlett laid his own coat upon the body likewise. Then slowly up the hill they passed, and rested now and again above the steep places.

" A wisht home-comin' as ever a body heard tell on," commented Gaffer Polglaze ; " an' yet the Lard's good pleasure's allus right if you lives long enough to look back an' see how things was from His bird's-eye view of 'em. A tidy skuat * o' money tu they tells me. Who be gwaine to come by that ? "

" Her give it under hand an' seal to her brother."

" Theer's another 'mazin' thing for 'e! Him drownded in salt, an' her in fraish! We lives in coorious times, to be sure—very coorious times, awin' to civilization."

" Bear yourself more sorrow-stricken, Gaffer. Us be in sight o' the house."

Mary Chirgwin met the mournful train, directed them to bring the body of Joan into the parlour, where a place was prepared for it, and then turned to Bartlett. She was trembling and very pale, for one of her complexion ; but the woman's self-command had not left her.

" The auld man's like wan daft," she said hurriedly. " He must be doin', so he rushed away to Newlyn to tell 'em theer. He ban't himself 'tall. You'd best to go arter en now this minute. An' theer's things to be done in Penzance—the doctor an' the crowner an'—an' the coffin-maker. Do what you can to take trouble off the auld man."

" Get me my coat, an' I'll go straight 'way. 'Tis thrawed awver the poor faace of her."

Two minutes later Mr. Bartlett followed his master ; but Uncle Sampy had taken a considerable start of him. The old man was terribly shocked to hear the news, for he had clung to a theory that Joan was long since in London. Dread

* *Skuat*, windfall, legacy.

and fear came over him. The thought of beholding this loved corpse was more than he could contemplate with self-control. A great nervous terror mingled with his grief. He wished to avoid the return from the valley, and the first excuse for so doing which came to his mind he hurriedly acted upon. He declared it essential that the Tregenzas should be told instantly, and hastened away before Mary could argue with him. Only that morning they had heard of Grey Michael's condition; but Uncle Chirgwin forgot it when the blasting news of his niece's death fell upon him. He hurried snuffling and weeping along as fast as his legs would bear him, and not until he stood at their cottage door did he recollect the calamities which had overtaken the fisherman and those of his household.

Uncle Chirgwin began to speak hastily the moment Mrs. Tregenza opened the door. He choked and gurgled over his news.

"She'm dead—Joan. They've found her in the brook as the waters went down. Drownded theer—the awnly sunshine as ever smiled at Drift. Oh, my good God—'tis a miz-maze to drive us all out of our senses. An' you, mother—my dear, dear sawl, my heart bleeds for 'e."

"I caan't cry for her—my tears be dried at the roots o' my eyes. I be down-danted to the edge o' my awn graave. If my man wasn't gone daft hisself, I reckon I should 'a' gone. Come in—come in. Joan an' Tom dead in a night, an' the faither of 'em worse than dead. I shall knaw it is so bime-bye; 'tis awnly vain words yet. 'Iss; you'd best to see en now you'm here. He may knaw 'e, or he may not. He sits craakin' beside the fire, full o' wild, mad, awful words. Doctor sez theer ban't no betterin' of it. But he may live years an' years, though tedn' likely. Tell en as Joan's dead. Theer edn' no call to be afeared. He's grawed quite calm—a poor droolin' gaby—but his gumption be clean gone."

Uncle Sampy approached Grey Michael, and the fisherman held out his hand and smiled.

"'Tis Farmer Chirgwin, to be sure. An' how is it with 'e, uncle?"

"Bad, bad, Tregenza! Your li'l darter—your Joan be dead—drownded in the flood, poor sweet lamb."

"You'm wrong, my son. Joan's bin dead these years 'pon years. She was damned afore her mother conceived her. Hell-meat in the womb. But the 'Lard is King,' you mind. Joan—'iss, fay; her mother was a Hittite—a lioness o' the Hittites; an' the mother's sins be visited 'pon the childern, 'cordin' to the dark ways o' the livin' God."

"Doan't 'e say it, Michael. She died lovin' Christ. Be sure o' that."

The other laughed loudly, and burst into mindless profanity and obscenity. So the purest liver and most cleanly thinker has often cursed and uttered horrible imprecations and profanations under the knife, being chloroformed and unconscious the while. Uncle Chirgwin gazed and listened open-mouthed. This spectacle of a shattered intellect came upon him as an absolutely new manifestation. Any novel experience is rare when a man has passed the age of seventy; and the farmer was profoundly agitated. Then a solemn fit fell upon Grey Michael, and as his visitor rose to depart, he quoted from words long familiar to the speaker—weird utterances, and doubly weird from a madman's mouth in Uncle Chirgwin's opinion. Out of the wreck and ruin of youthful memories Michael's maimed mind had now passed to these later, strenuous days of his early religious existence, when he fought for his soul and lived with the Bible in his hand.

"Hark to me, will 'e? Hark to the word o' God echoed by his worm. 'He that heareth, let en hear; an' he that forbeareth, let en forbear, for they are a rebellious house.' An' what shall us do then? Theer was a man as builded a heydge around a guckoo, thinkin', poor fool, to catch the bird; but her flew off. That edn' the Lard's way. 'Make a chain; for the land is full o' bloody crimes, an' the city is full o' violence.' 'An' all that handle the oar—the mariners, an' all the pilot's o' the sea—

shall come down from theer ships;' an' me amongst the rest. That's why I be here now, wi' bitterness o' heart an' bitter wailin' for my dead bwoy. 'As for theer rings, they was so high that they was dreadful; an' theer rings were full of eyes round about.' Huntin' damned sawls, my son—a braave sight for godly folks! That's why the rings of 'em be so full of eyes. They need be. An' theer wings whistle like a hawk arter a pigeon. 'Because o' the mountain o' Zion, which is desolate, the foxes walk upon it.'"

He relapsed into absolute silence, and sat with his eyes on the fire. Sometimes he shook, sometimes he nodded his head; now he frowned, then grinned vacuously at the current of his thoughts.

Mr. Chirgwin took his leave of Thomasin; prayed that she might be supported in her tribulation; and so departing, met Amos Bartlett, who was standing outside the cottage awaiting him. The man gave a forcible and blunt description of his morning's work, which brought many tears to Uncle Chirgwin's eyes; then, together, they walked to Penzance, there to chronicle the sudden death of Joan Tregenza, and arrange for those necessary formalities which must precede her burial.

The spectacle of Tregenza's insanity which, to an educated observer, had, perhaps, presented features of some scientific interest, and appeared strange rather than tremendous, fell upon the ignorant soul of Uncle Chirgwin in a manner far different. The mystery of madness, the sublimity and horror of it, rise only to tragic heights in the untutored minds of such beholders as the farmer; for no mere manifestation of mental disease is presented to their intelligence. Instead, such persons consider that they stand face to face with the infinitely more terrific apparition of God speaking directly through the mouth of one among his chosen insane. In their estimation a madman's utterance is pregnant, oracular—a subject worthy of most grave consideration and appraisement, a privilege to hear.

CHAPTER IX.

MARY CHIRGWIN would allow none but herself to perform the last offices of kindness for her cousin. In poor Joan's pocket she found a wet, crumpled mass of paper, which might have been dried and read without difficulty; but Mary lacked curiosity to approach the matter. She debated with herself as to how her duty stood in connection with the communication from John Barron, then took it in her hand—not without a sensation of much loathing—and burnt it to ashes. The act produced considerable and unforeseen consequences. Her own mundane happiness was wholly dependent on the burning of the letter; and a man's life likewise hung upon the incident; but these results of her conduct were only brought to the woman's understanding in the light of subsequent events. Then, she directly read God's hand in the circumstance. Another discovery saddened Mary far more than that of the letter, which had caused her little surprise. Around Joan's white body was a strange amulet—the glen-ader. She had sewed it upon flannel, then fastened the ends about herself, and so worn the snake-skin at all seasons since the finding of it. The fact was nothing; the condition of mind which it indicated brought grief to the discoverer. She judged that Joan was little better than a heathen after all; she greatly feared that the girl had perished but half believing. Any soul which could thus cherish the slough of a serpent must most surely have been wandering afar out of the road of faith. The all-embracing credulity of Joan was, in fact, a phenomenon beyond Mary's power to estimate or translate ; and her present discovery, therefore, caused her both pain and consternation. But as she had burnt the letter, so she likewise destroyed all evidence of her cousin's superstitious weakness ; and of neither one nor the other did she speak when the farmer returned to his home.

He was sadly crushed and broken ; and the spectacle of his loved one, lying silent and peaceful, brought with it deep grief for him.   Not until he had seen her and held her dead hand did he begin slowly to realize the truth.

"Her mother do lie at Paul, 'cordin' to the wish o' Michael ; but I seem as Joan had best be laid 'long wi' the Chirgwins at Sancreed.   If you'll awnly give your mind to the matter and settle it, I'll go this evenin' to wan plaace or t'other an' see the diggers," said Mary.

"Sancreed for sartain.   Her'll be nearer to us, an' us can see wheer she be restin' 'pon Sundays.   Sancreed's best an' fittest, for she was Chirgwin all.   They be comin' to sit 'pon her to-morrow marnin'.   Please God He'll hold me up agin' it ; but I feels as if I'd welcome death to be 'longside my li'l Joan again."

He wept an old man's scanty tears; and Mary comforted him, while she smothered her own sorrows entirely before his.   She spoke coldly and practically ; she fetched him a stiff dose of spirits and a mutton-chop, freshly cooked.   These things she made him drink and eat, and she spoke to the old man while he did so, larding the discussion of necessary details with expressions of hope for the dead.

"Be strong an' faace it, uncle.   God knaws best.   I lay the poor lovey was took from gert evil to come.   You knaw so well as me.   You can guess wheer her'd be now if livin'.   She'm in a better home than that.   I s'pose the buryin' might be two days off, or three.   I'll step awver to Sancreed bime-bye, an' if the undertaker come, Mrs. Bartlett can be with him when he do his work."

"''Iss; an' I've said as 'tis to be oak—braave, bold, seasoned oak—an' polished, wi' silvered handles to it. Her should lie in gawld, my awn Joan, if I could bring it about."

"Ellum be more——" began Mary, then held her tongue upon that detail and approached another. "Shall us ask Mrs. Tregenza? Sorrer's gripping her heart just now; but a buryin's a soothin' circumstance to such as she. An' she could carry her son in mind. Poor li'l Tom won't get no good words said above his dust; us can awnly think 'em for en."

"She might like to come if her could get some o' the neighbours to bide along wi' Michael. He'm daft for all time; but 'tis said as he'll be childlike wi' it, thank God. I let en knaw 'bout the lass, an' he rolled his head an' dropped his jaw like to a feesh, an' said as tweern't no news to en; which maybe it weern't, for the Lard's got His awn way wi' the idiot. The sayin's of en! Like as not Thomasin'll be here, if 'tis awnly to get the rids of Michael for a while."

The coroner's inquest found that Joan Tregenza had come by her death from drowning upon the night of the flood; the tragedy filled an obscure paragraph or two in local journals. Joan's funeral was fixed for two days later, and Mrs. Tregenza decided that she would attend it.

At a spot where fell the shadow of the church when the sun sank far westerly on summer days, they dug the grave in Sancreed churchyard. Round about it, on slate slabs and upright stones, appeared the names of Chirgwins not a few. Her maternal grandparents lay there, her uncle, Mary's father, and many others. Some of the graves dated back for a hundred and more years.

On the morning of the funeral Uncle Sampy, while waiting for the bearers, tied scraps of crape around the stems of his tall geraniums. He had forgotten the ancient custom until that moment.

Six men carried Joan's oaken coffin to Sancreed, while

there walked behind her Uncle Chirgwin, Mary and Mrs. Tregenza, Mr. Bartlett, his wife, Gaffer Polglaze, and other labourers and farm maidens. A few of the Drift folk and half a dozen young children came in the wake of the procession proper; and that was all. The mourners and their dead proceeded along the high lanes to Sancreed; and conversation was general. Uncle Chirgwin tugged at his black gloves and snuffled, then snuffled and tugged again; Mary walked on one side of him; and Mrs. Tregenza, in new and heavy black bought for another, found the opportunity convenient for the display of varied grief, as she marched along on the farmer's right hand. Her condition, indeed, became hysterical, and Mary only soothed her with difficulty. So the party crawled within sound of the minute bell, and presently reached the church. An undertaker buzzed here and there, issuing directions; the old clergyman met the dead at the lych-gate, and walked before her up the aisle, while those who had a right to attend the service, clustered in the pews to right and left of the trestles. Upon them lay Joan. The words of the service sounded with mournful reverberations through the chill echoes of an un-warmed and almost empty church; and then the little sister, sleeping peacefully enough after her one short year of storm, was carried to the last abode of silence. Then followed an old man's voice, sounding strangely thin in the open air, the strain-ing of cords, the whispering and hard breathing and shuffling of men, the grating of oak on a grave-bottom, the up-drawing of the ropes that had lowered the coffin. Genuine emotion accom-panied the obsequies of Joan Tregenza, and her uncle's sorrow touched not a few to visible grief and sympathy; but there was no heart to break for the heart which had itself come so near to breaking; there was no mighty well-spring of love to be choked with tears for one who had herself loved so much. A feeling, hidden in some minds, expressed by others, latent in all, pervaded that throng; and there was not one among those present save Sampson Chirgwin but felt that Providence, harsh till now, had dealt kindly by Joan in dealing death to her.

Upon the flowerless, shiny lid a little staring plate of white metal gleamed up at the world above like an eye, and met the gaze of the mourners, as each in turn, with Mrs. Tregenza first, peered down into Joan's grave before departing. After which all went away. The children were shut out of the churchyard; the old clergyman disappeared to the vestry. A young, florid man, with pale hair, tightened his leather belt, turned up his sleeves, watched a grand pair of biceps roll up as he crooked his elbows; then, taking his spade, set to work upon the wet mound he had dug from the earth the day before, to clear those few square feet of space below. As he worked he whistled, for his occupation held no more significance to him than an alternative employment—the breaking of stones by the highway side. He could see the black heads of the mourners bobbing away upon the road to Drift, and stopped to watch them for a moment. But soon he returned to his labour; the earth rose foot by foot, and the strong young man stamped it down. Then it bulged and overflowed the full hole, whereupon he patted and hammered it into the customary mound, and slapped upon it sundry pieces of sodden turf, with gaping gashes between their edges. The surplus soil he removed in a wheelbarrow; the boards he also took away, then raked over the earth-smeared, bruised grass about the grave, and so made an end of his work.

"Blamed if I ever filled wan quicker'n that," he thought with some satisfaction. "I reckoned the rain must fall afore I'd done; but it do hold off yet seemin'ly."

The man departed, grey twilight fell, and out from the gathering darkness, like a little wound on the breast of the great Mother, that new-made grave and its fringe of muddy grass stood forth, crude of colour, raw, unsightly, in the monochrome of the gloaming.

At Drift that important meal which follows a funeral was enjoyed with sober satisfaction by about fifteen persons. Cold fowls and a round of cold beef formed the main features of the repast; Mary poured out tea for the women at her end of the

table, while the men drank two or three bottles of grocer's
sherry among them. The undertaker and his assistants followed
and ate what was left when the funeral assembly dispersed.
Mrs. Tregenza was about to depart in the fly specially ordered
to take her home when Mr. Chirgwin's lawyer, who joined the
company after the funeral, begged she would stay a little longer.

"I learn that you are the deceased's step-mother, madam;
and as you stand related to the parties both now unhappily
swept away by Providence—I mean Thomas Tregenza and
Joan—it is sufficiently clear that you inherit directly the
bequest left by the poor girl to her brother. I framed her little
will myself. Failing her own child, her property went to Thomas
Tregenza, his heirs and assigns; those were the words. The
paper is here; the sum mentioned lies at interest of three per
cent. Let me know when convenient what you would wish to
be done."

So the pile of money, at a cost terrible enough, had reached
Mrs. Tregenza after all. She had been drinking brown sherry
as well as tea, and was in a condition of renewed tears approaching to maudlin when the announcement reached her. It steadied
the woman. Then the thought that this wealth would have
been her son's made her weep again, until the fact that it was
now her own became grasped in her mind. There are a sort of
people who find money a reasonably good support in all human
misfortune; and if Mrs. Tregenza did not entirely belong to
that callous company, yet it is certain that this sudden afflux of
gold was more likely to assuage her grief than most things.
She presently retired, all tears and care; but at intervals, when
sorrow rested to regain its strength, the lawyer's information
recurred, and the distractions of mind caused by the contemplation of a future brightened by this wealth soothed Thomasin's
nerves to an extent beyond the power of religion or any other
force which could possibly have been brought to bear upon them.
She felt that her own position must henceforth be exalted in
Newlyn, for the effects of the combination of catastrophies led
to that end. Her husband was the sole care she had left, and

physicians foretold no great length of days for him. The lugger would be put up to auction, with the drift nets and all pertaining thereto. The cottage was already Tregenza property. Thomasin therefore looked through the overwhelming misery of the time, counted her moneys, and felt comforted without knowing it.

CHAPTER X.

THE HOME-COMING OF JOE.

A FORTNIGHT and four days after the funeral of Joan Tregenza there blew a south-west wind over Newlyn, from out a grey sky, dotted with watery blots of darker grey. No added light marked the western horizon at sunset, but the short, dull day simply fell headlong into night; and with darkness came the rain.

About five o'clock in the afternoon, when the flicker and shine of many lamps in little shop-windows brightened the tortuous streets, a man, carrying a big canvas bag on his back, passed rapidly through the village. He had come that day from London upon the paying off of his vessel; and while he left his two chests at the railway station, he made shift to bring his sea-bag along himself, and that because he was bound for the white cottage on the cliff, and the bag held many precious foreign concerns for Joan Tregenza. It had been impossible to communicate with the sailor; and he did not write from London to tell any of his return, that their pleasure and surprise on his appearance might be the more complete. Now a greater shock than that in his power to give waited the man himself. The sailor's parents lived at Mousehole, but Michael's cottage lay upon the way, and there he first designed to appear.

Joe Noy was a very big man, loosely but strongly set together, a Celt to the backbone, hard, narrow of mind, but possessing rare determination. His tanned, clean-shaven face was broader at the jaw than the eyes, and a lowering heaviness

of aspect, almost ape-like, resulted when his features remained
in repose. The effect, however, vanished when he spoke or
listened to the speech of another. That such a man had proved
fickle in love was a thing difficult of belief to the mind familiar
with his character. Solid, sober, simple, fearing God and
lacking humour, the jilting of a woman was an offence of all
others least likely to have been associated with him. Yet
circumstances and some unsuspected secrets of disposition had
brought about that event; and now, as he hastened along, the
vision of the dark woman he once loved at Drift did not for an
instant cross his thoughts, for they were full of the fair girl he
meant to marry at Newlyn. To her at least he had kept
faithful enough; she had been the guiding-star of his life for
hard upon a year of absence; not one morning, not one night,
in fair weather or foul, had he omitted to pray God's blessing
upon her. A fatalism, which his Luke Gospel tenets did not
modify, was strong in the sailor. He had seen death often
enough in his business, and his instincts told him, apart from
all religious teaching, that those who died ripe for salvation
were but few. Every man appeared to be an instrument in
God's hand, and human free-will represented a condition quite
beyond the scope of his intelligence to estimate or even conceive.
Had any justified in so doing asked of him his reasons for
desertion of Mary Chirgwin, the man would have explained
that when inviting her to be his wife he took a wrong step in
darkness; that light had since suddenly shone upon him, as
upon Saul; and that Mary, choosing rather to remain outside the
sure fold of Luke Gospeldom, by so doing made it impossible
for him to love her longer. He would have added that the
match was doubtless foredoomed according to the original
arrangements of the Almighty.

Now Joe came back to his own; and his heart beat faster by
several pulses, and his steps quickened and lengthened as
through darkness and rain, he sighted the lamp-lit cottage
window of the Tregenzas. Thereupon he stopped a moment,
brought his bag to the ground, mopped his forehead, then

raising the latch, strode straight into the kitchen without a knock of warning. For a moment he imagined the room, lighted only by a dull glow of firelight, to be empty; but then, amidst familiar objects, he noted one not familiar—a tall and roomy armchair. This stood beside the fireplace, and in it sat Grey Michael.

"Why, so 'tis! Mr. Tregenza sure 'nough!" the traveller exclaimed, setting down his bag and coming forward with hand outstretched. "Here I be at last, arter nine months o' salt water! An' Newlyn do smell pleasant in my nose as I come back to it, I tell 'e!"

The other did not take Joe's hand. He looked up vaguely, with an open mouth and no recognition in his expression; but Noy as yet failed to note how insanity had robbed the great face of its power, had stamped out the strength of it, had left it a mindless vague of limp features.

"Who be you, then?" asked Mr. Tregenza.

"Why, blamed if you abbun forgot me! I be Joe—Joe Noy come back-along at last. My ivers! You, as doan't forget nothin', to forget me! Yet, maybe, 'tis the low light of the fire as hides me from 'e."

"You'm a mariner, I reckon?"

"I reckon so, if ever theer was wan. An' I'll be the richer by a mate's ticket 'fore the year's dead. But never mind me. How be you all—all well? I thot I'd pop in an' surprise 'e."

"Cruel fashion weather for pilchur fishin' us have had—cruel fashion weather. I knawed 'tweer comin', same as Noah knawed 'fore the flood, 'cause the Lard tawld me. 'Forty years long was I grieved wi' this generation.' But man tries the patience o' God these days. We'm like the Ruan Vean men—'doan't knaw, an' won't larn.'"

"'Iss, fay, mister, true 'nough; but tell me 'bout 'e all an'—an' my Joan. She've been the cherub aloft for me ever since I strained my eyes for the last peep o' Carnwall when us sailed. How be my li'l Joan?"

The other started, sat up in his chair, and gripped the left arm of it, while his right hand extended before him, and he jolted it curiously, with all the fingers pointing down.

"Joan—Joan? In hell—ragin', roastin' hell—screechin' I lay, like a cat in a bonfire. 'Tis lies they'll tell 'e 'bout her. She weern't drownded—never. The devil set sail 'pon auld Chirgwin's hayrick, so they sez, an' her sailed 'long wi' en. But 'theer rings, they was so high that they was dreadful, an' theer rings were full o' eyes round about.' She'm damned; my son—called, not chosen. 'The crop o' the bunch' they called her—the crop o' the devil's bunch she was—no cheel o' my gettin'. Her'll burn for a million years or better—all along o' free-traadin'. Free-traadin'! curse 'em—why doan't they call it smugglin', an' have done?"

Joe Noy had fallen back. He forgot to breathe; then Nature performed the necessary act, and in a moment of the madman's silence his listener sucked a long, loud breath.

"Oh, my gracious powers! what's fallen 'pon en?" he groaned aloud.

"God's strong, but the devil's stronger, you mind. Us must pray to the pit now. 'Our devil, which art in hell.' Ha! ha! ha! He hears fast enough, an' pokes up the black horns of en at the first smell o' prayer. Not but what my Tom's aloft, in the maintop o' Paradise. I seed en pass 'pon a black wave wi' a grey foamin' crest. An' the white sawl o' my bwoy went mountin' and mountin' in shape o' a sea-bird. Men dies hard in salt water, you mind. It plays wi' 'em cruel, like a cat wi' a mouse. But 'tis all wan. 'The Lard is King, an' sitteth 'tween the cherubims,' though the airth's twitchin' all the time—same as a crab bein' boiled alive."

Noy looked round wildly, and was about to leave the cottage. Then it struck him that the man's wife and daughter could not be far off. What blasting catastrophe had robbed him of his mind, the sailor knew not; but once assured of the fact that Michael Tregenza was hopelessly insane, Noy lent no credit to any of his utterances, and of course failed to dimly guess at those facts upon which his ravings were based. Indeed, he heard little after the first rambling outburst, for his own thoughts were busy with the problems of Tregenza's fate.

"Sit down, mariner. I shan't sail till marnin,' an' you'm welcome. Theer be thots in me so deep as Levant mine, but I doan't speak 'em for anybody's hearin'. Joan weern't none o' mine, an' I knawed it, thanks be to God, 'fore ever she played loose. What do 'e think o' a thousand pound for a sawl? Cheap as dirt—eh? 'Thou hast covered thyself with a cloud, that our prayer should not pass through.' Not as prayers can save what's lost for all eternity 'fore 'tis born into time. He ruined her; he left her wi' cheel; but ban't likely the unborn clay counts. God Hisself edn' gwaine to damn a thing as never drawed breath. Who'd a thot the like o' her had got a whore's forehead? An' tokened at that—tokened to a sailor-man by name o' Noy. Let'n come home—let'n come home an' call the devil as did it to his account! Let the Lard see to't so that man edn' 'lowed to flourish no more. I be tu auld an' broken for any sich task. 'For the hurt o' the darter o' my people I am hurt.' "

He spoke no more upon that head, though Noy, now awake to fear and horridly conscious that he stood in the shadow of some tremendous ill, reaching far beyond the madman, asked him frantically what he meant. But Michael's mind had wandered off the subject again.

"I seed en cast forth a net, same as us does for macker'l, but 'twas sawls, not feesh, they dragged in the bwoat; but braave an' few of 'em. The devil's nets was the full wans, 'cause——"

At this moment Thomasin came in, saw a man by Mr. Tregenza, but did not realize who had returned until she struck a light. Then, approaching, the woman gasped her surprise and stood for a moment dumb, looking from her husband to the sailor, from the sailor back to her husband. The horror on Noy's face frightened her; indeed, he was now strung to a pitch of frantic excitement. He saw that the woman was altogether clad in black, that her garments were new, that even her bonnet had a black flower in it; and, despite his concern, he observed an appearance of prosperity about her, though her face belied it, for Mrs. Tregenza was very thin, and far greyer and older too than when he saw her last. He took the hand she stretched, shaking, towards him; then a question burst from his lips.

"For God's sake speak an' tell me the worst on it. What terrible evil be here? He'm—he'm daft seemin'ly; he's spawk the awfulest mad words as ever comed from lips. An' Joan—doan't 'e say it—doan't 'e say 'tis true she'm dead—not my li'l treasure gone dead; an' me, ever since I went, countin' the days an' hours 'gainst when I should come back to her?"

"Ay, my poor lad, 'tis true—all true. An' worse behind, Joe. Hip and thigh us be smitten—all gone from us. My awnly wan drownded—my awn bwoy; an' Michael's brain brawk down along o' it. An' the bwoat an' nets be all sold, though, thanks to God, they fetched good money. An' poor Joan tu—'pon the same night as my Tom—drownded—in the gert land-flood up-long."

Grey Michael had been nodding his head and smiling as each item of the mournful category was named. At Thomasin's last words he interrupted angrily, and something of the old, deep tones of his voice echoed again.

"'Tis a lie! Dedn' I tell 'e, wummon, 'tweern't so? The devil took her—body an' bones an' unborn baaby. They say she was found in the river; an' I say 'tis false. You may groan an' you may weep blood, but you caan't chaange the things that have happened in time past—no, nor more can God A'mighty."

His wife looked to see how Joe viewed this statement. A great local superstition was growing up round Grey Michael, and his wild utterances (sometimes profanely fearful beyond the possibility of setting down) were listened to greedily as inspirations and oracles. Mrs. Tregenza herself became presently imbued with something of this opinion. Her deep wounds time promised to heal at the first intention, and the significance now attributed to her insane husband grew to be a source of real satisfaction to her. She dispensed the honour of interviews with Michael, as one distributes great gifts.

The force of circumstances and the futility of fighting against fate impressed Thomasin mightily now, as Noy's wild eyes asked the question his lips could not force themselves to frame. She sighed and bent her head and turned her eyes away from him, then spoke hurriedly.

"I doan't knaw how to tell 'e, an' us reckoned theer weern't no call to, an' us weern't gwaine to 'tell; but these things be in the Lard's hand, an' theer edn' no hidin' what He means to let out. A sorry, cruel home-comin' for 'e, Joe. Poor lass! her's done wi' all her troubles now, an' the unborn cheel tu. 'Tis very hard to stand up 'gainst, but the longest life's awnly short, an' us ban't called 'pon to live it more'n wance, thank God."

Here she gave way to tears and dried the same on a white pocket-handkerchief with a black border.

"'Tis all so true as gospel," declared Grey Michael, rolling his head round on his neck and laughing. "An' my auld wummon's fine an' braave, edn' her? That's 'cause I cleared a thousan' pound in wan trip. Christ was aboard, an' He bid me shoot the nets by moonlight off the islands. He do look arter His awn somethin' butivul, as I tawld en. An' now I be a feesher o' men, which is better; an' high 'mong the salt o' the airth, bein' called to walk along wi' James an' John' and the rest."

"He sits theer chitterin', ding dong, ding dong, all the wisht day. Tom's death drove en cracked, but 'e ban't no trouble, 'cept at feedin' times. Besides, I keeps a paid servant girl now," said Mrs. Tregenza.

Joe Noy had heard neither the man nor the woman. From the moment that he knew the truth concerning Joan, his own thoughts barred his ears to all utterances.

"Who weer it? Tell me the name. I want no more'n that," he said.

"'Tis Anne Rundle's darter," answered Mrs. Tregenza, her mind on her maid.

"The man!" roared Noy—"the man who brot the thing about—the man what ruined—— O God o' hosts, be on my side now! Who weer 'e? Give me the name of en. That's all as I wants."

"Us doan't knaw. You see, Joan was away up Drift wi' the Chirgwins; an' theer she was took when they found her arter the drownin'. She never knawed the true name of en herself, poor dear. But 'twas a paintin' man—a artist. It comed out arter as he'd made a picksher of her, an' promised to marry her, an' stawl all she'd got to give 'pon the strength of the lie. Then theer was a letter——"

"From the man?"

Mrs. Tregenza grew frightened at the thought of mentioning the money, and now adroitly changed the first letter from Barron, which was in her mind when she spoke, to the second, which Joan had received from him on the night of her death.

"'Iss, from him; an' Mary Chirgwin found it 'pon the dead frame o' the poor girl. But 'twas partly pulp, along o' the water, and Mary burned it wi'out readin' a word—so she said, at least, though that's difficult to credit, human nature bein' as 'tis."

"Then my work's the harder; but I'll find en, s'elp me God, even if us be grawed grey afore we meet."

"Think twice, Joe. You caan't bring back your lass, not now. 'Tis tu late."

"No, not that; but I can—— I'm in God's hand for this. Us be tools, an' He uses all for His awn ends. I sees whereto I was born now; an' the future be writ clear afore my eyes. Thicky madman theer said the word; an' I lay the Lard put it in en for my better light. Er said, 'Let'n come home an' call the devil as did it to account.' He was thinkin' o' me when he said it, though he dedn' knaw me."

"'Iss, 'tis generally allowed he be the lips o' God A'mighty now. But you, Joe—doan't 'e waste life an' hard-won money huntin' down a damned man. Leave en to his deserts."

"'Tis *me* that be his deserts, wummon—'tis me, in the hand o' the God o' vengeance! That's my duty now standin' stark ahead o' me. The Lard's pleased to pay all my prayers an' good livin' like this here. His will be done, an' so it shall to the dregs of it; an' if I be for the pit arter all, theer's wan livin' as gaws along wi' me."

"That's worse than a fool's thot. Bide till you'm grawed cool anyways. 'Tis very hard, this coil falling 'pon a virtuous member like what you be; but 'tedn' a straange tale 'tall. The man was like other men, I doubt; the maid was like other maids. You thot differ'nt. You was wrong; an' you'll be wrong again to break your heart now. Let en go—'tis best."

"Let en go! Blast en! I'll let heaven go fust! Us'll see what a wronged sawl's patience can do now! Us'll see what the end of the road'll shaw. O God o' the righteous, foster this here man's bones in his body, an' eat his life out of en wi' fiery worms! Tear his heart-strings, God o' hosts; rob en of all he loves; stamp his foul mind wi' memories till he shrieks for death an' judgment; punish his seed for ever; turn his prayers into swearin'; torture en, rot en sawl an' body till You brings me to en. Shaw no mercy, God o' heaven, but pile agony 'pon agony mountains high for en; an' let mine be the hand to send his cussed sawl to hell; for Christ's sake. Amen."

"Oh, my Guy Faux, theer's cussin'! An' yet 'tedn' gwaine to do a happard * o' good; an' you wouldn' be no happier for knawin' sich a prayer was granted," said Thomasin.

But Grey Michael applauded the outburst, and his words ended that strange spectacle of two men, for the time both mad.

"Hallelujah! hallelujah! Braave prayin'! Braave savour for the Lard's nose—sweeter than the blood o' beasts! You'm a shinin' light, cap'n—a trumpet in the battle, like the sound o' the sea-wind when it begins to sting afore heavy weather, an' the waters roll to the top o' the bulwarks an' awver. 'The snorting of his horses was heard from Dan'—sea-horses us calls 'em nowadays. Mount an' ride! mount an' ride! 'Cursed be the man that trusteth in man,' saith the Lard; but the beasts be truer, thanks to the dark way o' God, who's spared 'em the

* *Happard*, halfpennyworth.

curse o' brain paarts, but stricken man wi' a mighty intelligence. 'Twas a fine an' cruel act, for the more mind the more misery. 'Twas a damned act sure 'nough! Doan't 'e let on 'bout it, mate; but theer'll be clever surprises at Judgment, an' the fust to be damned 'll be the God o' Hosts Hisself for puttin' o' brains in weak heads. Then the throne o' Heaven 'll stand empty—empty—the plaace 'tween the cherubims empty; an' they'll call 'pon me to fill it so like's not. Tarraway, I shall be named, same as the devil in the droll—a purty word enough tu."

He broke into laughter, and Joe Noy, saying a few hasty words to Thomasin, departed.

CHAPTER XI.

A NIGHT VISIT.

He who less than an hour before had hastened hot-footed through the Newlyn streets; he whose habitual stern expression had softened before the well-known sights and smells of the grey village, whose earnest soul was full of happiness under the rain of the night, now turned back upon his way and skulked through the darkness with a murderer's heart in him. The clear spectacle of his revenge blinded lesser presentations, and even distracted his sorrow. There was no space now vacant in Noy's brain to hold the full extent of his loss; and the fabric of happiness which for weary months on various seas he had been building up in imagination, and which a madman's word had now sent spinning to chaos, yet remained curiously with him, as an impression stamped by steadfast gazing remains upon the eye. It recurred as of old : a joy ; and not till the former emotion of happiness had again and again reappeared to be blunted, as a dream at waking, by the new knowledge, did truth sink into this man's mind and become a part of memory. Now he was dazed, as one who has run hard and well to a goal, and who, reaching it, finds his prize stolen. Under these circumstances, Joe Noy's natural fatalism—an instinct beyond the power of any religion to destroy, appeared instant and strong. Chance had now fed this idiosyncrasy, and it grew gigantic in an hour. But the religious habit made him turn to his Maker in this pass, and the merely primitive passions, which were now breaking loose within him, he regarded as the direct voices of God. They proclaimed that solitary duty the world still held for him; they marked out his road to the lurid end of it.

Thus Noy's own furious lust for revenge was easily and naturally elevated into a mandate from the Highest—into a message echoed and reiterated upon his ear by the multitudinous voices of that wild night. The rain whispered it on the roof-trees, the wind and sea thundered it; out of elemental chaos the awful command came, as from primal lips which had spoken since creation to find at last the ultimate destination of their message within a human ear. To Noy, his purpose, not yet an hour old, seemed ancient as eternity, a fixed and deliberate impression which had been stamped upon his mind at a period far earlier than his life in time. For one end had he been created—that by some sudden short cut he should hurry to its close a vile life, fill up God's bitter curse upon this man, destroy the destroyer, and speed a black soul into the torment awaiting it.

Irresolute and deep in thought as to the course of his future actions, Joe Noy walked unconsciously forward. He felt unequal to returning to his home in Mousehole after what he had learned at Newlyn: and he wandered back, therefore, towards Penzance. A glare of gas-lamps splashed the wet surface of the parade with fire; while below him, against the sea-wall, a high tide spouted and roared. Now and again, after a heavy muffled thud of sea against stone, columns of glimmering, grey foam shot upwards like gigantic ghosts out of the water. For a moment they towered in the air, then, wind-driven, swept hissing across the black and shining surfaces of the deserted parade.

Noy stood here a moment, and the cold wind cooled him, and the riot and agony of the sea boiling against the granite face of the breakwater chimed with the riot and agony of his mind, whose hopes were now rent in tatters, riven, splintered, and disannulled by chance. He turned a moment where the Newlyn harbour light flashed across the darkness to him. From his standpoint he knew that a line drawn through that light must fall upon the cottage of the Tregenzas beyond it on the shore, and, fixing his eyes where the building lay hidden, he stretched out his hand and spoke aloud.

"May God strike me blind and daft if ever I looks 'pon yon light an' yonder cot again till the man be dead!"

Then he turned, and was about to seek the station, with a vague purpose to go straight to London at the earliest opportunity, when a wiser thought arrested this determination. He must learn all that it was possible to learn concerning the last days of Joan. Mrs. Tregenza had explained her step-daughter's life at Drift. To Drift, therefore, the sailor determined to go; and the stress upon his mind was such that even the prospect of conversation with Mary Chirgwin—a thing he had certainly shrunk from under other circumstances—caused him no uneasiness.

Over the last road that Joan had ever walked, and under similar conditions of night and storm, he tramped up to Drift, entered through the side gate, and surprised Mr. Chirgwin and his niece at their supper. As before with the Tregenzas, so now again in company of Uncle Sampy and Mary, Joe Noy formed the third in a trio of curious significance. Though aware that the sailor was due from his voyage, this sudden apparition of him at such a time startled his former friends not a little. Mary indeed was unnerved in a manner foreign to her nature, and the candle-lighted kitchen whirled in her eyes as she felt her hand in his. Save for an ejaculation from the old man which conveyed nothing beyond his astonishment, Noy was the first to speak; and his earliest words relieved the minds of his listeners in one great particular—he already knew the worst that had happened.

"I be come from Newlyn, from the Tregenzas. Thomasin have tawld me of all that's falled out; but I couldn' bide in my awful trouble wi'out walkin' up-long. I reckon you'll let the past be forgot now. I'm punished ugly enough. You seed her last, dead an' alive; you heard the last words ever she spoke to any of her awn folks. That drawed me. If I must ax pardon for comin', then I will."

" Nay, nay, my poor sawl; sit you down an' eat, Joe, an
take they wet boots off awhile. Our hearts have bled for 'e
this many days, Joe Noy, an' never more'n now."

" I thank you, uncle. An' you, Mary Chirgwin—will 'e say
as much? 'Tis you I wants to speak with, 'cause you—you
seed Joan arter 'twas awver."

" I wish you well, Joe Noy, an' if I ever done differ'nt 'tis
past an' forgot. What I can tell 'e bout her poor lass, as lived
the end of her days along wi' me an' uncle, you've a right to
knaw."

" An' God bless 'e for sayin' so. I comed rough an' ready,
an' thrust in 'pon you ; but this news be but two hour auld in
my head, you see, an' tedn' easy for such as me to make choice
o' words at a time like this."

" Eat, my son, an' doan't 'e fancy theer's any here but them
as be friends. Polly an' me seed more o' Joan through her last
days than any ; an' I do say as she was a lamb o' God's foldin'
beyond all manner o' doubt; an' Polly, as feared it wasn't
'sactly so, be of my 'pinion now. Them as suffered for the
sins o' other folk, like what she done, has theer hell-fire 'pon
this side o' the grave, not 'tother."

" I lay that's a true sayin'," declared Noy, shortly. " I won't
keep 'e ower-long from your beds," he added. " If you got a
drink o' spirits I'll thank you for it ; then I'll put a question or
two to she—to Mary Chirgwin—if she'll allow ; an' then I'll get
going."

The woman was self-possessed again now, although Joe's
voice and well-remembered gestures moved her powerfully and
made it difficult to keep her voice within absolute control.

" All you can ax that I knaw, I'll tell 'e, though Joan shut
her thots purty close most times. Us awnly got side views of
her mind, and them not often."

" Tho man," he said. " Tell me all—everythin' you can call
home—all what her said of him."

" Fust she thot a 'mazin' deal 'bout en," explained the farmer ;
" then time made her mind get stale of en, an' she began to see

us was right.   He sent money—a thousand pound, an' I, poor
fool, thot Joan weern't mistook at fust.   But 'twas awnly
conscience money; an' now Thomasin's the better for 't by
will."

But this sensational statement was not appreciated.   Joe's
mind being elsewhere.

"You never heard the name of en?"

"Awnly the christening name, as was 'Jan.' You may
have heard tell she got a letter the night she passed. Us found
the coverin' under the table next day, an' Mary comed across
the letter itself in her pocket at the last."

"'Tis that I be comed for. If you could tell so much as a
word or two out of it, Mary? They said you burnt it, an' the
crowner was mighty angry, but I thot as p'raps you'd looked at
it all the same, awnly weern't pleased to say so."

"No," she answered. "'Tis true I found a letter, an' I
might 'a' read some of it if I would, but I judged better not.
'Tweern't fair to her like."

"Was theer anything else as shawed anything 'bout en?"

"No—awnly a picksher of a ship he painted for her. I
burnt that tu; an' I'd 'a' burnt his money if I could. He
painted her—I knaw that much; she tawld us wan night—a
gert picksher, near as large as life. He took it to Lunnon—for
a shaw, I s'pose."

"I'd think of en no more if I was you, Joe," said Uncle
Chirgwin. "Leave the likes of en to the God of en. Brace
yourself agin' this sore onset, an' pray to Heaven to forgive all
sinners."

Noy looked at the old man and his great jaws seemed to
spread laterally with his thought.

"God have gived the man to me! that's why I be here: to
knaw all any can teach me. I've got to be the undoin' o'
that devil—the undoin' an' death of en. I'll be upsides wi' the
man if it takes me fifty year to do it. Awnly 'more haste, more
let.' I shall go slow an' sure. That's why I comed here fust
thing."

Mr. Chirgwin looked extremely alarmed and Mary spoke.

"This be wild, wicked talkin', Joe Noy, an' no mort o' sorrer as ever was can excuse sich words as them. 'Tedn' no task o' yourn to take the Lard's work out His hand that way. He'll pay the evil-doer his just dues wi'out help from you."

"I've got a voice in my ear, Mary—a voice louder'n any human voice; an' it bids me be doin' as the instrument of God A'mighty's just rage. If you can help me, then I bid you do it ; if not, let me be away. Did you read any o' that theer letter—so much as a word ; or did 'e larn wheer 'twas writ from ?"

"If I knawed, I shouldn't tell 'e, not now. I'd sooner cut my tongue out than aid 'e 'pon the road you'm set. An' you a righteous-thinkin' man wance ! "

He looked at her, and there was that in his face which showed a mind busy with time past. His voice had changed and his eye softened.

"I be punished for much, Mary Chirgwin. I be punished wi' loss an' wi' sich work put on me as may lead to a terrible ugly plaace at the end. But theer 'tis. Like the chisel in the hand o' the carpenter, so I be a sharp tool in the Lard's grip."

"Never ! You be a poor, dazed worm, in the grip o' your awn evil thots ! You'm foxing * yourself, Joe ; you'm listenin' to the devil an' tellin' yourself 'tis God—knawin' 'tedn' so all the while. Theer's no religion as would put you in the right wi' sich notions as them. Listen to your awn small guidin' voice, Joe Noy ; listen to me, or to Luke Gosp'lers, or any sober-thinkin', God-fearin' sawl. All the world would tell 'e you was wrong—all the wisdom o' the airth be agin' you, let alone Heaven."

"If 'twas any smaller thing I'd listen to 'e, Mary, for I knaw you to be a wise, strong wummon ; but theer ban't no mistaken' the message I got down-long when they told me what's fallen 'pon Joan Tregenza. No fay ; my way be clear

* *Foxing*, deceiving.

afore me ; an' the angel o' God will lead my footsteps nearer an' nearer till I faace the man. Windin' ways or short, 'tis all wan in the end ; 'tis all set down in the Book of the Lard."

"How can the likes o' you dare to up an' say what be in the Book o' the Lard, Joe?" asked Uncle Chirgwin, roused to words by the other's sentiments. "You've got a ghastly, bloody-minded fit on you along of all your troubles. But doan't 'e let it fasten into your heart. Pray to God to wipe away these here awful opinions. Else they'll be the ruin of 'e, body an' sawl If Luke Gosp'ling brot 'e to this pass in time o' darkness an' tribulation, 'tis a cruel pity you didn't bide a church member."

"I wish I thot you was in the right, uncle," said the sailor, calmly; "but I knaws you ban't. All the hidden powers of the airth an' the sea edn' gwaine to keep me from that man. Now I'll leave 'e ; an' I'm sorry, Mary Chirgwin, as you caan't find it in your heart to help me, but so the Lard wills it. I won't ax 'e to shake my hand, for theer'll be blood on it sooner or later—the damnedest blood as ever a angry God called 'pon wan of His creatures to spill out."

"Joe, Joe, stay an' listen to me ! For the sake of the past, listen !"

But Noy rose as Mary cried these words, and before she had finished speaking he was gone.

CHAPTER XII.

THE SEEKING OF THE MAN.

Thus the sailor, Noy, wholly imbued with one idea, absolutely convinced that to this end it had pleased Providence to give him life, went forth into the world that he might seek and slay the seducer of Joan. After leaving Drift he returned to Penzance, lay there that night, and upon the following morning began a methodical visitation of the Newlyn studios. Five he called at, and to five artists he stated something of his case in general terms; but none of those who heard him were familiar with any of the facts, and none could offer him either information or assistance. Edmund Murdoch was not in Newlyn, Brady had gone to Brittany; but at the seventh studio which he visited, Joe Noy substantiated some of his facts. Paul Tarrant chanced to be at home and at work when he called; and the artist would have told Joe everything which he wished to learn, but that Noy was cautious and reserved, not guessing that he stood before one who knew his enemy and entertained no admiration for him.

"Axing pardon for taking up any of your time, sir," he began, "but theer'm a matter concerning a party in your business as painted a maiden here, by name o' Joan Tregenza. She weern't nobody—awnly a fisherman's darter, but the picksher was said to be done in these paarts, an' I thot, maybe, you'd knaw who drawed it."

Tarrant had not heard of Joan's death and indeed possessed no information concerning her, save that Barron had prevailed upon the girl to sit for a portrait. The question, therefore, struck him as curious; and one which he put in return, merely to satisfy his own curiosity, impressed Joe in a similar way. His suspicious nature took fright, and Tarrant's dark, bright eyes seemed to read his secret and search his soul.

"Yes, a portrait of Joan Tregenza was painted here last spring, but not by a Newlyn man. How does that interest you?"

"Awnly sideways. 'Ted'n nothin' to me. I knaws the parties, an' wanted to see the picksher if theer weern't no objection."

"That's impossible, I fear, unless you go to London. I cannot help you further than to say the artist lives there, and his picture is being exhibited at an art gallery. Somebody told me that much; but which it is I really don't remember."

This was enough for Noy. Ignorant of the metropolis or the vague import of the words "a picture gallery," he deemed these directions amply sufficient, and, being anxious to escape further questioning, now thanked Tarrant, and speedily departed. Not until halfway back again to Penzance did he realize how slight was the nature of this information, and how ill-calculated to bring him to his object: the man he wanted lived in London, and had a painting of Joan Tregenza in a picture gallery there.

Yet, upon these directions, Joe Noy resolved to begin his search, and as the train anon bore him away to the field of the great quest he weighed the chances and considered a course of action. Allowing the ample margin of ten picture galleries to London, and assuming that the portrait of Joan once found would be easily recognized by him, the sailor considered that a fortnight of work should bring him face to face with what he sought. That done, he imagined that it would not be difficult to learn the name and address of the painter. He had indeed asked Tarrant this question point-blank, but the artist's accidental curiosity and Joe's own caution combined to prevent any extension of the interview or a repetition of the question. A word had at least placed him in possession of John Barron's name, but chance prevented it from being spoken, as chance had burnt Barron's letter and prevented his name appearing at the inquest. Now Noy viewed the task before him with equanimity. The end was already assured, for, in his own opinion, he walked God-guided; but the means lay with him, and he felt that it was his duty to spare no pains or labours, and not to hesitate from the terrible action marked for him when he should reach the end of his journey. Mary's last words came to his ear like a whisper which mingled with the jolt and rattle of the railway train; but they held no power to upset his purpose or force to modify his rooted determination. Her image occupied his thoughts, however, for a lengthy period. Then, with some effort, he banished it, and attempted a calculation of ways and means, estimating the capabilities of his money.

Entering the great hive to accomplish that assassination, as he supposed, both planned and predestined for him before God made the sun, Noy set about his business in a deliberate and careful manner. He hired a bedroom in a mean street near Paddington, and, on the day after his arrival in London, purchased a large map and index of the city which gave ample particulars of public buildings and mentioned the names and positions of the great permanent homes of art. By the help of newspaper advertisements he ascertained where to find some of the numerous private dealers' galleries, and likewise learned what public annual exhibitions chanced to be at that time open. Whereupon, though the circumstance failed to quicken his pulse, he discovered that the extent of his labours would prove far greater than he at first imagined. He made careful lists of the places where pictures were to be seen, and the number quickly ran up to fifty, sixty, seventy exhibitions. That he would be able to visit all these Joe knew was impossible, but the fact caused him no disquiet. The picture he sought and the name of the man who painted it must be presented to him in due season. For him it only remained to toil systematically at the search, and allow no clue to escape him. As for the issue, it was with the Lord.

London swept and surged about Joe Noy unheeded. He

cared for nothing but canvases and the places where they might be seen. Day by day he worked, and went early to rest, weary and worn by occupation of a nature so foreign to his experience. Nightly his last act was to delete one, or sometimes two, of the exhibitions figured upon his lists. Thus a week passed by, and he had visited ten galleries and seen upwards of five thousand pictures. Not one painting or drawing of them all was missed or hurried over; he compared each with its number in the catalogue, then studied it carefully to see if any hint or suggestion of Joan appeared in it. Her Christian name often met his scrutiny in titles, and those works thus designated he regarded with greater attention than any others; but the week passed fruitlessly, and Joe, making a calculation at the end of it, discovered that, at his present rate of progression, it would be impossible to inspect more than half of the galleries set down before his funds were exhausted. The knowledge quickened his ingenuity, and he discovered a means by which future labours might be vastly modified and much time saved. He already knew that the man responsible for Joan's destruction was called John; his mind now quickened with the recollection of this important fact, and henceforth he did a thing which any man less unintelligent had done from the first: he scanned his catalogues without troubling about the pictures, and only concerned himself with those canvases whose painter had "John" for their Christian names. He thanked God on his knees that the idea should have entered his mind, for his labours were thereby enormously lightened. Notwithstanding, through ignorance of his subject, Joe wasted a great deal of time and money. Thus he visited the National Gallery, the Old Masters at the Academy, and various dealers' exhibitions where collections of the pictures of foreign men were at that season being displayed.

The brown sailor created some interest viewed in an environment so peculiar. His picturesque face might well have graced a frame, and looked down upon the artistic throngs who swept among the pictures; but the living man, full of almost tragic interest in what he saw, labouring along, catalogue in hand, dead to everything but the art around him, seemed wholly out of place. He looked what he was: the detached thread of some story from which the spectator only saw this chapter broken away and standing without its context. Nine persons out of ten dismissed him with a smile; but occasionally a thoughtful mind would view the man, and occupy itself with the problem of his affairs. Such built up imaginary histories of him and his actions, which only resembled each other in the quality of remoteness from truth.

Once it happened that at a small gallery, off Bond Street, the sudden sight of precious things brought new emotions to Joe Noy—sentiments and sensations of a sort more human and more natural than those under which he was at present pursuing his purpose. Before this spectacle, suddenly presented in the quietness and loneliness of the little exhibition, that stern spirit of revenge which had actuated him since the knowledge of his loss, and which, gripping his mind like a frost from the outset, had congested the gentler emotions of sorrow for poor Joan and for himself—before this display of a familiar scene, hallowed beyond all others in memory, the man's relentless mood rose off his mind for a brief moment like a cloud, and he stood, with aching heartstrings, gazing at a large canvas. Sweet to him it was as the unexpected face of one dearly loved to the wanderer; and startling in a measure also, for, remembering his oath, to see Newlyn no more until his enemy was dead, it seemed as though the vow was broken by some miracle, and that from the heart of the roaring city he had magically plunged through space to the threshold of the home of Joan.

Before him loomed a picture like a window opening upon Newlyn. The village lay there in all the flame and glory of sunset lights. The grey and black roofs clustered up the great dark hill, and the gloaming fell out of a primrose sky over sea and land. The waters twinkled full of light to the very fore-front of the canvas, and between the piers of the harbour a fisher-boy was sculling his boat. Between the masts of stone-schooners at the quay, Joe saw the white cottage of the Tregenzas, and there his survey stopped, for at this spectacle thought broke loose. No man ever paid a nobler tribute to a good picture. Very long he gazed motionless, then, with a great sigh, moved slowly forward, his eyes still turning back.

The day and the experience which it brought him marked a considerable flux of new impressions in Joe's mind—impressions which, without softening the rugged aspect of his determination, yet added other lines of reflection. Sorrow for what was lost fastened upon him, and an indignation burnt his soul that such things could be in a world designed and ordered by the Almighty. Revenge, however, grew no less desirable in the light of sorrow. He looked to it more and more eagerly as the only food which could lead to peace of mind. His road probably embraced the circumstances of an ignominious death; but none the less peace would follow—a peace beyond the power of future life on earth to supply. Thus, at least, did his project then present itself to him. Thought of the meeting with his enemy grew to be a luxury, which he feasted upon in the night watches after fruitless days and the investigation of endless miles of pictures. Then he would lie awake and imagine the inevitable climax. He saw himself standing before the man who had ruined two lives; he felt his hand close over a knife or a pistol, and wondered which it should be; he heard his own voice, slow and steady, pronounce sentence of death, and he saw terror light that other man's face as the blood fled from it. He rehearsed the words he should utter at that great juncture, and speculated as to what manner of answer would come; then the last scene of all represented his enemy stretched dead at his feet, and himself with his hands linked in iron. There yet remained the end of the tragedy for him—a spectacle horrible enough in the eyes of those still left to love him, but, for himself, empty of terror, innocent of power to alarm. Clean-living men would pity him; religious men would see in him an instrument used by God to strike at a sinner. His death would probably bring some wanderers to the fold; it must of a surety be long remembered as the greatest sermon lived and preached by a Luke Gospeller. Lulled by the humming woof and warp of such reflections his mind nightly passed into the unconsciousness of sleep; and quickened by subsequent visions, the brain retraversed these imaginings with an added gloom, and that tremendous appearance of reality proper to the domain of dreams.

Thus the days sped and grew shorter as December waned. Then, at the end of the second week of his labours, Noy chanced to read that an Exhibition at the Institute of Painters in Oils was about to close; and not yet having visited that collection, he set out on the morning of the following day to do so.

CHAPTER XIII.

"JOE'S SHIP."

ACCORDING to his custom Noy worked through the exhibition catalogue for each room before entering it. The hour was an early one, and but few persons had as yet penetrated to the central part of the gallery. For these, however, an experience of a singular character was now in store. Wandering hither and thither in groups, and talking in subdued voices after the manner of persons in such a place, all were suddenly conscious of a loud inarticulate cry. The sudden volume of sound denoted mixed emotions, but amazement and grief were throned upon it, and the exclamation came from a man standing now stiff and spell-bound before "Joe's Ship," the famous masterpiece of John Barron. The beholders viewed an amazed figure which seemed petrified, even to an expression on his face. There are countenances which display the ordinary emotions of humanity in a fashion unusual and peculiar to themselves. Thus, while the customary and conventional signs of sorrow are a down-drawing slant to the corners of mouth and eye, yet it sometimes happens that the lines more usually associated with gratification are donned in grief. Of this freakish character was the face of Joe Noy. His muscles seemed to follow the bones underneath them; and now beholding him, the surprised spectators saw a man of gigantic proportions gigantically moved. Yet, while sorrow was discernible in his voice, the corners of his mouth were dragged up till his lips resembled a half-moon on its back, and the lids and corners of his eyes were full of laughter wrinkles, while the eyes themselves were starting and agonized. The man's catalogue had fallen to the ground; his hands were clenched; now, as others watched him, he came step by step nearer to the picture.

To estimate the force of the thing upon Noy's hungry heart, to present the chaos of emotions which gripped him at this, the goal of his pilgrimage, is impossible. Here, restored to him by art, was his dead sweetheart, the sum and total of all the beauty he had worshipped, and which for nearly a year of absence had been his guiding star. He knew that she was in her grave, yet she stood before him sweet and fresh, with the moisture of life in her eyes and on her lips. He recognized everything, to the windy spot where the gorse flourished on the crown of the cliff. The clean sky told him from whence the wind blew; the grey gull above was flying with it, upon slanting wings. And Joan stood below in a blaze of sunshine and yellow blossom. A reflection from the corner of her sun-bonnet brightened her face, though it was shaded from direct sunlight by her hand; her blue eyes mirrored the sea and the sky; and they met Joe's, like a question. She was looking away to the edge of the world; and he knew from the name of the picture, which he had read before he saw it, the object she regarded. He glared on, and his breath came quicker. The brown petticoat with the black patch was familiar to him; but he had never seen the gleam of her white neck below the collar, where it was hidden from the sun. In the picture an unfastened button showed this. The rest he knew—her hair turning at the flapping edge of the sun-bonnet; her slight figure, round waist, and the shoes, whose strings he had been privileged to tie more than once. Then he remembered her last promise— to see his ship go down Channel from their old meeting-place upon Gorse Point; and the memory, thus revived by the actual spectacle of Joan Tregenza looking her last at his vanishing vessel, brought that wild cry to Noy's lip with the wringing of his heart. He was absolutely dead to his environment, and his long days of silence suddenly ended in a futile outpouring of words addressed to any who might care to listen. Passion surged to the top of his mind—rage for his loss, indignation that the unutterably fair thing before them had been blotted out of the world while he was far away, without power to protect her. For a few moments only did the man lose his self-control, but in that brief time he spoke; and his listeners enjoyed a sensation of a nature outside their wildest experiences.

"O Christ Jesus! 'tis Joan—my awn li'l Joan, as I left her, as I seed her alive!"

He had reached a point separated from the picture by a few feet only. Here he stood and spoke again, now conscious that there were people round about him.

"She'm dead—dead an' buried—my Joan—killed by the devil as drawed her theer in that picksher. As large as life; an' yet she'm under ground wi' a brawken heart. An' me, new-comed off the sea—— "

"It's 'Joe's Ship' he means," whispered somebody; and Noy heard him.

"'Iss, fay, so 'tis; an' I be Joe—I talkin' to 'e; an' she'm shadin' her eyes theer to see my vessel a-sailin' away to furrin paarts! 'Tis a story that's true, an' the God-blasted limb what drawed this knawed I was gone to the end o' the airth outward bound."

A man from the turnstile came up at this moment, and inquired what was the matter. His voice and tone of authority brought the sailor back to the position he occupied; he restrained himself therefore, and said no more. Already Noy feared that his passion might have raised suspicions, and now, turning and picking up his catalogue, he made hasty departure, before those present had opportunity to take much further notice of him. The man hurried off into the rattle of the busy thoroughfare, and, in a moment, he and his sorrows and his deadly purpose had vanished away.

Meantime the curator of the gallery, a man of intelligence, improved the moment, and addressed some apposite reflections to those spectators who still clustered around John Barron's picture,

"It isn't often we get such a sight as that. Many people have wondered why this great work was called as it is. The man who has gone explains it, and you have had a glimpse of the picture's history—the inner history of it. The painting has made a great sensation ever since it was first exhibited, but never such a sensation as it made to-day."

"The beggar looked as though he meant mischief," said somebody.

"He knows the model is dead apparently; but there's another mystery there too, for Mr. Barron himself isn't aware of the fact. He was here only the day before yesterday—a little pale shadow of a man, like a ghost in a fur coat. He came to see his picture, and stopped ten minutes. A gentleman was with him, and as he left the gallery I heard the artist say that he had quite recently endeavoured to learn some particulars of his model, but had failed to do so as yet."

CHAPTER XIV.

THE FINDING OF THE MAN.

THE gratification of his desire and fulfilment of his revenge, though steadfastly foreseen by Joe Noy from the moment when first he set foot in London and began his search, now for a moment overwhelmed him at the prospect of their extreme propinquity. Had anything been needed to strengthen his determination on the threshold of a meeting with Joan's destroyer, it was the startling vision of Joan herself from which he had just departed. No event had brought the magnitude of his loss more cruelly to the core of his heart than the sudden splendid representation of what he had left behind him in her innocence and beauty; and, for the same reason, nothing could have more thoroughly fortified his mind to the deed now lying in his immediate future.

Noy's first act was to turn again to the gallery with a purpose to inquire where John Barron might be found; but he recollected that many catalogues contained the private addresses of the exhibitors, and accordingly consulted the list he had brought with him. There he found the name, and also the house in which the owner of it dwelt—

"JOHN BARRON,
No. 6, Melbury Gardens, S.W."

Only hours now separated him from his goal, and it seemed strange to Noy that he should have thus come in sight of it so suddenly. But his wits cooled, and with steady system he followed the path long marked out. He stood and looked in

at a gunsmith's window for ten minutes, then moved forward
to another. At the shop-fronts of cutlers he also dawdled, but
finally returned to the first establishment which had attracted
him, entered and, for the sum of two pounds, purchased a small,
five-chambered revolver and a box of cartridges. He then went
back to his lodging, and set to work to find the position of
Melbury Gardens upon his map. This done, the man marked
his road to that region, outlining with a red chalk pencil the
streets through which he would have to walk before reaching it.
Throughout the afternoon he continued his preparations, acting
very methodically, and setting his house in order with the
deliberation of one who knows that he is going to die, but
not immediately. Sometimes he rested from the labour of
letter-writing to think and rehearse again the scene which was
to close that day. A thousand times he had already done so;
a thousand times the imaginary interview had been the last
thought in his waking brain: but now the approach of reality
swept away the unreal dialogues, dramatic entrances, exits
and events of the great scene as he had pictured it. The present
moment found Noy's brain blank as to everything but the
issue; and he surprised himself by discovering that his mind
now continually recurred to those events which would follow
the climax, while yet the death of John Barron was unac-
complished. His active thoughts, under conditions of such
excitation as the day had brought upon the top of his discovery,
travelled with astounding speed, and it was not John Barron's
end, but his own, which filled the imagination of the sailor as
he wrote. The shadow of the gallows was on the paper, though
the event which was to bring this consummation still lay some
hours deep in unrecorded time. But, for Noy, John Barron
was as good as dead, and himself as good as under sentence
of death.

Grown quite calm, fixed in mind, and immovable as the
dark sea cliffs of his mother-land, he wrote steadily on until
thought sped whirling forward to a new aspect of his future:
the last. He saw himself in eternity, tossed to everlasting

flames by his Maker, as a man tosses an empty match-box, after it has done its work, into the fire. He put down his pen and pictured it. The terrific force of that conviction cannot fairly be set before the intelligence of average cultured people, because, whatever they profess to believe in their hearts, the truth is that, even with forty-nine Christians out of fifty, hell appears a mere vague conceit meaning nothing. They affirm that they credit eternal torment; they confess all humanity is ripe for it; but their pulses are unquickened by the assertion or admission, because in reality they believe nothing of the sort. Nor can educated man so believe; for that way madness lies; and he who dwells over long and closely upon this unutterable dogma, will anon himself feel the first flickering of the undying flame. It scorches, not his body, but his brain, and a lunatic asylum presently shuts him from a sane world.

But with primitive opinions, narrow beliefs, and narrow intelligences hell can be a live conceit enough. Among Luke Gospellers and kindred sects there shall be found such genuine fear and such trembling as the Church called Orthodox never knows; and to Noy the tremendous spectacle of his everlasting punishment now made itself actively felt. A life beyond death—a life to be spent in one of two places, and to endure eternally, was to Joe as certain as the knowledge that he lived; and that his destination must be determined by the work yet lying between him and death appeared equally sure. Further, that work must be performed. There was no loophole of escape from it, and had there been such he would have blocked it against himself resolutely. Moreover, as the will and desire to do the deed was an action as definite in the eye of Heaven as the accomplishment of the deed itself, he reckoned himself already damned. He had long since counted the whole cost, and now it only seemed more vast and awful than upon past surveys by reason of its nearer approach. Now he speculated curiously upon those meetings which must follow the world's dissolution; he wondered if murderers do ever meet and hold converse in hell fire with their victims. Then again he fell to writing, and presently completed letters to his father, his mother, to Mrs. Tregenza, and to Mary Chirgwin. These he left in his apartment, and presently going out into the air, walked with no particular aim until darkness fell. Hunger now prompted him, and he ate a big meal at a restaurant, and drank with his food a pint of ale. Physically fortified, he returned to his lodging, left upon the table in his solitary room the sum he would that night owe for the hire of the chamber, and then, taking his letters, went out to return no more. A few clothes, a brush and comb, and a small wooden trunk was all he left behind him.

Joe Noy purchased four stamps for his letters and posted them. They were written as though the murder of John Barron had been already accomplished, and he thus completed and despatched them before the event, because he imagined that, afterwards, the power of communicating with his parents or friends would be denied him. That they might be spared the horror of learning the news through a public source, he wrote it thus, and knew, as he did so, that to two of his correspondents the intelligence would come without the full force of a novelty. Thomasin Tregenza and Mary Chirgwin alike were familiar with his intention at the time of his departure, and to them he therefore wrote but briefly; his parents, on the other hand, for all Joe knew to the contrary, might still be ignorant of the fact that he had come off his cruise. His letters to them were accordingly of great length; and he set forth therein with the nervous lucidity of a meagre vocabulary the nature of his wrongs, and the action which he had taken under Heaven's guidance to revenge them. He stated plainly in all four of his missives to Newlyn, Drift, and Mousehole, that the artist, John Barron, was shot dead by his hand, and that he himself intended suffering the consequent punishment as became a brave man and the weapon of the Lord. These notes then he posted, and so went upon his way that he might fulfil to the letter his written words.

Following the roads he had studied upon his map, and

committed to memory, Noy soon reached Molbury Gardens, and presently stood opposite No. 6, and scanned it. The hour was then ten o'clock, and lights were in some of the windows, but not many. Looking over the area railings, the sailor saw four servants—two men and two women—eating their supper. He noted, as a singular circumstance, that there were wine-glasses upon the kitchen table, and that they held red liquor and white.

Noy's design was simple enough. He meant to stand face to face with John Barron, to explain the nature of the events which had occurred, to tell him, what it was possible he might not know, that Joan was dead; and then to inform him that his own days were numbered. Upon these words Joe designed to shoot the other down like a dog, and to make absolutely certain of is death by firing the entire contents of the revolver. He expected that a private interview would be vouchsafed to him if he desired it; and his intention, after his victim should fall, was to blow the man's brains out at close quarters before even those nearest at hand could prevent it. At half-past ten, Noy felt that his weapon was in the left breast-pocket of his coat ready for the drawing; then ascended steps which rose to the front door of John Barron's dwelling, and rang the bell.

The man-servant whom he had seen through the area railings in the kitchen came to the door, and, much to Noy's astonishment, accosted him before he had time to say that he wished to see the master of the house.

"You've come at last, then?" said the man.

Joe regarded him with surprise, then spoke. "I want to see Mr. John Barron, please."

The other laughed, as if this was an admirable jest. "I suppose you do, though that's a queer way to put it. You talk as though you had come to smoke a cigar along with him."

In growing amazement and suspicion, Noy listened to this most curious statement. Fears suddenly awoke that, by some mysterious circumstance, Barron had learned of his contemplated action, and was prepared for it. He stopped, therefore, looked about him sharply to avoid any sudden surprise, and put a question to the footman.

"You spoke as though I was wanted," he said. "What do you mean by that?"

"Blessed if you're not a rum un!" answered the man. "Of course you was wanted, else you wouldn't be here, would you? You're not a party as calls promiscuous, I should hope. Else it would be rather trying to delicate nerves. You're the gentleman as everybody requires some time, though nobody ever sends for himself."

Failing to gather the other's meaning, Noy only realized that John Barron expected some visitor, and felt therefore the more determined to hasten his own actions. He saw the footman was endeavouring to be jocose, suspected he was drunk, and therefore humoured him, pretending at the same time to be the individual who was expected.

"You're a funny fellow, and must often make your master laugh, I should reckon. 'Iss, I be the chap what you thought I was. An' I should like to see him—the guv'nor—at once if he'll see me."

The footman chuckled again. "He'll see you all right. He's been wantin' you all day, and he'd have been that dreadful disapp'inted if you 'adn't come. Always awful particular about his clothes, you know, so mind you're jolly careful about the measurin', 'cause this overcoat will have to last him a long time."

Taking his cue from these words, Noy, still ignorant of the truth, made answer—

"'Iss, I'll measure en all right. Wheer is he to?"

"In the studio—there you are, right ahead. Knock at that baize door, and then walk straight in, 'cause he'll very likely be too much occupied to answer you. He's quite alone—leastways, I believe so. I'll come back in quarter'n hour; and mind you don't talk no secrets, or tell him how I laughed at him behind his back, else he'd give me the sack for certain."

The man withdrew, sniggering at his own humour, and Noy, quite unable to see rhyme or reason in his remarks, stood with an expression of bewilderment upon his broad face, and watched the servant disappear. Then his countenance changed, and he approached a door covered with red baize, at which the passage terminated. He knocked, waited, and knocked again, straining his ear to hear the voice he had laboured so long to silence. Then he put his revolver into the side pocket of his coat, and afterwards, following the footman's directions, pushed open the swing door, which yielded to his hand. A curtain hung inside it, and, pulling this aside, he entered a spacious apartment with a glass roof. But scanty light illuminated the studio from one oil-lamp which hung by a chain from a bracket in the wall, and the rays of which were much dimmed by a red glass shade. Some easels, mostly empty, stood about the sides of the great chamber; here and there on the white walls were sketches in charcoal and daubs of paint. A German stove appeared in the middle of the room, but it was not burning; skins of beasts scattered the floor; upon one wall hung the "Negresses bathing at Tobago." For the rest the room appeared empty. Then, growing accustomed to the dim red light, Noy made a closer examination until he caught sight of an object which caused him to catch his breath violently and hurry forward. Under the lofty open windows which rose on the northern sides of the studio, remote from all other objects, was a couch, and upon it lay a small, straight figure shrouded in white sheets save for its face.

John Barron had been dead twenty-four hours, and he had hastened his own end, by a space of time impossible to determine, through leaving his sick-room two days previously that he might visit the picture-gallery wherein hung "Joe's Ship." It was a step taken in absolute defiance of his medical men. The day of that excursion had chanced to be a very cold one, and during the night which followed it John Barron broke a blood-vessel, and precipitated his death. Now, in the hands of hirelings, without a friend to put one flower on his breast or close

his dim eyes, the man lay waiting for an undertaker; and while
Joe Noy glared at him, unconsciously gripping the weapon he
had brought, it seemed as though the dead smiled under the
red flicker of the lamp—as though he smiled and prepared to
come back into life to answer this supreme accuser.

As by an educated mind Joe Noy's estimate and assurance
of the eternal tortures of hell cannot be adequately grasped in
its full force, so now it is hard to set forth, with a power
sufficiently luminous and terrific, the effect of this discovery
upon him. He, the weapon of the Almighty, found his work
finished, and the fruits of his labours snatched from his hand.
His enemy had departed, and the fact that he was dead only
made the case harder. Had Barron escaped from him alive,
he could have suffered it, knowing that the sure end lay in
the future at the determination of God; but now that end
appeared before him accomplished, and it had been attained
without his assistance. His labour was lost, and his longed-
for, prayed-for achievement rendered impossible. He stood
and scanned the small, marble-white face, then drew a box of
matches from his pocket, lighted one and looked closer. Worn
by disease to mere skin and skull, there was nothing left to
indicate the dead man's wasted powers; nothing to suggest
one whose word had possessed fascination so tremendous. The
end of Noy's match fell red-hot on John Barron's face. Then
he turned as footsteps sounded. The curtains were moved aside
and the footman reappeared, followed by another person.

"Why, you wasn't the undertaker after all!" he explained.
"Did you think the man was alive? Good Lord! But you've
found him any way."

"Iss, I thot he was alive. I wanted to see en livin' an'
leave en——" he stopped. Common sense for once had a word
with him, and convinced him of the folly of saying anything
now concerning his frustrated projects.

"He died last night—consumption—and he's left money
enough to build a brace of ironclads, they say; and never no
will, and not a soul on God's earth is there with any legal

claim upon him. To tell the truth, we none of us never liked him. He was a low-bred man for all his money."

"If you'll shaw me the way out into the street, I'll thank you," said Noy.

The undertaker was already busy making measurements. Then, a minute later, Joe found himself standing under the sky again; and the darkness was full of laughter and of voices, of gibing, jeering noises in unseen throats, of rapid utterances on invisible tongues. The supernatural things screamed into his ears that he was damned for a wish and for an intention; then they shrieked and yelled their derision, and he understood well enough, for the point of view was not a new one. Given the accomplishment of his desire, he was prepared to suffer eternally; now eternal suffering must follow on a wish barren of fruit, and hell for him would be hell indeed, with no accomplished revenge in memory to lessen the torment. When the voices at length died, and a clock struck one, Noy came to himself and realized that, in so far as the present affected him, Fate had brought him back to life and liberty by a short cut. Then, seeing his position, he asked himself whether life was long enough to make atonement, and even allow of ultimate escape after death. But the fierce disappointment which beat upon his soul like a recurring wave, as thought drifted back and back, told him that he had fairly won hell-fire and must abide by it.

So thinking, he returned to his lodging, entered unobserved and prowled the small chamber till dawn. By morning light all his life appeared transfigured, and a ghastly anti-climax faced the man. Presently he remembered the letters he had posted over night, and the recollection of them brought with it sudden resolves and a course of action.

Half an hour later he had reached Paddington station, and was soon on his way back to Cornwall.

CHAPTER XV.

STARLIGHT AND FROST.

BORN of the sunshine, on a morning in late December, grey ephemera danced and dipped and fashioned vanishing patterns against the green of the great laurel at the corner of Drift farmyard. The mildness of the day had wakened them into brief life, but even as they twinkled their wings of gauze, death was abroad. A sky of unusual clearness crowned the Cornish moorland, and Uncle Chirgwin, standing at his kitchen door, already foretold frost, though the morning was still young.

"The air's like milk just now, sure 'nough, an' 'twill bide so till noon, then, when the sun begins to slope, the cold will graw an' graw to frost. An' no harm done, thank God."

He spoke to his niece, who was in the room behind him; and as he did so, a circumstance of very unusual nature happened. Two persons reached the front door of the farm simultaneously, and a maid, answering the double knock, returned a moment later with two communications, both for Mary Chirgwin.

"Postman, he brot this here, miss, an' a bwoy from Mouzle brot t'other."

The first letter came from London, the second, directed in a similar hand, reached Mary from the adjacent fishing hamlet. She knew the big writing well enough, but showed no emotion before the maid. In fact, her self-command was remarkable, for she put both letters into her pocket, and made some show of continuing her labours for another five minutes before departing to her room that she might read the news from Joe Noy.

He, it may be said, had reached Penzance by the same train which conveyed his various missives, all posted too late for the mail upon the previous night. Thus he reached the white cottage on the cliff in time to see Mrs. Tregenza and bid her destroy unread the letter she would presently receive; and on returning to his parents, himself took from the letter-carrier his own communications to them, and burnt both immediately. He had also despatched a boy to Drift that Mary might be warned as to the letter she would receive by the morning post; but the lad, though ample time was given him to reach Drift before the postman, loitered by the way. Thus the letters had arrived simultaneously, and it was quite an open question which the receiver of them would open first.

Chance decided; Mary's hand, thrust haphazard into her pocket, came forth with Noy's epistle recently despatched from Mousehole; and that she read, the accident saving her some suffering.

Thus wrote Noy:

"DEAR MARY,

"You will get this by hand afore the coming in of the penny post. When that comes in there will be another letter for you from me, sent off from London. It is all wrong, so burn it, and don't you read it on no account. Burn it to ashes, for theer's a-many reasons why you should. I be coming up-long to see you arter dinner, and if you can walk out in the air with me for a bit I'll thank you so to do.

"Your servant,

"J. NOY.

"Burn the letter to dust 'fore anything else. Don't let it bide a minute, and doan't tell none you had it."

Curiosity was no part of Mary Chirgwin's nature. Now she merely thanked Heaven which had led to the right letter, and so enabled her unconsciously to obey Joe's urgent command. Then she returned to the kitchen, placed his earlier communication in the heart of the fire, and watched while it blackened, curled, blazed, and finally shuddered down into a red-hot ash. She determined to see him and walk with him, as he asked, if he returned with clean hands. While the letter which she had read neither proved nor disproved such a supposition, the woman yet felt a secret and sure conviction in her heart that Noy was coming back innocent, at least, of any desperate action. That he was in Cornwall again, and a free man, appeared to her proof sufficient he had not committed violence.

Mary allowed her anxiety to interfere with no duty. By three o'clock she was ready to set out, and looking from her bedroom window as she tied on her bonnet, she saw Joe Noy approaching up the hill. A minute later she was at the door, and stood there waiting with her eyes upon his as he came up the path. Then she looked down, and to the man it seemed as though she was gazing at his right hand, which held a stick.

" 'Tis as it was, Mary Chirgwin—my hands be white," he said. " You needn't fear, though I promised if you ever seed 'em agin as they'd be red. 'Tedn' so. I was robbed of my hope, Mary. The Lard took Joan fust; then He took my revenge from me. His will be done. The man died four-an'-twenty hours 'fore I found en—just four-an'-twenty li'l hours—that was all."

" Thank the Almighty God for it, Joe, as I shall till the day of my death. Never was no prayer answered so surely as mine for you."

" Why, maybe I'll graw to thank God tu when 'tis farther to look back 'pon. I caan't feel 'tis so yet. I caan't feel as he'm truly dead. An' yet 'twas no lie, for I seed en, an' stood 'longside of en."

" God's hand be everywheer in it. Think if I'd read poor Joan's letter an' tawld 'e wheer the man's plaace of livin' was ! "

" 'Iss, then I'd have slain en. 'Tis such li'l things do mark out our paths. A gert picksher o' Joan he drawed—all done out so large as life; an' I found it, an' it 'peared as if the dead was riz up again an' staring at me. If 'tis all the saame to you, Mary, us'll go an' look 'pon her graave now, for I abbun seen it yet."

They walked in silence for some hundred yards along the lanes to Sancreed. Then Noy spoke again.

" How be uncle? "

" Betwix' an' between. The trouble an' loss o' Joan aged en cruel, an' the floods has brot things to a close pass. 'Twas the harder for en, 'cause all looked so more'n common healthy an' promisin' right up to the rain. But he's got the faith as moves mountains; he do knaw that sorrer ban't sent for nort."

" An' you? I wonder I'm bowldacious 'nough to look 'e in the faace, but sorrer's not forgot me neither."

" 'Tis a thing what awver-passes none. I've forgived 'e, Joe Noy, many a long month past, an' I've prayed to God to lead 'e through this strait, an' He have."

" 'Tis main hard to knaw what road's the right wan, Mary."

" 'Iss, fay, an' it is; an' harder yet to follow 'pon it when found."

" I judged as God was leadin' me against this here evil-doer to destroy en."

" 'Twas the devil misleadin' 'e an' takin' 'e along on his awn dance, till God saw, an' sent death."

" 'Iss; an' I be damned for nort but evil thots."

" Thanks to the mightiness of His mercy, Joe, He's left 'e time to repent. 'Twas the God *us* worships, you mind, not Him of the Luke Gosp'lers, nor any other 'tall that brot 'e out o' this pass. Theer's awnly wan real, livin' God; an' you left Him for a sham."

" An' I'm punished for't. Wheer should I turn now? I've thrawed awver your manner o' worship, an' I'm sick o' the Gosp'lers, for 'twas theer God as brot all my trouble 'pon me. He caan't be no God worth namin', else how should He 'a' treated that poor limb, Michael Tregenza, same as He has. That man had sweated for his God day an' night for fifty years. An' see his reward."

" Come back, come back to the auld road agin, Joe, an' leave the ways o' God to God. The butivul, braave thing 'bout our road be that wance lost 'tedn' allus lost. You may get night-foundered by the way, yet wi' the comin' o' light theer's allus a chance to make up lost ground agin an' keep gwaine on."

"A body must b'lieve in somethin', else he'm a rudderless vessel seemin'ly, but wi' sich a flood of 'pinions 'bout the airth, how's wan sailor-man to knaw what be safe anchorage an' what ban't? If Gosp'lers be liars, an' 'tothers likewise all awver the world, why is it sure that you o' Drift ban't liars tu?"

Mary argued with him in strenuous fashion, and increased her vehemence as he showed signs of yielding. She knew well enough that religion was as necessary to him in some shape as to herself.

Already a pageant of winter sunset began to unfold fantastic sheaves of splendour, and over the horizon line of the western moors the air was wondrously clear. It faded to intense white light where the uplands cut it, while, above, the background of the sky was a pure beryl gradually burning aloft into orange. Here waves of fire beat over golden shores, and red clouds extended as an army in regular column upon column. At the zenith, billows of scarlet leaped in feathery foam against a purple continent, and the flaming tide extended from reef to reef among a thousand aërial bays and estuaries of alternating gloom and glow until shrouded and dimmed in an orange tawny haze of infinite distance. In the immediate foreground of this majestic display, like a handful of rose-leaves fallen out of heaven, small clouds floated directly downwards, withering to blackness as they neared the earth and lost the dying fires. Beneath the splendour of the sky the land likewise flamed, the winding roadways glimmered, and many pools and ditches reflected back the circumambient glory of the air.

In a few more minutes Mary and Joe reached Sancreed churchyard, and soon stood beside the grave of Joan Tregenza.

"The grass won't close proper till the spring come," said Mary; "then the turf will grow an' make it vitty; an' uncle's gwaine to set up a good slate stone wi' the name an' date an' some verses. I planted them primroses 'long the top myself. If wan abbun gone an' blossomed tu!"

She stooped to pick a primrose and an opening bud; but Joe stopped her.

"Doan't 'e pluck 'em. Never take no flowers off of a graave. They'm all the dead have got."

"But they'll die. Theer's frost bitin' in the air already. They'll be withered come marnin'."

"No matter for that," he said; "let 'em bide wheer they be."

The man was silent awhile as he looked at the mound. Then he spoke again.

"Tell me about her. Talk 'bout her doin's an' sayin's. Did she forgive that man afore she died, or dedn' she?"

"'Iss, I reckon so."

Mary mentioned those things best calculated in her opinion to lighten the other's sorrow. He nodded from time to time as she spoke, and walked up and down with his hands behind him. When she stopped, he asked her to tell him further facts. Then the light waned under the sycamore trees, and only a red fire still touched their topmost boughs.

"We'll go now," Noy said. "An' she died believin' just the same as what you do—eh, Mary?"

"Uncle's sure of it—positive sartain 'twas so."

"An' you?"

"I pray that he was right. 'Iss, fay, I've grawed to b'lieve truly our Joan was saved, spite of all. I never 'sactly understood her thots, nor she mine; but she'm in heaven now I do think."

"If bitterness an' sorrer counts, she should be. An' you may take it from me she is. An' I reckon I'll come back to what she died believin' tu, if I may hope for awnly the lowest plaace. I'll come back an' walk along to church wance agin wi' you, wance 'fore I goes back to sea. Will 'e let me do that, Mary Chirgwin?"

"You'm welcome to come along wi' me next Sunday if you mind to."

"Now us'll go up the Carn an' look out 'pon the land and see the sun sink."

They left the churchyard together, climbed the neighbouring eminence, and stood silently at the top, their faces to the west.

A great pervasive calm and stillness in the air heralded frost. The sky had grown strangely clear, and only the rack and ruin of the recent imposing display now huddled into the arms of night on the eastern horizon. The sun, quickly dropping, loomed mighty and fiery red. Presently it touched the horizon and its progress, unappreciated in the sky, became accentuated by the rim of the world. A semicircle of fire, a narrowing segment, a splash, throbbing like a flame—then it had vanished, and light waned until there trembled out the radiance of a brief after-glow. Already the voices of the frost began to break the earth's silence. In the darkness of woods it was busy casing the deep mosses in ice, binding the dripping outlets of hidden water, whispering with infinitely delicate sound as it flung forth its needles, the mother of ice, and suffered them to spread like tiny sudden fingers on the face of freezing water. From the horizon the brightness of the zodiacal light streamed mysteriously upwards into the depth of heaven, dimming the stars. But the brightness of them grew in splendour and brilliancy as increasing cold gripped the world; and while the stealthy feet of the frost raced and tinkled like a fairy tune, the starlight flashed upon its magic silver, powdered its fabrics with light and pointed its crystal triumphs with fire. Thus starlight and frost fell upon the forest and the Cornish moor, beneath the long avenues of silence, and over all the unutterable blackness of granite and dead heather. The earth slept and dreamed dreams, as the chain of the cold tightened; all the earth dreamed fair dreams, in night and nakedness—dreams such as forest trees and lone elms, meadows and hills, moors and valleys, great heaths and the waste, secret habitations of Nature, one and all do dream: of the passing of another winter, and the on-coming of another spring.

THE END.

PRINTED BY WILLIAM CLOWES AND SONS, LIMITED, LONDON AND BECCLES.

October 1897.

NEW & RECENT BOOKS PUBLISHED BY A. D. INNES & COMPANY BEDFORD ST. MDCCCXCVII.

THE ISTHMIAN LIBRARY: A Series of Volumes dealing popularly with the whole range of Field Sports and Athletics.

Edited by B. FLETCHER ROBINSON, and Illustrated by numerous Sketches and Instantaneous Photographs. Post 8vo, cloth, 5s. each.

Vol. I. **Rugby Football.** By B. FLETCHER ROBINSON, with chapters by FRANK MITCHELL, R. H. CATTELL, C. J. N. FLEMING, GREGOR MACGREGOR, and H. B. TRISTRAM, and dedicated by permission to Mr. ROWLAND HILL.

Vol. II. **The Complete Cyclist.** By A. C. PEMBERTON, Mrs. HARCOURT WILLIAMSON, and C. J. SISLEY.

Vol. IV. **Rowing.** By R. C. LEHMANN, with chapters by GUY NICKALLS and C. M. PITMAN.

Vol. V. **Boxing.** By R. ALLANSON WINN.

Other volumes are in preparation, and will be duly announced.

NEW BOOKS PUBLISHED BY

A. D. INNES & CO.

By F. H. S. MEREWETHER.

Through the Famine Districts of India.

Being an Account by Reuter's Special Correspondent of his experiences in travelling through the Famine Districts of India. Profusely illustrated, demy 8vo, price 16*s.*

By Sir JOSEPH FAYRER, Bart., K.C.S.I., M.D.

The Life of Sir Ranald Martin, C.B.

A Brief Account of the Life and Work of the Great Indian Sanitary Reformer. Crown 8vo, cloth, price 6*s.*

From the Letters of Major W. P. JOHNSON.

Twelve Years of a Soldier's Life.

Edited by his Widow. Being an Account of the experiences of a Major in the Native Irregular Cavalry in India and elsewhere, with portrait. Crown 8vo, cloth, price 6*s.*

By Lieutenant-Colonel ROSS-OF-BLADENSBURG, C.B.

The Coldstream Guards in the Crimea.

Being a Sketch of the Crimean War, treating in detail of the operations in which the Coldstreams took part. With numerous Maps. Crown 8vo, cloth, price 6*s.*

By Professor W. T. LAWTON.

The Successors of Homer.

Being an Account of the Greek Poets who followed from Homer down to the time of Aeschylus. Crown 8vo, cloth, gilt top, price 5*s.*

By GEORGE COOKSON.

Poems.

Crown 8vo, cloth, gilt top, price 4*s.* 6*d.* net.

By B. DALY COCKING.

A Primer of French Etymology.

Designed (1) as a Guide for Students who are able to consult larger works, (2) as a Note-book for Teachers, (3) as a Handbook for Examinees, especially in the Cambridge Higher Local Examinations. The volume contains chapters on the Formation of the French Language, with annotated specimens selected from various stages of its growth. Royal 18mo, price 1*s.* 6*d.*

EIGHTEENTH CENTURY LETTERS

EDITED BY R. BRIMLEY JOHNSON

With introductions by eminent scholars and photogravure portraits of the writers. Crown 8vo, half parchment, gilt top, price six shillings each volume.

Vol. I.—Swift, Addison, Steele.
With an introduction by STANLEY LANE POOLE.

Vol. II.—Johnson and Chesterfield.
With an introduction by GEORGE BIRKBECK HILL.

Other volumes will be duly announced.

The voluminous and interesting correspondence of the Eighteenth Century—when letter-writing was indeed an art—can only be read at present in more or less elaborate and expensive complete editions, or in small anthologies containing at most half-a-dozen letters by the same writer.

The aim of the present series is to present a selection of this inexhaustible material in groups, each sufficiently large to create an atmosphere. No attempt has been made to seek out one-letter men, or to unearth a neglected genius; but the leaders of thought and action—in so far as they wrote good letters—are represented by their most characteristic work, collected from all authentic sources.

The choice of particular letters has been governed by literary rather than historical or even biographical considerations; and each volume should be readable and complete in itself; illustrative at once of style and manners. To this end elaborate annotation seems tiresome and out of place, and incidental references to trifling persons and events are deliberately neglected. The notes are designed to elucidate, not to interrupt, the narrative.

Letters in foreign languages, almost all diplomatic correspondence, and philosophical or literary essays published as letters are omitted; while on the other hand selections have been sometimes made from letters in journal form.

It is hoped to cover the whole century; and the volumes will be ultimately arranged, though not originally published, in chronological order; the rule of birth date being in some cases slightly modified for the union of friends or writers of one class.

RECENT BOOKS.

HISTORY.

By A. HILLIARD ATTERIDGE, Special Correspondent of the *Daily Chronicle* with the Dongola Expeditionary Force.

Towards Khartoum.

The Story of the Soudan War of 1896. With numerous Maps and Illustrations from Photographs taken by the Author. Demy 8vo, buckram, price 16s.

Mr. Atteridge's letters to the "Daily Chronicle" contained no more than the skeleton of the present work, which is in no sense a reprint of them.

By Lieutenant-General MCLEOD INNES, V.C.

The Sepoy Revolt.

A Critical Narrative, covering the whole field of the Indian Mutiny, its causes and course, till the final suppression. With numerous Maps and Plans. Crown 8vo, cloth, 5s.

The picturesque aspects of the Indian Mutiny have been frequently treated. The purpose of this volume is to convey in a clear and compendious form the underlying causes as well as the immediate circumstances which led up to the Revolt; and the true relation and importance of its various phases.

By General Sir CHARLES GOUGH, V.C., G.C.B., and ARTHUR D. INNES, M.A.

The Sikhs and the Sikh Wars.

With 13 Maps and Plans. Demy 8vo, cloth, 16s.

An account of the rise of the Sikh State; of the struggle with the British, the most stubborn in our Indian record; and of the subsequent Annexation. With especial reference to current misapprehensions as to Lord Gough.

By Lieutenant-Colonel ROSS-OF-BLADENSBURG, C.B., late Coldstream Guards.

Dedicated, by permission, to H.M. the Queen.

A History of the Coldstream Guards, from 1815 to 1885.

With numerous Coloured Plates, Drawings, and Maps by Lieutenant NEVILE R. WILKINSON. Crown 4to, cloth, gilt top, two guineas net.

An account of the famous regiment since Waterloo; with the history of the political events and the campaigns with which it has been associated.

The *Times* says:—"This magnificent volume. . . . A model of what such a work should be."

By C. R. B. BARRETT.

Dedicated, by permission, to General H.R.H. the Duke of Connaught, K.G.

Battles and Battlefields in England.

With an Introduction by H. D. TRAILL, and profusely Illustrated by the Author. Super royal 8vo, buckram, gilt top, 18s.

Compiled from a thorough examination of the authorities, and personal inspection of the ground.

"A remarkably good book of its kind."—*Sketch.*

v

RECENT WORKS OF HISTORY.

By G. BOISSIER (de l'Académie Française).
Cicero and His Friends.
Translated by A. D. JONES. Crown 8vo, cloth, 5s.

M. Boissier's work in the French is familiar to historical students: but it has been felt that a translation would make it available for many more readers. The addition of an index and analytical contents increase its advantages for reference.

By J. S. RISLEY, M.A., B.C.L.
The Law of War.
A Study of the Legal Obligations and Conditions applying to Belligerents or Neutrals in Times of War. Demy 8vo, cloth, 12s.

Compiled primarily for the use of the ordinary reader rather than the technical student.

First Review.—"The book . . . is admirably done. It avoids technicalities and . . . is admirably suited to serve as a guide and first introduction to a most instructive subject."—*Scotsman.*

NEW AND REVISED EDITION.

By Lieutenant-General McLEOD INNES, V.C.
Lucknow and Oude in the Mutiny.
A Narrative and a Study. With Numerous Maps, Plans, etc., and an Index. Demy 8vo, cloth, 12s. net.

A critical narrative of the causes and course of the Mutiny, with a full account of the operations in Oude and the siege of Lucknow, from personal knowledge.

"A most valuable contribution to the history of the great crisis."—*Times.*

"Recent literature concerning the Indian Mutiny has brought us nothing so valuable. . . . His knowledge of India and her people is accurate and profound. . . . The facts are marshalled with consummate skill. In this book General Innes has rendered invaluable service in regard to the military history of the Mutiny and of the Indian Empire."—*Army and Navy Gazette.*

By Dr. WILHELM BUSCH, Professor at the University of Freiburg, in Baden.
England under the Tudors.
Vol. I. Henry VII. (1485-1509). Translated from the German by Miss ALICE M. TODD and the Rev. A. H. JOHNSON, sometime Fellow of All Souls College, Oxford, under the supervision of, and with an Introduction by Mr. JAMES GAIRDNER, Editor of the "Paston Letters." Demy 8vo, cloth, 16s. net.

"Since a body of Oxford Tutors published a translation of Ranke's English History just twenty years ago, no more important step has been taken to give English readers access to recent German work on English History than in the book now before us. . . . The general value of what we hope will ultimately be the best general text-book of Tudor History is too well known to scholars to make it worth while to dwell upon it here."—*Speaker.*

By ARTHUR D. INNES, M.A., Author of "Seers and Singers," etc.
Britain and her Rivals.
1713-1789. A Study dealing chiefly with the Contests between the Naval Powers for Supremacy in America and India. With numerous Plans, Maps, etc. Large crown, buckram, 7s. 6d.

The *Pall Mall Gazette*, in a review headed, "History as it Should be Written," says: "The book is indeed just what was most wanted : . . . a great deal more than a popular work in the usual sense of the term, seeing that it is accurate and thoughtful, besides being eminently readable."

RECENT WORKS OF TRAVEL, ETC.

By GWENDOLEN TRENCH GASCOIGNE.

Among Pagodas and Fair Ladies:

Being an Account of a Tour through Burma. With numerous Illustrations from Photographs. Medium 8vo, buckram, 12*s.*

"Whoever wants to tread in imagination 'the road to Mandalay,' and visit that 'cleaner, greener land' of which Mr. Kipling sings so alluringly, could not do better than take the authoress of this book for his guide."—*Glasgow Herald.*

By G. F. SCOTT ELLIOT, F.S.S., F.R.G.S.

A Naturalist in Mid Africa.

Being an Account of a Journey to the Mountains of the Moon and Tanganyika. With numerous Illustrations from Photographs and Sketches by the Author, and Three Coloured Maps. Medium 8vo, buckram, 16*s.*

"Mr. Scott Elliot is a good geographer, and a first-rate naturalist, and his book is a worthy addition to the library which has already been written on East Africa."—*Times.*

By ROBERT K. DOUGLAS.

Society in China.

An Account of the Everyday Life of the Chinese People, Social, Political, and Religious. Crown 8vo, cloth, 6*s.* (Library Edition, with 22 Illustrations. Demy 8vo, cloth, 16*s.*)

Mr. Henry Norman, in "People and Politics of the Far East," says: "Professor Douglas's book tells the truth about China in so indisputable and entertaining a manner, and he speaks with so much authority, that there is very little left for any one else to say. I have omitted from this volume much of my material about China, and my experiences there, simply because Professor Douglas's work has covered the ground finally."

By Rev. W. F. COBB, D.D.

Origines Judaicæ.

An Inquiry into Heathen Faiths as affecting the Birth and Growth of Judaism. Demy 8vo, cloth, 12*s.*

"We cannot help feeling very grateful to our author. He has obtained a competent knowledge of what recent investigation has revealed in Egyptology and Assyriology, and he has brought his stores of knowledge to interpret the old Testament religion and history, and by his conception of 'Menotheism,' if not by the coining of the word, he has brought a welcome illumination to the obscure subject of the primitive Hebrew religion."—*Daily Chronicle.*

With an Introduction by the Very Reverend F. W. FARRAR, D.D., Dean of Canterbury.

The New Life in Christ Jesus:

Thoughts of a Huguenot Mystic. Translated by JULIAN FIELD. Demy 8vo, cloth, gilt edges, 5*s.*

RECENT BELLES LETTRES.

By CLIFFORD HARRISON.

The Lute of Apollo.

An Essay on Music. Fcap. 8vo, cloth, gilt top, 5s. net.

"No real lover of music will fail to give an easily accessible and honoured corner on his or her favourite bookshelf to this little volume. It has a unique charm which no words of mine can properly define or describe."—*Ladies' Pictorial.*

By MAIDIE DICKSON.

The Saga of the Sea Swallow.

Illustrated by J. D. BATTEN & HILDA FAIRBAIRN. Fcap. 4to, cloth, gilt top, 4s. 6d. net.

"The narrative is told with the most engaging circumstantial vividness, and it held us as we read."—*Academy.*

By COSMO MONKHOUSE.

In the National Gallery.

The Italian Schools from the Thirteenth to the Sixteenth Century. Illustrated with numerous examples specially prepared for this work. Crown 8vo, buckram, gilt top, 7s. 6d.

"One of the most popular handbooks yet issued on the development of Italian art as exemplified by the works in our National Collection. The author's name is a guarantee of the precision of the facts he produces, and of the excellence of the writing by which they are connected. The book is illustrated by a good number of excellent reproductions of the principal pictures."—*Magazine of Art.*

By A. J. BUTLER.

Dante: his Times and his Work.

A Popular Treatise dealing with the great Poet. Crown 8vo, cloth, gilt top, 3s. 6d.

"The work should be interesting and profitable both to every Dante student and to every general reader who wishes to acquire a knowledge of a most interesting epoch of modern history, and of one of the most interesting figures of any epoch."—*Illustrated London News.*

By ARTHUR D. INNES, M.A.

Seers and Singers.

A Study of Five English Poets (BROWNING, TENNYSON, WORDSWORTH, MATTHEW ARNOLD, and Mrs. BROWNING). Cloth antique, extra gilt top, 5s.

"Never were great poets and their gifts to us dealt with in a more reverential and yet discriminating fashion. Comments and criticism are alike delicate and suggestive. All followers of the great five should possess this little book, whose dainty get-up is still its least charm."—*Pall Mall Gazette.*

www.ingramcontent.com/pod-product-compliance
Lightning Source LLC
Chambersburg PA
CBHW032141110726
47902CB00003B/652